Praise *Crip*

Praise for *I Paint the Sky*

'An emotional journey that's as startling as it is touching.' —*Wild Sage Book Blog*

'Brimming with page-turning tension.' —*S. Glum, Award-Winning Author of 'A River of Crows'*

'A stunning tour de force set against the backdrop of the American west.' —*R. Samborn, Award-winning Author of the 'Painted Souls' Series*

'I stayed up until the wee hours of the morning seeking the conclusions of the characters' journeys.' —*Ashley Reads for Fun*

Praise for *The Lantern Creek Series*

'A Wild Ride... That's Well-Worth the Price of Admission.' —*Kirkus*

'Twin Peaks Meets Hart of Dixie.' —*Book Riot*

I Paint the Sky

LAURA KEMP

LOST MERIDIAN

I Paint the Sky
By Laura Kemp
Published by Lost Meridian Press
www.lostmeridianpress.com
Copyright @ 2024 by Laura Kemp
All rights reserved

ISBN Large Print Edition 979-8-9906588-2-0

Cover Design: Denise Birt
Connect with the author online at www.laurakemp.net

To my wild Dakota family-
Grandpa Carlos and Cowboy Frank-
Your dreams became mine.

And rise with me forever
Across the silent sand
And the stars will be your eyes
And the wind will be my hands

-Far From Any Road
B. and R. Sparks

Chapter One

Summer, 1855
Kansas

E mily Ives watched Independence vanish like a piece of thread pulled tightly between the gentle swell of hills. She'd spent three days in a dusty camp, waiting to cross the Missouri River, and most of the fourth on a plank seat behind people she barely knew.

She felt the jolt of the rutted road cut through her back and settle in her stomach, where the baby moved with its usual tenacity.

She straightened her spine, hopeful the pain would subside when another lurch pulled a small cry from her lips.

Clementine May twisted on the box spring, her dark eyes worried and patted at her neck and the mass of hair bunched there.

"Be careful, Jake," she scolded, and Emily put a hand to her mouth, not wanting to worry them when they had been so kind as to offer her safe passage to Fort Kearny.

"I can't make the road any smoother, Clem," Jake said, his tanned face scrunched up in a way that said he was mad - although such a thing was unlikely. In the brief time Emily had known the Mays, she'd never seen a sour word pass between them.

In fact, they seemed very much in love, which was why she took notice of them in the crowded wagon yard, watching them for more than an hour before Clementine realized she was not only following them, but alone and heavy with child.

The baby was not due for another two weeks, of that, Emily was certain.

The night she conceived this child was burned into her mind like a brand, and she'd been counting the hours and minutes and seconds until it would be released from her body, grateful only because people took pity on her.

"Jake'll make you a bed when we stop for dinner," Clementine said. "I'll put some blankets down and you'll be quite comfortable."

Emily ducked her head, looked beneath the canvas cover and saw people walking beside their wagons, hats pulled low to shield them from the sun. They were ten abreast, now that the path was wide, dust rising like smoke behind them. She heard words rise from the prairie as locusts would, some making sense- some a jumble that told her these people were strangers to this country.

She knew how they felt, having come from the flatlands of southern Michigan to this alien world of endless sky and grass, the smell of manure always present and the promise of a better life seeming to mock her every minute she remained on the plank seat behind the Mays.

She felt the wagon jolt, heard the horses whinny and turned to see Jake tap them with his reins.

Emily bit her lip, worried that he needed to make up time and was only pretending to accommodate her by riding in the wagon with his wife.

The others were walking, would she be forced to as well?

He seemed like a good man, but his kindness would only last so long.

Like her husband's.

"Thank you," she answered, a longing for the little town she'd left behind making her chest hurt.

She remembered Carrie, a childhood friend she'd run races with behind the schoolhouse, and her older brother - a young man with hair the same color as Clementine's.

There was talk he might court her, and the gossip did not displease her because James was attractive in a

3

simple way, his childlike eyes seeming to moon over everything she said.

Emily sat on the plank seat behind strangers she'd met only three days before, wondering if she should have allowed James to marry her- knowing what the answer would be.

Another jolt sent her tumbling to her knees and Clementine turned quickly.

"Jake!" she cried. "Stop!"

Emily cried out, a strong pain in her stomach, and put her hand there, felt a dampness on her dress and between her legs.

"Clementine," she whispered, her fear turning to panic.

"Her water broke," Clem cried, and Jake pulled on the reins, bringing the four red oxen to a stop so quickly Emily fell backwards against a sack of meal.

Her mother almost died giving birth to both her and her sister, but she'd hoped she would be spared, wondering if this was punishment for what she'd done to Marvin.

She heard wagons rolling by, the smell of hot beasts in the sun making her gag and recognized a man's voice, inquiring as to why they'd stopped.

She'd heard it before, speaking to Jake while she rested inside the wagon and knew they'd made a bargain to ride together until they reached California.

"Her water broke," Jake replied as Clem slid onto her knees beside Emily. "The baby's coming."

Silence- followed by a soft curse and Emily cried out, her pain roiling in her stomach.

"Try and be still," the voice said, and Emily pulled back, horrified to see the strange man had crawled through the back of the wagon and was now kneeling over her.

"Mr. Merritt," Clem said, her face twisted. "Can you get help?"

"I *am* the help," he replied.

Clem shook her head, put her hand to her mouth.

"I'm the oldest of six," he said sharply. "Pa worked the mines and that left only me to bring my brothers and sisters into the world."

"Surely," Clem began again, her voice wavering. "There must have been a midwife."

"There *wasn't*."

Emily clamped her eyes shut, numb with shame.

"The baby's coming fast," he said.

Emily gritted her teeth, felt the remaining water from her womb wet the plank floor beneath her.

"Emily," she heard Clem say. "Stay awake."

But she couldn't, and time seemed to slow to a crawl as she writhed in pain, wondering why the baby hadn't come when Mr. Merritt said it would.

"It's turned the wrong way," he said, and she tried to focus on his face, Clem's face, the sun making strange shapes on the floor as it bled through the tiny holes in the canvas.

"Clementine," she said weakly, the sound of tack

jangling on the passing wagons reminding her that life went on.

"We need clean linen," Mr. Merritt said. "And whiskey, if you have it."

Emily imagined Clem's indignation even as her eyes slid closed, her body tumbling down the same hole that had welcomed her mother.

"Marvin," she whispered, fear of what might be waiting on the other side of the darkness making her panic. "Forgive me."

Chapter Two

Summer, 1854
Michigan

The muslin bolt felt soft beneath Emily's fingertips. She drew out a measuring stick and cut the length to suit the purpose of the lady standing in front of her, a woman who had always thought herself better than everyone else.

"That will do," the woman said sharply, her small, pinched eyes searching for something over Emily's shoulder. "I would like to speak with Patricia."

Emily looked up. "My mother?"

"Yes," the woman repeated while smoothing the topmost ruffle on her enormous skirt. "She's here, isn't she?"

Emily nodded, used to giving this woman what she wanted, and turned to look awkwardly over her shoulder.

"She went to the back room but should return at any moment."

The woman pressed her lips together, watched closely while Emily carefully folded the linen and placed it inside the brown paper they used to wrap parcels.

"And how is your father?" the woman asked, her sharp eyes softening in the slightest.

Emily looked down, her cheeks flushing when she remembered how this woman had once admired Gerald Ives. "He is well, thank you."

The woman smiled, touched her pearl brooch and then the tip of the hat placed so nicely on her head, a gift from the man she married because Emily's father wouldn't have her.

A moment passed and Emily took a breath, drew her honey blond braid over her shoulder and smoothed it while she waited.

It seemed forever before she heard her mother's footsteps, her smile vanishing when she turned the corner and saw who stood at the counter.

"Josephine," she said, the word clipped. "How may we help you?"

The woman raised her chin. "I am afraid there has been a mistake regarding the wheat my husband purchased last week. It seems you have charged us too much."

Emily sighed, unable to hide her annoyance, and Patricia's gaze cut to her quickly.

"You must be mistaken," she countered slowly. "Our prices are the best in the county and my daughters are always quite careful—"

"Nevertheless," Josephine interrupted, one finger raised. "An error has occurred, and we expect to be compensated."

Emily's breath gathered in her cheeks, her skin prickling as the woman who could have bought and sold their store three times over argued about a dime.

"I'm sure you are wrong," Patricia straightened her shoulders, perhaps thinking of those long-ago days when they argued over something far more important.

"Well..." Josephine huffed; her thin lips pursed. "We will just have to see about that. I know my husband was charged almost seven dollars for a barrel of wheat and—"

"Excuse me," a voice interrupted, and Emily raised her head, surprised that someone had entered the store without ringing the bell that hung above the door.

The man stood behind Josephine was tall, with a muscular build. His hair seemed to dance between a shade of russet and red, his tan face lean and strong.

Emily caught his eye, which seemed to dance brightly with a slow, green fire.

Josephine turned, the feathers in her hat quivering and the man bowed slightly, a smile on his face that seemed to fascinate the older woman.

9

"I don't believe I know you," Josephine said, and Emily hid a smile behind her hand.

"You are correct in your assumption," the man replied. "I rode into town ten minutes ago."

Patricia nodded slightly. "Welcome to Fairview, Sir."

The stranger smiled again, his eyes running the length of Emily.

"I'd say the town is well-named."

Patricia glanced at her daughter, then the stranger, her eyebrows raised.

"I couldn't help but overhear your discussion. I just came from the north country and wheat is going for seven dollars and fifty cents a barrel there."

Josephine looked at the man, her back stiff, her hands clasped in front of her and did not know what to say.

"And that is finely ground."

The woman huffed, the feathers twitching again as she looked between Patricia and the stranger.

"I do not understand—"

"This lady has given you a good price. And a fair one, and I don't think you will get a penny's worth for the trouble you aim to cause," he paused. "Not that you need it."

Emily giggled behind her hand, saw her mother glance at her in annoyance as Josephine drew herself to her full height.

"You are indignant and rude," she said. "And I don't care about the prices in the north. Here in

Fairview, we *help* our neighbors, and this mercantile's prices are outrageous."

The stranger stepped closer, looked down at the counter and the neatly folded parcel. "But not enough to keep you from purchasing enough linen for a new dress."

Emily heard her mother draw in her breath.

"Sir—" Patricia began.

"I apologize," he said, the merriment in his eyes belying the situation. "This was none of my business."

Josephine nodded, the feathers on her hat floating on air as if they had lives of their own. Then she pushed past the stranger and out the door, her shoes making a clomping sound that spoke to her mortification, her parcel forgotten.

Emily kept her mouth covered, another laugh bubbling up in her throat.

A moment passed, then two, before Patricia rounded the counter and stood before the stranger, her face speaking of the satisfaction the encounter had given her.

"Thank you," she said. "That woman is always trying to get a rise from us. And often succeeds."

The stranger bowed his head slightly.

"I hate to see people taken advantage of. Especially hard-working folks such as yourself."

Emily lowered her hand, looked into his eyes and knew she had never seen anything like them in her life.

"Thank you," she smiled, her heart beating quickly, the collar of her dress suddenly tight. "I've wanted to tell that old goat to shove off for as long as I can remember."

Patricia gasped.

"Emily!"

The stranger leaned his head back, laughed in a way that tickled Emily's spine right down to the small of her back.

"It's rare to find a woman who speaks her mind so freely."

"Is it, then?" Patricia shook her head. "We wouldn't know."

Marvin smiled, stood straight again and took a step back as the bell above the door rang, announcing the arrival of two more customers.

"And what is your name," Patricia asked, noticing for the first time how her daughter and the stranger were watching each other. "So that we may thank you."

The man smiled again, his eyes on Emily in a way that made her skin burn.

"Marvin Jones." he said. "And I'm pleased to make your acquaintance."

Chapter Three

Emily sat at the dinner table, the clink of knife and spoon against china plates making her more uncomfortable than she already was.

Marvin sat across the table and beside her younger sister Maddie, his eyes on Emily and she felt her cheeks flush, wanting him to keep looking and stop at the same time.

Her father had insisted he come to dinner after hearing what had happened at the store. He was much obliged, after all, and Marvin was new to town.

Marvin agreed, telling them he wasn't sure where he would have got his evening meal and Patricia scolded him, a hint of color in her cheeks that surprised her daughter.

"Are you staying at Patterson's Boardinghouse?"

He nodded, took a slow sip of water and Emily

found her eyes drawn to the rise and fall of his Adam's apple.

"Just until I can purchase a plot down by the creek and put up a shanty."

"A shanty?" Gerald repeated.

"I've a mind to farm out there," Marvin said. "And I hope to build a proper home one day."

Gerald looked down at his plate, cut his meat and then brought it to his mouth, chewing slowly as he spoke.

"Farming's hard work."

Marvin nodded. "So is running a store. Even with such capable help. We all need to make our way in whatever way we can make it."

Emily's father continued to chew.

"Where do you come from, Mr. Jones?" he asked, his blue eyes lowered in the slightest and Emily saw Maddie shift in her seat, uncomfortable with what she suspected would be a singular line of questioning.

Gerald Ives was a straightforward man, and this stranger had taken him by surprise by both defending his family to a woman he'd never met, and his blatant fascination with Emily, a young woman he barely knew.

Marvin cleared his throat, a piece of salt pork skewered on the end of his fork.

"I come from Presque Isle, sir. In the north country."

Patricia smiled. "I have a cousin there. Married to a

man named Marchand with three daughters. Have you heard of them?"

"I can't say that I have," Marvin shook his head. "But if her daughters are as lovely as yours, Mrs. Ives, I count myself poorer for our lack of acquaintance."

Emily glanced at her sister, who suddenly dabbed at her mouth with her napkin as Gerald cleared his throat.

"And what made you leave?" he asked. "It's a good long trip."

"That it is," Marvin agreed. "I guess you could say I wanted a change of scenery. An adventure, so to speak."

"Adventure!" Maddie burst out, a silly trill to her voice and Emily raised an eyebrow.

"Yes," Marvin turned to the girl beside him. "Haven't you ever wished for something out of the ordinary to happen to you? Something you never could have expected?"

"Why... I couldn't imagine," Maddie stammered, looking to her sister for help and Emily straightened her back, sat her fork on her plate and leveled him with a stare not unlike her father's.

"I have."

Gerald and Patricia looked at her uneasily, their inability to imagine a life outside of Fairview plain for all to see.

"Ah, Miss Emily, I see we are kindred spirits," Marvin smiled while popping the salt pork in his mouth and Emily felt the familiar tightness of her collar as Maddie glanced down at her lap.

"Kindred spirits?" Patricia echoed. "I must say, Mr. Jones, this has been an unusual day."

Marvin nodded. "I would agree, Mrs. Ives."

Emily smiled, bowed her head and finished her meal in silence, listening while the others talked of farming and weather and the price of wheat in Presque Isle even as her mind lingered on the places she'd dreamed of- a land where she could live freely beneath her own piece of sky.

It wasn't long before dinner ended, and Emily stood, began clearing dishes from the table while the others sat talking to Marvin.

It seemed rude to excuse herself, but she needed a breath of air, a moment to think about the tightness of her collar and the way her skin seemed to press against the fabric of her cotton dress, making her want to un-button it.

Moving to the kitchen, she went to the sink, closed her eyes and plunged her hands into the warm basin water.

"Miss Ives," she heard the voice behind her, the face so close it stirred the hairs on the base of her neck, and she turned, stunned to see Marvin be-side her.

"Call me Emily," she said quickly, undone by how close he was as he took a wet dish from her hand and began to dry it with a cloth she'd laid on the counter. "There is no need—"

"I don't mind helping," he said. "And I wanted to speak with you."

She turned, looked through the doorway and saw her parents in the front room with Maddie, who lingered in the doorway, trying to pretend she wasn't eavesdropping.

"Whatever for?" she asked, her skin prickling again as his elbow brushed hers.

"I'd like to walk with you after we are finished here."

"Walk?" she repeated, unsure where they would go aside from the main street, and she didn't want that.

"Yes," he said. "If you will allow it."

"My father—"

"Has given his permission."

"He has?" she asked in wonderment, having never known her father to be anything but suspicious where the intentions of young men were concerned. "You are certain?"

She saw Marvin smile, saw how his teeth came together to make an appealing picture that could catch a woman off guard and hoped she hadn't offended him.

"If you don't want to walk with me, I will take that as my cue to leave. So, please... speak your mind as you did earlier in the store."

"Yes," she said quickly, drying her hands on the towel. "I will walk with you."

She heard him release his breath and wondered at how quickly things could change. Four hours ago, she'd been unaware of this man's existence, and now he was going to parade her through Fairview as if they were courting.

"Shall we, then?" he asked, holding out his arm and she tucked her hand into his elbow, unnerved by the warmth of his skin as she made her way to the front door, her father's silhouette in the parlor as he told them to be back within the hour.

She quickly grabbed her straw hat, tied it beneath her chin as Marvin took her shawl from the hook beside it.

"Yes, Sir," Marvin called, his tone cheerful and Emily stepped outside, the evening air caressing her face as he placed the shawl over her shoulders.

The road that ran in front of the store was empty, the livery stable across from it occupied by three men who were tending to their horses. She did not see anyone she knew, and so quickened her step.

"Do you want to walk towards the creek," he asked, "I don't think anyone will see us there."

She lowered her head, embarrassed.

"I understand this is sudden," he said. "But I must say you have captured my interest."

She looked up at him quickly, undone by how he was watching her.

"I can't imagine why," she said, thinking again of Carrie's brother and how he would stand before her, twisting his hat like a wet dishrag.

Marvin stopped walking, turned her so that she was looking up into his eyes.

"You are an enchanting woman, Emily Ives. And an artist and a poet, as well."

She felt herself straighten, disturbed that he knew so much about her.

"Who told you—"

"Your father."

She looked down, her cheeks red. "I enjoy writing things down in my journals. And drawing the things that catch my eye."

"And what has caught your eye, Miss Emily?"

"Mr. Jones—"

"You must know that men desire you."

"I know nothing of the sort," she said, her tone rising. "And I do not intend to entertain such a notion with someone I've known less than a day."

"Miss Ives—"

"You are too forward, sir," she scolded, not knowing where her anger had come from, feeling like he might not deserve it. "You were rude to Josephine Reynolds in our store, and you are acting like a cad to me, right here in the middle of the street."

Marvin smiled, began walking again while tucking her arm back in his elbow.

"I will not argue that point."

Emily cleared her throat, suddenly uncomfortable to be with him in the gathering darkness.

"I do not think—"

He stopped again, turned her towards him and Emily looked down the street, saw that they had left the store and livery stable behind.

"Thinking will get you into trouble, Miss Ives."

"Emily," she said suddenly, wanting him to say her name in the way she was used to hearing it. "My name is *Emily*."

"Emily," he repeated, watching her for a moment before turning back towards the river. "I apologize for my behavior. If you want to go back, I'll take you."

"Mr. Jones—"

"Marvin."

She cleared her throat again. "I don't know what I want. I've *never* known—"

"That's not true," he said softly. "You know. I can see it in your eyes."

She stood straight, tried to breathe the air in through her nose and found that she was lightheaded.

"I saw the same thing in myself when I left Presque Isle," he said. "I wanted adventure, that was certain, but I was only one of a passel of boys, not expected to make much of myself and when my folks died, my brothers turned me out. Said they weren't going to give me a stake until I grew up and got myself a wife."

Emily felt her mouth go dry, unsure she had heard him right.

"Is that what you are doing, Mr. Jones? Searching for a wife so you can get your farm back?"

"Miss Ives—"

"It certainly seems so—"

"No," he whispered, and something in the word made her stop. "I'm never going back."

She met his gaze, unbelieving.

"I don't want to be where I'm not wanted. And I don't want to waste another minute on something that's not worth it."

She looked at him, unable to speak.

"Do you know I wanted to walk with you the second I saw you wrapping up that awful woman's package today," he paused. "I just wasn't sure how to ask."

She frowned, took a step back even as her heart began to imagine a life apart from her parents and the store and a boy who would rather twist his hat than say she was beautiful.

"I think," she began, her gaze drawn to the curve of his mouth. "I think you have that part figured out."

"Do I?" he asked, his face close to hers and she wanted to look down the street again, to see if anyone was watching but it didn't matter.

She took a breath, the tight feeling in her chest again as Marvin closed the distance between them.

"May I?" he asked, his hand rising to her cheek as his lips sought hers.

She closed her eyes.

"Yes."

Chapter Four

Emily felt blinding sunlight stroke her lids as her head rolled from side to side. She heard voices, recognized them as Clementine and Jake May and had some recollection of what had happened in the wagon bed.

Her dress had been wet, the pain excruciating as the man named Merritt knelt at her side, telling her the baby was turned the wrong way. She remembered drinking whiskey, something she had smelled on Marvin's breath many times, and it made her head swim, the pain somewhat bearable as darkness encased her skull like a hood.

Time passed slowly after that, and she awoke every now and again, aware that the wagon was moving and saw patches of sunlight under the side of the canvas. She heard rain once, and thunder, and the small, mewling cry of a baby- one she could hardly believe was hers.

Or Marvin's...

She remembered how badly he wanted a son, how he'd talked to her mother and father about it at supper the night he'd asked for permission to marry her.

"We'll give you a bushel of grandchildren," he'd laughed, and Emily looked down, uncomfortable with the way her father stared at him. "Starting with a boy, of course."

Maddie blushed, took a quick drink of water and Emily wondered if she thought about her own wedding night and what sort of man would be lying beside her.

The wagon jolted again, and she let out a moan, the muscles in her lower back and abdomen aching with a pain she feared would never go away.

She moved her hand to her face, felt sweat on her forehead as the familiar smell of manure mixed with warm wind and grass met her nose.

"Emily," Clem said softly, and she opened her eyes, saw her climbing through the cinched canvas at the back of the wagon. "How are you feeling?"

Emily opened her mouth, licked her dry lips and tried to sit up.

"Stay where you are," Clem put a hand to her cheek. "Thank goodness your fever broke."

Emily took hold of her hand, stopping her. "What happened?"

Clem's eyes widened in surprise.

"You had a baby."

"A baby?" she echoed, remembering the storm and the cries, wondering where the child was and if it would be given back to her.

"A little boy," Clementine smiled, her eyes moving to the corner of the wagon and Emily tried to sit up, to see what she was looking at and saw a bundle of blankets tucked neatly beside a sack of meal.

"A son," she said, imagining how Marvin would react to the news, suspecting he would use it as an excuse to go to the tavern and not come home until morning.

"He's healthy and strong," Clem smiled. "And has the brightest red hair I've ever seen.

Emily caught her breath, thinking of her husband and the child who would forever remind her of him. A moment passed in silence, a moment where Clem shifted on the wagon bed, her dark eyes worried as she glanced again at the bundle of blankets in the corner.

"Mr. Merritt was a wonder to behold. I never knew a man to be of any help in situations like these, but we certainly would have been in a world of trouble without him."

Emily tried to think of something to say even as scorching shame swept her body, making her hot.

"I should thank him," she said, and Clem smiled.

"All in good time. Mr. Merritt's sister has been nursing him."

Emily put her hand to her forehead, wanting Clem

to stop talking and wanting her to continue so she wouldn't have to face what was in front of her.

"What will his name be?" Clem offered after a moment.

"His name?" Emily repeated.

"We need something to call him."

Emily shook her head, not wanting to think about that right now.

"What's wrong?"

She turned her head to the side, gazed beneath the canvas and saw that the ten wagons abreast had now become five. The recent rain had settled the dust, the sky that hung above them seeming to waver between blue and gray.

"Does he look like his father?" Clem asked and Emily looked over quickly. "You talked about someone named Marvin."

"Clem—"

"You asked him to forgive you."

Fear rose in her chest, fear for what might happen if they discovered the truth.

"You told us your husband died."

"He did," she said, her mind spinning as the wagon rolled to a stop. "Last Christmas. But there were words I spoke that I shouldn't have. And when a person faces death, those things come to mind."

Clem started, and Emily knew her words had shocked her.

"Whatever happened between you," Clementine took her hand. "It's not the baby's fault."

25

Emily licked her lips again, embarrassment staining her cheeks.

"I'm sorry, Emily," Clem said again. "We just want to help you. We've been together for almost a week now and it only seems fitting that- "

"We agreed to take her to Fort Kearny and that's the end of it," Jake said, at the back of the wagon now and uncinching the canvas.

Emily tightened her jaw, hurt by his words but knowing she had brought them on herself. She looked at the bundle of blankets again, knowing a baby boy lay nestled in the folds, a child that was already being nursed by another woman and knew she would need to take care of him.

"Bring him to me," she whispered, and Clem gave a brief nod, maneuvered around barrels of bran and bacon, sacks of strong-smelling coffee and a butter churn before scooping up the infant.

Emily heard a soft sound as Clem lifted the blankets and knew the baby had been sleeping and was just now waking up.

"Here you are," she said, placing the bundle in Emily's arms and she moved the cloth aside, looking down on the face of her son.

His eyes were closed, his fists struggling against the swaddle and Emily watched him yawn, saw that the fine hair on top of his head was indeed as red as Marvin's and was surprised by the fierce love that swept over her.

She remembered holding Maddie this way when

she was a baby, a tiny thing that she and her father cared for when her mother was sick.

She remembered the soft cries she would make when she was hungry, remembered the bond they had always shared because of that time spent together and wished for the same thing with this child.

"You won't be like him," she whispered, unable to believe this tiny person belonged to her. "I won't let it."

"Emily," Clem whispered, and she shifted her weight, felt the baby move and watched him open his eyes.

"They're blue," she smiled, her fingers touching the little nose and mouth, the forehead that wrinkled as sunlight touched his skin.

"All babies are born with blue eyes," Clem said, glancing again at Jake, who was peeking beneath the sides of the canvas as he rolled them up.

"Yes," Emily said, the thought of putting him back in the corner beside the butter churn as foreign as returning to Marvin. "But I think they will stay this color."

Clementine smiled, adjusting the swaddling around him. "That would be nice."

Emily touched his forehead again, feeling for the first time like everything was good and right and as it should be if only because her son would never know his father.

"James," Emily said, looking up at Clem. "We'll call him James."

Chapter Five

R uth Merritt put a hand above her eyes, strained to see the horizon in front of her and the line of wagons that seemed to move in place against the sky. She squinted, thinking she might see the May's wagon in the row beside them, wondering when the baby's mother would be able to take care of him.

The thought gave her a start, made her heart turn cold for a moment.

Caleb was able to get him turned, had delivered him squalling and squirming even as Emily lay like a dead person in the corner of the wagon.

She remembered Clementine May bringing the bundle to her, having heard, no doubt, that she had lost an infant daughter just over a month before.

She'd cradled the tiny thing, praying she could still feed him.

She turned to her brother, his skin tanned from a life spent outdoors, his dark blond hair streaked from the sun.

He returned her gaze, his gray eyes reminding her of their mother.

"Are you thinking about the boy?" he asked, his callused hands gripping the bridle of the oxen he led, and she looked down at her feet as they tapped the hard soil.

"It's a good thing you're doing," he continued, his hat shading his eyes as he squinted against the sun. "The mother was bad off."

Ruth nodded, remembering how she had stood holding the oxen, their brown gelding tied to the side along with their cow, waiting while Caleb went to see why the wagon had stopped.

Clementine May was waving her hands, pointing into the bed and Ruth watched her brother break into a run, his long strides taking him there in seconds.

She stood watching while he climbed inside, stood listening to the woman's screams and knew what was happening.

She had gone through the same thing just two months earlier.

Ruth put a finger to her lips, chewed on the edge of her finger to keep the tears from smarting her eyes.

Caleb would notice, would start wondering if it had been a mistake to bring her.

She would have to pretend she was all right and not think of the newborn who had stopped breathing three weeks after her birth, or the man who denied them both even as he courted another girl from across the river.

"When we stop for the noon meal, you can tend to the boy," Caleb said, glancing sideways as he scratched the stubble that had begun to darken his jawline.

Ruth nodded, pulled her sunbonnet over her head, remembering the moments spent with the unnamed baby in the bed of their own wagon, his small mouth at her breast.

"Be careful," her brother said.

"What do you mean?" she asked, straining again for a glimpse of the May's wagon and the bundle she laid so carefully in the corner of the box.

"Don't think of your daughter."

She felt the sharp sting in her eyes again.

"Or her father."

Ruth bunched her hands into fists and hated that he said that to her, hated the knot of shame and regret that twisted her stomach.

"He was your friend," she began, thinking of their days spent throwing stones across the rolling waters of the Ohio, his hand in hers as they climbed the high bluffs.

"Not anymore."

Yes, Ruth thought. Those days were gone.

"I'm not thinking of him. And I'm not thinking of that boy. His mother will be well soon and it's all for the best."

She saw her brother glance at her again, saw his mouth tighten in a way she recognized.

"That girl will likely need your help even after she wakes up."

"Caleb—"

"She's very weak."

"I know."

"Remember who he belongs to."

She drew her bottom lip into her mouth.

"Clementine said her husband died at Christmas. Said she whispered his name right before she fainted and that she wanted him to forgive her—"

"I heard what she said."

"Why doesn't she wear a wedding ring?" she asked. "Do you suppose something happened to make her take it off?"

Her brother made a noise that said it was none of their business.

"Clementine says they're leaving her at Fort Kearny where an uncle will take her to the north country."

Her brother frowned. "The north country is full of Sioux."

She paused, thinking of the child again.

"What do you suppose would happen if the uncle doesn't come? We can't leave her there, all alone when she's already weak and sick and probably scared..."

She turned then, saw her brother's jaw working in a way that said he was thinking hard on something and wondered at his regrets.

31

"Caleb, "she began, "I didn't... I'm sorry—"

"I know," he said, turning to her with the smile that could charm the fuss out of anyone, the smile she'd hardly seen since that day in June the summer before. "You don't need to say sorry to me, Ruthie. Not ever."

She touched his shoulder, her heart softening beneath the grief they shared.

"I'll do it just the same."

Chapter Six

Emily stood in the parlor of her home, dressed in a white gown cinched tightly at the waist and a full, billowing skirt made of satin with lace trim. The bodice sat low on her shoulders and lay gathered at her breast with a pale pink rose.

The sleeves were short, just above her elbows and revealed her smooth skin as she turned, trying to catch a glimpse of herself in the small mirror that hung on the far wall.

"You're beautiful," her mother said, bending slightly to adjust her veil, which sat secured with a pearl comb just beneath the crown of her head.

She turned again, loving the sound her skirts made when they swept the carpeted floor and looked at her sister.

Maddie stood in a corner, her own ruffled dress a

shade of saffron, a bouquet in her hand that she held for Emily as they waited for the reverend to arrive.

Marvin, who had asked for her hand in marriage only a month before, insisted their courtship be short. He wanted to get settled into the shanty and there was much work to be done.

"It needs a woman's touch, darling," he said as they strolled the same path they'd taken on their first walk together.

Emily looked up, her heart beating quickly as the sunset painted the sky a soft orange, thinking of the times he'd reached for her hand, his finger stroking the soft skin of her palm.

He'd kissed her, too- often and in the dark, his hands seeking her face- and then her waist as he pulled her against him.

Emily resisted at first, the feeling of his body over-whelming, but as his lips continued their gentle progress, she began to feel an uncoiling inside of her-self that said this was right and good and what engaged couples were meant to do.

"I can't wait until our wedding night," he whis-pered to her as they sat to supper not long after she'd accepted his proposal, Maddie's eyes lifting when Emily told him to hush. "You won't believe what I will show you, my darling."

Emily had sipped her soup, her cheeks red, won-dering how he knew these things and how many women he had shown them to.

The thought made her cross well into the night,

and when Marvin asked her to walk with him in the dusk as they always did, she refused.

"Emily," her mother said as she settled herself on the parlor sofa. "Why ever not?"

She looked at her father then, who sat reading his paper, unwilling to meet her eyes but unsettled just the same.

"I'm tired," she lied, her blue eyes rising to Marvin's, and she knew he was angry even as his lips hardened into a thin smile.

"Come outside with me," he repeated. "We need to talk."

She stood there, in the parlor she would one day get married in, her chin raised as she thought of the other women he had kissed and touched and told how beautiful they were.

"Go," Gerald spoke from behind his paper.

She frowned, unused to this treatment from her father and grabbed her straw hat and shawl- followed her fiancé into the gathering darkness and down the street where they wouldn't be heard.

"What's wrong with you?" Marvin asked once they were alone. "I've never seen you this way before."

Emily shook her head, "I should be ever so grateful if you would *show* me how to behave, Marvin. Just as you will show me how to become a proper wife on our wedding night."

"Darling—"

"How do you know I won't show *you* a thing or

two?" she spat, surprising herself and he grabbed hold of her elbow, squeezed.

"Don't say such things."

"I'm supposed to speak my mind, aren't I? It was one of the things you first admired about me."

He narrowed his eyes.

"Not in this way."

"Why?" she asked, glancing down the street again, hoping it was empty. "Is it because I'm a woman?"

"Yes," he hissed. "I expect to find my bride untouched."

She gritted her teeth, yanked away with such force it surprised him.

"And what am I to find on my wedding night? A man who is comparing me to all his other conquests?"

Marvin shook his head, his breath heavy and she knew he was trying to control his anger.

"Are you jealous, sweetheart?"

"Don't call me that!"

He took another coarse breath.

"Did you really think I'd never been with a woman? I'm *twenty-six* years old."

Emily stood still, the summer breeze blowing her long hair and wondered what her parents and Maddie were thinking as they sat in the parlor with the windows open, straining for the sound of their voices in the still of the evening.

"I—" she stammered. "I don't know what I thought..."

Marvin's fingers loosened, became tender again as he pulled her closer.

"My dear," he whispered, touching her face. "You must know that I was a different man before I met you."

She looked into his eyes, unsure she wanted to hear the rest.

"My brothers thought I would run the farm into the ground, and I admit that I gave them reason to believe it," he paused. "I did things I shouldn't have with people who were beneath me. But I swear to you, Emily Ives, you are the first woman I have ever, or *will ever,* love."

"Marvin," she whispered, her shame choking her. "I'm didn't think... I'm so-"

"It's alright," he said, kissing her cheeks now, the strange feeling building inside her stomach again. "I sometimes forget how young you are. And I know you're angry because you love me. And I can forgive you for that reason."

She nodded; tears she'd held inside falling freely now.

"I promise you will be the only woman I think of on our wedding night," he looked at her intently. "And every night after."

She smiled, the tightness in her chest lifting then even as it built again now, in the parlor of her home just before her wedding.

"Are you feeling well?" Maddie asked, coming

closer, her dark hair curled in a way that made her look like a doll. "You look pale."

"I'm fine," she said, her heart hammering.

"This is such an exciting day," she said. "Aren't you excited, Em?"

She nodded quickly, unsure why she should be frightened when the door opened, and the reverend walked in.

He was tall and skinny, looking something like Ichabod Crane from the Sleepy Hollow book she'd read, and she covered her mouth to hide her smile.

"Are you ready, Emily?" he asked, turning to look for the groom and at that moment the screen door opened, the quickening steps announcing Marvin's arrival.

She'd expected him earlier, had thought he would want to talk with her parents a little bit before they were married but he had stayed at the shanty until her mother sent Maddie to make sure everything was as it should be.

Emily waited anxiously for her sister to return, hopeful that everything was all right and when she entered her bedroom, telling her Marvin was taking extra care with his appearance, she wilted in relief.

And now he was here, walking around the corner of the dining room, his russet hair slicked down, a cotton shirt and dark pants painting a picture that seemed unfamiliar and when he saw her, he stopped, unable to conceal his astonishment.

"Are you ready, Mr. Jones?" the reverend asked,

and he nodded, took his place by Emily's side as they said words meant to bind them together forever.

And then Marvin was placing a golden band on her finger, and she was placing one on his, and then the preacher said they were husband and wife, and Emily drew a deep breath, expecting to feel different.

Marvin came closer, put his hand on her cheek, kissing her softly in front of these people.

Maddie had told her, after their mother went to the kitchen, that Marvin had stayed so long at the shanty preparing the bedroom for them, for *her*, because he did not want his bride to spend her wedding night in a room that wasn't finished.

"He loves you," Maddie assured her as she took her hand and squeezed. "He's trying to make everything perfect for your arrival."

Emily thought back to this now, as she stood in the dining room surrounded by food that had been prepared by the ladies from the church auxiliary.

It seemed the line of people waiting to greet Marvin would never end, and still she needed to greet them and be kind when her mind was on the room that was now finished and the bed they would share.

She thought about it as Carrie came through the front door, smiling in a way that reminded her of their foot races behind the schoolhouse.

"Em," she said, her black hair done up like Maddie's, her dress a rich blue. "It seems like I haven't seen you in ages. And now you are married! Let me meet this man who has stolen you away."

"How is James?" she asked, wondering if he would come, knowing he wouldn't.

"Heartbroken, of course," Carrie frowned. "He had hopes of standing in Marvin's place."

Emily blushed, looked down.

"I'm the one you should be fretting over," Carrie continued. "My only wish was that you would one day be my sister and now that hope has vanished."

Emily took her friend's hand, squeezing it as Marvin approached from behind.

"This must be the Caroline I've heard so much about," he nodded, the charm he seemed to use at will in full evidence here.

"I am the very one," Carrie replied, her eyes sparkling and when he turned to greet someone else moments later, she began to giggle.

"My brother does not hold a candle to him," she said. "You are lucky."

Emily smiled; her earlier fears forgotten because Carrie found Marvin handsome.

And then she was moving again in an endless circle between the parlor and dining room as more people arrived, her father's eyes following when she came close.

"Emily," he said, the warmth she had always known taking a distant turn.

"Pa," she replied, her eyes on the people moving from room to room.

"Are you enjoying yourself?" Gerald asked, his manner formal and she did not know how to answer, suddenly aware that he might be thinking of her wedding night as well.

"Of course," she smiled, bowing her head as someone passed, pressing closer to Gerald when he took hold of her elbow.

He turned to her, his blue eyes promising all the things gathered from her happy childhood and she leaned forward, kissed him on the cheek.

She felt his smile beneath her lips as he reached over to pat her hand.

"I hope you are happy."

She closed her eyes, stayed where she was for a moment with her face pressed to the side of his neck.

"My Emilou."

"Yes," she whispered, unable to remember the last time he'd called her that.

"You have married a fine man."

She nodded, not wanting to break away.

"You belong to him, now."

She looked up, her blue eyes questioning.

"Your life will be apart from ours."

Her pulse quickened; her confusion deepened with her father's words.

"Pa-"

He patted her arm, his eyes seeming to glisten when her mother came from some far corner.

"Emily," she said. "It's time to see you off."

She nodded, knowing what her mother meant and before long they stood alone in the parlor, thinking of

41

the visitors that seemed to have come and gone so quickly.

A bag had been packed with some of her clothing, and tomorrow afternoon her father would bring over the furniture they'd bought as a wedding present.

Maddie stood by the door, her eyes down and Emily wondered why her mood matched her father's.

"Come, darling," Marvin said, suddenly at her side as he picked up her bag. "I'm anxious to show you our new home."

Emily nodded. She'd already seen the shanty, had tried to imagine the house it would one day become and couldn't picture it.

As if sensing her thoughts, Maddie spoke.

"The room is ever so cheerful, Em. I made a rug in secret and Marvin put it beside the rocking chair."

She smiled, her sadness deepening.

"Thank you."

Turning to her mother, she asked, "When will you expect me at the store?"

Her mother glanced sharply at Marvin.

"Why... I—"

"We're not sure," he said, his tone light. "There's work to be done at our new home."

Emily took a slow breath, her temper peaking.

"Are you saying I won't be working at the store?"

Gerald cleared his throat, clearly disturbed as Marvin held up a hand.

"I don't see how you could possibly have time."

Emily took a step aside, removed his hand from her arm as Gerald stepped forward.

"You assured me you had discussed this with her," he said. "You told us it was Emily's decision to leave."

Marvin gave a light laugh. "It was our decision. And a sound one at that."

"*Our* decision?" Emily echoed, her emotions churning, and Maddie put a hand on her arm, squeezed lightly.

"It's bad luck to argue on your wedding night," she laughed, her eyes darting between her father and Marvin. "I'm sure we will need you at the store sooner rather than later."

Marvin cleared his throat, nodded quickly. Then they were climbing into the wagon, and he was urging his old mare on while Emily sat perfectly still on the high seat; her knees clenched together as they rolled down the darkened road.

Marvin was silent, and Emily guessed that he was angry with her for contradicting him.

Halfway to the shanty, she saw him straighten on the seat.

"I thought you would not want to work once we were married."

She turned to look at him, shook her head.

"We never discussed it."

He tapped the reins, and the horse took off at a fast walk.

"Am I obliged to discuss everything with you? Or can I assume you want to be a proper wife?"

She glanced at him out of the corner of her eye. Minutes passed before she found the words.

"To be a proper wife, I must have a proper husband."

He turned to her.

"You'll know what I'm made of soon enough."

She swallowed, her stomach in knots, her knees still pressed together as they rolled to a stop in front of the shanty.

"Emily," Marvin's voice startled her, and she looked down, surprised to see that he now stood beside the wagon. "Are you coming inside?"

She nodded, took his hand and climbed down. Once inside, she saw that a small fire had been built.

"Who lit the stove?" she asked, and he smiled.

"I have friends who are always willing to lend a hand."

She pressed her lips together, wondering why the thought did not comfort her and then glanced around the room.

The space was small, a faded curtain dividing it from the corner where their bed awaited. The rocking chair Maddie had spoken of was pulled close to the wood stove, a red and blue crocheted rug beside it.

She remembered the quilt her mother had given them, imagined lying beneath it with Marvin and felt her legs weaken.

"Dearest," Marvin said, his hands on her shoulders now. "I'm sorry I didn't discuss the store with you."

She drew a breath in through her nose.

"Do you forgive me?" he asked, his hands falling to her bare arms, and she felt gooseflesh rise there.

"Marvin—"

"It will never happen again," he said, stepping closer.

She gave a shy smile.

"You cannot imagine how much I want you. How long I've waited for this moment."

She clasped her hands in front of her, wondering how to answer when he gently turned her and began to undo the hooks on the back of her dress.

"Marvin," she said, shocked that he would begin before they had unhitched the mare or put her things safely away. "The horse should be put up. And my journals shouldn't stay in the damp—"

"Hush," he smiled, his mouth on the curve of her neck, his lips parting and Emily felt his tongue on her skin as the wedding dress slid to the floor in a pile of silk and crinoline.

"Please," she said, wanting him to stop for a moment as he worked at her corset, undoing it as his hands slid down her stomach and between her legs, his fingers seeking the place she knew he must touch. "Stop—"

He pulled back, looked at her with displeasure.

"There's no stopping this," he whispered. "I will be as tender as I can."

Her slip fell to the floor, her flushed skin exposed

to his gaze as he pulled his shirt from his trousers. Soon he was naked in the firelight, and Emily felt her eyes drawn to the place between his legs, surprised that desire and fear could exist together.

"You are so beautiful," he said, his voice soft. "I've never seen a woman who is your equal."

She felt herself stiffen even as he drew aside the curtain, leading her to the bed before lowering her onto it.

Then he was on top of her, his hands in her hair, his bare chest pressed to hers and she began to respond to him, the feel of his mouth opening, his warm tongue exploring places he had never dared to on their evening walks.

"Yes," he whispered into her ear as she began to move against him. "You know what to do."

Emily smiled, her hands splaying across his back, the kerosene light playing off his hair, all thoughts of her parents and the store and the mare waiting outside in the damp air leaving her.

There was only this place, and this bed, and this man- his skin against hers as he whispered that she must be still because he couldn't wait any longer.

And then his hands were on her knees, easing them apart and she felt her back stiffen as he began to push something inside of her.

She arched upwards, her hands circling to his stomach in an attempt to push him away or at the very least, make him move slowly.

"Em," he rasped. "I can't wait."

She heard his breath come in heavy rasps, his arms

holding her down as he reached between her legs to the place where their bodies touched.

She felt a sharp pain and let out a gasp, one Marvin covered with a kiss. He stayed that way for a moment before pulling back, his head hanging beside hers and she didn't dare move, didn't dare breathe for fear the pain would continue and she would displease him.

"Emily," he whispered. "Are you all right?"

She stared at the ceiling; every breath labored and nodded.

She felt his smile against her skin, felt him begin to move inside of her and gritted her teeth, wondering when the wanting she had felt earlier would come back and listened to his staggered breath, the squeak of the bed springs giving her something to focus on.

"God," he rasped, and she closed her eyes, trying to think about something else even as the pain began to lessen, a spark of heat building beneath it.

She held onto the ember, trying to keep it from dying in the wind and made a low noise, one that seemed to excite her husband.

"You're more than I hoped for," he whispered into her ear, his movements sharp now and she bit her lip to keep from crying out as he groaned, his head arching back in a moment of pure abandon Emily wished they could share.

And then he was still, his body limp and damp against her and she wondered what had happened to the small flame that had been burning inside of her.

She looked away, felt shame seep into her bones

because she had wanted it to go on, wanted to move and feel the ember grow into a flame and now it was over.

"My darling wife," he said, lifting his face from her neck, his eyes wide with a wonder she'd never seen before. "How can you be so perfect?"

She moved then, to the side and away from him and he looked at her, his face seeming to take on a shadow.

"How did it feel?" he asked.

She pressed her face into her arm, feeling like she should hide herself from the man who had just touched every part of her.

"Emily?" he asked again, an edge to his voice. "Tell me what's wrong."

She felt tears now and had no idea if she was happy or sad or an odd mixture of the two as he pulled her against his chest.

"I'm sorry it happened so fast."

She nodded against his skin, his words filling the darkness that had settled around her heart.

"I will be gentle next time. I will show you how a woman can feel what a man does."

She looked up, wondering if the other women had felt it.

"Did your mother tell you nothing?" he asked. "About this?"

She clenched her jaw, suddenly angry.

"Nothing," she said quickly.

"Well," he shook his head. "I am sorry for that."

She felt the stab of his disappointment.

"Did I do something wrong?"

He touched her cheek, shook his head.

"I did... because you felt something that I did not. Something *happened* to you that didn't happen to me."

Marvin drew in his breath, rolled over to sit up on the edge of the bed.

"I must tend to the horse," he said while pulling his pants back on. "Tomorrow will be busy, so you'd best get some sleep."

She lay there, unbelieving, thinking that he should lie with her and hold her and talk about what had happened between them.

"With any luck you have already conceived a son."

"Do you?" she began, pulling the blanket to her chin. "Do you think it is possible?"

He turned to her, touched her hair as if he were touching spun gold.

"You are young and eager to please me. All these things make me happy- make me believe you'll soon be pregnant."

She looked at him, unsure what to say.

"I may be gone for a little bit."

She drew in her breath, cold water running inside of her veins.

"Where are you going?"

He smiled while buttoning up his shirt and ran a hand through his hair.

"Don't wait up."

She looked at him for a long moment, watched his smile fade to nothing before he turned and walked outside into the darkness.

Chapter Seven

Emily sat in the darkness, holding James to her breast when Ruthie Merritt poked her head through the opening in the canvas.

One leap and she was inside, a fistful of her gingham dress in her hand as she maneuvered around the barrels and sacks that had become her new home.

"I'm so sorry," Emily said, her voice small. "I should be able to take care of him."

"No, you shouldn't," Ruthie said, her hair falling over her shoulders in two long braids that made her seem younger. "You're worked up about meeting your uncle, is all. Once he's feeding, you'll have no trouble."

She'd been inside the wagon most of the morning trying to get James to nurse, and when Clementine had discovered her, suggesting she use some milk from the Merritt's cow before offering Ruthie herself.

"Don't you think?" the young woman repeated, and Emily looked up, nodded, her mind wandering to Fort Kearny and what would happen when they discovered only parts of her story were true.

Her uncle was one of those- and something of a black sheep on her mother's side, having left home when Patricia was only a girl.

Once every month or so a letter would arrive, telling of his adventures as a guide and tracker in the unorganized territories and what sort of people he had met living amongst the natives.

Patricia would shake her head, passing the letter to Gerald, who chuckled at something while Maddie and Emily waited patiently on the sofa, hoping they could see what was written.

"Rand was always wild," Patricia said. "Pa never knew what to do with him."

"He acts like a perfect rogue," Gerald laughed, and Patricia hushed him, her eyes moving to her daughters. "Does he even have a home?"

"It's in the Black Hills," she explained patiently. "French Creek to be exact. He went west to seek his fortune and now works as a guide helping emigrants to Sacramento and Oregon."

Gerald shook his head, unable to imagine a life apart from the one he was living.

"Maybe he will make his way here," Patricia had mused. "He must be to Kearny and Laramie quite often, to mail so many letters."

Gerald huffed, adjusted his paper.

"He is certainly a wild ruffian. Maybe our Emilou will write a story about it."

Emily smiled, her eyes shifting to Maddie, who took the letter from their mother.

"As silly as that story would be," Gerald continued. "I believe this is a warning not to venture far from home."

Maddie nodded, and Emily believed her sister meant it even as a strange desire to see The Black Hills began to grow inside of her.

"Emily?" Ruthie asked, her voice bringing her back to the wagon bed and the baby she couldn't feed. "Can I have him?"

Emily started, then handed James to her.

A moment later she had unfastened her dress and the child was happily nursing, his little hands kneading her breast before falling to his side in satisfaction.

"He just needs to latch on," Ruthie said. "And my milk's already come in."

Emily nodded, trying to swallow her sorrow. "What happened to your baby?"

Ruthie did not look at her, touched James's head.

"My daughter died three weeks after she was born. Doctor said it was pneumonia."

Emily pressed her lips together. "I'm sorry."

Ruthie glanced up, a sad smile dusting her lips.

"Her father wanted nothing to do with us. I don't even think his folks knew I was pregnant."

Emily folded her hands, waiting until she chose to say more.

"My brother was fit to be tied. And when Caleb's mad, you'd better watch out!"

Emily stiffened, thinking of the man who'd delivered James, a person she hadn't seen since.

"Pa died in the mines when I was twelve and Ma followed four years later," she paused, touched James's head again, her finger lingering on the space between his eyes as he continued to suckle. "Caleb was looking after me and doing a poor job of it."

"Is that why you left home?" she asked.

Ruthie looked at Emily again, her brow creased.

"Caleb's wife mentioned it once," she paused, and Emily felt a strange lump in her throat. "But then she got sick. And I lost the baby and..."

She trailed off, unsure what to say and Emily looked down.

"We decided to leave the past behind us. Everyone else was settled and I'm good with a gun. Say, how old are you, anyway?"

"Nineteen," Emily replied, trying to imagine the little thing in front of her shooting anything. "My birthday's in September. How many are in your family?"

"Two sisters and three brothers. I'm seventeen and Caleb is eight years older. He took up Pa's job after he died and then again after our farm went bust."

Emily's heart softened for the man who'd seen so much at such a young age.

"And you can shoot, you say?"

Ruthie nodded. "I hit what I aim at, generally."

Emily smiled, thinking she might need some lessons with a rifle if she planned to live in the north country. "Can you teach me?"

The girl looked up, adjusted James in her arms.

"Teach you to shoot *and* nurse a baby?"

Emily nodded.

"Not sure I have that much time on my hands."

Emily smiled, not sure if she was joking but enjoying her company just the same.

"We can't waste daylight on either count. Kearny is only a week's ride."

The thought made her go still even as Ruth burped the baby and handed him back to her.

"I'll make a deal with you. You get to shooting proper and we'll take Caleb's gelding and Clementine's mare and go have us a little hunting party."

Emily laughed, her spirits lifting for the first time since leaving Independence.

"You should come to our fire when we make camp tonight. My brother plays the fiddle and there might be dancing."

"Midwife, coal miner *and* fiddler," she smiled. "Your brother is a man of many talents."

Ruth grinned. "You have no idea."

Emily paused. "I really couldn't-"

"Why not?"

She sat with James in her arms, having no excuse

aside from the uncomfortable feeling she was sure to have when she saw Caleb Merritt again.

"It's my brother, isn't it?" Ruthie asked, and Emily looked down.

"I haven't seen him since James was born, and it wasn't a typical introduction—"

"He's awful, isn't he?" Ruthie interrupted. "He should have come to see you right away."

"No," Emily laughed. "I didn't expect—"

"He's been so worried about you slowing down the wagons and us not getting over the mountains in time. You heard about that party eight years back that got stuck in the snow and ended up eating their dead folks!"

Emily swallowed. She'd heard about it all right, which made her more determined than ever to prove she wasn't a burden.

"I don't know why he talks about such things, he used to be a lot sweeter than he is now. Why, he was a regular dandy when he met his wife. And the fun we used to have when he'd play his fiddle! And to think I had to beg him to bring it along. Probably on account of how much Celia loved it."

"Oh—"

"But if he knows you're coming, he might play a song or two."

"Ruth—"

"Please come," she said, her eyes holding Emily's and it made her pause.

"I," she began, looking past Ruthie and into the memory of everything she'd left behind. "I suppose—"

"Good!" she clapped her hands together. "I'll tell Caleb."

Emily tried to return the smile, wondering why she felt like she'd just swallowed a whole hive of bumblebees.

Chapter Eight

Emily looked down at the simple gold band on her finger, then rolled over onto her side and away from her husband, his soft snores echoing against the walls of the shanty.

It was August and she'd been married for two months. They'd spent the summer fixing up the claim and getting in a garden. It was late to be planting, but Marvin hoped for a good harvest that would see them through the fall months.

They'd even purchased a cow and a handful of chickens and now Emily was milking in the mornings and collecting eggs in the evening.

Marvin also began building a shelter for the hogs he hoped to buy, saying there was nothing like pork to liven up a meal and they could begin making money if the market prices were high enough.

It was then she asked to work at the store again,

sure her father would pay her a wage now that she was married, but Marvin just shook his head, saying it wasn't quite time.

Her parents came to visit the day after their wedding and she stood in the small space, knowing there was no room for them, her heart lifting when her father told her he was going to order a new stove from Chicago.

Marvin, who'd come home late the night before and was just waking up, held his hand out to Gerald. The older man responded slowly, telling them he would like Emily to pick it out from the catalog in their store, and that it would take some time to arrive.

She'd nodded, as eager as a girl on Christmas morning, and when he'd finally brought it in the wagon, Emily stood by the front door, crying.

Marvin helped connect the stovepipe, remarking about how happy he was, but when supper came, his mood darkened.

"You made quite a show in front of your father today," he said, and Emily didn't know if he was having fun at her expense or truly angry.

"What do you mean?" she asked, taking a bite of the stew they'd been eating for leftovers since the day before yesterday.

He pointed at her with his fork, still chewing, and she found the way he spoke repulsive.

"You wept," he said. "Over a stove."

Emily took a deep breath, trying to hold her temper. She knew what would come later that night, knew that he would lay with her and hold her and kiss her and do the same things they had on their wedding night.

She knew she would put her arms around his neck, trying to feel that tiny spark again, wondering when it would come and how Marvin could feel it over and over when she did not.

She knew he was cross about what was happening in their bed and an argument over a stove should be avoided.

"Of course, I did," she said, unable to hide her annoyance. "It is hard to cook over a fire and Father knows I've always wanted one."

Marvin continued to chew; his eyes fixed on her.

"And Emilou always gets what she wants."

Emily stopped eating, dabbed at her mouth with her napkin.

"Your parents will think you're unhappy."

She straightened her shoulders, took a breath before dropping her eyes.

"Are you?" he asked.

She continued to cut her meat with her fork and knife.

"Is it something I'm doing?" he asked, and she looked up.

"I'm lonely, Marvin," she said. "I want to work at the store."

"I need you here."

"I want to see my parents. And Maddie. And my friends."

"Friends?"

"Yes," she said. "I work all day in the shanty and on that shelter for the hogs, not to mention milking and cooking and then I'm so tired all I can do is sleep."

"Really," he said, a harsh edge to his voice. "Are you sure?"

She looked up at him, uncomfortable. "Yes—"

"I beg to differ, my sweet. You go to bed, but you do not sleep. No, you lie there beneath me while I try to be the proper husband you wanted so badly."

"Marvin—"

"Every night you remind me of my failings."

She shook her head.

"I've been with other women."

She felt her heart freeze in her chest.

"I've never failed to please them and yet you deny me the thing I want most."

She threw her napkin down, stood up. "I haven't denied you anything! I lie with you every night, listening to you take pleasure from me while I feel *nothing!*"

He looked at her closely.

"You feel nothing?"

She raised her chin. "Would you rather I pretend? Because Maddie once told me I could make a career on the stage."

He laughed lightly and Emily waited, the cow lowing in the pasture, the sound of crickets beginning to prick the evening air, the wind so hot she thought she would suffocate.

"Will you pretend now, Em?"

"Marvin—" she began, ashamed.

"Do you think that's what I want," he asked, emotion coating his voice. "I thought you'd be with child by now."

She looked down at her lap.

"A woman is most fertile when she takes her pleasure from a man."

She swallowed, her voice a whisper. "Then I fear I will never conceive."

He did not answer, just cleared his throat and wiped his mouth with his napkin before placing it beside his plate. Standing up, he walked towards the door.

"Where are you going?" she asked.

Marvin turned quickly, took a step towards her and she started, backed away.

"I've a mind to go to town."

"Town?" she repeated helplessly. "Why?"

"I suspect I will find something there to amuse me."

She swallowed, unbelieving. "*Amuse* you?"

"Don't wait up for me."

"Marvin—"

"Perhaps you will feel something while I am gone."

"What do you mean?"

"When you are alone."

"Alone?" she asked, disbelieving. "How—"

"If you place your hand where I do, and do the

things that I do, we'll know if you feel anything or if you're simply unable to."

"Unable?" she said weakly. "I don't understand."

"If you are frigid," he said bluntly. "Then we'll know you're at fault."

He grabbed his hat and stood in the doorway, waiting for her to say something and she could only wonder how they'd strayed so far from crying over a stove.

"Marvin."

He waited.

"Please don't go. I'm sorry—"

He shook his head. "I don't think you are."

Then he was gone, the darkness closing up to consume him while she stood watching the road, wondering if she had just been abandoned or if he would return after sampling the women who lived above the Lamplight Saloon.

She eyed the cabinet where he kept his whiskey and got a glass from the cupboard. She knew her father and mother would be horrified, knew Maddie might giggle and take a sip herself, and poured a glass.

Sitting in the rocking chair, Maddie's rug at her feet, she thought about her life and the sorrow that had consumed her since marrying Marvin.

Her thoughts turned to James, and she quickly finished her glass, her mind fuzzy as she poured herself a second.

He wasn't handsome, but his heart was kind, and she couldn't imagine him speaking to her the way

Marvin had, couldn't imagine backing away when he stood, afraid of his temper.

She wondered where he was now, wondered if she could ask Carrie about him if she came to call.

But she never came to call.

No one did.

Marvin made sure of that.

She looked at her second glass of whiskey, half gone now.

Marvin had left for town over an hour ago and she imagined him lying naked with a girl from the Lamplight, his face contorting like it did when he was on top of her, his breath coming in spurts and was glad someone else was enduring it tonight.

The woman would know how to move in the right way, know how to make the right noises and if she didn't feel anything- she would pretend.

She looked down at her lap, her hand close to the place Marvin always touched and wondered if she should do the same.

Then we'll know you're at fault...

Was it because of her they hadn't conceived a child?

She wished she'd talked to her mother, wished Patricia had told her what would happen between a husband and wife and could not imagine having the conversation.

She poured another glass, her mind swimming, and took a long drink, anger coursing through her because Marvin should have shown her what to do instead of laying the blame at her feet.

She sat her glass down, her eyes heavy and placed her hand between her legs, her fingers moving in slow circles as she began to do the things Marvin did, praying no one would see her.

But who would see her, in the middle of nowhere with the wind blowing hot and her husband off with a whore.

She drew her hand back, unsettled, then touched herself again.

She remembered the small spark she felt on their wedding night, back when she was unaware of her husband's nature. She remembered wanting more and moved her hand more quickly.

Her head fell back, the whiskey erasing her shame as she felt a heat build beneath her fingertips, certain this was what Marvin meant, relief coursing through her because if she could feel even this small thing, she was not frigid.

Her eyes slid closed, her lips parted as she began to make the sounds Marvin did, unable to understand what would happen when this thing reached its end and for the first time saw how a man and a woman could enjoy lying together in the dark.

A moment passed, then two as she moved her hand in a way that pulled a small cry from her throat, her toes curling against the plank floor when the door swung open.

She sat up, her eyes wide as Marvin came into the

room, a look on his face that said he was pleased with what he saw.

"Em," he grumbled, swaying on his feet. "What're you doing?"

She pulled her hand away, straightened her skirt and stood, the whiskey giving her courage.

"What you couldn't!" she cried, one finger in his face.

"Ah," he said, shutting the door behind him. "Then you are not frigid."

Emily raised her chin, ashamed that she wanted to finish what she'd been doing.

Marvin stepped closer, the smell of whiskey on his breath, his eyes taking in her empty glass and the bottle that sat beside it.

"Have you been drinking, Mrs. Jones?"

Emily took a step back, straightened her shoulders.

"And what if I have?"

"Then I would say we are in the same boat," he smiled, began taking off his coat, his fingers wandering to the buttons of his shirt.

"Marvin-"

"And I would say I am not angry with my wife. In fact, I would say I enjoy seeing her this way."

"And what way is that?" she asked, almost to the bed by now, her eyes drawn to her husband's bare chest as he shrugged out of his shirt.

She remembered, in their early days of courting, wondering what his body looked like beneath his clothes, entranced by the way his arms felt when he pulled her against him. She remembered feeling embarrassed - and then the way he had taken her quickly on her wedding night, leaving no room for discovery.

But now, with her fear dulled, she admired him for the virile man he was.

"What are you thinking, Emily?" he asked, his hands on the buttons of his pants and she could see that he was aroused through the fabric. For a moment she thought about the women at the Lamplight Saloon, wondering if he'd been with one before coming to her.

"Have you been with a whore?" she asked, taking a step towards him, her hands on his as he lowered his trousers.

"Yes," he said, his eyes on her. "But I was thinking of my wife."

She raised her hand and slapped him across the face.

"I could divorce you for that."

He winced. Then smiled again.

"I don't think you will."

She looked at him, considering what to do next.

"How do you know?"

He tilted his head, his tongue licking the corner of his mouth.

"You're all I think about, Emily. All I want."

"No-"

"To see you just now," he paused, reaching for her. "When I came in the door. You're so fucking beautiful.

I want to make you feel that way. Want to hear the sounds you were making."

"Then do it."

He stood still for a moment, hardly believing she was giving him permission, and then lunged for her, his hands on the bodice of her dress, ripping it from her shoulders and even though Emily knew she should be afraid, she wasn't.

She responded, her mouth open to his, her head back as he bit the soft skin of her throat. Then he was kissing her shoulders, and she pushed him towards the bed and made him sit down on it.

"I will be the husband," she whispered, his head at her breast as he drew a nipple into his mouth, suckling as a baby would. "And you will please me."

He fell backwards, and she stepped out of her ruined dress, crawled on top of him and took him inside of herself in a way she never had before.

Her husband began to moan, his hands on her hips, as he tried to guide her in the way she must move but she shook him off, rising and falling in the way that brought pleasure to the deepest part of herself.

He seemed to realize this because he stopped, his eyes wide with wonder as he watched her atop him, her hair loose, her skin awash in the glow of the fire that had grown low in the hearth.

"Emily," he gasped. "My God—"

She didn't hear him. This act was about her and what she must do to bring an end to the thing she'd first felt on her wedding night.

68

She moved steadily, her hands on his shoulders, holding him in place and in that way, he existed only to please her, and she was once again as powerful as she had once been on their evening walks.

"What do you want?" he rasped, "What can I give you?"

"I want a child," she moaned, the feeling that she had just stepped into a hot bath growing around the place where their bodies joined.

"Yes," he gasped, drawing her mouth to his, his tongue sweeping inside.

"And I want to work at the store," she pulled back, moving faster now, convinced he would give her anything.

"You can," he gasped, jerking beneath her. "Yes."

"And I want to see my family. And Carrie and James."

She felt her mistake at once, the whiskey bringing forth the name of the man she'd pictured even as she climbed on top of her husband.

Marvin took hold of her hips and stilled her, his fingers curling into her flesh as he used his weight to shift her over and beneath him.

"What are you doing?" Emily asked, her fear rising.

"Now I will be the husband," he said. "And erase that man's name from your mind."

She looked at him, her desire gone, replaced by hate.

"And you, having just been with a whore."

He drew his hand back, slapped her as she'd

slapped him, and Emily felt blood on the inside of her mouth.

"Marvin—" she gasped but he put his hands around her throat, began to squeeze.

"I don't love a whore, Emily. And yet you say the name of the man you would have married." He paused, looking down on her even as he began to move inside of her again. "I'll kill him, Emily. And it will be on *your* hands."

She opened her mouth, tried to say his name but her breath was gone, the room going spotty before her eyes.

Marvin loosened his hold, afraid for a moment that he'd gone too far, and she tried to wiggle free, but he held her down, this time by the shoulders.

"I'm not done, Darling," he breathed against her cheek, his tongue resting there, the skin beneath it throbbing from where he'd slapped her. "I want you to know why our fire burns so brightly tonight. Those journals you kept, the ones with your silly drawings and poems... I fed the stove you love so much with them."

Emily gasped, her arms flailing in an attempt to break his hold. Instead, she rose up as high as she could and spit in his face.

"You bastard—"

Marvin smiled, wiped the spittle from his cheek.

"Say you love me."

She clamped her mouth shut, and he put his own over it, bit her lower lip in a way that made her cry out.

"Say it," he whispered, still deep inside her but unmoving.

She turned her head to the side, tears stinging her cheeks.

"I will hold you here all night, Emily," he smiled, "And every night after and there is nothing your parents or Carrie or your darling *James* can do about it."

She whimpered, tried to move and found him as solid as anything she'd ever fought against.

"You are mine," he whispered, his hips rising and falling again as he held her down, his breath coming in the short pants she recognized and she went limp, closed her eyes and let him do what he wanted, the pleasure she'd once felt buried beneath mountains as cold as snow.

Chapter Nine

Emily sat looking out the hole in the back of the wagon where it was cinched, wondering if the dress she was wearing was festive enough for the fire Ruthie had spoken of when Clementine stuck her head through.

"How's James?" she asked, and for a moment Emily thought she was talking about someone other than the baby.

"He's sleeping," she said, watching the campfires glowing behind Clementine's head, figures moving in front of them, and she wondered if one of them might be Caleb Merritt.

She thought of his fiddle, imagined him playing a tune and smiled.

"Gather him up," Clem said. "Jake and I are going to the fire."

"But-"

"Ruthie'll feed him."

Emily's cheeks reddened.

"Caleb's been asking after you and it's high time you get acquainted."

Emily knew avoiding the man who had saved her and James was going to be harder the longer they traveled together.

And she didn't want to avoid him, she just burned with embarrassment at what he'd seen wondering what he would think of her traveling alone and without a husband.

"Come," Clem said. "We've camped at a lovely spot. The emigrants call it Alcove Springs."

"Oh?"

"We'll have music and dancing. And Jake has said there's a little waterfall."

Emily shifted, remembering the times she'd enjoyed the barn dances back home, the music playing as she spun with her friends from the schoolhouse, the boys watching from the side as her parents sipped punch from cut glass cups.

That time seemed far away, a life erased forever but if she could enjoy this one night, maybe she could carry it with her in the days to come.

"Let's go," Clem extended her hand and Emily gathered James in his blanket, stepped carefully from the wagon.

The night was unseasonably cool, a breeze blowing from across the prairie that brought the scent of wet earth and dry grass.

She saw the oxen standing close to the wagon, chewing the grass they'd been grazing on, heard the rise and fall of voices gathered around the other fires, the smell of meat cooking over an open flame making her mouth water.

"Jake's already set up next to the spring pool," Clem exclaimed. "I think they are cooking antelope for supper. Caleb shot one earlier and I heard Ruthie might boil some potatoes. And I have butter from that bucket of milk we've been jostling around for days."

She shifted James's weight, felt him stir and hugged him closer to her breast.

She remembered the morning after Marvin had held her down and slapped her and put his hands around her throat. He'd been tired and slow from the whiskey the night before, had rolled over and touched her stomach as she lay next to him.

"I'm sorry, my darling," he rasped, his eyes going wide when he looked at her face and Emily knew he saw a swollen cheek and cut lip.

He reached for her, held her lightly.

"I'm sure you're pregnant with our son," he whispered. "The way you were last night, when you were on top of me," he smiled. "I'll never forget that sight."

"Marvin-"

"I can't abide his name," he said, his eyes holding hers and for a moment Emily thought he might be sorry for what had happened. "I can't abide it in your mind or on your lips and that's why I acted like a cad."

She didn't answer.

"I promise to never act that way again if you forget he lives and breathes."

"You said you were going to kill him."

Marvin laughed.

"Best not to listen to me when I've been drinking."

Emily tried to smile, gave a small nod if only to get him to remove his hand from the place she never wanted to be touched again.

"Stay close to the shanty for a few days and rest," he said, sitting up now, his face shadowed. "I'll finish the shelter for the hogs."

She didn't answer.

"Will that suit you, Em?"

She tensed. Nodded.

"Good," he whispered. "We'll forget this ever happened."

"Emily!" She heard her name now, across the darkened plain that dipped towards a grove of trees and knew Ruthie Merritt had caught sight of her. "Over here!"

She adjusted James again, heard him gurgle and settle back against her chest, content to sleep, and quickened her pace.

The Merritt wagon sat on the western edge of a small meadow, just near a shelf of rock where a stream tumbled into a waterfall.

Another wagon was pulled close, and Emily wondered who might have joined them. She saw Jake May standing by the fire, cooking something on a metal spit that he was turning, and she knew it was the antelope Caleb had killed.

"Emily," Jake smiled, and Emily drew closer, saw another man standing just on the edge of the firelight.

She knew it was Caleb Merritt by the set of his shoulders, and the hat she'd seen him wearing from a distance. Aside from that, she had only a vague memory of his face, her delirium having erased all memory of his appearance.

He turned then, the soft glow illuminating his features and she swallowed, unsure what to say as Ruthie took her elbow.

He stood for a moment, his gray eyes taking her in before approaching at a measured pace and Emily realized he was just as uneasy as she was.

"Ma'am," he said, and she remembered his voice, deep and sure and strong, telling her what she must do to bring James into the world and felt tears prickle the inside of her eyelids.

"Mr. Merritt," she bowed her head, suddenly aware of her appearance even as she took in his.

He was tall, standing just higher than Jake, his hat hiding a generous amount of dark blond hair that seemed to be streaked by the sun. She looked down at his hands, the first that had ever held her baby, and felt a scalding shame at not introducing herself before.

"Mr. Merritt," she began. "I—"

"Call me Caleb."

"Caleb," she said, the name strange to her lips.

"How do you do?" she asked, but he didn't smile, just shifted his gaze to the baby in her arms.

"I'm well," he said, his mouth a straight line and Emily wondered if he was displeased. "How's the baby?"

"James is fine," she said, feeling like she was taking high tea with the Queen of England instead of talking to a strange man in the middle of a moonlit prairie.

"Good," Caleb said. "It was dangerous business starting on the trail so close to giving birth."

"I'm aware of that," she said, unsure if he was baiting her, the flickering light shadowing his face, making it impossible to read.

"I assume you have no family," he said, his gray eyes seeming to cut through her. "And the baby's father is gone."

"Caleb," Ruthie hissed.

He turned to his sister; his face hard.

"It's a question that needs to be asked."

"Not here," his sister said, turning back to Emily. "And not now."

He paused before speaking.

"It's a question that needs to be asked even if no one else will," he paused. "A man has a right to see his son."

A long moment passed, one in which brother and sister stood facing each other while Emily glanced between, uncertain what she'd gotten herself into.

"Maybe you're right," Ruthie finally said, "But

Emily is my guest tonight and I'll thank you to mind your *darned* manners."

He raised his eyebrows, a hint of a smile playing on his lips and something in it made Emily straighten her shoulders.

"I'm perfectly capable of answering any question he may ask."

Caleb stepped back, crossed his arms against his chest.

"It's true I have no family to speak of," she said, her blue eyes catching hold of his, her gaze never wavering. "And while there was a man who contributed to the making of this child, he is certainly no father," she paused, unsure if she should say more. "Nor will he ever get the chance to be."

Caleb cleared his throat. "Ma'am—"

"And while I do thank you for bringing him safely into the world, I also trust this matter is now at rest."

Caleb Merritt looked at her, his eyes awakening for a brief moment before the shadows closed around them again.

"Nothing's ever put to rest out here," he said, and Emily felt something cold stir in her chest.

She raised her chin, adjusted James's weight.

"Sit down by the fire."

She wrinkled her nose.

Caleb Merritt stood, unsure what to say.

"May I have the pleasure of your company at my fire, Miss..." he trailed off, and Emily knew she would have to answer.

"Ives," she said. "Emily Ives."

He smiled then, an honest to goodness transformation of his face and Emily felt as if she were falling and looked down quickly to make sure James was still in her arms.

"Has a nice ring to it," he said, tipping his hat. "Pleased to make your acquaintance, Miss Ives. Aside from the wagon bed."

"Caleb," Ruthie shook her head, pulled Emily closer to the fire, where she sank into the grass, undone by the encounter.

A moment passed before Ruthie spoke again.

"There's no excuse for him. Cold one minute. Hot the next."

Emily shook her head, listened to James as he began to make a low cry in his throat that said she would have to feed him soon.

"He's testing me," she said. "To see if I'm telling the truth."

"Of course, you are."

Ruthie smiled, then walked away to tend to the potatoes that were boiling over a second fire.

Emily sat in the grass, the ring of flame dancing around her, a half-moon slowly climbing the sky as Clementine came to sit beside her.

"Well," she asked. "What did he say?"

"We introduced ourselves," she said, her eyes on Ruthie as a young woman came to stand beside her, her black hair hanging loose, a colorful shawl wrapped around her shoulders.

"Who's that?" Emily asked and Clementine sighed, shook her head.

"Her name is Beatrice and she's riding to Oregon with her aunt and uncle. How she attached herself to us, I'll never know, aside from the fact that Mr. Merritt is here."

Emily laughed, lifted James from his position so he could see the firelight.

"Why would that matter?"

Clem smiled, leaned closer and whispered in her ear. "She has a mind to fetch a husband before Fort Hall. That's the jumping off point where she'll be forced to go with them."

"Oh?" Emily asked, her eyes sweeping over the woman who stood beside Ruthie. "She won't have any trouble finding a husband."

"Her uncle spoke to Jake, and he seems ready to jump as soon as Caleb gives the word. She's been something of a problem for them and they were hoping to unload her, so to speak."

"Is that why she's so friendly with Ruth?" Emily asked, watching as the young girl carefully stirred the pot, careful not to look directly into Beatrice's eyes even as the other tried to attract her attention.

Clem nodded, bent down to coo at James.

"I believe it would do Mr. Merritt some good to marry again."

Emily straightened her back.

"What happened to his wife?"

Clem shook her head, held out her arms for James,

and Emily gave him to her, hopeful she would be spared the indignity of handing him to Ruthie when he started to cry.

"I believe it was some sort of sickness."

Emily peered across the fire to where Caleb stood beside Jake, his tall frame illuminated, his hair catching the light.

She saw Beatrice gaze at him and wondered at the knot forming in her belly.

She sat that way for some time, the prairie wind blowing her hair as James gurgled happily from Clementine's arms. Then Ruthie was carrying a plate towards her, and she was savoring the antelope meat and potatoes they had so carefully prepared.

Ruthie sat down, as did Beatrice, who seemed unable to do anything on her own and Emily wondered where the aunt and uncle were and if they were enjoying their peace and quiet inside the wagon.

"Hello," Beatrice said, her voice high and light. "I don't think we've been introduced."

Emily shook her head, saw Caleb glance at them and wondered if he was thinking of the wife who died of sickness.

The thought made her sad, made her want to take James back and hold him but Beatrice was bending down, making faces at him while he chewed on his tiny fist.

"He's so handsome," she said, her dark eyes searching Emily's. "Does he take after his father?"

"His father doesn't matter," she said quickly. "He

abandoned us and was killed in a brawl near Chicago the day after Christmas."

"Oh!" Ruthie exclaimed. "You never told us that."

"Why would I?" she said, more sharply than she had intended. "I have no family aside from an uncle who lives with the Sioux. I never wanted your pity—"

"We don't pity you," Clementine said quickly, dropping her eyes and Emily knew she was lying.

"I'm sorry," she said, her gaze cutting to Beatrice, who'd put a hand over her mouth as though Emily's confession was the most scandalous thing she'd ever heard. "I shouldn't have said anything."

"It's none of our business anyway," Ruthie said, her gaze cutting to Beatrice, who cleared her throat.

"Did Mr. Merritt deliver this baby?"

Ruthie nodded, almost proud now. "Sure did. He had lots of practice with our brothers and sisters."

"Oh, my," Beatrice whispered. "That must have been frightening."

Ruthie laughed. "Caleb's not scared of a little old baby."

"I wasn't talking about a *baby*—"

"What're you all clucking about?" Jake said, a tin plate in his hand as he drew closer to the circle of women. "Has Clemmie told a secret?"

His wife shook her head and stood up, handed James back to Emily.

"Where's the music? I'm ready for some fun."

"My brother'll play, or I'll box his ears," Ruth said,

jumping to her feet and Emily looked at Beatrice again, a light in her eyes as she rose slowly.

"My Uncle Putt brought a fiddle as well," she said. "Perhaps he will take a turn so Mr. Merritt can enjoy the music."

James stirred, his little fists kneading Emily's chest, and she looked down, fear of having to feed him in front of Beatrice causing her to stand as well.

"I need to tend to him," Emily said, small cries rising in the night, and it made her skin prickle.

"Use our wagon," Ruthie said, and Emily paused before smiling her thanks.

"I won't be long," she said, her eyes shifting to where Caleb stood away from the others, bending to fetch something in the grass.

Moments later she was crawling in the back of the Merritt's wagon, smelling the coffee and spices that marked this space as their own, wondering if they laid on their back under the wagon, a gun between them.

She moved to a corner, determined to feed her son.

The sound of a fiddle being tuned filled the small space and she smiled in the darkness.

James went still, listening as well. Soon a second instrument joined the first and she frowned, annoyed that Beatrice had gotten her way.

"That must be Uncle Putt," Emily muttered, a picture of Beatrice dragging the poor man out of his wagon making her frown.

In no time at all she would be coaxing Caleb into a

dance, the firelight swirling around them, and he would be hard pressed to refuse such an offer.

Emily pictured them in each other's arms, and began to unbutton her blouse, a piece of green muslin she'd picked out of a catalog and sewn in the soft light of the room she shared with Maddie.

She remembered her father remarking on it, telling her she'd done a fine job with the needlework, his face soft and proud.

She bent her head, undone by the memory and guided James to her breast.

A rustling at the back of the wagon drew her attention and she shrank back, unsure who could see her when Ruthie climbed through.

"That woman," she said, dusting her hands as if they were dirty. "I've a mind to turn my gun on her if she doesn't stop mooning over Caleb. The last thing we need is another mouth to feed if he does get it into his fool head to take a wife."

Emily watched as she sat down beside her, watched as she helped guide James to the place where he should latch on.

"And Heaven knows he's a sucker for a pretty face. Celia was a sight, I tell you, but with more than an ounce of common sense, which I'm afraid Miss Beatrice is in sore need of."

Emily looked down, touched the top of James's head as he began to nurse. Now was the time he would always pull away, after that brief moment when hope began to build.

"I wonder what she did to be such a bother to her aunt and uncle," she said, hardly aware of Emily or the baby. "I suppose it must have been something wicked for them to want to get rid of her. And out here, of all places."

"Ruthie—" Emily began.

"I had better speak to Caleb and nip this thing in the bud before he drops a match and wonders how the fire started."

"Ruth—" Emily said, her son suckling, his little hands going still as they burrowed into the fullness of her breast.

"Why, I'm—" Ruth stopped, put her hand over her mouth, jumped to her knees, then to her feet. "He's eating! It must be the food. And the music."

Emily smiled, not caring what the reason was because now they could leave her in Fort Kearny, and she wouldn't have to beg a woman or milk a cow to take care of him.

"Ruth Elizabeth Merritt—" Caleb's voice called from the back of the wagon and Emily sat bolt upright as James began to wail, his head wobbling on his tiny neck and she wanted to take the closest thing and throw it at the man who'd ruined everything.

"Caleb!" his sister cried as he tried to climb through. "Stop-"

"It's my wagon," he said, surprised to see Emily in the half-darkness as she quickly buttoned up her dress.

"Miss Ives," he said quickly, his eyes on where her fingers worked furiously.

"Call me Emily," she said coldly. "We should be on friendly terms by now."

He tried to back out of the small hole, then stopped, his foot searching for a way out before thinking better of it.

"What're you doing in here?"

"Isn't it obvious?" she replied. "The better question is what are you doing here?"

"This is *my* wagon! And my sister left a pot of potatoes boiling over the fire and no one to tend it!"

Ruthie huffed, reached over to take a squalling James and immediately the baby quieted, her scent comforting him.

"I suppose Miss Beatrice could help. She certainly ate her fair share!"

Caleb shook his head. "You two certainly have some bees swarming around in your bonnets. I didn't see anything I hadn't already been introduced to in the bed of that wagon."

"How dare you!" Emily said, rising to her feet and stomping towards the man, who crawled quickly through the hole and stood on the other side, a strange smile on his face.

"I do apologize," he said, his tone light. "But I was just coming back to my own wagon to see if my own sister might be bothered to help me feed six extra people tonight. I had no idea you were in here."

"Didn't you hear me offer it to her?" Ruth asked, turning her back to her brother so she could continue nursing James. "Or were you distracted by that black-haired hussy!"

"Maybe," he grinned, tipping the edge of his hat. "The scenery is much nicer since their wagon pulled up."

Emily shook her head, feeling trapped in the small space while Ruth held her baby and Caleb blocked her escape.

"May I?" She stood looking through the cinched hole, wanting to run from her humiliation and take refuge with the Mays.

Caleb stepped aside, offered her his hand as she climbed through and she took it, wondering at the feel of his skin and why it should bother her when it was obvious he had eyes for the lovely simpleton who couldn't stir a pot of potatoes.

She stood for a moment in the grass beside him, waiting, but he didn't release her hand. Instead, he stepped back, smiled, and for the first time Emily realized he'd been drinking.

Memories of Marvin and his evenings at the Lamplight made her recoil but Caleb bent slightly, the sound of music filling the air.

"Do you care to dance, Miss Ives? Or Emily? Or whatever I'm supposed to call you."

She pressed her lips together, undone by how close he was and how desperately she wanted to feel like a nineteen-year-old girl again.

"I couldn't—"

"Yes, you could," he swung his hat off his head.

"We'll be parting ways soon and it would be a shame to not have one good memory to show for it."

"How do you know it'll be good?" Ruthie said from within the wagon, amusement in her voice even though she was cross with her brother. "It may be the worst thing that ever happened to her."

"Don't listen to my sister. Ma dropped her when she was young. Flat on her head."

She looked up to find him grinning. Then he was pulling her towards the fire and Emily put a hand to her hair, patted a stray piece while venturing a smile.

"You should do that more," he remarked, and she looked at him closely, undone by how different he was tonight, remembering that liquor made Marvin behave just the opposite.

But maybe Marvin had something inside of him that this man did not.

"Emily," Caleb said, the sound of her name on his lips making her feel like she'd tasted whiskey herself.

"Pretty over there, isn't it?" he asked, and she nodded, watching while Clem and Jake danced by the waterfall and the little stone shelf it toppled over.

She looked over her shoulder, saw Beatrice watching from the other side of the fire as she stood beside her uncle, strains of 'Laura Lee' filling the night.

Emily remembered listening to the same song at one of the barn socials. Her parents had danced as well, her mother beaming as though she were a girl again and Emily had leaned closer to Maddie, whispering how lucky they were to have parents who loved each other.

And now she was in the middle of nowhere, dancing to the same song with a man who'd delivered her baby only a few days before.

But it felt good and right and what she should be doing as he put his hand on her waist, the other closing around her fingers as they turned in time to the music.

"Where'd the smile go?" he asked, and she looked down, not wanting him to know he was amusing her.

"I suppose Miss Beatrice will be unhappy," she said, feeling the woman's eyes on her and at the same time wondering how James and Ruthie were doing inside the wagon.

"Don't concern yourself with other people's happiness," he said, and she looked up, saw the pain behind his words and wondered what had happened to the woman named Celia.

The name lingered on her lips, but she knew better than to say anything. Caleb was happy, lighthearted and half- drunk and she wasn't going to spoil it by mentioning his dead wife if for no other reason than she liked seeing Beatrice angry.

"My goodness," Clem said, her face beaming from her husband's arms. "This is a sight I never expected to see."

"I am a lucky man, indeed," Caleb nodded to Jake, who watched with more suspicion than his wife. "My only hope is that I will not cripple Miss Emily with my poor dancing."

Emily laughed, her eyes across the fire again and Beatrice nudged her uncle, who abruptly stopped playing. In an instant she was stalking around the edge, making her way towards Caleb who didn't seem to notice, but raised his hand and called for the man to play another song.

The uncle looked to his niece, shrugged his shoulders and began 'My Old Kentucky Home,' and she waited, wondering if he would change partners now that Beatrice stood beside them, waiting to be asked.

"I'll just finish this dance and return to my fiddle," he said, and her cheeks turned red as she puffed them out, unsure what to say. "I know your uncle would like to take a turn with his wife."

Emily thought she saw her say something, her arms stiff at her side as she slowly backed away, lost in the darkness beyond the fire.

But then there was the music, and Caleb's arms around her in a way that Marvin's had never been. She dared to look at him again, saw his eyes grow soft and leaned her head against his chest, the sound of his heartbeat making her feel safe for the first time since Marvin placed a ring on her finger.

"Were you feeding James in the wagon?" he asked, serious now.

"Yes."

He pulled back to look at her.

"He got scared when you came in, but I was feeding him by myself."

Caleb laughed. "No wonder you got so mad!"

She smiled, looked down. "Now you won't have to worry about us when we get to Fort Kearny."

Caleb stopped moving and she looked up at him, unable to tell what he was thinking.

"Easier said than done," he whispered, and she felt a small ball of warmth forming in her stomach, reminding her of her wedding night and the flame that came and vanished just as quickly.

He rested his chin on top of her head, content for the moment and she knew the others were looking at them, wondering what this could mean when his hands tightened around her back, pulling her against him.

Her heart beat quickly, torn between wanting to stay where she was and wanting to run away. She didn't know this man, just as she'd never known her husband.

She leaned back, tried to put space between them but he held her fast.

She looked up again, smelled the whiskey on his breath and remembered Marvin holding her down, the same scent surrounding her as his fingers tightened around her throat.

"Please," she whispered, trying to wiggle free and Caleb loosened his hold.

"What's wrong?"

"I need to go," she said, her voice so small she could barely hear it.

"Are you alright?"

She put her hands up, pushed against his chest.

"Stop!"

"Emily," he said, confused for a moment before letting her go. Then, in a low voice. "What did he do to you?"

Emily drew in her breath, shocked that he could see what she'd been trying to hide and felt Marvin's fingers around her throat, choking her.

"What did he do?" Caleb repeated, true concern in his voice and she shook her head, unable to answer because there were too many words and none all at once.

So, she remained silent, her eyes down because she couldn't look at the mess she'd made, couldn't stand to think Marvin had ruined this as well.

"You've been drinking, Mr. Merritt," she said, cold now. "There is nothing-"

"Bullshit," he said under his breath, and she stiffened. "The baby's father," he paused. "He hurt you."

She stepped away, turned from him and began to walk towards the May wagon. She felt his eyes on her, felt all of their eyes on her and moved, her shoulders stiff and after a minute had passed, she paused, the prairie wind at her back as a wolf howled against the moonlight.

Chapter Ten

Emily put her arms around her stomach, the swelling flesh reminding her of the night Marvin had died inside of her heart.

It became obvious she was pregnant after she missed her monthly cycle, and Marvin's temper changed almost instantly for the better.

He even drove her into town so she could work at the store the day after they finally finished the hog pen.

Her mother knew something was wrong, as did Maddie, who pulled her into the back room and asked all sorts of questions.

Emily tried to act as if everything was all right, knowing Marvin's anger would return if she told them their secret and still her sister seemed to know.

That night she ate with Gerald and Patricia at the old table, while Marvin did business in town, and she knew this loosening of his hold was a special gift to her- if only for the time being.

Emily chose to tell her family she was pregnant at dinner, chose to mistake their silence for joy until Maddie came over and put her arms around her, tears falling down her cheeks.

Then Marvin came to collect her, and Gerald grasped his hand, his face soft with emotion and Emily watched her husband, fearing him more than ever because shaking her father's hand was the worst thing he'd ever done.

One month turned into two, then four with Marvin attempting to be kind and Emily knew it was for no other reason than to protect their son.

"What if it's a girl?" she asked one night while knitting in front of the new stove, and he looked at her sharply.

"Then we'll try again for a boy," he said simply. "I won't rest until I have a son to carry on my name."

"And if we never have one?" she asked, wanting to hurt him.

He paused, looked at her for a beat. "Then there is no need for you, my sweet."

Emily's skin went cold, hating him more than she thought was possible even as they played at being a happy couple, as they would be tonight at the winter social held in the meeting hall just before Christmas.

Emily was surprised that Marvin suggested they go- but he was a vain man, anxious to show off his pregnant wife to the men he believed looked down on him.

They sat in the wagon beneath wraps and coats, the old mare plodding the road between their shanty and town when he asked the question she'd been waiting for.

"Will James be there?"

Emily shook her head. "I have no idea."

His hands tightened on the reins. "I don't believe that, Em. I believe you know exactly where James will be tonight."

She sat, nausea rising in her stomach and knew his kindness had come to an end.

"I don't believe James will be interested in a four-month pregnant woman even if he is still unmarried. Which I doubt he is."

Marvin turned to her, his face softening.

"James would steal you away from me even if he had ten wives and you were wearing nothing but a sackcloth."

She felt her cheeks heat, hopeful they wouldn't argue tonight.

"Marvin-"

"I am only saying that you are a beautiful woman, and any man who can't see that, even in your condition, cannot be mistaken for a man."

"Thank you," she said, and she felt her husband's hand slide to her knee, felt him squeeze and wished she could turn as cold as the snow that fell softly around them.

"I would take you now in this wagon if we wouldn't be missed," he whispered in her ear and Emily gritted her teeth, wishing there was a way to keep her husband from touching her.

They pulled up to the meeting hall a few minutes later, the sound of music spilling from inside, and Emily waited for Marvin to help her down, the picture of perfect chivalry when others were watching.

At once she was surrounded by her old life, by friends from the schoolhouse and people she had known from the store. Carrie was there, in a lovely red dress that only she could wear without looking scandalous.

"Oh, Em!" she exclaimed when she took off her cloak. "Maddie told me you were expecting but I didn't believe it. Not until I saw you for myself."

Emily nodded, smiling now because Marvin was tending the horse, and she had her friend to herself.

"Where is James?" she asked quickly.

Carrie laughed, pulled her aside. "What a question to ask! James is here, of course, with his new wife so you've missed that boat if you cared to hop aboard."

Emily drew a breath of relief.

"And why ever would you care with a husband as handsome as yours? The ladies in town are ripe with jealousy, especially now that you are with child."

Emily bit her lip, wanting to tell her what the dashing Marvin Jones was like behind closed doors, but she simply smiled, content to have them envy her if only for the evening.

"I'm just anxious to catch up with him," she lied. "Marvin would like to meet him since he didn't come to our wedding."

Carrie giggled behind her glove. "He was too heartsick to come. But not enough to keep him from snatching up Rachel Wilson. She was our schoolmarm's niece. Remember?"

Emily nodded, feeling like she'd been away from town for years instead of a few months.

"She was quiet and shy."

"*Dull as mud*, you mean," Carrie laughed. "But she's perked up since becoming a bride. I do suspect Ma and Pa will marry me off next."

Emily leaned closer, anxious for news.

"Is there a young man in particular?"

Carrie shook her head. "All the boys are awful. I've a mind to move away after my next birthday. My cousins live in Missouri and people are always heading west like that wild uncle of yours did-"

"Miss Carrie," Marvin said, suddenly at her shoulder and Emily felt the fine hairs on the nape of her neck rise.

Carrie bowed her head, a hint of color in her cheeks.

"Mr. Jones."

"You're a sight in that dress. All eyes are on you. Including my own."

Emily stirred, unsure if she should pretend to be insulted.

97

Carrie blushed, looked down and then up into his eyes again.

"I trust you are taking good care of my friend."

Marvin smiled, reached down to cover Emily's stomach with his hand.

"I should say so."

Carrie's eyes widened, shocked by the innuendo and Emily put her hand on his arm, embarrassed.

"Come," she said, wanting to get away. "Mother and Father are here. And Maddie."

Marvin bowed his head, and they moved through the large room, saying hello to the people they recognized, the scent of evergreen garlands surrounding them until they stood beside her parents.

Patricia Ives smiled, bent to kiss her daughter and then ventured to touch her stomach. Gerald just looked at Marvin, then his daughter with a vacancy in his eyes Emily feared would anger her husband.

"So good to see you both," he said stiffly, hugging his daughter as if his arms were made of wood. "I trust you are feeling well, Em?"

"Yes," she said softly, unsure what to do now that her family felt like strangers.

"We are hoping to see you at Christmas," he ventured, his eyes on Marvin and Maddie moved closer, put a hand on her father's arm.

"We had hoped so, too," Marvin said. "But Em's not feeling well, and she needs to rest."

"We would happily come to get her," Gerald said.

"Her mother is good at comforting her and the shanty is only two miles from town."

"Feels like twenty-" Patricia muttered and Marvin looked up quickly.

"I'm sure you, of all people, know the risks of bringing a child into the world."

Patricia's eyes flared in anger, and she lifted her chin, a gesture Emily realized she'd inherited from her.

"Mr. Jones," she began. "I'm sure I don't know—"

"I'll not risk my son's life for a silly tradition," Marvin said.

"Your *son*-" Gerald said. "How would you—"

"Every man wants a son," Marvin interrupted. "As I'm sure *you* know, Mr. Ives."

"Young man—" Gerald approached Marvin, his chest out and Patricia stepped in front of him.

"I think I see the Wilson family. We should speak to them."

"I will not be insulted by my own son-in-law," Gerald hissed, and Maddie tensed.

"Father—"

"Mark my words," he said, inches from Marvin. "I will see my daughter when I choose. You will not keep her prisoner on that shanty."

"Prisoner?" Marvin repeated. "She is my *wife*."

"And she is my child!" Gerald roared, his eyes on fire.

"It seems we've overstayed our welcome," Marvin turned to Emily. "We should go."

"No," she shook her head, her heart breaking at the sight of her father's face. "I want to stay."

Marvin smiled, his mouth stiff and took her elbow.

"My dear—"

"No!" she yanked away.

"My sweet—"

"Don't touch me," she hissed, and her parents froze, Maddie's face draining of color.

"It's time to go," he said, his voice cold and Emily straightened her shoulders, the way she'd felt that night as he writhed below her rising from the place she'd buried it.

"No," she said.

Marvin's face went hard, his color deepening.

"You are my wife," he said. "And will do as you're told."

"*No,*" she said, feeling Gerald tense beside her, ready to jump forward if Marvin came closer. "I will stay with my family tonight and then decide tomorrow if I wish to come back to the shanty."

"Emily," he said, his voice a growl as he took a step closer.

"What's going on here?" a voice from behind and Emily turned, saw Carrie and James and his new wife standing behind, their faces drawn up in concern.

"Ah," Marvin laughed. "I see you've come to rescue the woman who did not want to marry you."

Whispers, murmurs now, and Emily looked at James, took in his sweet, soft face and the brown eyes that had captured her interest, the same eyes she thought about as she laid beneath her husband at night.

She looked at his wife, the girl she'd gone to school with and felt shame round her shoulders before rage straightened them.

"I'll not have you speak to him that way," she said, her voice rising, and other heads turned, wondering what was going on in the corner of the meeting hall, Carrie's red dress drawing all eyes to where they were. "I'll not have you speak to my family as if I'm a horse you keep in a stall."

Marvin didn't move, didn't speak, but the coldness in his eyes said she had much to fear the next time they were alone.

"I'm staying in town tonight," she said. "And every night after."

Marvin tensed, his arm reaching for her as James stepped between.

"Don't touch her."

Rachel moved, her hand on his shoulder, her face white.

"I'll do what I want with my own wife," Marvin growled. "Tend to your own."

Others were coming over now, men she'd known from the store, men who were friends with her father and they surrounded Marvin, their voices low and powerful, telling him to keep his voice down and not harm anyone.

To go home.

He shook his head. "What man would leave without his wife?" He turned to the others as though it had all been a joke. "Which one of you would tolerate this insult?"

More murmurs before Lester, a large man Emily recognized from the livery stable, stepped forward.

"You will leave your wife in town tonight, Mr. Jones. You will leave your wife in town until she has a mind to come home."

Marvin laughed, put up his hands and backed away.

"I see where I stand now," he said, turning in a circle to face them all. "I see what my money has bought me in this town."

They stood silent, watching him and Emily took a cautious step between her sister and James, who looked at her with pity in his eyes.

"Go home, Mr. Jones," the large man said.

Marvin took another step backwards.

"And if you come back, I'll be waiting."

"Come back?" Marvin said, turning to the others again. "And take what was promised to me before God?"

The others stood silent, and Emily felt Maddie's hand slip into hers, felt her squeeze and had no idea what she'd just done.

"Take her, then. I've no more use for her," Marvin

said, and Emily looked up, saw her father moving towards her husband and put a hand on his arm, steadying him.

And then he turned, strode out of the building and she went to the window, watched him as he untied the horse and crawled into their wagon alone.

She watched as he drove by, his shoulders hunched, his hands gripping the reigns so tightly his knuckles blanched. It seemed he turned at that moment and looked in at her and Emily shrunk back, barely aware that Carrie was standing beside her.

"I'm so sorry," Carrie said, unshed tears shining in her eyes and Emily turned back to the window, not knowing what to say because the truth was too heavy. "We all thought he was a fine man."

"I didn't," James interrupted, and she dared a glance at him. "I knew something wasn't right and that's why I didn't come to the wedding. I'm sorry, Emily. I should have spoken up sooner."

She shook her head, her eyes shifting to Rachel, who seemed uncomfortable with her husband's confession.

"I wouldn't have believed you," she replied, wanting to be held by arms that wouldn't hurt her and turned back to the window.

"Do you want to leave?" Carrie asked, "We'll take you home."

Emily stood, watching the snow fall outside and shook her head.

Time passed, people came to speak to her, and she

nodded, thinking about Marvin and what he was doing out at the shanty. She touched her stomach, wondering what would become of her and the baby if she never went back.

Then her father and mother were there, telling her it was time to go, and she followed them outside into the snow as they walked the short distance to her house.

She stumbled on the steps, and her father steadied her, his hand warm on her arm. Once inside, she gave them her wrap and went to the front room, stood facing the place where she'd married the man she hated.

"Emilou," Gerald said, and she looked up, startled.

"I'm sorry," she said, "I should have told you..."

"Shhh," he said, the father she loved replacing the man Marvin had deceived. Then Patricia was there, and Maddie, and together they gathered around her as they wrapped her in their arms and Emily began to cry, began to think of all the ways Marvin could find to punish her.

"It's all right," her mother whispered, smoothing her hair. "It's over."

Emily went still, something in Patricia's words making her cold.

"No," she whispered, her eyes on the windows. "It's only begun."

Chapter Eleven

"Right there, look through that slot. Give a little squeeze on the trigger and you've got it." Ruthie Merritt said as they knelt in the grass, Emily in a new pair of bloomers she'd found in the wagon that gave her room to move freely.

Clem bought two pairs in Independence but was too scared to wear them, saying she would see how Jake acted after seeing them on Emily before doing the same.

Two days had passed since the fire at Alcove Springs, two days of avoiding Caleb for fear he would say something about her behavior.

They had crossed the Big Blue River on the first day out, the wagon rising like a boat and Emily had hung onto the sideboards, peering over because the water was murky and deep, and she feared what would happen if she had to swim.

But they made it across, the thick, tar caulking Jake and Caleb applied beforehand keeping all provisions dry, including herself and Clem and James.

Caleb came by after they made camp to talk to Jake about the upkeep of their iron wheels, his eyes settling on her at strange times, and she'd felt her cheeks heat up when she thought of him watching her.

Ruthie came along with her brother, and then again, the day after that to drink coffee after the noon meal, talking about everything that came into her mind, including her first shooting lesson.

"No time like the present," Emily said, and they stood, wandered from the wagon and into the high grass, Ruthie pointing towards a lone cottonwood tree that stood sentinel against the sky.

"Have you handled a gun before?"

Emily shook her head. "Pa had a rifle, but I never used it."

Ruthie smirked. "Forgot you were a town girl."

Emily laughed. "You make that sound like a bad thing."

"Doesn't have to be." Ruthie knelt in the dirt, swung her rifle around. "Aim at that mound of dirt in front of the tree over there. If you can hit it, and a bunch of prairie dogs pop out, we've got a start."

"I'll hit it."

"All confident now," Ruthie laughed, sitting in the grass and Emily watched her handle the rifle, watched her half cock the hammer and insert a paper cartridge in the front before flipping a lever that made a tiny slot spring up.

"This is Caleb's rifle. Good for hitting things at a distance."

Emily watched intently as her friend got up and knelt in the grass, the stock against her shoulder.

"I'm going to aim for the tree."

Emily squinted, "It's so far—"

"Not far enough," Ruthie smiled, her gray eyes dancing as Caleb's had around the fire.

Emily looked over her shoulder, saw the Merritt wagon standing against the dry, dusty earth and wondered what Caleb was doing and if he was thinking about firelight and fiddles.

Movement from her own wagon caught her attention and she saw Jake come out and shade his eyes, curious.

"Will your brother be mad that you took his gun?"

Ruthie laughed, readjusted the stock.

"Ever since you turned your back on him at Alcove Springs, he's been meaner than ever. I'll probably get skinned alive," she smiled out of the corner of her mouth. "Thank you very much."

Emily adjusted her weight on her knees. "He'd been drinking. And he was teasing me."

Ruthie raised the rifle, pulled the hammer back.

"What's wrong with a little teasing?"

A quick, sure pull to the trigger and the rifle

sprung forward, echoing across the plains in a way that made Emily cover her ears.

"Hit it!" Ruthie cried, her face glowing. "If that was an antelope we'd be having steaks for supper."

Emily laughed, watching as the young girl pulled on a lever and loaded another cartridge in the chamber.

"Your turn," she said, handing the rifle over. "Don't point it at anything you don't want to kill."

Emily took the thing in her hands, imagined Caleb shooting this very gun and wanted to prove herself worthy to use it. Looking through the sights, she tried to squint and focused on the tree, her arms aching from the rigid fit of the stock against her shoulder.

"Take a deep breath," Ruthie instructed. "Shoot while you're holding it."

Emily did as she was told, pulled the hammer back like she'd seen her friend do, and squeezed the trigger.

The rifle shimmied in her hands, but she held it still, absorbing the kick with her shoulder, her knees digging into the dirt.

Ruthie stood up, shading her eyes, and scanned the landscape.

"You came pretty close," she smiled down. "Not bad for your first time. Now I'll teach you to load it in case—"

"What the *hell* are you doing?"

Emily lost her grip on the rifle, turned to see Caleb glaring down at them.

Ruthie dusted off her skirt, crossed her arms.

"What does it look like?"

Caleb's jaw began working, his hat hiding his eyes, but Emily knew they were fixed on her.

"Are you stupid or just a damned fool," he grunted. "We've got to save those cartridges for hunting."

"And Emily needs to know how to shoot!" Ruthie insisted. "We're coming into Fort Kearny in a couple of days and—"

"Her uncle'll take care of her."

Emily swallowed, unable to reconcile this man with one she'd danced with only two days before.

"She still needs to know how to use a gun!" Ruthie cried, her cheeks red.

"Not with my rifle, she doesn't."

Emily got slowly to her feet, wiped her bloomers off where they were dirty.

"I'll stop wasting your shot, Mr. Merritt," she smiled, remembering that he wanted to see her do that more. "But I want to see if I hit that tree."

Caleb laughed. "If you hit that tree, then I'll eat my hat."

"Is that a promise?"

He crossed his arms. "I'll do it right after I set fire to those silly pants you're wearing."

Emily looked down, touched the fabric lightly.

"Jake likes them," she lied. "And I'm ever so much help around the campsite," she paused. "Come to think of it, I haven't seen Miss Beatrice outside today. Do you suppose she's still sleeping?"

Caleb cleared his throat.

"I'll just take a look at that tree."

"And I'll go with her," Ruthie spoke up.

"Like hell you will," he said. "Dinner needs cleaned up and I don't trust you two any farther than I can throw you."

His sister frowned. "Caleb—"

"I don't intend to eat my hat."

Ruthie shook her head and mumbled something under her breath about not having any fun.

"We'll be wanting some coffee when we get back," he said. "Be sure to make it how I like it."

Emily tried to hide her laughter, the tension of the last few days and the dustiness that seemed to cling to her skin lifting a bit with his humor. It seemed everything was lighter when Caleb was in a good mood, which was why Ruthie spent so much time at the May's wagon.

"I have a feeling the coffee won't go well with your hat," she said, turning before he could respond as Ruthie chuckled from behind.

"Ladies first," Caleb bowed, and Emily tugged at her sunbonnet, pulling it up over her head, aware that Caleb was following somewhere behind.

She stepped carefully over the sagebrush, the hot sun causing sweat to crawl down her neck and could not understand why she felt lighthearted.

She dared to think about a bath, something she had not had since they crossed the Big Blue and wished for a stream or lake to swim in.

"So, you don't know how to shoot?" Caleb asked, at her shoulder now and Emily dared a glance at him. He seemed as hot as she was, the collar of his cotton shirt and the buttons that went down the front dampened with sweat.

His hat was pulled low on his head, but he took it off to wipe at his brow. His hair was getting longer, and Emily remembered how she used to cut her father's in the back of the store.

She wondered if Caleb would let her do the same, or if he intended to grow it out until he looked like a bandit.

"I can cut your hair if you like," she offered, unsure why she would offer such a thing and he seemed caught off guard.

Shoving his hat back on his head, he grunted.

"You don't shoot, but you can cut my hair? That'll come in real handy when you're left at Fort Kearny."

She stopped, turned to face him, her hands on her hips, wondering why he was suddenly so cross.

"What are you getting at?"

He took a deep breath, his nostrils flaring out.

"I'm wondering how you aren't scared to death right now. I'm wondering how you intend to live if this wild uncle of yours doesn't show up."

"He'll show up."

"How do you know that? Did you get some letter I haven't heard about? Do you really expect us to leave you and James in the middle of nowhere with no protection?"

"There are soldiers at the fort."

"Strangers, you mean," he said. "Did you hear from him?"

She linked her hands in front of her, swallowed the lump in her throat and felt it settle in her chest.

"*Did you?*"

She looked down, her heart beating so fast she felt like it might come out of her mouth.

"I may have—"

"*May* have?"

She turned back towards the tree; grateful they were almost there.

"Uncle Rand may have sent word, or he may be there himself. I can wait for him. I'm in no hurry."

"In no hurry?" he asked, his voice rising. "And what if he *never* comes? Will the soldiers adopt you and James as one of their own?"

She took another deep breath, started walking again until she felt his hand on her shoulder, stopping her.

"Do you have any idea how Ruthie will feel? Or Jake? Or Clem?"

Emily shook her head. "Is that what you're thinking of, Mr. Merritt? Your sister and Jake and Clem? How will *you* feel after leaving us?"

He stood looking at her for a moment before taking his hat off again, wiping his face and she saw that her words had disturbed him.

"I'll move on, Miss Ives," he said coldly. "I'll settle in Sacramento like my wife wanted. I'll grow fruit trees as far as the eye can see and sleep under the stars every night."

She felt a stirring inside of her, a picture of this man lying in his yard beneath an orange tree, his hands behind his head, staring up at what God had given him. She thought about the brokenness he'd suffered, the wife who'd gotten sick, leaving behind dreams for him to follow alone.

"And in this land with fruit trees and stars and far-away oceans," she stopped, unsure if she should say more. "Are you alone?"

"I'll have Ruthie," he said, walking forward again.

"And another wife, I suppose," she called after him.

He stopped again, turned to look at her.

"That's none of your business."

She pressed her lips together, angry now.

"Just as what happens at Fort Kearny is none of *your* business. Just imagine me fat and happy in a little cabin beside a mountain, trading beads with Indians and riding war ponies."

He paused. "Emily—"

She laughed then, moving past him, his mood making her feel strangely alive.

"I'll race you to that tree."

He cocked his head to the side.

"You'll *what?*"

"Let's see if these bloomers are worth the scandal I endure by wearing them."

Caleb looked at her, scratched his chin and suddenly she was rushing towards the cottonwood that stood gripping the sky like a hand.

In one move he was off, jumping over sagebrush and grass, his arms pumping even though it was foolish to run in the heat.

Then they were at the tree, laughing as they came up against it, palms pressed to the trunk as they panted in its shade.

"That was stupid," he said as he tried to catch his breath.

"But fun," she said, feeling a bit of her old self coming back in the shade of this sentinel cottonwood with Caleb Merritt beside her. "And I have to say these bloomers did their job."

"How do you figure?"

"I won," she laughed,

"That's questionable," he said, his eyes on her as she pulled her sunbonnet down. "But I do see Ruthie's bullet hole."

"How do you know that's not mine?"

Caleb let out a slow breath. "Ruthie could shoot before she could walk. Kept all of us fed on squirrel and rabbit when I started working the mines."

Emily moved her hands on the bark, searching for the hole and felt a sadness when she thought of Caleb underground in the darkness.

"How long were you there?" she asked, realizing she had no idea where he came from or how far he had traveled to reach Independence.

"Too long."

Emily looked to the branches overhead, wanting to ask all sorts of questions and wanting things to remain unsaid so she wouldn't think of him when his wagon pulled away the day after tomorrow.

"Now, where's my bullet hole," she smiled, standing straight now, tracing the tree with her hands, running her fingers over the grooves in the cottonwood and imagined touching Caleb in the same way.

She stopped, memories of Marvin flooding her mind, causing her to pause but then they passed, a joy she couldn't explain replacing it.

"I don't see it," he said, his voice at her ear and she looked up, saw him peering around the trunk, a smile on his face that reminded her of Alcove Springs.

"You should do that more," she teased, her fingers skipping towards his, lingering there and she thought she saw him swallow.

He didn't say anything, just pulled her to him in one movement and she felt his arms on her back, crushing her against him.

Then his mouth was on hers, kissing her, his lips falling open, and she did the same, the tip of his tongue touching hers.

She wound her hands in his hair, heard him groan and wondered if she had let things go too far, wondered if he would be able to let her go or if he would force her into the grass and take her as Marvin had so many times in the past.

But she didn't care, didn't mind that his hands were on her waist now, that they were wandering lower, cupping her bottom through the fabric of her bloomers.

She turned her head, wanting him to touch her there, wanting him to lower her into the grass and undress her and felt his mouth on her throat, his tongue tracing a line to her earlobe when a noise made her tense.

Beads in a glass jar.

Caleb stopped, his hands stiffening, and whispered.

"Don't move."

She froze, her eyes moving to the base of the tree. A rattlesnake lay coiled in a clump, its head pulled back, its tongue tasting the wind.

"Caleb," she whispered, and felt the leather of his holster brush her fingers. She moved her hand, the cool metal of his revolver awakening her skin.

"What're you doing?" he hissed, frantic as his hands tightened on her waist.

She kept her eyes on the snake and knew it was getting ready to strike, knew every moment they stood frozen was a moment too long.

She imagined the rattler biting Caleb, imagining dragging him to the wagon and watching him die slowly in the back of it.

She thought of Ruthie, traveling alone to California, and the endless stars Caleb would never lie beneath.

The snake pulled its head back and Emily felt Caleb's weight shift, knew he was getting ready to throw her out of the way when she unsheathed his gun.

She pulled the hammer, hopeful the chambers were loaded, knowing they were.

The snake struck forward as Caleb pulled back, her finger squeezing the trigger and then the rattler flew into the air, landing a few feet away, half its head blown off as the body continued to writhe in the dirt.

"Oh, my God," Caleb cried, stumbling backwards. "Emily."

She gripped the revolver, her hand shaking, and then turned to him.

He went to the snake, stomped it into the dirt until it stopped moving.

Then he came back to her, reached down and took the gun while replacing it in his holster with a careful hand.

A moment passed before he pulled her to his chest and Emily felt him shaking, felt herself shaking and allowed him to hold her, his heartbeat racing beneath her cheek.

"Are you alright?" he asked, stroking her hair and she nodded, the fabric of his shirt scratching her cheek.

"I think so."

"We need to get back," he whispered. "The others heard that shot."

She nodded, unwilling to let go.

"You saved my life," he said, pulling back to look at her.

She didn't say anything, just stepped out of his arms before she collapsed at his feet and moved from beneath the tree and into the sagebrush, her gaze sweeping the baked earth.

Caleb followed, waiting a moment before touching her arm.

"What happened back there?" he asked.

She glanced at him briefly.

"I killed a snake."

He tried to laugh.

"I couldn't make that shot on my best day."

"Ruthie—"

"Couldn't either."

Emily looked up, the dusting of fear in her eyes and Caleb took her by the shoulders.

"You told my sister you couldn't shoot."

She nodded, felt her lip trembling and tried to hide it.

"What do you call what you just did?"

She took a breath, stepped away from him.

"Beginner's luck."

Chapter Twelve

Caleb couldn't think straight. All he could see was the rattlesnake's head as it pulled back to strike, all he could feel was terror when he thought of Emily being bitten.

Then the snake's head flew into the grass, the body writhing as though it was still alive.

He watched her walk in front of him and wanted to grab her, just as he'd wanted to during the campfire at Alcove Springs. He wanted to turn her around and make her tell him how in the hell she learned to shoot like that.

But more than that, he wanted to put his hands on her again, wanted to feel her body against him as her mouth opened against his.

He'd seen plenty of pretty women since Celia died- had more than a few show interest, but they hadn't gotten his dander up like this one had.

She traveled alone while nine months pregnant, was able to shoot the head off a rattlesnake and talked as though living at Fort Kearny was as common as washing those stupid bloomers of hers.

Caleb took off his hat and scratched the back of his head.

He'd seen the fear in her eyes at the campfire and knew it came from the whiskey she smelled on his breath, knew because he'd seen that look in women who'd found themselves on the rough side of their husbands.

Including his mother.

It bothered him that Emily might have been hurt by the man who was supposed to protect her, but Caleb was no better.

He'd done the same to Celia.

He thought of his wife now as Emily continued to walk ahead, unwilling to turn around after what happened under the cottonwood tree.

She had Celia's spunk, that was certain, but there was something else, some quality that made her see everything with childlike wonder.

Celia knew what she wanted from the day they met, had planned their life like it was a list of items they could buy at the mercantile.

Caleb wiped his sweaty brow, put his hat back on and thought of the wonderment he'd witnessed when Emily touched the trunk of the cottonwood tree.

He remembered her hands traveling up it, searching for the bullet hole that had become a joke between them. He remembered wishing her hands were on him, feeling a sense of shame when he remembered his wife.

But that hadn't stopped him from kissing her, tasting her, hadn't stopped him from wishing they hadn't been interrupted by a rattlesnake.

He wondered if he would have undressed her there and made love to her, wondered if she would even be able to so soon after giving birth.

He didn't want to hurt her, didn't want to add any weight to her sorrows, but the thought of leaving her alone in Fort Kearny was almost as bad as handing her over to some wild uncle he didn't know.

"Emily," he said, and she stopped, turned slowly. "I'm sorry—"

"Why?" she asked, and he didn't know if she was angry or teasing him again.

"I shouldn't have kissed you," he said. "That's not why I went out there."

She straightened her spine. "It wasn't why I went out there, either. But it happened. And I won't be sorry for it."

He stood, ashamed of what he'd said.

"I won't be sorry for anything ever again."

"I didn't mean that," he said. "I just—"

She came to him and put her hand on the side of his face.

Caleb drew his breath in, disturbed by how her touch affected him.

"You won't have to worry about me much longer,

Mr. Merritt. We can put everything behind us, and you can move on to your fruit trees and oceans and endless stars."

He hadn't meant to make her feel like that, but she was turning again, moving towards Clementine and Jake, who wanted to know what the shot was about while Ruthie came towards him, Beatrice close behind.

He looked at his feet, trying to avoid their gaze because what he wanted was to go after Emily and tell her he didn't regret it and that he would think of her when they left Fort Kearny.

And every day after.

"What in the world," his sister said, her face pinched with worry, and he went to her, ruffled the top of her head like he did when they were kids.

"Rattlesnake," he said matter-of-factly, and Beatrice gasped as though it just occurred to her that she might come into contact with one. "I shot it."

Ruthie looked at him for a beat, and he knew she was weighing the truth of his words.

"Ain't you a hero, then," she smiled, her eyes floating to Beatrice. "Did Emily faint in your arms?"

Caleb looked at Beatrice, who made an awkward giggle.

She was a pretty woman, standing in the shade of their wagon, her dark hair spilling over her shoulders, her smooth skin sure to blister and burn before the trip was over and Caleb couldn't help but see how unsuited she was to life on the trail. Or anywhere, for that matter.

He pictured her beneath the cottonwood tree, pictured kissing her and felt his heart turn to stone.

"Didn't seem to scare her," he said. "I think Miss Emily was made for life out here."

Beatrice smiled, swished her skirt from side to side. "Then she will have her fill of it when we leave her at that fort." A slight pause. "Shouldn't we start soon? It would be a shame to miss her uncle even by an hour."

Caleb looked at her, his jaw hardening.

"We'll make sure her uncle is there, no matter what day it is," Ruthie said, looking to Caleb for assurance. "We sure won't leave her."

He grabbed a cup of coffee and a piece of salt pork left out for him, patted the sides of the oxen and made a note to water them well and clean their noses before they pulled out.

"She wants us to leave. Says she'll be fine whenever he shows up because she's in no hurry."

"Isn't she brave," Beatrice mused, swishing her skirt and it made Caleb so angry he turned his back and walked to the other side of the wagon.

He stood there for a moment, trying to steady his tumbling thoughts when he heard a voice.

"She certainly has you all fussed up."

Caleb swung to face his sister, his face red.

"Miss Beatrice—"

"Emily," Ruthie smiled. "I know something happened out there under that tree. You've been sweet on each other since Alcove Springs. Everyone sees it. That's why Beatrice is so jealous!"

"Ruthie," he said, his thoughts wandering to how quickly Emily had unsheathed his gun, the accuracy of her aim.

"What?" his sister asked, her hands on the collar of his shirt, straightening it as though they were going to church instead of leading a team of oxen into the middle of nowhere. "You're a perfect mess and—"

"Emily shot the snake."

He watched his sister's face go slack, watched her eyes widen as though she hadn't heard him right.

"She couldn't even hold your rifle. Her aim was way left and—"

"She blew the head clean off."

Ruthie hugged herself, looked over her shoulder and lowered her voice.

"That's impossible," she whispered. "Even I couldn't do that."

Caleb looked at her, his heart beating quickly. "I should be dead right now."

She put a hand to her mouth.

"*Don't say that.*"

"It's true," he said, a troubled look in his eyes. "But why would she lie about knowing how to shoot? What's the reason?"

Ruthie shook her head, and Caleb peered around the side of their wagon, saw that Beatrice had gone back to hers and that the Mays were cleaning up their noon meal.

No sign of Emily meant she was probably tending to James.

"It's part of her act," he said, cold fear creeping in. "She's hiding from something. Or someone."

"She told us her husband left her at Christmas-that he died in a brawl near Chicago."

"Maybe he did," Caleb said, his eyes narrowing against the sun. "But we have no way of finding out. It's best to leave her and her secrets at Kearny."

"How can you say that?" Ruthie said, her voice rising.

"She's trouble."

His sister put her hands on her hips and balled them into fists.

"And you weren't any, I suppose? What if Ma had just left you off somewhere to fend for yourself?"

"That's different."

"No, it isn't!" she cried. "You can't bury your heart next to Celia."

He looked at her for a beat, then threw the rest of his coffee out. Slamming the cup on the axle, he pointed a finger at her.

"You were running around with Thomas when she got sick. And I was stuck in that tomb, trying to put food on our table when I should've been with *her*."

"It was the only work you could find."

"I should have tried harder."

"You did the best you could."

Caleb stopped, his eyes on the May wagon again, his breath catching when he saw Emily emerge from it. She stood for a moment, seeming to turn in his direction and he pulled back, fear burning his chest like a brand.

"Did I?"

Chapter Thirteen

Emily sat on the sofa in the front room, her embroidery in her lap, a fresh breeze blowing from the window and took a long breath.

She'd been with her parents for over three months now, sleeping beside her sister as she had before she married Marvin, wondering every day if he would come and take her away.

She'd seen him ride through town the week before while she was sweeping the front porch and hurried inside. Maddie had shuffled her off to the back room, watching the counter in case he decided to pay a visit.

But he didn't.

After some time had passed, she ventured to the porch again, only to see their old mare tied to the post in front of the Lamplight Saloon.

She'd felt relief then, knowing the whores would keep him occupied for some time, and as the afternoon wore on, he rode past the store again and stopped at the livery stable.

She wondered if Lester was still keeping an eye on him, making sure he stayed put until she walked home.

But by the end of the day, he was gone.

Emily closed the store, her fear settling in her stomach, making her worry for the baby.

It was moving now, and sometimes she would trace her wet skin as she soaked in the bathtub, watching the darkened windows for Marvin's face.

Her parents were worried as well, and most evenings her father would speak with Lester, who always visited after they'd finished their supper.

And still Marvin stayed away.

Emily waited through the winter, waited while the first tendrils of spring began to unfold around her, lifting her mood. She thought about when the baby would be born as she measured out sugar and flour and oats for their customers.

Those long, winter months seemed far away as she focused on her embroidery, her mind daring to hope when a knock sounded at the door.

Maddie looked up quickly and rose from her chair.

Emily's spine stiffened when she thought about why Marvin had been waiting when he could simply knock on the door.

She thought about the gun her father kept in the bureau drawer, the Navy Colt he'd used during his time under Governor Mason in the Toledo War and wished she could shoot.

The knock came again, and Emily moved quickly to the kitchen, waiting while Maddie opened the door, her breath escaping when she saw James.

She said his name, undone by how much she wanted to see him, and he came to her in a few, brisk steps, his face furrowed.

"Emily."

She stood as he took her hands in his, shocked that he would do such a thing while married.

"James," she said, catching Maddie's eye and her sister shut the door quickly and came to stand beside them.

"Maddie," he nodded to her. "I'm sorry I didn't call sooner."

Emily looked at the floor.

"I am too forward," he said, glancing down at his hands and backing away. "I should have sent word that I was coming."

"That's all right," Emily said, her eyes rising. "Would you like to sit down? Maddie, can you get us something to drink?"

"Oh, no," James said, turning to her. "I won't be long. Rachel is home, and I shouldn't keep her waiting."

Emily lifted her chin, her hands a knot at her waist.

"Why have you come?"

James took a step back, motioned for her to sit on

the sofa. She straightened her shoulders, moved past him to her seat and picked up her embroidery.

"I fear for your safety."

Emily cleared her throat, suddenly hot even as a cool breeze fanned her skin.

"Can you bring us something, Maddie?" she asked, and her sister waited for a beat before hurrying off to the kitchen.

"Why would you fear for my safety? Aside from the husband who wants nothing more than to keep me prisoner in that shanty?"

James sat down beside her, his elbow brushing hers and she felt a strange tingle where their flesh met, knowing it came from being so close to a man after months apart from her husband.

"Has he come to see you?" James asked, and Emily's eyes cut to him.

"No."

"I've heard he wants to take you back to the claim."

Emily felt her blood thicken, felt it turn cold until it ran like an icy sludge beneath her skin.

"What?" she whispered, glancing towards the kitchen. "I've been here almost four months. Surely, he would have done something by now."

"Rachel's brother visits the Lamplight at times. We do not approve, of course, but he told us he overheard Marvin say he would take you back to the shanty."

Emily put her embroidery down, folded her hands over her stomach.

"He swore he would do it before the baby was born."

"Did he, now?" she asked, wondering where Maddie could be, feeling like she might faint.

"Emily," he said, sensing her fear. "Are you well?"

"I'm fine," she lied, gazing into the eyes of the man she prayed could protect her.

"You must be careful. Keep Lester close. I'll send word if Liam hears more but I must get home. Rachel was against me coming at all—"

"Of course, she was."

His eyes widened. "What do you mean?"

She bit the inside of her mouth, wanting to strike him across the face for running back to his wife.

"Thank you for coming," she said, her eyes darting to the kitchen again, knowing Maddie was giving them privacy. "I appreciate the warning and will be ever so *careful.*"

"Please—" He touched her hand, leaned toward her. "I would have married you. You must know that."

She stiffened, anger rising from a place she hadn't known existed.

"But you didn't."

He pulled back, shocked.

"Marvin was courting you."

She picked up her embroidery again, her fingers pushing the needle with ferocity.

"I remember wondering if you cared because you never did anything but stare at me, twisting that *stupid* hat of yours."

"That's enough."

"When Marvin came along, he knew what he wanted, told me I was beautiful and if I'd had some shred of assurance that you wanted more than to moon over me—"

"Emily!" He raised his voice, his face blotted with shame, and she lowered her eyes.

"Please go," she said coldly, and he stood up, clasping and unclasping his hands before dropping to his knee in front of her.

"I blame myself for what happened."

"James—"

"I was a coward," he lifted his head to look at her. "I should have been bold. But you were so pretty, so *fun* when we were with friends. I never thought I stood a chance; never thought you would accept my proposal."

She looked at him, her face softening.

"Why ever not?"

"Emily—"

"I could run away," she said, her face hopeful. "My uncle lives out west—"

"Run away," he took her hands, rubbing the top of them. "Emily *no.*"

"I can't stay here," she lowered her voice.

"Of course, you can," James said, his brown eyes close to tears. "But you must be careful."

"No," she shook her head. "You don't know what he is capable of. I will never be safe while my husband is alive."

"While Marvin is alive," he repeated, looking over his shoulder at the kitchen. "What are you saying?"

She felt terror clog her throat, unsure why she would reveal her deepest desire to a man who had admitted his cowardice.

"If Marvin were gone," she pulled her hands away. "If he no longer lived on the shanty, or *anywhere* for that matter, I would rest easy."

"Rest easy?"

"My mind would be settled."

"Emily," he whispered. "What are you asking?"

She shook her head, placed her embroidery on the table beside her.

"Nothing."

"Yes," James said, his voice pleading now. "What would you have me do?"

"I'm not sure," she whispered, looking for Maddie, unsure why it mattered. "I'm only hoping that something could be done to settle my mind."

"You have no need to be disturbed," he said. "Now that I've warned you. You have your parents, and Maddie, and *Lester*. And myself, if need be."

She laughed then.

"And will you rush to my side if Marvin comes knocking? No, James, you will be at home, attending to the wife who didn't want you to come."

"Emily—"

"I will never be free."

He stood then, his face pale and took a step towards the doorway. Pivoting on his heel, he came back, anger twisting his face and she felt shame for putting it there.

"I'll take care of it."

She couldn't breathe.

"James—"

"I failed you once. I won't do it again."

She shook her head, stood up and he put his arms around her, drew her against him even as his lips found hers, and she pulled back, mortified.

"James—"

"Let me kiss you."

She looked back at the kitchen. "Rachel—"

"Let me forget," he said, drawing her into a corner. "If only for this moment."

Emily closed her eyes even as he pressed his lips to hers, his tongue tracing her bottom lip and she stiffened in his arms, her heart cold.

A noise from the kitchen startled them and he pulled away, a look of joy mixing with the shadows of his eyes.

Maddie stood holding a tray of cookies, two glasses of lemonade balanced on top of it.

"I'll be going now."

She stepped back from the door.

"I'll attend to the matter we spoke of."

"You needn't," she said, unable to let him leave with the thought in his mind. "I don't know what I was thinking."

He shook his head.

"I will do it." His gaze shifted to her sister.

"I apologize for the trouble, Miss Maddie. Give my regards to your mother and father."

Her sister nodded as he backed out the door.

"That was strange," she said, setting the tray down and closing the door. "Why did he come?"

Emily put a hand to her mouth, took a step away from the door.

"Rachel's brother was at the Lamplight," she said. "He overheard Marvin say he wanted to take me back to the shanty."

Maddie gasped, both hands covering her mouth.

"We must do something!"

She touched her sister's shoulder, wanting to protect her, wishing she'd taken that Navy Colt out of its drawer and learned to use it.

She thought of James, returning to a woman he didn't love while plotting to murder the husband of the woman he did.

"You're shaking," Maddie said, pulling away and Emily saw tears in her eyes.

"I'm scared."

"Of course, you are," she said. "We must tell Pa."

"This will kill him," Emily whispered. "He's so tired."

"Em-"

"We need to wait."

Maddie pulled back, her brown eyes questioning.

"Wait?"

Emily sat down again, looked at the needlework sitting on the table beside her.

"James will help."

"Help?" Maddie asked, sinking beside her sister.

Emily nodded. "In any way he can."

Maddie sat silently, her eyes on her lap. Then she reached over to where the tray of cookies sat and picked one up, took a small bite.

Maddie?" Emily asked, taking her hand.

"Yes," her sister replied, taking another bite. "Let's wait."

Chapter Fourteen

Emily sat in the wagon bed with James, watching the prairie slip by on either side, the threat of rain causing her to draw the sides halfway down even as the heat suffocated her.

Dust curled on either side, kicked up by the oxen, and she wished for a storm if for no other reason than to settle the earth.

James cooed from her arms, and she looked down at him, touched the crease between his eyes, which were still as blue as the day he was born.

He was almost two weeks old, and growing heavier every time she picked him up- which meant he'd gotten his fill of Ruthie's milk.

And now her own.

"How far?" she called to Clem as she walked beside the wagon, but she knew by the excitement that seemed to have set fire to the air, that Fort Kearny was near.

"We should be there within the hour."

Her thoughts moved to Caleb, and then Ruthie, hoping she wouldn't cry when they left, praying Uncle Rand would be there so she would be able to look them in the eye when their wagon pulled away.

Caleb had been by that morning to talk to Jake, his eyes skipping over her, and she felt a lump in her chest, feeling like she might have ruined something by telling him she didn't regret what happened beneath the cottonwood tree.

They hadn't spoken since their kiss, but she'd thought about it more than once, touching her lips in the darkness of the wagon, imagining his mouth there.

Thunder rumbled, making her tense as James turned to see where the noise had come from.

"It's all right," she whispered, kissing his head and the soft, red hair that grew there. "Uncle Rand will be waiting."

"Are you sure?" Clem asked, her words making Emily sit up straighter.

"Of course," she lied. "I sent the letter ages ago and mail comes regularly to the fort."

"It comes once a month," she corrected. "And you said he serves as a guide in the mountains."

Emily frowned, her courage failing with Clem's words.

"If he isn't there when we arrive, he'll be along shortly."

Clem laughed.

"That word doesn't mean the same thing out here as it does back east."

"That's true," Jake said, turning from where he led the oxen. "You may be waiting a long time."

Loud voices made her jump, and she leaned out the side again, caught sight of thunderclouds rolling across the prairie and in the distance, a strange, disjointed assembly of buildings that resembled toy blocks scattered on a golden blanket.

"There's the fort," Clementine said, pointing.

Emily leaned farther out while Jake urged the oxen on. The gentle creatures kept their pace, unaware that good grain, cold water and new shoes awaited.

"We may have to stay for supper if this storm hits," Jake said, and Emily did not know whether that made her feel better or worse. "I know Miss Beatrice is itching to move on and will probably convince Caleb and Ruthie to pull out fast."

She thought of Beatrice and felt a twist in her gut, hoping Caleb did not settle for a woman like her and instead waited for someone who would lie on her back with him and watch the stars.

The thunder rolled again, and James began to cry. She looked down at him, imagining the three of them napping beneath an orange tree and felt a shock settle in her chest.

The image was real, pleasant, and not half as frightening as waiting for Rand at Fort Kearny.

She frowned, thinking her comfort should come from her uncle, not someone she'd known for all of two weeks, half of which she'd spent avoiding him.

James cried out again and she rocked him, heard him gurgle and leaned out of the wagon to get a better look.

Lines of wagons waited outside the main building, and she saw people dashing to get inside before the storm hit. Soldiers in uniforms leaned on their rifles, unconcerned with getting wet and she wondered if they knew Rand and where he might be at that moment.

"Emily!"

She looked up, saw Ruthie jump onto the back axle and climb through the cinched canvas.

"Didn't want to miss saying goodbye to you!"

Emily laughed, her fear lifting.

"Where's Caleb?"

She waved her hand and walked unsteadily to where Emily sat.

"He's perfectly fine leading a pair of dumb cows. There are a lot of people in the fort, and I thought...". she trailed off. "I might not see you and Jimmy."

Emily swallowed her distress. She hadn't thought about losing Caleb and Ruthie or Jake and Clem in the crowds.

"Jimmy?" she asked, trying to hide her discomfort.

Ruthie kneeled in front of her, touched his red hair and smoothed it down.

"James is too proper. He'll end up being a Jimmy for certain."

Emily smiled, liking the sound of that.

"You'll need to talk to one of the soldiers right away. See if a letter came."

She nodded, turning James as he strained to find where Ruthie's voice was coming from.

"I will," she said, silence settling uneasily between them.

"How'd you learn to shoot like that?"

"Excuse me?" Emily said, startled.

"Caleb said you shot the head off a rattler."

"Well—"

"He tried saying it was him but he's a terrible liar. And shot, if you ask me—"

"Ruthie—"

"No sense denying it. But it doesn't add up since you couldn't hold that rifle worth a darn."

"I held it just fine!"

"You're not fooling me," she said, smiling now. "No matter how you try. Clem knows it, Jake knows it, and Beatrice sure as heck knows it and that's why she can't wait to get you away from my brother."

"Ruthie!"

"I know something happened under that cotton-wood tree, but it isn't any of my business. What I do know is he'll be a sorry excuse for company if you don't patch things up."

"There's nothing to be said."

Ruthie clucked her tongue, held her arms out for James and Emily handed him to her.

"Course there is. Now go and say it."

Emily laughed. "I'm sure I'll take a moment to wish him a safe journey."

Ruthie sighed, rubbed her nose with James's as he tried to grab a fistful of her hair.

"He likes you, is all. And that's *something* because he's hardly cracked a smile since Celia died, let alone carried on the way he did at Alcove Springs."

"I don't—"

"Please," she said, serious now. "I can't stand to see those shadows in his eyes again. If all you do is set his mind at ease about your uncle, then I'll be content. I deserve that, at least."

Emily looked down, knowing she was right, wanting to tell Caleb what was in her heart but fearful of what that might mean.

The wagon lurched to a stop, and she knew her time inside of it was over.

She heard Clem call to her from outside, saying she was going into the fort with Jake, and Ruthie stood, ready to hand James back to her and Emily felt fear peak in her chest.

"Wait," she said suddenly.

Ruthie froze, her eyes large.

"I need to tell you something, but you can't say anything to Caleb."

"What?" Ruthie asked. "*Why?*"

"Just knowing me puts you in danger. Puts you *both* in danger."

"Emily—"

"My parents and sister are gone. And I told you my husband died—"

"In a brawl outside of Chicago," Ruthie interrupted, holding James tightly. "Emily, what are you saying?"

She drew a deep breath, her words wavering.

"He's alive."

Ruthie went to her knees. "Why does that scare you?"

Emily took hold of Ruthie's arm.

"My husband used to put his hands on me, used to... *take* me against my will and I had a friend who said he wanted to help me... but Marvin *stopped* him and," she paused, despair thickening her throat. "The only thing I could do was run away, the only way to honor him was to name James after him."

Ruthie's eyes grew large. "What happened?"

Emily drew a deep breath, those dark days after James made his promise coming to life in her mind.

"He went to our shanty, intent on killing my husband but...."

Ruthie covered her mouth and Emily looked away, remembering the moment Lester had run into town saying a body had been found in Crooked Creek.

"Is it my husband?" she'd asked, her words wild with hope, and Lester looked at her with the same pity everyone did.

"It's James, Miss Emily."

She remembered trying to control her terror, remembered asking him what had happened.

"He was kicked by a horse."

Her stomach turned over at the thought, trying to imagine what Marvin had done to make it look that way.

She remembered his funeral, remembered standing beneath the cemetery trees in her black dress before walking to the meeting hall with her family.

They'd sat in a row beside Carrie, eating sandwiches prepared by the Ladies Auxiliary and Rachel came to her, asking to walk for a bit and she'd followed her into the street.

"Did your husband kill him instead?" Ruthie asked, her words so low Emily could hardly hear them.

"The sheriff said he'd been kicked by a horse. His wife didn't believe it. I didn't, either."

"His *wife?*"

Shame rose in her chest, and she lowered her eyes.

"It was wrong of him to go out there, wrong of me to let him go but I was so *scared,* Ruthie."

"Of course, you were," she said, reaching out to squeeze her shoulder. "Sounds like that fella should've married you, anyway."

Emily shook her head.

"I didn't love him," she said. "I know that, now. But he loved me, and I *used* him—"

Ruthie bent down, looked into her eyes. "He was the one who decided to go out there, knowing he might meet up with trouble. Sounds like he knew what he'd signed up for."

Emily felt her words like a cold salve on burned skin.

"Marvin told me he was going to kill him."

"Em—"

"He'll do the same to Caleb if he finds out we kissed under that cottonwood tree."

"You *kissed* my brother?"

"Ruthie, that's not the point right now-"

"I'll be cow-kicked!" she exclaimed, shifting Jimmy's weight again. "No wonder he's been such a grump, with a broken heart and all—"

"I didn't break his heart-"

Ruthie rose up on her knees, covered Emily's hand with her own.

"You've gotta stay with us now! We can protect you and Jimmy-"

"My husband was shot in the shoulder and the leg. If he's alive, he'll need time to recover."

"But—"

"Uncle Rand will be here. And we'll go to a place Marvin Jones will never find me."

Ruthie shook her head, desperate.

"You need to leave, Ruthie. You need to take Caleb and go, and I know it was foolish to kiss him, but I wanted to believe my life could be different-"

"It *can* be different."

Emily looked down, unable to meet her eyes.

"Don't make me lie to my brother."

145

"You have to, at least until you're so far he won't turn back."

"There's no such place."

Emily's eyes began to smart, thinking of the man she'd danced with at Alcove Springs, his eyes alight in the darkness and knew he wanted something different, too.

"Make him go," she said. "I was selfish with James. I won't do the same thing to Caleb."

"*Why not*?" Ruthie begged, the first drops of rain hitting the canvas. "He's a grown man and can make up his mind—"

"Because" she interrupted, her words a revelation. "I love him."

Chapter Fifteen

Emily stood with her baby in her arms, the blanket she'd used to shield him tied into a sling as he strained for a look at his new surroundings, his face scrunched up as though he might cry.

People were moving about inside of the store, driven inside by the storm and so she went to a corner, stood until a soldier approached her from behind.

"Do you need something, Miss?"

He was tall, with a white mustache and kind face.

"Yes," she said. "I need to know where you keep your letters."

He stopped, looked her up and down, his eyes searching behind her for a brother or a husband as James began to whimper.

"The post office is in another building," he said. "Are you well, Miss?"

Emily's cheeks reddened, embarrassed that he would assume she was in distress simply because she was alone.

"My uncle is Rand Albright and he's a guide in the mountains. I'm expecting a letter."

The soldier smoothed his mustache, shook his head.

"I have not heard that name. But my assignment is new. Let me inquire."

Emily felt people brush against her and pulled back. She hadn't seen Clem or Jake since she ran for the fort but had expected to find them in the lines of people buying goods.

She turned again, scanning the faces for someone familiar and clutched James to her chest.

"What is your name, Miss?"

She opened her mouth, felt a man press his hands into her shoulders as he moved behind her.

"Miss?"

"Her name is Emily Ives," Clem's voice steadied her, and she gulped in a breath, turned to see her friend.

The soldier nodded, bowed slightly.

"If you stay here, Miss, I will be back shortly."

Emily nodded, clutching James tighter.

"You look pale," Clementine said. "We waited by the staircase, but you bolted right past us like your bloomers were on fire."

"I'm sorry," Emily smiled, rocking a gurgling James and Clem held out her arms. He stilled almost at once and Emily wondered if he felt her distress, her fear that the soldier with the white mustache would return without a letter.

"Will you be staying through supper?" Emily asked, wondering where they would possibly eat, how *she* would possibly eat.

"Jake says no," she said, her eyes catching hold and in them Emily saw sadness. "I think Caleb and Ruthie want to push on. And Miss Beatrice and Putt and the aunt we've yet to see will do whatever Caleb tells them to."

"I see," Emily said, her heart falling even as she faced the inevitable.

And so, she waited with Clem and James while the soldier looked for a letter, waited while Jake came by and spoke to her, handing her a satchel and some money to buy provisions with.

"Jake," she said, shaking her head. "I couldn't-"

"It's the least we can do," he said, his dark eyes softer than she'd ever seen them. "Clem won't sleep unless you're settled. I won't either, to be honest."

Emily smiled, looked to her friend and the baby cooing in her arms and did not want to leave them. For a split second she considered riding the rest of the way with them, hopeful that Marvin had found some new woman to occupy himself with.

If he was even alive...

He had a way of making trouble for himself and could have wound up on the wrong side of someone meaner than him.

Her heart lifted, the freedom she imagined when James promised to help her returning in a flood of joy that threatened to send her to her knees.

"Thank you," she said, and Clem nodded, telling her she would return after they bought what they needed.

They moved off then, James still in her arms and Emily realized they did not want to leave and were probably waiting as anxiously as she was for the soldier with the white mustache to return.

And then he was there, a letter in his hand and Emily grabbed it so quickly she cut her finger.

"Is there anything else you need?" the soldier asked, and she shook her head quickly, confident now that she had a satchel and some money and a letter from Uncle Rand.

She looked up, saw sunshine streaming through the window and knew the storm had passed. People were beginning to move to other buildings and so she drew further into her corner, turned her back and tore open the letter.

My Dear Emily,

I am sorry to hear of your troubles, and most distressed by the fate of your family. Sister Patty was always the best of us, and I pray she is at peace now.

I am unable to meet you at Kearny. A speculating party has procured my guidance through the Black Hills, and I must see to my homestead on French Creek.

I can return by mule to Laramie, and then due east down the trail.

Speak to Sergeant Jack Hawkins about provisions. I will settle accounts when I return.

Ehawee is good with babies.

Fondly, Uncle P.R.

Emily gripped the letter with shaking hands.

Uncle Rand was in the Black Hills. He would return after he settled accounts on his homestead and with his speculating party. There was a man named Jack Hawkins who could help her, but she would be waiting some time for her uncle to return.

She didn't know whether to laugh or cry, and so stood in her corner, holding her piece of paper while Clem wandered the building with Jimmy, Jake straggling after and felt the knife's edge of fear pierce her heart.

They would pull out of this place later today, leave her behind and if something happened to her uncle on his way to Kearny-

"Is it good news or bad news?"

She jumped, turned quickly and found herself staring into Caleb's eyes.

They looked almost silver, with a touch of blue and she realized she'd never really looked at his face even before they kissed under the cottonwood tree.

"Uncle Rand is in the Black Hills," she said, a tiny lift to her chin that dared him to react. "He'll go back to Laramie by mule and then come this way when his business is settled."

Caleb stood still, so still Emily could not tell if he was angry or relieved.

"And what'll you do in the three months it takes him to wander this way?"

She pressed her lips together, folded the letter quickly and shoved it in her skirt pocket. "There's a soldier named Jack Hawkins who will help me. He knows my uncle—"

"And what if Jack Hawkins has been assigned to another post?"

"My uncle wouldn't have left his name if he wasn't here."

"Soldiers get new assignments all the time."

"He's here!" Emily said, her voice rising, and Clem turned to look at her, an exasperated expression on her face when she saw Caleb.

"Getting riled up, aren't you, for a woman who's in no particular hurry to go *anywhere*."

Emily stood looking at him, her heartbeat in her throat.

"And you're getting awfully riled up for a man who couldn't care less."

Caleb tilted his head, the trace of a smile on his lips.

"I'll help you find this Jack Hawkins. And then I'll be about my business."

"I don't need—"

Caleb came closer, touched her arm.

"Let me help you."

Her skin danced under his fingers, and she looked down, swallowed in order to steady her voice.

"Thank you."

He nodded briefly, moved off in the direction of the counter and asked the man behind it a question.

"Emily," Clem said, beside her now and she held out her arms, taking James back. "What did the letter say?"

Emily took the letter out of her pocket, handed it to her friend, who read it with a worried expression.

"Who is P.R?" she asked. "Your uncle's name is Rand."

Emily put her hand on her friend's arm, grateful for her concern.

"His first name is Phineas. He always signed his letters to mother that way. That's how I know this is real."

Clem nodded quickly, trying to smile.

"He'll come to get me when he returns from Laramie. Sergeant Jack Hawkins will look after me until then."

Clem glanced at Jake, who shook his head slightly.

"Caleb is asking after him."

Jake was shaking his head. "We bought enough food to get us through to Laramie. I added some extra in case..." he trailed off, looking at his wife. "In case you needed to ride along."

Emily's heart soared, grateful Jake didn't see her as a burden even as thoughts of her uncle settled in her mind, making it firm.

"Thank you, Jake," she said. "But even if I do ride to Laramie, there's a good chance I would miss Uncle

Rand on the trail. I should stay here, where I told him I would be, or you may find yourself hauling me all the way to Sacramento."

"Wouldn't be a bother," Clem said, and Emily smiled, bent close to hug her.

"You've done so much already. I'll send word as soon as I'm settled."

Clementine nodded as Jake put an arm around her shoulder.

"If something should happen, send a letter to Fort Hall. That's the last outpost before we turn for Sacramento."

She smiled her thanks, knowing there was nothing these people could do if something went wrong.

Then Caleb was there, his eyes settling on Jake in a way that told Emily he did not like leaving her, and that small flame burned in her chest, making her think about Jimmy growing strong under this man's watchful gaze.

"Hawkins is on the parade grounds."

Emily looked at her friends, nodded as Clementine turned quickly and walked away.

"Be safe," Jake said. "And write to us."

"I will," she said. And then Caleb walked towards the door.

It was bright outside, the air crisp after being washed by the rain. She took a deep breath, readjusted her baby's weight and followed Caleb down the staircase and towards the center of the Fort, a large lawn where several soldiers stood.

"How will we know him?" she asked, hurrying to keep up.

"He has a large Walker with four white socks."

"A large... what?" Emily asked, and Caleb turned, a slight tug to the corner of his mouth.

"A Tennessee Walker with four white hooves."

"Oh," she nodded.

"You don't know much about horses."

"Pa kept some at the livery stable, but we only used them for visiting."

"Well, you'd best start learning."

James gurgled, waved his arms and Emily turned him, one eyebrow raised.

"You've never held him, have you?"

Caleb looked confused.

"A horse?"

"The baby!"

He laughed, turned and walked towards the parade ground again.

"Probably not a good time to start."

She caught his hand and he turned at her touch, his eyes torn between worry and amusement.

"Please hold him."

"Emily—"

"You were the first person in the world to do it," she paused, wanting to see her baby in his arms more than anything else. "I wasn't able to see it then."

He looked at her with the same intensity he had earlier, and she was aware that the other soldiers were watching them, that the people wandering around with sacks of flour and rice and cloth were watching and perhaps from some high window, Clem and Jake and Ruth as well.

"Please," she said, emotion making her voice waver.

Caleb looked at the ground, blinked hard.

"Come with us."

She lost her breath.

"Please, Emily."

"I can't."

"Yes, you can. We'll write to your uncle and—"

"And what?" she asked, "Will I stay in Laramie? Or go on with you to California?"

Caleb put a hand to the back of his head, turned away and then pivoted back.

"Do you *want* me to go to California?"

He paused, a pained expression on his face and whispered, "I don't know."

She shook her head, pushed past him, blindly looking for the man whose horse had four white hooves.

"Emily—" he reached for her elbow, but she shrugged him off, imagining Rachel's husband standing in front of her, his hands twisting his hat, his head bashed in by whatever weapon Marvin had chosen to use against him.

"Let me go."

The soldiers began to stir, their eyes on the exchange.

"I'm sorry," Caleb said, reaching for her again. "But I need to know what happened back east."

"Nothing happened. My husband died at Christmas. My family was killed in a fire. I have to come west to live with my uncle whether I like it or not."

"Bullshit!" he said, his voice rising, and she wanted to slap him for speaking to her like he had at Alcove Springs. "Tell me why the smell of whiskey makes you run like a scared rabbit, or how you blew the head off a rattler when you told Ruthie you couldn't shoot."

"I said that was beginner's luck. And no woman likes the smell of liquor—"

"Stop *lying* to me!"

"All right!" she cried. "It's not that I don't want to tell you. I *can't* tell you!"

"Yes, you can," he said, his tone low, his eyes on the soldiers. "We can go back to the wagon. We can talk there."

She shook her head, the baby wiggling wildly now, his small cries rising.

"I didn't tell you because I wanted to protect you," she said. "I *need* to protect you."

"You don't have to be afraid," he said. "You can trust me."

"No," she said, feeling faint now, afraid that James would slip from her grasp. "I can't trust anyone."

"Emily," Caleb asked, his eyes seeking answers when a young soldier with a handlebar mustache came to his side, tipped his hat.

Emily locked her knees, wanting the soldier to stay and wanting him to go.

"Ma'am," he said, his tone soothing with a hint of southern drawl. "Is everything in order?"

She bowed her head, took a deep breath and felt her mind clear.

"Yes."

The soldier glanced at Caleb, pulled himself to his full height, the brass buttons on his uniform glancing off the sun.

"It seems there might have been a misunderstanding."

"No," Caleb interrupted, his eyes holding hers. "We understand each other perfectly."

Emily felt the needle prick of his remark and readjusted James.

"We were just looking for Sergeant Hawkins. My uncle Rand—"

"Randall Albright?" The soldier laughed, and Emily looked at him, saw him twirl his mustache. "Well, that's some pumpkins!"

Emily looked at Caleb, but he would not meet her eyes.

"I'm Sergeant Hawkins," he bowed slightly. "And you are?"

"Emily Ives."

"And you are?" He turned to Caleb, who dug his boot into the earth.

"A friend."

Sergeant Hawkins raised an eyebrow, twirled the other end of his mustache.

"Odd way to show it," he muttered, and Caleb stiffened, his nostrils flaring before Emily spoke up.

"My uncle will collect me when he returns from Laramie. He said you could help me with provisions."

Hawkins stepped back, looked her up and down, his eyes settling on James, who had just settled down again.

"Rand wants me to provide for you and a baby for upwards of the time it takes to return from Laramie?"

"Yes," Caleb stepped in, clearly uncomfortable. "And if you can assure me the lady will be taken care of, I'll be on to shoeing my oxen."

Hawkins smiled, then bowed to Emily. "I can assure you; the lady will be taken care of."

Emily's spine stiffened and she looked at Caleb, who was staring at Hawkins.

"Where will she sleep?"

The young soldier laughed, tipped his hat.

"I will get to work on that detail at once. I can assure you she will be comfortable," a slight pause. "And I would like to see the letter from Rand, to make sure all affairs are in order."

Emily nodded, took the letter from her pocket and handed it to Hawkins, who continued to twirl his mustache while reading it.

Caleb stood, rocking from one foot to the other and Emily knew he wanted to see but was too proud to ask.

"Are you satisfied, sir?" Hawkins said once he had

finished. "Is there anything else I can do to set your mind at ease?"

Caleb looked at Emily, his eyes begging her to tell him, and she looked down, certain the only way to save him was to remain silent.

"I'd like for the lady to have a revolver," he said, and she looked up, saw that he was staring at the horizon instead of her. "Just to make sure all affairs are in order."

Hawkins laughed, bowed slightly. "I can assure you—"

"You can't assure me of anything," he said, his voice cold. "And so, I'd like to see you hand your revolver over to the lady."

Emily felt her cheeks heat up and Hawkins chuckled.

"Just give my Colt to her right now?" he said, his voice reminding her of a man who carried his fair share of pride. "Is she even capable of handling a firearm?"

Caleb stared at him, his eyes never wavering.

"Quite capable."

A nervous laugh, and Hawkins straightened his shoulders, looked down on Emily as if to shake off Caleb's remark. Then he unholstered his gun, handed it to her as though he didn't mind at all.

"Anything else, then?"

"No," Caleb said after a moment had passed. "It was a pleasure traveling with you, Miss Ives. Good luck."

She nodded, her heart beating quickly and looked

down at her feet, fearing what she would do when he was gone- and when she looked up, he was.

She stood looking in the direction he had gone for a few moments before Hawkins' laughter startled her.

"You two certainly entertained the crowds."

Emily's cheeks burned as James's small cries turned into a wail.

"Let's find you a place to nurse him," Hawkins smiled, touching the top of the baby's head. "There is an empty barrack room that will work until I can find something more comfortable."

"Thank you," she said, the gun still in her hand and Hawkins looked at it, a small smile creeping to his lips.

"I can relieve you of the firearm, Miss. The gentleman was quite insistent, but I can assure you—"

"I'll keep it," she said quickly while shoving it into the waistband of her skirt.

Hawkins' smile never faltered, but his eyes went cold.

"As you wish," he said. "If it had been my favorite revolver I wouldn't have given in so easily. And I will see about getting you some food."

"I have money," Emily said, reaching into the satchel. "I can pay—"

"No need," Hawkins bowed slightly. "Any friend of Randall Albright is a friend to me."

Chapter Sixteen

Emily sat beside her husband in the wagon they had once shared, her back stiff from trying not to touch him, Lester behind on the plank seat, and stared ahead.

She'd agreed to ride with him under the condition that he would grant her a divorce, a strange predicament born from her walk with James's wife following his funeral.

Rachel had taken her to the street, accused her of things that were true and when Emily tried to walk away, she spit on her, pulled on her arm and caused her to fall.

She'd gone down hard on her side, her stomach cramping in a way that made her worry for the baby. And so her mother put her in bed, watching for any signs of bleeding. Sheriff Bates thought it best they call on Marvin, who had waited in the parlor with Lester and Gerald.

Emily hadn't wanted to see him, had told Maddie and Patricia to send him away but he'd offered her a choice- a short ride in exchange for her freedom.

"He wants to explain himself," Maddie said. "Lester will go along, of course."

"No."

"If you do this, you can be rid of him forever."

Emily hadn't believed it, had told her to get him to write it out and Marvin agreed, his name signed on a piece of paper her father locked up in the back room of their store.

The day was clear, the sun shining, when she finally agreed to ride with him. He'd pulled up in their wagon with their old mare as Lester came forward, his hand extended.

"I'll need your sidearm, Mr. Jones."

Marvin laughed, shook his head and handed over the revolver Emily recognized- the one with the chip in the handle he claimed once belonged to his father.

Gerald came to the porch, and Emily knew he had left the store on purpose to see her off.

"If you're not back within the hour Sheriff Bates will come for you."

Marvin nodded, climbed into the wagon as Lester helped Emily up.

And now they were almost a mile from town, the road curving towards the creek where James had died, and she prayed he wasn't taking her there.

Emily put her hand on her stomach and Marvin turned, his green eyes following.

"How are you feeling?" he asked, his tone quiet, respectful.

She looked straight ahead. "I'm well."

"And how is the baby?"

"Fine."

"He will be born in early summer, I suspect."

Emily pressed her lips together.

"I know you want a divorce, and I don't blame you. I did things to you no wife should endure, spoke to you in a way your father should horsewhip me for."

Emily heard Lester turn on his plank seat and glanced down at him. He held a revolver in his lap, his thumb hovering near the hammer.

"Do you expect an argument?" Emily asked, turning to look at her husband for the first time.

"No," he said softly, "I only want you to listen."

She sat silently, the squeak of the springs beneath her seat grating her nerves.

"My brothers disowned me because I drank too much," he said softly, and Emily watched his hands as they gripped the reins, the knuckles white. "If I was ever in a sour mood, I turned to women and whiskey."

She took a long breath and he glanced at her.

"It's no excuse-"

"Then why does it sound like one?"

He paused.

"I haven't had a drop since the Christmas social."

"Then why did Liam hear you swearing in the Lamplight that you would bring me home before the baby was born? Do you expect me to believe you weren't drinking or sampling the whores while you were there?"

"Liam was mistaken."

"I don't believe he was," she said, praying he would turn the wagon around.

"Are you afraid of me, Emily?" her husband asked, and she felt his eyes on her.

"Would you blame me?" she replied, "I'm only here because you agreed to a divorce in writing in front of my father and Lester and Maddie."

Marvin sighed, flicked the reins and the old mare picked up her pace.

"We'll have to fix that then, won't we?"

Lester grumbled again and Emily turned to look at him, her eyes questioning when a sharp pop startled her.

She watched the bullet hit Lester in the temple, watched the other side of his head explode in a spray of red mush.

Blood flew in her face, and she screamed, trying to back away as the old mare whined, tossed her head.

"Marvin," she gasped, unable to breathe.

He was looking at her, a smile on his face, the revolver she thought he'd given to Lester hanging from his hand.

"What did you do?" Emily gasped as Lester toppled over and rolled into the wagon bed with a sickening thud.

"Taking back what belongs to me," he smiled, smacking the horse again. "Hid this gun in the jockey box. Even broke off that bit you remembered from the one I handed that beast."

Emily looked at her apron pocket, wondering if she could reach the shears she kept for cutting ribbon, the ones Maddie suggested she bring, before Marvin could get to her.

She knew he wouldn't shoot her; knew he would never risk the life of his baby and so slowly ran her fingers down her leg and towards the pocket.

He turned and she grabbed for the shears, plunging them into the flesh of his forearm. He screamed in rage, grabbing for her as the mare stopped suddenly.

Marvin toppled to the side, fell against the brake lever as Emily braced her foot against the toe board and jumped from the wagon.

She landed heavily, a pain low in her stomach and then spun in a circle. The road to town stretched behind, weaving between scattered woodland and the long rushes that lined Crooked Creek.

She took off at a shuffling run as a black smudge appeared in the sky above the towering trees.

She heard Marvin jump from the wagon, heard him come up beside her and tried to move faster.

"Now I see your true nature."

She turned, watched him pull the shears from his arm and toss them in the reeds. The wound began to bleed, but he didn't seem bothered by it.

"Fortunately, you are weak," he said. "The harm you aimed to cause won't amount to much."

She turned from him, shuffled down the road and towards town, the pain in her stomach stronger now.

"You shouldn't have jumped from the wagon."

"Pa," she gasped, her stomach cramping and she doubled over, "Ma..."

Marvin stood in place as she tried to stand, Lester's blood drying on her face and blouse and sticking to the side of her neck.

She swatted at it, felt it smear against her cheek and lost her breath.

She went down on one knee, tried to get up and fell to both, her hands splayed on the ground in front of her.

"Emily—" Marvin said from behind. "It is no use."

"The Sheriff—"

"Will be busy attending to matters in Fairview."

She put her hand up, tried to push him away and began to crawl towards town, the dark smudge speaking of a horror she couldn't find words for.

"What do you suppose it could be?" Marvin observed, following a few paces behind as she crawled, his shadow stretched by the midday sun.

Emily didn't answer, her hands gripping dirt and grass as she crawled down the road.

"Seems that smoke is coming from the mercantile."

She stopped, put her head down and felt the earth rock beneath her.

"Your father was working today, wasn't he? Along with Patricia and Maddie?"

Emily gasped, knowing it was true, knowing that Marvin had done something to start the fire and crawled on, gasping for breath.

"You'll tire out eventually, my love. And then you'll get back in the wagon and we'll start our new life."

"L-Lester..." she gasped. "Y-you killed him."

Marvin laughed. "What of it?"

"You *killed* him!"

"Just like you sent your dog to kill *me*."

"I didn't," she managed, stopping again, spots dancing before her eyes. "I never asked him to do anything."

Marvin clucked his tongue, shook his head.

"He paid me a visit, nonetheless, played me false by promising a message from you. It was fortunate I had my spade handy when he chose to draw on me."

"Stop!" Emily cried, crawling again, her breath in pants as the smell of smoke reached her nose.

"He didn't die quickly; I'll tell you that."

Emily laid down, placed her cheek against the dirt, her tears mixing with it.

"Did you fuck him, Emily?" Marvin asked, on his knees beside her now, his breath fanning the hair on the side of her face.

She shook her head, squeezed her eyes shut.

"Made him work for free, I see."

She lay in the dirt, Lester's blood on her face, wishing she could die and felt her head grow fuzzy, unable to think or move or even keep her eyes open until time stopped completely, and she woke up with a start in the wagon bed several hours later.

Lester's body was gone, and she heard voices. Recognizing one as Marvin's, she rolled over to her back.

A man spoke on the other side of the wagon, and she went still, listening.

"The job in town is done."

"Does Bates suspect anything?" Marvin asked.

"Far as anyone thinks, Mr. Ives's cigar fell into a scrap bin by mistake."

Emily felt bile rise in her stomach, knowing her father would be blamed for the death of his family.

"And what of my wife?"

The man laughed. "I hauled that other wagon to the creek like you said. Tipped it over and put those bloody shears beside it. Far as anyone knows, she went into the water an' drowned."

"Lester will be missed."

"They can miss him all they want," the other man said. "Without a body there ain't no crime."

Marvin laughed.

"That's what I like about you, Slant. Now get rid of him so we can be on our way. Sophie at the Lamplight told me this place was haunted and the old man in the woods is crazy."

A slight pause.

"Don't know how you get all these ladies in your pocket. Wish I did-"

Marvin laughed.

"Time and patience, my friend. And a dream

worth dying for."

Emily tried to move, felt a rope bite at her wrist and saw that she'd been tied to the brace.

"Where you gonna take her?" Slant asked, and Emily sat up, peeked over the top of the wagon and saw Marvin and a skinny man standing beside an old cabin, Lester's body lying off to the side.

"To the place I told you about," Marvin answered.

"You gonna deliver that baby in the middle of nowhere?"

Silence followed, and Emily gritted her teeth, scanned the wagon bed for something to use. The sky was fading, the moon beginning to rise but enough light remained for her to see that her situation was desperate.

"Get the man buried," her husband ordered. "I'll be back when my business is settled with your share."

The man grunted.

"Seems to me I deserve my share right now."

"Seems to me I could shoot you and dig two holes instead of one."

The man grunted again, and Emily heard a scuffle, knew they were dragging Lester's body.

She closed her eyes, thought back to the days when she used to play with James and Carrie down by the creek. In the course of their adventures, they'd discovered an old knothole in an oak tree, and promptly began dropping pennies into it, both found and given until a great treasure grew. When it was time to retrieve them, she remembered Carrie reaching inside, and then James, each without luck.

But Emily had bent her hand in a way they couldn't, reaching for the coins until she touched them with her fingertips.

"There's something the matter with you," Carrie giggled, and James nodded, swiping the coins from her as he raced towards the store and the penny candy her father kept in glass jars.

She smiled at the memory, the children racing through the woods and the laughter they carried as far away as the moon.

She pulled on the rope, felt the binding give in the slightest. Another tug and it loosened.

There's something the matter with you.

She yanked hard, felt her wrist begin to bend and gritted her teeth.

Another twist and the rope slid past her wrist, then the fleshy part of her palm and finally, her fingers.

The burn from the rope felt like fire and she brought her wrist to her mouth, tasting blood before she rolled to her side and began to crawl to the other side of the wagon.

She sat up slowly, saw her husband and Slant like dark shadows in front of the cabin as they carried Lester's body around back.

She waited, watching as they disappeared and then stood slowly, perching on the sideboard, her foot stretching blindly for the wheel.

Coming against it, she gripped the edge and rolled over to the ground.

She put her arms up, deflecting the brunt of the fall from her stomach and landed on her back.

"Dig the hole," Marvin's voice rose above the noises of the night. "I'm getting her out of here."

Emily got unsteadily to her feet and scanned for a hiding spot. The woods stood only twenty yards away and she crouched down, moved towards it only to be yanked back by her skirt.

Turning quickly, she saw the fabric wedged in the wheel axle.

She pulled quickly, felt the skirt tear as Marvin's voice sounded from the other side of the wagon.

She knew it would take him a moment to realize she wasn't in the bed and ran for the trees.

A moment passed before she heard her husband's voice.

"Emily!" he screamed into the night.

She didn't turn, just dropped to her knees. The wild grass came to her shoulders, and she crawled on towards the woods.

"Emily!" he screamed again, closer this time and she pulled herself forward, the tree line within a few feet as she scrambled on our fours into the tangle of trees.

The ground was rough, briars reaching from every direction to snag at her skin, and she pressed down on her tongue to keep from crying out.

Then she heard him, heard his boots hitting the ground in a synchronized pattern and knew he'd spotted her.

She struggled to her feet and saw him at the edge of the trees, scanning the darkened landscape for her.

She moved deeper into the forest as quietly as she could, weaving around fallen logs until she found one she could hide against.

It was soft, the green moss that blanketed it skimming off as she straddled it. Then she was pulling her skirt behind her, rolling into a ball and scooting into the undergrowth as her husband shouted her name again.

Soon everything became quiet.

She felt the baby move and gripped her stomach, barely breathing for fear her husband would hear it.

"Come out, my sweet," Marvin sang from the other side of the log, and she scrunched up as far as she could, ready to lash out if he reached over the top.

"Gotcha!"

She jumped, felt his hand close around her arm and sunk her teeth into his flesh.

"Bitch!" he screamed, grabbing a handful of hair and yanking her to her feet.

Emily stood, her head thrown back, and looked into the darkened face of her husband.

"I see I need to keep you on a short leash."

"I'll run away," she hissed in his face. "I'll kill myself and the baby."

He laughed then, "Maybe I'll beat you to it."

She swallowed, unable to form a thought beyond this dark forest and the man holding her and the wagon that was waiting to take her away.

"Please," she whispered. "Let me go."

"Begging now?" he clucked his tongue. "It doesn't become you. And I know you would gut me the minute I turned my back. No... my love... we are going on a long journey together as husband and wife."

A bullet whizzed by her cheek, grazing Marvin's shoulder.

He grunted, took a faltering step back and drew his gun.

"Get out of my woods," a voice boomed, and Emily felt Marvin pull her against him, the gun pressed to the side of her head.

"I'm just taking my wife home," he called, "She wandered off."

A pause.

"If your wife wandered into my woods after dark she most likely did it on purpose."

Marvin laughed again. "She's not right in the head. I'd be obliged if you'd help me since you were the one who shot me. She's pregnant and likely to hurt herself and our baby."

Another blast rang out, splintering a small tree that stood beside them.

"Shit!" Marvin cried. "Are you trying to kill me?"

The man laughed. "If I was trying to kill you, you'd be dead."

"My wife—"

"Has a gun pressed to her head. And you've yet to pull the trigger."

"Wait!"

Another shot rang out and Marvin went down to one knee, releasing her.

One glance and she knew her husband could not walk, and so she yanked her arm away, her heart in her throat as the stranger walked from the woods, his revolver pointed at Marvin.

She watched her husband aim, ready to shoot and the next moment the man fired again, and Marvin fell back, motionless.

Emily stood between the two figures, her ears ringing from the gunfire, praying she was safe when the stranger approached. The next moment he bent down, lit a lantern that lay at his feet.

His face illuminated, she saw a white beard, blue eyes and a lip stuffed with chewing tobacco.

"Ma'am," he nodded, not bothering to ask why she was covered in blood, his gun still pointed at Marvin, who lay where he'd fallen, blood pooling around his back.

"P-Please," she whispered, her eyes on the man. "Shoot him again."

The man holstered his gun.

"I'm outta shot."

She shook her head, hugged herself as a cool breeze rose from the forest.

"Just came out here to walk the edge of my property, not get tangled up in a lover's spat."

"We're not lovers," she said, and the man's gaze dropped to her stomach.

"Married, then."

Emily looked at him, thinking he might be a cross between Daniel Boone and Santa Claus.

"You don't understand," she reached for his arm, touching it. "I need him to be *dead.*"

The man looked down at Marvin, scratched the top of his head.

"He will be soon enough."

Chapter Seventeen

Emily sat on the small bed Sergeant Hawkins had provided for her, in a room that stood in a long row of other rooms and listened to the soldiers talking about her through the wall.

She looked down at James, who was sleeping in her arms, and was grateful she'd been able to feed him.

She thought of Ruthie, said a small prayer of thankfulness that she had gotten Caleb to leave and tried to imagine what they were doing.

They would be about four miles away by now and Emily wondered why they hadn't decided to camp at the fort overnight.

She drew a long breath, let it escape slowly and knew it was because Caleb wanted to get away from her.

And she couldn't blame him.

He'd asked her to come with him, and Emily could

only imagine what he'd overcome inside of himself to say those words.

And she'd demanded answers.

Stormed away from him.

All because she loved him.

Her mind reeled at the thought, trying to make sense of what she knew to be true.

Caleb was strong, and handsome, and a hard worker, and honest, and full of fun when he was able to see beyond the past.

But he was also hard, wounded, impossible to read and naive when it came to the damage Marvin could inflict.

She thought of their kiss, thought about lying in the dark with him like she had with Marvin and wished she'd gotten in the wagon.

She bit her lip, looked down at her sleeping baby and placed him on the bed.

She stood, began pacing the room.

Hawkins had visited earlier with food, and she thanked him, wondering how long he would stand there, twirling his mustache and if she could really trust him.

But Rand had left her in his care.

Which meant she could.

She thought of Clem and Jake and knew they were unhappy with her. Jake had purchased extra food, had invited her to ride to Laramie and still she'd refused to leave.

She glanced at James, then went back to the window, the soldiers' voices carrying to her room.

"She's a pretty piece of flesh," one said.

Mumbled responses, followed by a laugh and a voice she recognized as Hawkins.

"She's under my care and protection, gentlemen."

More laughter.

"She seemed under the *care and protection* of the man on the parade grounds," another voice said. "And someone fathered that baby."

"I'll thank you to leave the lady's virtue out of this," Hawkins scolded, and Emily put a finger to her lips, chewed on a nail. "You should concern yourself with what's coming across from Kansas, not who shares her bed."

"Why?" a voice replied. "It's more appealing than thinking about a bunch of border ruffians."

Another bout of laughter and then a door opened.

They stood on the stoop, and Emily saw them through the window, saw them casting glances at her door and she pulled back, looked at James again and knew he was sleeping soundly.

The sky was growing dark, the air cool from the rainstorm that had passed earlier, and Emily watched the soldiers through the wavering glass. Hawkins had given her a pitcher filled with water and a basin with a wash rag, but she didn't feel comfortable taking off her dress.

She remembered the night she escaped from Marvin, remembered following the man who called himself Quinn back to his cabin.

It seemed a woman had lived there at one time, and Quinn gave her a pitcher and bowl much like the one she was staring at now. He'd gone to another room, allowed her to pull a curtain across the doorway while she washed Lester's blood from her face and neck and hands.

He'd handed her a nightgown, surprised that it fit around her stomach before offering her some stew he'd saved for supper.

Halfway through the meal she broke down and covered her face, unable to tell him about her mother and father and Maddie, unable to speak at all because she couldn't breathe, and he'd led her to a cot and covered her with a blanket.

"There's time to talk tomorrow," he said, turning from her and taking the kerosene lamp and Emily faced the wall, weeping silently for most of the night.

When she dreamed, she saw Marvin lying in the woods, the ground dark beneath him as he bled out. She saw Quinn in front of her, pointing the gun at his face before pulling the trigger.

She remembered sitting up in bed, Quinn lighting the lamp because she had screamed.

"You're scared of your own shadow," he observed. "Only cure I know is to learn to shoot."

She shook her head. "I can't-"

"I'll teach you."

And he'd kept his promise.

Emily thought back to the week spent in his company, thought back to the afternoon they ventured to where Marvin's body had been only to find it gone.

Cold fear pressed through her body, but Quinn just shook his head.

"Critters most likely dragged him off," he said. "Or that fella he was with."

Emily wanted to tell him that no animals had taken her husband away.

"I told you he needed to be dead," she whispered, and Quinn looked at her.

"He is."

"No," she shook her head. "I need to know it... need to *see* that he's dead."

Quinn scratched his white beard, his face softening.

"Even if he ain't, we'll make sure he never finds you."

Emily remembered them planning her escape, remembered writing her first letter to Rand and she'd given it to him, asked if he could take it to town.

But Fairview was a long way off, and Quinn didn't go there often.

"I need to mail this letter," she told him. "And I need to see the store."

And so, a plan was born between them as she stood in the woods, shooting his revolver again and again and again.

"God gave you a gift," Quinn said after she'd hit

her mark cleanly. "Others don't catch on so well or so quick."

Emily felt pride swell inside of her, wondering how her time in the shanty would have changed if her father had taught her to use his Navy Colt.

"My rifle's got a broken flint, or I'd set you on that next," Quinn smiled. "I suspect you'd shoot as sure."

She stood looking out the window, remembering the man who had saved her life, longing for the one who would lead her to a new one and knew she'd made a terrible mistake.

A light knock on the door and she jumped, smoothed her skirt as though she was expecting company and went to answer it.

The soldier with the white mustache stood on the stoop. He bowed slightly, asked how she liked her room and if there was anything he could get for her.

"I'm comfortable, thank you," she said, wondering for the first time what she would do while waiting for Rand. She thought of Caleb and Ruthie, rolling west in their wagon and wanted to be with them so badly she thought she might cry.

"I'm glad to hear you are well."

Emily tried to smile, then nodded quickly.

"I will take my leave," he bowed slightly. "Good evening, Mrs. Jones."

She looked up at him.

"What did you call me?"

The soldier smiled, tipped his hat. "Mrs. Jones, Ma'am."

She felt her heartbeat scatter against her ribs. "My name is Ives. You knew as much when you brought my letter from the post."

"Ma'am?"

"Why did you call me Mrs. Jones?"

The man looked past her as if trying to remember something.

"I'm sure I heard Sergeant Hawkins mention it when he was making arrangements for your provisions. I thought perhaps you preferred—"

"Hawkins?" she interrupted.

"He's making his nightly rounds and will be here shortly," he said quickly. "I apologize if there has been some sort of mistake. I'm sure he can sort the matter out."

She took a step back into the room, looked at James sleeping in the pile of blankets behind her.

"Thank you," she said quickly. "I must tend to my son."

He looked over her shoulder, raised his eyebrows.

"Ma'am—"

"Goodnight."

She shut the door in his face, ran over and grabbed James off the bed. Closing her eyes, she allowed herself a moment before grabbing the revolver.

Marvin was alive, might even be at the fort and Hawkins had known, had mistakenly mentioned her real name.

He'd been shot three times, once in the leg. But with the right doctor or nurse to tend to him... It'd been almost a month since he'd bled out in the woods behind Quinn's cabin, enough time to make a recovery and find his way to Kearny.

She stuffed the revolver in the waistband of her skirt and turned down the lamp.

Moving to the window, she looked out as James began to squirm.

She cupped the back of his head and rocked him, searching for any sign of Hawkins, and opened the door.

The night was quiet, a warm breeze blowing from beyond the ramparts when she stepped into the darkness.

She heard voices from the row of barracks, listened to horses neighing, yellow light falling from windows as campfire smoke drifted like dust in the air.

She knew the trail followed the Platte River and ran west on the far side of the fort, knew that Caleb and Ruthie and the Mays lay somewhere in the darkness that had spread across the prairie.

A familiar voice pierced the night and she drew back, ducked behind the barrack wall, listening as two soldiers paused on the other side of it.

"I already checked on Mrs. Jones."

A long pause, and Emily peeked around the corner, saw the man with the white mustache talking to Hawkins, who had removed his hat and was running his fingers through his long, curly hair.

"Did you call her by that name when made your visit?"

"Yes," the man replied. "And she seemed taken aback. Something is amiss here—"

"You're damn right," Hawkins slapped his hat on his knee.

"I thought-"

"I don't want you to *think*, Slocum," Hawkins roared. "I want you to follow *orders!* I told you to check in on Miss Ives... Not Mrs. Jones."

James began to fuss, began to rub his face against her chest as if he wanted to nurse and she unbuttoned her dress so he could smell her skin.

"Sir," Slocum said. "I am at a loss—"

"Where is she now?"

"She was tending to her baby. She seemed over-wrought."

"Dammit," Hawkins cursed, and she saw him turn sharply towards her room.

James let out a small whimper and Hawkins paused, turned slowly towards where she was hiding.

"Was that a child?" he whispered.

"A child?" Slocum echoed, making his way to the wall as Emily slipped around the opposite corner.

"A baby," Hawkins paused.

"There are children at the campfires, sir."

"That is too far away," Hawkins said, rounding the corner.

Emily didn't wait to hear his response, but crept along the wall, one hand grasping the handle of her gun even as she heard Hawkins' voice, following her in the darkness.

"Her husband has come to collect her," he said, and Emily wondered if his words were meant for her to hear. "She ran away with their child and is bound for a lunatic asylum."

"She did not seem unstable."

"You saw the spectacle on the parade grounds. It has come to my attention that she is a woman of loose morals."

"You don't say," the voices were fading now, and Emily continued to move forward, her eyes adjusting to the darkness as James squirmed in her arms.

"Shhh," she cooed, shoving a finger in his mouth and he began to suckle.

She moved quickly then, the gates of the fort looming in front of her, and beyond- a landscape dotted with campfires that seemed as bright as lightning bugs.

"Who goes there?" a man called from behind and she spun, saw someone step from the darkness and tightened her grip on the gun.

"It's me," she said, feeling dumb, James squirming against her finger.

"Ma'am?" he asked, moving forward and she straightened her shoulders.

"I'm going to my wagon," she said, and the watchman came closer, rifle in hand.

"Do you always carry a gun?"

She swallowed, ready to shoot if he came closer.

"I'm alone with a baby."

The soldier chuckled. "I see that."

"Then let me pass."

"Were you left behind?" he asked, and in the distance, she heard voices rising, knowing Hawkins had discovered her empty room and would track her to the gates.

"No," she said. "I had business at the fort, but my campsite is near."

"Weren't you the woman arguing with that man today?" the watchman said, smirking now. "Planning to pay him a visit?"

Emily nodded, moving away and the soldier waved his rifle, the smell of liquor on his breath as she dashed into the darkness.

Holding James tightly, she sprinted towards the river.

She remembered crossing the Big Blue, remembered the water lapping at the sideboards and prayed the Platte was more forgiving.

Moments later her feet found water and she plunged into it, the mud suctioning over the top of her shoes as she began to wade across.

James gave a sharp cry, and she reached down, wiped the water from his face, waves lapping at her shins as she struggled forward.

"Shhh," she cooed, sticking her finger in his mouth again but he pulled away, screamed into the night.

Hawkins was at the riverbank now, calling her name and Emily looked over her shoulder, saw him pause at the water's edge, a half dozen soldiers beside him.

"Let her go," one of them said. "It's not worth getting your feet wet."

Emily kept moving, the mud pulling at her shoes, James against her chest even as the wind tried to snatch his cries away.

"She took a man's child!" Hawkins cried, trying to rally the others. "Don't you hear him screaming?"

Emily stopped, readjusted James against her breast and he latched on- silence descending over the river.

In the distance she heard laughter and the lowing of cattle and on the far reaches of the prairie - a fiddle.

She bent her head, overcome with the need to call out Caleb's name.

"Are you going to help me?" Hawkins demanded.

"We'll find her in the morning," one of them said.

"They may be gone!" Hawkins roared, closer now and Emily knew he had entered the river.

"Then she's gone," one of them said. "It's no skin off my nose if she wants to kill herself out here."

She dared to move, dared to inch closer to a brush covered island and sat down amongst the brambles before scooting inside of them.

A wind blew against her wet clothes, making her shiver and still James nursed, his silence their salvation.

Emily tried to look at the far bank, tried to make out Hawkins and was certain she saw another man standing beside him.

She narrowed her eyes, tried to see if the man was

really there, if it was her husband and knew he'd found her.

She pulled the revolver from her waistband and raised it, knowing she would hit her mark.

God gave you a gift...

If that's what killing was called.

James moved against her breast, his fingers kneading her flesh and she looked down at him, then up at his father.

A moment passed before she lowered her gun.

The soldiers weren't coming, the man who stood beside Hawkins had withdrawn to the bank and so she crawled through the bramble and brush to the far side of the island, kicked off her shoes and waded into the stream again.

It wasn't long before Fort Kearny was nothing more than a distant glimmer.

She looked at her son, sleeping now, and readjusted her hold on the revolver. The prairie was silent, camp-fires burning to embers, the memory of the distant fiddle haunting her.

"Caleb," she whispered, praying his heart would hear her. "Find me."

Chapter Eighteen

Caleb sat by the campfire, his mind clouded with worry and tried to listen to what Beatrice was saying. She'd invited herself to supper, had taken every opportunity to be close to him while they were eating, and he knew it was because Emily was gone.

The thought hit him in the chest, and he coughed into his fist.

He remembered leaving her at the fort, remembered the look in Hawkins' eyes that said he couldn't be trusted and still there was nothing he could do short of slinging her over his shoulder and carrying her back to the wagon.

They'd already caused a stir with their argument, and he doubted he would have left the fort without a bullet in his back.

These thoughts made him pensive, and he'd been

quiet all afternoon as they moved west, sometimes raising his hand to touch the side of the oxen, sometimes watching Ruthie as she walked ahead of them, her head bent.

When they stopped for the night, only five miles from the fort, he let his mind wander to what Emily might be doing and if Hawkins had made good on his promise to take care of her.

"Are you alright?" Beatrice asked, scooting closer, her black hair spilling over her shoulders, her bright eyes dancing in the firelight and Caleb knew any other man would take advantage of the situation.

He glanced at her wagon, knew Putt and her aunt were making their own supper and would not come to fetch her.

"I'm fine," he answered, picking at the rice and beans Ruthie had heated up over the fire, his fiddle resting at his feet.

"Play a song," she said, her shoulder brushing his and he caught Ruthie's eye as she sat eating her own food on the other side of the fire.

She frowned, pushed her hair behind her ear and looked away.

Caleb knew she was worried, knew she loved James as much as she'd loved her own infant daughter and hated that he'd been taken away from her.

But more than that, he hated what had been taken from him.

The thought jarred him, making him think of

Celia and he cleared his throat, pulled away from Beatrice.

"I will after supper."

She clicked her tongue at him. "All you've done is push your food around, so we may as well have some music to liven things up."

He looked at her, unaware that he hadn't eaten and sat his plate in the grass.

"Should I fetch Clementine and Jake?" Beatrice asked, and Caleb knew they were eating their own small meal on the other side of the wagon, content to be alone with their thoughts. "Everyone is so somber tonight!"

Caleb didn't answer, just took the fiddle out of its case, tuning the strings while standing up and walking to the fire's edge.

He began to play- the song low and melancholy and existing only in his mind, and before long Beatrice came to stand beside him, her face drawn up.

"She's gone, Caleb."

He stopped abruptly, lowered his fiddle.

"I know that."

"You must accept it."

He caught sight of Ruthie and felt grief well up inside him.

"I left her and James well- protected, and that's a comfort."

Beatrice pulled away, her face pinched.

"I was talking about your *wife*."

Caleb looked down, knowing she had a right to be

angry with him, feeling angry at himself as Ruthie fidgeted from her place on the wagon tongue.

"Do you love her?" Beatrice asked.

Caleb swallowed, ran a hand over his head and wished he'd taken Emily up on that haircut.

He looked past the young woman standing beside him, remembering the way she'd looked in the firelight at Alcove Springs, and again under the cottonwood tree.

He thought of James growing tall and strong, thought about lying beside her in the soft light of morning and turned to Beatrice.

"That's none of your business."

She puffed out her cheeks, pressed her lips together.

"She's *married!*"

He felt his anger rise in his throat.

"Her husband died at Christmas."

Beatrice put her hands on her hips, glanced at Ruthie.

"No, he didn't! I heard your sister and her talking in the wagon before she went inside the fort. They were telling all sorts of secrets!"

Ruthie stood then, threw her plate in the grass and rushed to the other side of the fire.

"You little sneak!"

Beatrice raised her chin. "I was simply walking by and there you both stood, plain as day-"

"Strange how you could see us plain as day while we were *inside* the wagon."

Beatrice started swishing her skirt back and forth, her mouth open as if she wanted to say something.

"That's what I thought," Ruthie cried. "You were spying on us!"

"So, what if I was," she spat. "Caleb should know the truth!"

"Beatrice," Caleb managed, feeling like his heart had stopped beating as he laid his fiddle in the grass. "What are you talking about?"

She turned to him, a frightened look in her eyes.

"Her husband is alive and searching for her! He's crazy and would kill you for what you refuse to admit to me."

"What I refuse to admit?" he repeated. "I'm not sure what you're accusing me of, but even if her husband is alive, she's hardly in danger surrounded by soldiers."

"Things aren't always what they seem," Beatrice said, a strange smile on her face. "Sergeant Hawkins made my acquaintance when I was carrying my parcels. He was stopped by a skinny man who said a Mr. Jones was waiting to speak with him."

"Jones?" Caleb asked, scratching the back of his head.

"It's her married name!" Beatrice blurted; her cheeks puffed. "She said so herself! The sergeant is sympathetic to her husband's cause, of course. As any decent person would be when a woman acts in such a way."

Ruthie lunged forward, grabbed her elbow and twisted it.

"You're positively rotten! Why didn't you tell us before we left her there?"

Beatrice stumbled backwards, yanked her arm free.

"Why would I tell you anything? You've been against me from the start," she turned to Caleb, her shoulders heaving "And Jones *is* a common name, but this man said the provisions he'd been given weren't adequate because he needed enough for his wife and baby and was nursing an injured leg-"

Ruthie gasped, put her hand over her mouth.

"It's *him*!"

Caleb turned to his sister.

"What do you mean?"

"Caleb—"

"*What's she talking about!*"

Ruthie froze, covered her face only to have Caleb yank her hands away.

"Look at me!" he ordered.

"Caleb—" Beatrice spoke from behind and he turned to her, pointing a finger in her face.

"You knew she was in danger and didn't say a word," he spat. "You're probably hoping her husband killed her already."

"No," she shook her head. "I was afraid for you."

Caleb ran a hand through his hair, turned to his sister again.

195

"Tell me what she said."

Ruthie was sobbing, her breath coming in pants.

"She made me promise," she cried. "I begged her, Caleb... I said you had a right to hear the truth, but I didn't know her husband was really there."

Caleb bent down then, put his hands on either side of her face and looked into his sister's eyes.

"If you ever loved me, Ruthie, if you ever cared for me at all you need to tell me exactly what she said."

Ruthie nodded, her tears running between her lips and began to speak.

"Her husband used to do terrible things to her. He killed the man she named her baby after, and she was afraid he'd hurt *you*-"

Caleb heard her words, felt like he was falling.

"He killed a man?"

Ruthie nodded, wiped her cheeks.

"That's why she wrote to her uncle. She thought he could protect her by taking her to live with his Sioux wife in the hills. She said her husband took three bullets before she escaped. Two to the shoulder and one to the leg."

"The leg—" Caleb repeated, his head swimming.

"She knew he'd need time to recover, that's why she thought Rand would get to the fort first."

Her brother spun on his heel, put a hand to the back of his neck as Clem and Jake came to the fire, their faces questioning.

"Caleb—" Jake began, and he shook his head, turned back to his sister.

"You let me leave her there."

"She *begged* me to leave her, begged me to make you go—"

"Why the *hell* would she do that?"

Ruthie's face went red, her hands balled into fists at her side.

"Because she *loves* you, you nincompoop!"

He stood looking at her, then walked in a circle, muttering to himself.

"Her uncle won't be back for weeks."

Clem's eyes cut to her husband.

"Is Emily in danger?"

Too numb to respond, Caleb looked around the fire and saw fear, confusion and hopelessness in the faces of the people gathered there.

"*Is she?*" Clem demanded, and Jake stepped forward, his gaze fixed on the man in front of him.

"What do you need me to do?" he asked, and Caleb met his stare.

"Saddle your horse."

Chapter Nineteen

Emily lay curled in a ball on the far side of the
Platte River, her feet and skirt covered in mud,
shivering as the night wind blew from the
prairie and tried to comfort James.

She waded upstream until she could no longer see
the lights of the fort, waded until the voices of the soldiers died on the wind before crossing to the other
side. She held James to her breast, allowed him to nurse
until he fell into exhaustion.

She walked past campfires, careful not to be seen,
stopping only when she reached a thicket of locust
trees that clung to the bank and laid down.

Tucking James against her body, she curled around
him, the gun in her hand and tried to sleep.

It didn't come.

She opened her eyes, looked at the stars and
thought about the people she loved- living and dead-

and remembered Quinn driving to town with her letter to Rand while she waited in the cabin.

The day had been long, and Emily spent her time shooting, her marks getting better and cleaner until she heard Quinn call from the distance.

She turned, saw Carrie sitting beside him on the wagon seat and knew he'd done as she asked.

Her friend got down quickly, her face pale as she pulled her into an embrace.

"Everyone thinks you're dead."

Emily stepped away, took her hands.

"We need to leave it that way."

"The Sheriff—"

"Can't protect me. I have to go west."

Carrie's eyes went wide. "To your uncle?"

Emily nodded.

"My cousins in Missouri will help you."

Emily smiled, tears in her eyes and Quinn came up from behind, laid his hand on her shoulder. "I'll get her there."

She hadn't asked him to take her, had said she could find passage on a train or steamboat, but he'd shrugged, saying he didn't have much to do besides mourn a wife who wasn't coming back.

Emily looked at the stars, sleep teasing her mind and remembered that long journey by wagon and the places they camped, the things they had talked about and wondered what had become of the man once he'd turned for home.

He bought her a new dress outside of St. Louis,

made sure she got plenty of food and rest, remarking once how he wouldn't mind seeing California for himself and her heart almost leapt from her chest.

"Will you come with me?" she asked, but he shook his head, saying he would not leave the grave of his wife or the home they built together.

She'd mourned his answer even as he drove her to the door of Carrie's cousins, a newly-married couple who had welcomed her, assuring her they would stay in the wagon yard until she found passage to Kearny, giving her a warm bed and bath before mailing her final letter to Rand.

Emily wondered what these people would think of her now, alone and afraid and clinging to a baby in the middle of the Nebraska prairie, waiting for a man who didn't know she needed him- running from a man who would never stop hunting her.

The thought made her shiver, made her burrow further into the thicket.

She remembered the fiddle music, held onto the hope that Caleb was near and closed her eyes.

Hours passed, and she slept at last, disturbed by dreams where Marvin walked with her under the elm trees as her parents' store burned behind them. She saw Rand and Ehawee before a black mountain, saw their cabin hidden behind a copse of trees and the single strand of smoke rising from the chimney and turned at the sound of a horse's hooves.

She saw a buckskin against the sunset, saw him

coming towards her and felt James squirming in her arms.

Her eyes flew open and she curled into a ball, certain that Hawkins had rallied the soldiers in order to drag her back to Kearny.

It was dark, the horizon beginning to curl at the edges as two figures galloped by.

They were speaking to each other, and in the jumble, she thought she recognized a voice.

"Caleb-" she whispered, sitting up.

They were moving away, unaware of her in the locusts and she clutched James to her chest, crawled from thicket and struggled to her feet.

"Caleb!" she screamed, praying it wasn't a dream.

They kept riding, the prairie wind stealing her voice and she took out the gun, fired a shot into the air.

They slowed, turned their horses sharply.

She stood, shivering, her muddy clothes stuck to her body, the wind pierced by the most beautiful sound she'd ever heard.

"Emily!"

She covered her face as James began to cry.

Hooves pounded the ground and she struggled forward.

Caleb jumped from his horse.

The next second he had her in his arms, crushing her against him.

"Thank God," he said, his voice breaking.

She tried to speak; her breath short as Jake rushed up from behind.

"I'll take the baby to Ruthie," he said, and Emily held him tightly, not wanting to let go.

"He's real cold, but we'll get him warm," Jake assured her, and she kissed James's head, handed him over before pressing against Caleb again.

"Are you hurt?" he asked, his hands running down the length of her back and arms as if to see if anything was broken.

"I'm all right," she whispered, and the next moment he leaned down, kissed her soundly on the lips.

"We almost missed you."

She smiled, the heat from his body seeping into her bones.

"I would've shot you first."

He chuckled under his breath, then bent down to pick her up.

She wanted to protest, but her muscles ached, and she'd started to shiver and so she allowed him to mount his horse with her in his arms, a feat he seemed to handle with ease.

Once in the saddle, he wrapped his arms around her, rested his hands on the pommel.

"Ready to go home?" he asked, and she smiled, covering his hands with her own.

"More than you know."

Chapter Twenty

Marvin lay in the dirt, his shoulder a pulsing ball of agony and waited to die. That bitch of a wife, the one he desired above all others, had run off with the old man into the woods, leaving him here for the buzzards and he couldn't believe she'd done it after everything he'd given her.

He'd bought a shanty, fixed it up nice and fucked her every chance he got, something any woman would appreciate.

Marvin thought back to the other women he'd been with and knew he was a capable lover, knew they all believed his sincerity, and still *this* one... the one he'd given his name to, hated him with a depth that seemed endless.

He wondered if Slant knew he was hurt, wondered if the gunshots had scared him off and cursed his cowardice.

He looked at the stars through the circle of tree-tops and thought back to the farm he'd left in Presque Isle, thought back to his brothers and how they had turned him out, told him to not come back until he'd made something of himself.

His head was getting light, his blood wetting the back of his shirt and the hair at the nape of his neck.

He thought about his days spent in Sunday School, lined up on the hard bench beside his pa and brothers while the preacher rained down fire and brimstone.

He wondered if he really would go to hell for ordering that store to be burnt while Gerald and Patricia were inside of it.

He liked Patricia, thought she was a handsome woman and would have gladly played the adoring son-in-law if not for her bastard of a husband.

He'd hated him from the start, had looked down on him just like his brothers and there was nothing Marvin loathed so much as to see the arrogance in his eyes.

As if he wasn't fit to wipe Emily's boots.

He'd seen in her eyes as well, especially when he was fucking her, trying to please her, and she would grit her teeth, looking at him like he was trash.

He felt blood pool in the back of his throat, turned his head to the side and spit it out.

"Slant?" he called, his voice cracking, knowing he would die sometime in the night.

An hour passed, and then another. A coyote

laughed in the distance, followed by its pack until it reminded him of a group of children giggling in the darkness.

Marvin thought about the coyotes surrounding him here, his breath growing shallow, wishing the old man had finished him off when he had the chance.

But he had no more ammunition, so couldn't kill him like Emily had wanted.

He has to be dead...

He would prove her wrong even if he had to crawl back to that coward Slant's wagon, even if it meant hunting her down and gutting her from throat to groin after she delivered their son.

A figure appeared between the trees, and for an instant he thought it might be Emily, the height and form were so similar.

"So, you've come back, have you?" he rasped, his hope rising, and he hated himself for it.

"Marvin?" The voice was small, timid, and as a breeze blew across his face, he smelled a familiar scent.

And then she was there, on her knees before him as she took his face in her hands, his disappointment out-weighed only by the hope that she might lead him to her sister.

He felt blood gather in his throat again and swallowed it, her name a garbled whisper.

"Maddie..."

Chapter Twenty-One

Caleb stood looking out at the prairie, the day long and hot as he led his team of oxen along the Platte River Valley.

They'd arrived at the campsite just after dawn, Clementine running to meet them. She'd taken Emily into her wagon, had undressed her and washed her with a cloth and cold water before helping her into an old nightgown.

Jake started moving items, making space for her but Caleb stopped them, saying she would ride with him now.

The pair exchanged glances, an understanding settling between them that seemed to worry Clem.

Caleb tried not to see it, tried to distract himself by spreading blankets on the wagon bed, the idea that Emily would stay here lifting his mood despite Clem's haunted eyes.

He went to her, half asleep, beside the campfire and told her he'd made a place for her. She smiled, slid into his embrace freely now as he walked her to the wagon.

He helped her climb through the back, watching as she laid down on the bed he prepared and when she looked up at him, he thought she was the most beautiful thing he'd ever seen.

"Does this mean you want me to go to California?"

He looked at her for a moment, ran his thumb along her cheek.

"I'd say the chances are good."

She smiled, turned her lips into his palm.

"Uncle Rand?"

Caleb chuckled.

"What about him?"

A shadow seemed to cross her face, and Caleb wondered if she'd set her heart on her wild uncle and his Sioux wife, the dark mountains rising up to welcome her as she rode her Indian pony.

His mind tangled on the thought, piercing it like the thorns he'd combed from Belle and Blue's hair yesterday.

Then the look was gone, and she was Emily again, and he knew he'd never wanted anything so much in all his life.

Including Celia.

He thought back to his days in the mines, thought of the darkness and silence and the shame he felt for leaving his wife alone.

He'd been away for two weeks when their neighbor brought word that she was sick.

He'd asked if it was serious- money was scarce and the job wouldn't wait for him.

The neighbor nodded, his eyes dark and worried and Caleb went to the foreman, but he just laughed, told him not to come back.

He'd ridden as fast as he could, arriving at daybreak.

But it was too late.

She'd died an hour before.

Caleb remembered her face, so still and beautiful, and knew she'd been watching the doorway for his return as Ruthie took his hands, telling him she'd died peacefully and without regret, but her eyes said different.

He'd failed her.

Just as he'd failed the child growing inside of her.

No one knew she was pregnant, and after the death of Ruthie's baby the following spring, he knew it was time to move on.

He cleared his throat, trying to suppress the memory and saw that Emily had fallen asleep, the blanket pulled to her chin, and marveled that she and James had survived when so many others hadn't.

He stood up, climbed out of the wagon and surveyed the landscape. If they joined with a larger party, they would be harder to find.

And Hawkins knew what he looked like.

He ran a hand through his hair and saw Ruthie, James in her arms, ready to go.

He nodded to her, cinched up the back and was just turning around when he saw Beatrice.

She'd been waiting for him, had probably been eavesdropping and the thought made him angry and irritated and just this close to telling her to go to hell.

Instead, he took a breath, remembered that it was her nosy nature that had saved Emily's life.

"Beatrice," he nodded.

She smiled widely.

"Is she alright?"

She stood on tiptoe, trying to see through the opening and he touched her shoulder, led her around the side.

"She's sleeping."

"Her husband will come looking for her, you know."

He nodded.

"Likely so."

She frowned, swished her skirt from side to side, a habit that annoyed him.

"Guess it was a good thing I told you what I heard," she said, following him to the front. "So, we can keep her safe until we get to Laramie."

"Beatrice-"

"I'm sure he'll never agree to a divorce-"

Caleb touched her shoulder again, his voice low.

"I'm taking Emily to California."

Her eyes grew large, and she shook her head.

"She has a husband."

He grunted, his irritation growing.

"Women leave their husband's for far less."

She stood, dumbfounded. "He'll hunt you down."

Caleb had been thinking about that, had tried to untangle the web his mind was weaving and came to one conclusion.

"Then I'll be ready."

She stood still, as serious as he'd ever seen her.

"He'll kill you, Caleb. And your sister."

He drew a quick breath, disturbed by her words.

"I'd like to see him try."

"He'll try all right," she said. "And he has friends to help him. Why, that Hawkins was stationed at Kearny, and we had no idea."

Caleb looked at her, a strange appreciation growing within him.

"Can I tell you something, Miss Beatrice," he began, and she seemed taken aback because she touched her hair, pulled it over one shoulder.

"Of course."

"You are a handsome woman."

She smiled, her color rising.

"Why, thank you," she said. "Coming from you, that is high praise indeed."

"And nothing would make me happier than to see you settled with a good husband."

"Goodness," she began again. "Mr. Merritt—"

"But I won't mislead you. My intentions are set on Miss Ives."

She frowned. "You mean Jones…"

Caleb looked up at the sky, his patience wearing thin.

"The facts remain," Beatrice continued. "She is married, and I am *not*."

He smiled- the nice, wide, fat one he'd used on Celia when she was mad at him.

"You won't stay that way for long."

"Goodness—"

"With a face as pretty as yours, I'm sure you could distract Sergeant Hawkins if he did come poking around."

Beatrice glanced down, dug the toe of her shoe into the dirt.

"He's a dandy, you know."

She looked up. "Oh?"

"Nothing compared to me, of course," he smiled again, put his hat back on his head. "But passable."

"Now you're teasing," she laughed.

"Guilty as charged."

Beatrice giggled, swayed from side to side again. "If he did happen to come by, I suppose he would be riding that horse I saw him on yesterday?"

Caleb nodded, walked towards the oxen and she followed.

"It was a beautiful animal."

She clasped her hands in front of her.

"I told him as much when he was carrying my parcels."

"You did?"

"He was flattered."

"I'm sure he was," he agreed, adjusting the harnesses, his eyes meeting Ruthie's across the oxen's back. "And did you take notice of that fine mustache he likes to twirl?"

She giggled again. "He seemed so refined."

Caleb cleared his throat. "I suppose he comes from money. West Point and all that."

Beatrice swallowed, turned towards her own wagon.

"I believe I'll walk outside today- see if I can spot him."

Caleb patted Belle and she turned her head, mooed at him.

"He may spot you first."

Beatrice put her fingers to her lips, her color high.

"You will be a soldier's wife yet."

"Mr. Merritt—"

"Let me know if you see him, so we're not taken by surprise."

She giggled again.

She smiled to herself, took off with a shuffling step and Caleb knew he'd just hired the best lookout money couldn't buy.

And now the day was almost done, and no one had seen Hawkins, or a man riding with him who might be Emily's husband.

Caleb adjusted his hat, thinking of what he would say to the man who'd hurt her so badly, realizing the next moment he wouldn't do much talking.

He imagined Marvin hitting Emily, imagined him putting his hands around her throat and felt rage roil inside of him.

He walked beside Belle and Blue, their steps lighter after the new shoes and fresh grain from Kearny and watched the river flowing to their right.

He remembered seeing Emily's muddy dress, thinking for one terrible moment it was blood, and knew she'd crawled through the Platte River to escape.

She had gumption, that was certain.

Something Celia lost and never found again.

He tried to imagine his wife on this journey and knew it would be very different. She had a cheerful disposition, but would fall into melancholy for no reason, staring past him and refusing to talk.

Caleb squinted up at the sky, sweat running down his back and pooling at the base of it. He was ready to stop to make camp and have supper, ready to wash up with the cold water he'd stored in their barrels.

He was ready for Emily to wake up and sit beside him- ready to hold her hand and ask questions, her answers easing all the doubts Beatrice had placed in his heart.

He saw Celia's face again, cold and still as she lay in the bed they shared, Ruthie's small voice telling him she'd passed without worry or regret.

Caleb knew his wife had plenty of regrets, knew she wanted a life they could hold like a fixed rope, strong and secure.

And he'd left her alone, causing her melancholy to return.

He looked over the tops of the oxen's backs to his sister again, her auburn hair hanging in the two braids she favored, and knew she had enough gumption for all of them.

"Ready to stop?" he asked, and she looked up, lost in thoughts of her own.

"I'm beat," she said, adjusting James so he could look out at the featureless prairie, and he gurgled his happiness. "This baby's getting bigger by the minute."

"That's a good thing," he smiled.

"Sure is," she kissed the top of James's head.

Caleb pulled on the harness, and the oxen came to a stop. Behind them the May wagon slowed as well, followed by the others who looked to him to measure their days.

Just as Celia had, her melancholy returning worse than before when he'd spoken about going back to work in the mines.

He remembered Ruthie's face when he ran through the front door, scared he would see something she didn't want him to.

He'd stood, too numb to speak to her before removing his hat and entering the room.

You can't blame yourself...

But he had.

She knew you were coming, knew that you loved her...

He'd loved her without ceasing for the past year, had thought of her when he woke in the morning and when he laid down at night, thought of her when he made the decision to come west, imagining their life in a land where sadness couldn't touch her.

He rubbed at his forehead, the question that had haunted him a hundred times burning inside his throat.

"Ruth," he said slowly, not sure he wanted an answer, knowing he would need one if he wanted a future.

She glanced at him, her smile wide, James's tiny fist wrapped around her finger.

"Did Celia end her life?"

Her smile vanished.

"Caleb—"

"I saw it in your eyes that day."

She looked down, then came around the oxen, touching their noses as she passed, and stood in front of him.

"She was so lonely."

"That's not what I asked."

Ruthie took a breath, her face as sad as he'd ever seen it.

"She didn't eat or sleep after you left, just sat in that chair and looked out the window, waiting for you to come back."

Caleb swallowed, the despair he'd felt that day rising to the surface.

"She'd convinced herself that something awful was going to happen. I kept telling her you were safe, but she dreamed every night that you were buried alive."

Caleb felt his chest tighten and bent over, his hands above his knees.

Ruthie touched his back, let the moment pass before she spoke again.

"She left all the chores to me, and one day I was out chopping firewood for the stove," she paused, lowering her eyes. "When I came back inside, she was lying beside that chair she always sat in. I tried to wake her up and called for the doctor."

"Ruthie—"

"Later that night I found an empty bottle in the pantry," she paused. "I threw it out."

Caleb stood up, took a deep breath through his nose.

"Was it laudanum?"

She nodded, and Caleb remembered the doctor giving her a bottle, hoping it would cure her melancholy.

"Why didn't you tell me?"

She shook her head. "Same reason I didn't tell you about Emily's husband."

"I don't need my little sister to protect me."

She puckered her nose. "You sure as hell do."

"Ruth—"

"You're the only person who's stood by me

through thick and thin, so shut up and listen to what I have to say."

He tried to laugh, the noise dying in his throat.

"Celia was crazy about you and it's not your fault she got sad, just like it's not your fault you had to take that job and I don't want that hanging over your head for the rest of your life."

Caleb looked down, his love for her easing the pain of her words.

"She was pregnant."

Ruthie didn't answer at first and so he raised his eyes and found hers filled with tears.

"Oh, Caleb—"

"She was so happy when she told me," he said. "She wanted a little girl... wanted to name her Alice."

His sister came to him, James on her hip, and put her forehead against his.

"She shouldn't have done that to you. Or the baby."

He put his arm around her shoulder, turned her into his chest.

"And mine fought so hard, even though she was so little."

He cleared his throat, not wanting to say anything else, wishing Celia had remained the girl he'd fallen in love with- grateful she hadn't.

"I'm sorry you had to keep that secret," he whispered.

"You had your own to bear," she said, her gaze

drawn to a figure in a white nightgown as she climbed from the back of the wagon.

Caleb's eyes followed, his heart lifting at the sight.

"It's gotta be different this time."

"Ruthie-"

"Promise me, Caleb."

Emily stood watching them, a blanket thrown over her shoulders and Caleb turned back to his sister.

"I promise."

Chapter Twenty-Two

Emily sat at the fire beside Clementine, her baby in her arms, and watched the sun melt like ice at the horizon's edge.

She'd slept most of the day, content with the knowledge that Ruthie was caring for James and Jake was keeping watch and Caleb wanted her to go to California.

She dreamed of the fruit fields and endless stars; their corner of the sky pulled brightly above as she pressed her lips to his.

And now she sat in Clem's old nightgown, a blanket around her shoulders, eating fried salt pork and potatoes, watching the man she desired stoke the fire.

The man she *loved...*

She smiled and looked down at her plate, trying to

make sense of the sensation that made her feel like she'd jumped out of her skin.

She thought she loved Marvin, had felt affection for James, but this thing that had been building between her and Caleb since that first evening at Alcove Springs was much different.

He bent low before her, the fabric of his shirt pulled tightly against his shoulders, and she imagined unbuttoning it and placing her mouth on his skin.

Marvin was the only man she'd ever seen, and she wondered how Caleb's body would differ, wondered if his kisses would linger and where, when they had no rattlesnakes to interrupt them.

She remembered his mouth running the length of her throat, his hands tightening on her bottom.

She smiled again, and covered it with her fingers.

"You're in good spirits," Clem observed, and Emily took another bite of potatoes, unsure how to explain herself.

"I suppose I'm happy because I know we will be traveling together," she said, hoping her friend didn't blame her for the danger she'd put them in.

"You will not live with your uncle, then?" Clem asked, taking a bite of her food, dabbing the corners of her mouth.

She shook her head, wondering how she would explain her sudden change of plans to Rand in the letter she was going to leave at Laramie.

But he'd run away, too. And married an unlikely woman.

"And your husband?" Clem asked, taking another bite, her question sincere but it bothered Emily.

She looked down, unsure how to respond.

"I'm sorry to ask such a thing, Em," Clementine said, her voice soft. "I know you can't answer it."

She looked at her friend, straightened her shoulders and noticed that Caleb had turned to listen as well.

"As soon as we get to California, I'm going to ask a judge for a divorce."

Caleb nodded, his jaw set. "If he doesn't end up on the wrong side of my Colt first."

"I hope it doesn't come to that," Jake said from his place across the fire, and she looked away, remembering when she knelt in the river, her gun pointed at Marvin.

She looked down at her son and felt the food thicken in her throat.

She could have been mistaken about the man in the river, could have let terror twist her mind into seeing things that weren't there, but her heart knew different.

There was a feeling that existed between them that no bullet could kill.

She touched James's nose, watched him yawn before settling back into his blanket and remembered their long night in the thicket.

Tears stung her eyes and she blinked hard, putting her plate aside as Caleb came to stand in front of her, the words they had yet to speak weighing between them.

"Will you walk with me?" he asked, and she glanced at Clem, who nodded while holding her arms out for the baby.

Clearing her throat, she stood, suddenly embarrassed to be in an old nightgown with the sun setting behind her.

Caleb seemed to be thinking the same thing because he didn't know where to put his eyes.

"We won't go far," he assured her. "I know you're-"

"I'll go wherever you go," she said, and he seemed startled, his eyes darting away before settling on her again.

And then he smiled, not the tight ones she'd seen in the past, but the real ones Ruthie had told her about, like the one she'd seen at Alcove Springs.

Emily's stomach fluttered, and she couldn't help but think of what she had done in the rocking chair after drinking the bottle of whiskey.

She looked at Caleb, wondering if he would think badly of her.

He'd been married, had obviously been with Celia in the way she'd been with Marvin and if he'd pleased her...

Heat spread through her body, unable to imagine him failing in that regard.

He noticed her hesitation.

"Emily?" he asked, and she looked at Clementine,

looked at Jake as he eyed them from the edge of the circle and held out her hand.

He took it slowly, his thumb running the length of her palm as he led her to a cluster of rocks that sat on a high point beyond their wagons.

They walked silently, and once Emily looked over her shoulder, wondering what Clem and Jake were thinking as they sat eating their dinner.

Then she turned back to Caleb, everything else forgotten, her heart pounding because he was going to ask her questions she didn't want to answer.

Once at the rocks, they sat with their shoulders touching, his hand in hers and she took a breath, the sunshine washing over them like an ocean of gold.

"No rattlesnakes in sight," he joked, and she looked at the sky, pulled brightly at the corners, the scent of hard earth and sweat and the soap he used settling around her.

She'd seen him bathing once, not long after James was born, in a small creek that ran into the Big Blue while she lay in the back of the wagon. She'd wondered if it was him, the slope and sway of his body somehow familiar.

She took a deep breath, absorbing everything that made her feel safe, praying she hadn't made a mistake by pinning her hopes on a man she barely knew.

"About your husband," he began, and she took a breath, raised her head and looked into her eyes. "Did you mean what you said about divorcing him?"

She nodded, hoping it was what he wanted to hear.

"It'll be hard," he said.

"I don't care," she said. "I want to start over."

"With me?" he asked, and she started, suddenly shy.

"Yes."

"You don't know me from Adam."

She sat up straight, knowing he was right.

"I know enough."

He nodded, looked out at the horizon as if he was settling something in his mind.

"If that man comes looking for you, I won't wait around for a judge to tell me you're mine. He'll end up gone... one way or another."

She bent her head, nodded.

"There's something I need to tell you," he said after a moment had passed, and she turned to him, fear building inside her chest.

"My wife died last June," he said softly. "On a Thursday."

"Caleb—"

"I blame myself for what happened to her."

She looked at him, confusion in her eyes, and took his hand.

"I fell in love with her the first moment I saw her wading in the river with that silly group of girls she ran around with. I loved her every second between then and the night she died two years later."

Emily drew a breath, pain piercing her chest and

knew she had to listen, knew this was the price she would pay for loving him.

"I loved her when I saw her lying dead on our bed and when they lowered her into the ground. I loved her when I went to sleep and when I woke up with the idea of taking Ruthie with me. I loved her when I was selling our house and packing up, wondering how things might've been different if we'd come west when she wanted to."

"What do you mean?" Emily asked, her heart hurting for the man beside her, ashamed that she'd added any weight to the sorrows he carried.

"She killed herself."

The prairie wind seemed to die in her ears, and she drew a quick breath, her fingers tightening around his.

"I always suspected it," he said. "She was happy when we were first married, but during the winter, her sadness took hold and there was nothing I could do to stop it."

"I'm so sorry," Emily said, feeling helpless and he looked at her, smiled in a way that said she only needed to listen.

"It got worse when I started looking for work in the mines, so the doctor gave her a bottle of laudanum. He thought it would help, but I never liked what it did to her."

Emily nodded, thinking back to the women who came to their store seeking bottles of the bitter liquid that seemed to cure everything.

She remembered Patricia pulling her and Maddie

aside and telling them in a low voice who they could sell to and who should get theirs from a doctor.

"I loved her with everything I had, and I still didn't know her heart- didn't understand how that sadness went straight to her bones like a winter chill."

"Caleb," she whispered, no other words behind it and still he held her hand as if it was the only thing in the world.

"I thought a child and some money would make her happy. I was working on both when she drank that bottle dry."

She turned to him, watching his profile in the fading light.

"Was she pregnant?"

He looked down at his boots, his silence the only answer she needed.

"I'm so sorry," she whispered.

"When I held James for the first time it was like," he paused. "I'd finally done something *right*."

She touched his face.

"You saved my life. Saved my baby's life-"

"Emily," he whispered, touching his forehead to hers. "I need to know your heart."

She pulled back, and he paused, his face softening and she realized he'd simply been waiting all this time for the truth.

"I married Marvin quickly," she paused, trying to gather everything that had happened into words. "Too quickly.... But he was charming at first, and made my father believe he would take care of me. And... I loved him."

She watched Caleb for any sign of anger or jealousy, but he simply looked out at the prairie, his face still.

"I wasn't allowed to see my parents or work in their store. I never left the shanty except for one time at Christmas when we went to a social. It was there my father confronted him for the liar that he was."

Caleb laced his fingers with hers, brought her hand to his mouth and kissed it.

"I left him that night and never came back," she paused, fear making speech difficult. "He threatened to come and take me back to the shanty. But there was a man I'd known since childhood, a man who wanted to help."

She paused, shame washing over her.

"He went to the shanty on his own, but Marvin was waiting and he..." she stopped, pushing her hair behind her ear with a shaking hand.

Caleb waited a moment, allowing her to collect herself.

"Was this the man you named James after?"

She pressed her lips together, nodded quickly, the story of Marvin and Lester and Quinn and Slant falling free from some secret place where she'd hidden it, the truth of her husband's existence, something she could barely admit to herself.

"I saw Marvin standing in the river beside

Hawkins, but I couldn't shoot him. I couldn't kill him then and I can't kill him now and I don't know why."

He looked down at their hands, stroked her knuckle with this thumb.

"Is it because I'm weak? Or frigid... like he used to say when he'd force himself on me?"

"No, Em," he whispered, "You're none of those things."

"Then what is it that keeps me from killing him when I know it would set me free... set *us* free?"

Caleb glanced over his shoulder, and she followed his gaze, surprised to find several campfires burning when it seemed they'd left only moments ago.

"Your son."

She drew a breath, looked out at the horizon.

"You can bring yourself to kill your husband, but you can't murder his father."

She felt something held tightly inside of her suddenly release and closed her eyes.

"You're a good woman, Emily Ives. No matter what you may think of yourself."

She took a breath, blinked hard.

"I loved Celia, but I've never been more scared than when I was riding to Kearny last night."

She pressed her lips together, lost in the picture his words created.

"Not even when I was coming back from the mines, or when I saw Ruthie's face in our doorway."

She drew a breath, turned to look at him. "Caleb—"

"I love you," he said, tipping her chin with his index finger. "I don't know how it's possible, but I see you and feel like I'm burning from the inside out."

She felt pain pierce her chest, the secret only Marvin knew holding her heart like a fist.

"You have to know... there's something wrong with me."

"There's nothing wrong with you."

"I can't feel the things other women do, when they lay with a man. Marvin used to get so mad at me... I felt it once, on our wedding night, and once when I was alone but... it never came back."

"Em—"

"I may never be like Celia."

He raised his hand, touched the side of her face.

"Don't compare yourself to her."

"I can't help it," she whispered. "You deserve more—"

"Stop," he said. "You said yourself that Marvin was a liar."

She looked at him, her eyes questioning.

"I intend to prove it."

The next moment his mouth covered hers, coaxing it open and she obeyed, her head falling back.

She felt him explore gently, his tongue touching hers before moving away and she moaned low in her throat, a need she couldn't explain causing her to push into him.

Then his hand was in her lap, his fingers seeking her through the nightgown.

She stiffened, ready for the cold feeling that always accompanied Marvin's touch and prayed he wouldn't turn from her.

He broke away from her mouth, his lips next to her ear as his fingers bunched the fabric, working their way beneath it.

"I won't do anything you don't want me to," he said. "Say the word and I'll stop."

She nodded, knowing she wouldn't have to because he would hate her once he discovered the truth.

She remembered the few times she had tried to pretend, remembered Marvin's sweaty face, his body moving again and again as he sought to please her. She'd tried to make a noise, tried to move in a way that said she felt the same things, but Marvin's eyes saw through her.

She was a liar, too.

Caleb's hand was on her thigh now, his fingers reaching for the place that had belonged only to her husband and she tightened her knees. Caleb's hand stilled, sliding down before gently cupping them, and she felt her legs fall wide of each other as if of their own accord.

"There are a lot of ways to please a woman," he said, his lips feathering her neck now, his tongue trailing to her earlobe as his fingers began to move in slow, rhythmic circles.

She sat still, hardly believing what he was doing-the wagons so close she could hear Ruthie talking to Jake. She bit her lip, the slow burn that had begun on her wedding night spiraling out in a way that seemed to pierce a deeper part of her body.

She gasped, then covered her mouth with her hand.

The next moment Caleb was removing the blanket from her shoulders, spreading it on the ground in front of the rocks where they wouldn't be seen.

She swallowed, unsure what was going to happen and then moved to the blanket, aching to be touched by him.

"God, I want you," he whispered, stretching out beside her, his fingers continuing to move beneath her nightgown. "But you're not ready."

She looked at him, understanding that he was worried about the baby even as his hand sought what he wanted.

He unlaced the front of her nightgown, his mouth falling to the swell of her breast. She felt a tender pain shoot through her as he took a nipple into his mouth and she sighed, her hand curling in his hair.

He pulled away, pushed himself lower, his tongue trailing to her belly button until his face hovered between her legs.

She closed her eyes, remembering a time Marvin had wanted to use his mouth in the same way but she had refused, forcing his face back to hers.

"Caleb," she managed, trying not to think about the others, desperately wanting to feel that thing that had begun on her wedding night, the low ember which had now spread to her legs and thighs and stomach.

Then he touched her with his breath, followed by his lips until his tongue began to taste what she had denied her husband.

She looked at the stars, a moan rolling in her throat, all thoughts of what was happening at the campsite forgotten.

"You're beautiful," Caleb whispered, and she bit her lip, wanting him to continue, her hips rising to meet his mouth in a way that seemed primal.

His finger slid inside of her, and she gasped, surprised to feel only a dull pain, muted by desire. She let out a small cry, his name on her lips as he moved his hand and mouth in a way meant to bring her closer to the stars- a place where nothing existed apart from the ending she'd sought for so long.

She laid beneath him, expecting the feeling to die away but instead it grew stronger until she no longer cared what the others might hear. She felt her voice break free from her throat, her fingers tangled in his hair as her hips rose, her toes curling against the earth as they had in the rocking chair.

She gasped, her body locked in place, her teeth finding the back of one hand, and allowed herself to feel everything Marvin had denied her.

She wanted to speak, to make sense of the thing that had happened to her with words, but she couldn't. Instead, she laid beneath him, her body slowly loosening until she lay like a rag doll on the blanket.

Caleb did not move at first, but turned his lips to her thigh and she felt him smile against her skin.

"Well?" he asked. "Is he a liar?"

She nodded, one arm over her face, her flushed skin cooling in the evening air.

"What did you feel?"

"I can't say," she whispered. "There are no words."

He moved then, stretching himself out beside her.

"You are far from frigid, Emily Ives. In fact, you may burn our house down once we get to California."

She smiled, Marvin and Celia forgotten, her deepest shame erased in the pleasure she'd drawn from him.

And when they were able to be together as a man and woman should...

She looked at Caleb and wanted to touch him, wanted to hear him make the sounds she had, knowing she was the cause of them.

"Is it true that a man can be pleased in the same way?" she asked, and he smiled, touched her face before rolling slowly onto his back.

"You tell me."

Chapter Twenty-Three

Maddie Ives sat on the horse behind Marvin, her hands clasped around his waist, wondering how she had come to be where she was and pushed the fear aside.

She couldn't think that way, couldn't question anything this man told her to do, or she would walk into the hills and put a bullet in her head.

She'd made the decision to follow him months ago, after he came to see her when she was working alone in the store.

And before that, if she was perfectly honest, when she'd caught him gazing at her across the table when he was supposed to be courting her sister.

Her thoughts tangled on Emily.

They'd slept in the same room since they were girls, telling secrets about what sort of man they would fall in love with, never guessing it would be the same person.

Maddie had resisted Marvin for some time, even as she felt his eyes roving over her, his hand brushing hers as he walked past, his touch promising something reserved only for her sister.

She'd come to the shanty on his wedding day, searching for him and he'd taken her hand, coming closer until he stood next to her. He'd kissed her, softly and on the cheek, but it had shocked her, made her think of herself in a way she never had before.

Emily had always been the lively one, the pretty one, the one who was going to write stories one day and who had silly men like James falling over themselves while Maddie stood in the background- quiet and afraid of the things that seemed to excite other people.

But Marvin had said strange words to her that day in the shanty and then later, at the store, telling her she was more beautiful than her sister.

He'd also confided that Emily was failing as a wife.

"You would be different," he whispered. "I can tell by looking at you."

She lay awake that night, wondering if Marvin was touching her sister while he thought of her.

It was the week before the winter social when she finally met him in secret- in the back room of the store after they had closed for the night. Her parents were sleeping, Gerald softly snoring when she crept past their room.

Marvin was waiting outside the back entrance, eager to touch her and kiss her and undress her while her sister waited alone and pregnant at the shanty.

Maddie led him to the room where they kept the fabrics and empty sacks of cornmeal, and they had laid down on top of one.

It took only a short time to lose everything she'd been told to save, but Marvin seemed pleased with her responses, telling her she was nothing like her sister and Maddie smiled, vanity usurping her shame.

He came every week after, waiting in the same place, doing the same things to her on top of the cornmeal sacks and each time it seemed she felt more and cared less about what others might think.

There was a time she worried she might be pregnant, after Emily had come home to live with them again, and she stopped seeing Marvin because it was getting harder to sneak out at night while she shared a room with his wife.

But then Patricia had moved Emily to the spare room, and Maddie had continued her visits, her fear vanishing when her bleeding began.

She tightened her arms around Marvin, placed her lips on his back between his shoulder blades and he stiffened, pulled away in the slightest and she felt the sting of his rejection, followed by a piercing fear.

If he should leave her out here on the high prairie with no family aside from a sister she had betrayed...

She wondered if Emily would be happy to see her,

thinking she had escaped the fire and knew she would never move past the despair she felt for starting it.

"What are you thinking?" Marvin asked, as he often did, when she was quiet.

She stared off into the dusk, the campfires dotting the hills like fireflies and thought of her sister.

They'd been watching the wagons for some time-had caught up with them on a blustery day three days ride from Kearny but no one noticed two riders amongst the cluster of immigrants crowding the trail.

"What is the matter?" he asked again.

"I'm tired," she answered, turning to look behind at Hawkins, who followed at a short distance.

He'd left the fort under the pretense of scouting for Pawnee who had stolen some mules, but she knew he was in league with Marvin, knew they had a plan she was unaware of and didn't dare ask about.

"We'll stop when the sun sets," he answered. "And I have some of the candies you like in my knapsack."

Maddie smiled, put her face against his back again and this time he did not pull away, but relaxed against her and she felt her heart lift, knowing he'd been thinking of her.

It had been a hard journey- Marvin had taken over a week to recover from his wounds well enough to sit on a horse. He was still on the mend, still walking with a limp but the doctor she and Slant had found outside of Chicago had done a remarkable job for an equally remarkable price.

And still the delay had given Emily one hell of a start.

They'd gone to Independence together, asking questions and paying anyone who would give them information.

They found people willing to talk, and Maddie told Marvin she felt sure Emily was running towards Nebraska Territory and their wild Uncle Rand.

"She used to talk about his cabin on French Creek all the time," she said." Rand and his wife and those dark mountains were all she dreamed about. She never cared about us or the store, or *James*..."

She regretted those words, knowing they hurt Marvin, but when they arrived at Kearny just before Emily, a letter from Rand had been waiting.

Maddie remembered Hawkins handing it to Marvin, remembered his excitement and the care he took folding the letter back up, resealing it as if it had never been opened.

He'd been happy that night, kissing her, telling her how beautiful she was while making love to her in one of the rooms Hawkins had provided. But soon his tenderness vanished, and he'd turned her away from him, taking her from behind in a way that made them seem like animals.

She'd asked him to stop, told him he was hurting her, but he went on as if he didn't hear- and when it was over she lay down on the bed and cried.

He touched her hair for a moment, seeming to regret his actions before leaving to find Hawkins.

She'd asked about the sergeant when he returned, and Marvin had shrugged, saying they knew each other from boyhood but that didn't seem possible.

Just as everything did until he started paying.

She'd asked him once where he'd gotten so much money, and he told her it was his share of the family farm.

She didn't ask anything after that, choosing to follow the man who'd come to fill every waking moment with a hope she didn't dare question.

She thought back to the week before she set fire to the store. Her behavior had sparked the suspicions of her father, who was sitting in the front room, smoking his pipe when she came down the stairs.

He'd asked her where she was going and she lied, telling him she needed a glass of milk from the kitchen.

He'd locked the front door the next night, keeping the key in his room and she'd tried going out the back before finally opening a window and crawling down the lattice that hung thick with ivy.

Marvin had been waiting in his usual place, his eyes narrowing when she told him what her father had done.

"He'll take you away, Maddie," he had said. "Mark my words, you will never see me again."

The thought was enough to terrify her, and even as she climbed on top of him, doing the things Emily couldn't, she knew she would run away.

The fire was Marvin's suggestion, meant to make

her parents think she was dead, but she hadn't planned on them walking in when she was lighting the bolts of fabric in the room where Marvin had taken her virginity.

Slant had come along as well, helping her while Marvin rode out of town with Emily and he had used a club her father kept behind the counter to strike them and Maddie had screamed, knowing it was useless.

Later that evening, she'd hidden in the woods by the creek before making her way to the cabin Slant told her about.

"Madeline," Marvin said again, his voice laced with concern. "Why do you keep looking behind?"

"Why did my parents come into the store that day?" she asked suddenly. "I was supposed to work alone so they could watch for Emily."

Marvin clucked his tongue. "No need to worry about the past, my love. They were probably checking on you because they were worried."

"But you said—"

"Never mind what I said," he said, his tone sharp. "It's better they're gone and not trying to stop us from making our new life together."

She bit her lip, tried to suppress the memory of that awful day, the black smoke rising against the blue sky as Marvin took her sister for a ride, promising Maddie he would let her go after the baby was born and they could raise him as their own.

It's quite obvious you cannot bear a child...

It was then Maddie understood he wanted her to be pregnant.

I thought your sister was barren at first... because she didn't take pleasure from me...but maybe it is something within your family...

Maddie thought about his words many times after, hoping and praying she would become pregnant now that she had nothing else to offer.

"I wonder why Hawkins is coming with us," she said, annoyed that she had given up her horse, knowing it was slowing them down.

"You know how he feels about his Walker. He won't risk losing him on a ride like this. And we need him, my love."

"A ride like this?" she asked, her senses peaking, the campfires looming closer, and she felt her heart quicken, knowing her sister was nearby.

She'd caught a glimpse of her and the baby when she was hiding in the room Hawkins had given her, arguing with a man on the parade grounds and wondered who he was.

He was tall, with a head of dark blond hair that needed cutting. From her hiding space she could see that he was handsome and understood that her sister must have tricked him like all the others.

She'd opened the window, listened as they argued and knew he loved her, anger bringing her heartbeat to her temples.

She thought of James again, remembered him lingering in their front room as she listened around the corner. They had been plotting Marvin's murder, and Emily had encouraged him, allowing him to kiss her even though he was married.

Maddie remembered running to the shanty, telling Marvin all she knew and he'd kissed her, telling her for the first time how much he loved her.

"We are heading into a dangerous country, my sweet," he said, turning to her. "There are Sioux and buffalo and strange, fierce storms. Hawkins knows the area and is familiar with the hostiles. We may need his help to get over the mountains."

"Mountains?" she asked, not understanding what he was asking of her, and he sighed, clucking her under the chin.

"I sometimes forget how simple you are."

She tried to laugh, not understanding what he meant and why he would say it in the way he did.

"Your sister knows I am alive. We must take her by surprise if I am to have a life with my son."

She looked at him.

"If *we* are to have a life, my sweet, silly girl."

She stiffened behind him, a strange understanding seeping past the infatuation she'd felt since he first told her Emily was a failure.

"Is that why you need me?" she asked. "To trick her?"

He clucked her under the chin again.

"Are you going to kill my sister?"

"No... no," he cooed. "I do not want her to die. I just want her to suffer."

Maddie pulled away.

"You want it, too."

She shook her head.

"Years of living in her shadow while your father doted on her... his darling Emilou."

Maddie felt tears prickle her eyelids, the same sting she'd felt since childhood rising to the surface. Yes, her father had favored Emily but that wasn't her sister's fault.

Was it?

"She will understand how you have felt all these years."

"She will?"

"Don't tell me you didn't envy her... didn't want James to court you instead."

She had admired James, yes... but did she love him?

"And all you did was work in that store while she danced and had fun. Why, she even tricked me, Maddie."

"Tricked you?"

"She made me believe she loved me, then refused to be a proper wife. Do you know she asked the man in the woods to shoot me again to make sure I was dead?"

"No—"

"After every moment we have shared, can you ever imagine me hurting you?"

She drew in her breath.

"Are you thinking of the way I laid with you the

other night?" he asked, his green eyes on her in a way that made her feel like she was floating.

"Marvin—"

"I'm sorry I hurt you, my sweet. Sometimes my anger gets the better of me when I think of all I have lost. I promise I will never use you in such a way again."

She smiled, allowed him to draw closer to her and kiss her, his mouth opening, and she felt the strange, desperate wanting that seemed to never go away rise up inside of her.

He pulled away, kissed her forehead lightly.

"Now we must be quiet and see what they are about," he turned to Hawkins, who seemed annoyed to be riding such an old horse.

But Maddie knew he would do what Marvin said once he had his money.

And Hawkins feared him.

As everyone did.

She wondered if she should be scared as well when he leaned over, whispered in her ear.

"I can't wait to lay you down beneath the stars and make love to you properly. We will send Hawkins away on some errand."

She nodded, ready to send him away now as a voice carried to their ears.

She tensed, knowing that Emily or the man she had tricked could easily shoot at them if they revealed their location and stayed silent.

It was her sister's voice, followed by the man's, and

it seemed to be coming from a cluster of rocks that sat away from the wagons.

She leaned forward and Marvin hushed her, turned to silence Hawkins as well as they drew the horses into a copse of cottonwoods.

Soon the voices stopped, and the figures seemed to vanish into the night, sliding down on the other side of the rocks.

Maddie felt Marvin tense in front of her, noticed his breath coming in short pants and knew he was holding his anger in check.

"Marvin," she whispered.

"Shut up!" he hissed at her, and she pulled back, startled.

After some time had passed, he drew the horse away, moved to the other side of the wagons and up the trail. Moments later they were crossing the river, followed by an annoyed Hawkins who began asking questions.

"Was that your wife?" he asked. "Why the devil didn't you take her?"

Marvin grumbled something.

"Do explain yourself, sir."

Marvin slid from his horse in one fluid motion and strode towards Hawkins. The next moment he'd pulled him off the horse, slammed him into the ground while Maddie watched in horror.

"My wife was fucking another man," he hissed. "And your suggestion is to walk up and just *take* her?"

Hawkins sputtered something, and Marvin slammed him into the ground again.

"I will not lose my son!"

Hawkins took his hands, tried to pry them off of his jacket.

"Our prize is in the mountains, and I swear to God, you will not ruin this for me."

"Marvin," Maddie whispered while sliding from the horse.

Marvin turned, his eyes wild in the weakening light, and seemed to come to his senses.

He released Hawkins, took a step back and ran a hand through his hair.

"I apologize, Madeline," he said. "I was not expecting to find Emily like I did. But I should have known better."

Maddie clasped her hands in front of her, wondering what her sister would think if she found them lying together.

"That man will pay for it, I assure you," he said, more to himself than her or Hawkins. "But we must bide our time if we hope to make the most of our advantage."

"Bide our time?" Hawkins asked, his voice almost a whisper. "I was not prepared—"

"You will be paid handsomely, Jack," Marvin said, helping him up, clapping him on the back like they were old friends. "And tonight, I'll share some of that candy I bought for Maddie at the fort."

"Candy?" Hawkins laughed, looking at Maddie as he picked up his hat and dusted it off. "I don't—"

"I trust I have your help in this matter," Marvin said. "I would hate to tell your men you were lost while scouting."

"Lost," he repeated. "I was only helping you on account of your friendship with my dear sister. Of course, I expect to be compensated but it was more for principal than—"

"There are others waiting to help us who would gladly take your share."

"My *share?*" Hawkins put his hat back on. "What the devil are you talking about? My share of *what*?"

Marvin laughed, swung back on top of his horse and extended his hand to Maddie.

"You'll see."

Chapter Twenty-Four

Caleb sat atop his gelding, Jake May beside him, watching the yellow hills and the tall, burnt grass that seemed to bend in the wind. It had been three days since he and Emily had laid together in front of the rocks, three days of trying to make sense of how his world had suddenly turned upside down.

"You're a sorry sight," Jake said, amusement in his voice. "Supposed to be looking for antelope but you're staring at the sky like it's gonna fall down on you."

Caleb glanced at his friend, tall in the saddle, his hat pulled low and was grateful for his companionship.

They had decided to go hunting that afternoon, and Caleb welcomed the distraction even as Emily and the others continued their slow journey west.

He worried when they were separated but knew

they needed fresh meat. Others in the train had reported scurvy and they were best to nip it in the bud right now.

"You were gone a spell the other night," Jake said. "We thought the Pawnee might have stolen you like they did those mules at Kearny."

Caleb cleared his throat, embarrassment making him jumpy where he wouldn't have been before.

"I fully intend to marry her."

Jake put his head back, squinted into the sun. "That'll be a trick."

"The husband's good as gone."

Jake smirked. "You sure?"

"Nothing's certain out here."

Jake laughed. "Damn straight."

"I love her," Caleb paused, uncomfortable. "And whatever you think happened between us, I'd never take advantage of her."

Jake held up two fingers and winked. "Scout's honor?"

"She just had a baby."

Jake laughed. "I'm not as stupid as I look, Merritt."

Caleb cleared his throat, scanned the horizon and the low, rolling hills that rose from the edge of the prairie. They were coming into Sioux Territory- the great Nebraska plains stretching far to the north before spilling against the Black Hills.

They'd written Rand a letter, intending to give it to the men at Laramie.

The fort was over a week's ride, but the women were excited about Chimney Rock, which was visible to them now and rose like a church spire on the far edge of the plain.

Emily had suggested a picnic when they stopped for the noon meal yesterday. She'd also wondered about fresh meat, an absentminded comment on her part- but it stuck in Caleb's mind as a far better reason to hunt than scurvy.

She'd moved for good from the May wagon to his, and they slept together underneath it at night, nestled in each other's arms and with James between them, a thing that irritated Ruthie.

"I'll not have that baby in the middle of your kissing and hugging," she said, her face flushed as she wrung out their laundry. "He needs a good night's sleep."

Caleb laughed, pulled on one of her braids.

"What makes you think we're doing any of that?" then, with a narrowing of his eyes. "She's a married woman, you know."

Ruthie shook her head; flung the laundry against a flat stone she'd been using. "If the good Lord wants her married to that bastard, I'll go live with the buffalo."

Caleb pulled her other braid.

"You'd probably smell better."

She laughed, hit the other side of the rock so hard the water splashed him in the face.

"I'm doing *your* laundry. It's a wonder Emily touches you at all!"

He smiled, stroked his chin.

"A wonder indeed."

Ruthie stood straight, her hands on her hips. "I'll have Jimmy next to me tonight. And tell Em you need that haircut she's been promising."

"Jimmy?"

She shrugged her shoulders. "We like the sound of it."

Caleb smiled.

He did, too.

Later that night Emily draped a linen around his shoulders, Clem's scissors in her hand, and cut his hair as she used to cut her father's in the back of the store.

She'd bent, pressing her lips to the side of his neck and he'd taken her hand, kissed her palm in a way that made him feel like he was watching Celia in the river all over again.

He put his hand to his head, the newly cut hair distracting him when he was supposed to be hunting.

"I think I see something out there," Jake said, pointing to the low hills and what looked like a sprinkling of pepper against the yellow grass.

Caleb nodded, dismounted and slid his rifle out from where he'd held it against the pommel. He thought of the fresh antelope meat making Emily smile and steadied the barrel against his saddle.

He'd been a good hunter back in Ohio, had hit his mark more often than not before Ruthie learned to shoot and he'd started in the mines.

Jake slid from his saddle, peered through the sight of his own rifle and waited.

One squeeze of the trigger and the rifle kicked back against Caleb's shoulder.

The herd scattered and Jake took aim, squeezed off a second shot.

"I think we got one," Caleb said, lowering his rifle.

"I surely did," Jake said. "Clem will be thanking me tonight for our fresh meat."

Caleb laughed, clapped his hand on his friend's shoulder.

"I'm sure we can both take credit and reap the rewards."

Jake laughed, swung back into his saddle as the two took off at a slow gallop.

Two hundred yards and they came up on the dead antelope, a large female that would feed them for the next few days.

"We need to gut her quick," Jake said, pulling his hunting knife from his belt and Caleb bent to help, remembering all the times Ruthie had stood and held the legs while he cut into the meat that would feed their family.

He thought of his brothers and sisters, lost to time and settled with families of their own and wondered what they would think of him now.

Minutes passed, the hot sun beating on the back of his neck, and he looked over his shoulder, caught sight of the wagons and imagined Emily's face when he came home with supper.

"Yes, sir," Jake said as he cut at the flesh, the warm innards of the antelope spilling onto the baked earth. "We'll certainly get a kiss or two out of this old girl—"

A shadow fell across the ground, and they stood quickly, sidearms drawn.

Two spotted ponies faced them, the riders lean and dark-skinned. They wore leather vests lined with beads, their faces creased from the sun and Caleb knew they were Sioux.

They sat holding the manes of their ponies, their legs gripping the sides, a quiver of arrows slung across their shoulders, knives sheathed at their belts along with what looked to be Navy Colts.

"Put your gun down, Jake," Caleb instructed, holstering his revolver as his friend did the same.

For a moment they stood watching each other, unsure what to do when the taller of the two spoke in slow, halting English.

"The dark hills belong to Waken Tanka."

Caleb looked at Jake, who shook his head slightly.

"We're just passing through," Caleb said, his fingers hovering over the handle of his revolver, his thoughts floating to the wagons.

"He will take whoever crosses into the north country," the second man said, the eagle feather that was tied to his black braids blowing in the wind. "We have already seen three riders pass into a land that is forbidden to them."

"We don't know anything about that."

The shorter of the two grunted.

"They are not from your people?"

Caleb looked at Jake, the antelope bleeding between them.

"No. But we'll give you our meat," he said, and Jake glanced at him sharply, his eyes narrowing. "As a token of peace."

"We do not want your kill," the tall Sioux said. "Take what is yours and tell the others in your wagons not to go beyond this place."

Caleb stood, watching them, every muscle in his body tense.

They turned the horses in a circle, stopping only when they faced them again.

"Waken Tanka paints the sky. You must decide if it is for war or peace."

One last glance at the men and they galloped off, the riders seeming to move as one with their animals until they vanished into the hills, the only sign of their passing a trail of dust that rose like smoke from the earth.

Jake took his hat off, wiped at his sweaty forehead and Caleb saw that his hands were shaking.

"What the hell was that?" he asked.

"A lucky break," Caleb said, eyeing their antelope as Jake bent to scoop up his knife.

Moments passed before Jake spoke, his voice low as he worked.

"We'd best skin out quick," Jake continued, "I don't like leaving the wagons with Sioux this close."

Caleb nodded, his throat suddenly dry.

"What was all that talk about Waken Tanka and painting the sky for war? Who the hell even paints a sky?"

"Someone a lot bigger than us. Next time we hunt closer to the trail."

Jake nodded, bending down to continue his work.

"Who do you think those three people were? Riding this far from the Platte?"

Caleb watched the knife slice the antelope's flesh, wondering what sort of land he'd wandered into.

"Damned if I know," he said, his mind on Marvin and who might be with him. "And I don't intend to find out."

Chapter Twenty-Five

Emily sat with Clementine, dusk darkening the sky, and watched for Caleb.

Beatrice sat beside them, her uncle walking the perimeter of the wagons with his rifle, on edge because the men weren't back yet.

She held James to her chest as he squirmed to see behind him and she wondered if he was missing Caleb, too.

Clem let out a sigh, reached out to stoke the fire with the stick she'd been using, a pot of potatoes boiling above it.

"I'm getting tired of these things," she grumbled, cross because Jake was gone, and Emily tried to act cheerful.

"They're getting us fresh meat and I know they won't stop until they bring some back."

Clem glanced at her out of the corner of her eye and gave the coals another poke.

"I know you're as worried as me," she said. "We moved almost fifteen miles today. You hear stories of people who get lost and don't find their folks for days... or *ever.*"

"Clem—"

"They should just camp tonight instead of trying to find us in the dark. And I'm no good at hitching up those oxen! Oh, why didn't one of them stay behind?"

Emily took a breath, wishing for a bit of Gerald's common sense and her mother's good nature. She even longed for Maddie to be sitting beside her, telling her everything would be all right and felt tears stinging her eyelids.

"People leave to hunt all the time," she said, trying to steady her voice. "They probably went farther from the trail than expected and are circling back."

Beatrice shifted beside them.

"Uncle Putt said he saw Sioux on the high rocks today. Who knows but they might have run into some."

Clem stabbed the fire so hard her stick broke in two. "If they're not back by daybreak I'm riding into Laramie to tell the soldiers."

Emily's eyes widened, wondering if her friend would really do such a thing.

"That's three days ride—"

"My mare is good for it," she snapped. "And it's

better than sitting around, wondering what happened."

"Goodness!" Beatrice exclaimed. "All this fuss for a little fresh meat and a picnic at Chimney Rock. Land's sake-"

"Hush your mouth," Clem stood suddenly, and Emily drew James against her, wondering if the two men had run into something besides Sioux on the north plains.

The thought made her nauseous, made her think of the last three days and how happy she'd been walking beside Caleb as he led the oxen, sharing meals on the wagon tongue, and lying in his arms at night.

She couldn't count how many times she'd stolen a kiss, or how often he'd touched her as though it was his right to do so.

And never in a way that made her feel afraid. Instead, it was a simple gesture, repeated until it became a habit and felt as natural as what they'd done in front of the rocks.

She felt heat build in her cheeks as Beatrice and Clem continued to bicker, embarrassed by where her thoughts had taken her.

She still struggled to understand what she'd felt beneath him... or on top of him for that matter. And yet it felt right- like things people who were in love were supposed to do.

She felt a smolder of guilt and looked out at the prairie, then back again at Beatrice, who crossed her arms, moved away from Clem as she sat stoking the fire with half her stick.

Emily eyed the fiddle Caleb had laid on the wagon seat before he left, telling her he would play a tune at supper, and she wondered if she should pick it up and attempt some chords.

Music had led her to camp when she stood alone in the Platte River- maybe it would do the same for him.

She bit her lip, remembered Caleb's words about being afraid on his ride to Kearny and understood how he felt.

"What're you all moping around for?"

She turned to see Ruthie standing behind her, hands on her hips, a pink shawl wrapped around her shoulders.

Emily smiled, turned James so he could see her, and he began making noises in his throat.

"Your brother and Jake aren't back yet."

"You worried about them?" she asked, heading to the fire to stoke it herself with the other half of the stick Clem had tossed aside. "Caleb's been in tighter spots than this! One time he left me alone for three days while he was chasing after Celia."

Emily cleared her throat, but Ruthie didn't notice, just poked at the fire from the other side.

"He wasn't paying attention to her, so she took up with some fella just to make him jealous. Rode all the way to the next county in his new buggy and you'd better believe my brother was fit to be tied! Went out on our good horse and brought her back, fussing all the way. Good thing I could shoot my own squirrels and skin them. Both those boys would be back by now if I'd gone along-"

"Ruthie," Emily said. "I think the potatoes are done."

Clem looked at her, then threw her hand over her mouth and burst out laughing.

The two women looked at each other, uncertain if she'd lost her mind and Emily stood, handed James to Ruthie.

"Clem," she said, approaching her slowly. "Are you alright?"

She bent over, laughed again.

"Ruthie's right. Jake's been gone way longer than this back home. No reason to worry. But here... it just seems like something is watching us."

"Pshaw!" Ruthie laughed. "Nothing's watching us but some critters hoping to steal what's left of our supper. And maybe Emily's husband."

"Ruthie," Emily gasped, and Beatrice glanced sharply at her.

"She's right," the woman said. "We never thought of that."

"Stop!" Emily cried, distraught now. "Ruthie, sometimes your thoughts need to stay *inside* of your head!"

"No," Clem interrupted. "This has nothing to do with Marvin. It's like we're not supposed to be here. Like the land doesn't *want* us to be here."

"I've heard stories about things called Skinwalkers that take the shapes of animals and-"

"*Enough*," Emily interrupted, her heart racing. "Plenty of folks have passed by this place before. There's nothing different- nothing *strange*—"

"You're wrong."

Emily turned, startled by a voice she did not recognize.

A woman appeared beyond the firelight, her blue dress familiar to those who had spent the last month traveling with her, if only from a distance.

"Aunt Rose," Beatrice said, her face white. "You should stay in the wagon."

The woman came closer, her face illuminated by the flames.

An angry, red line cut her left cheek in two, stopping just short of her dark eyes.

"I figured it was time to show my face," she said, and Emily realized she'd never taken her sunbonnet off during the day, but had stood apart from the others, raising a hand in greeting but never joining them at their fire or on their walks beside the oxen.

Beatrice told the others that she was sickly and afraid of catching cholera, which was why she chose to boil her water and take her meals alone.

She was old and set in her ways, she'd said- always anxious to get to their new home and find a proper husband for her niece.

"You seem surprised," she said, a soft lilt to her

voice that made her words seem like silk, and Emily suspected she'd used it to her advantage.

"Ma'am," Ruthie said. "We weren't expecting—"

"A whore who was cut up by one of her customers, and then turned around and shot him dead? Well, I'm all those things."

Clem glanced at Emily, her eyes wide, and took a step back.

"Rose—" Beatrice said, putting her hand on the woman's shoulder. "Mother—"

Emily started, unsure she'd heard her right, and the woman turned, her eyes challenging them to speak against her.

"It's true."

Clem stood, her mouth open, gasping as the potatoes began to boil over.

"Sakes alive!" she called, using her skirt to remove the pot and it landed on its side, the lid toppling over as frothy water puddled out.

"I've startled you and ruined your supper," Rose said, and from behind Emily saw Putt approach, his face slack.

"Rose," he said. "What have you done?"

"I'm tired of hiding when I might be of some help. My face won't change no matter where we go."

She paused, looked around at the people who had gathered near the fire.

"Guess I need to speak my piece."

Ruthie crossed her arms.

"Guess you do."

Rose stared at her for a moment, then raised her chin.

"You said this land gave you a bad feeling, Mrs. Clementine," she began. "I feel it, too."

"Really?" Clementine asked, her voice strangely hopeful.

"When my daughter talked of Skinwalkers, she wasn't mistaken. My mother was half Navajo, and she told us stories about the things that could happen if someone wandered into the wrong place."

"Oh, dear," Clementine sighed, her eyes darting between the pot of spoiled potatoes and Rose. "Do you think Jake and Caleb found themselves... in one of those places."

Rose glanced at her, and continued speaking.

"Truth of the matter is my daughter here was raised apart from the brothel where I used to work. Thanks to Putt, she went to a fancy school where she took on airs. But we'll soon stomp that nonsense out of her."

"Mother," Beatrice sighed, and Rose held up her hand.

"Quiet, girl. In the course of my time at the Golden Goose, I saw a lot of ornery characters. One was the fella that broke that bottle and came after me with it. Luckily Bea was home from school and able to pull my derringer, or I'd be cut to ribbons right now."

Emily's eyes flew to Beatrice, who had taken a step back.

"You killed him?" Clem looked at the girl, her face white. "Really and truly?"

"We both had our part," Rose said. "But the law wouldn't see it that way, so I had to take my girl and run right then and there. Putt was good enough to help us get this far and will see us to Oregon."

"Rosie," the man said, and Emily understood that he was in love with her and had been since the time he'd sent Beatrice to the fancy school.

"I overheard you saying you wanted to ride into Laramie, Mrs. Clementine. I'm here to say that's a sort of trouble we can't have any part of."

Clem smoothed her skirt, opened her mouth to speak, but Rose interrupted her.

"It's bad enough Mr. Merritt asked Bea to look for that sergeant, bad enough she took a fancy to him but bringing soldiers here is another kettle of fish altogether."

"Mother's face is on posters now," Beatrice said. "I saw one in Kearny."

Ruthie came closer, adjusted James to her other hip. "They're looking for you, then?"

Rose nodded, a small smile playing against the corner of her ruined mouth.

"Miss Emily and I are, how do you say it, birds of a feather?"

Emily's spine stiffened, aware that everyone was looking at her.

"I'm just asking that any soldiers who come this

way be sent in another direction. Including Sergeant Hawkins."

Beatrice looked down, dug her toe into the earth and Emily suspected she wanted to do just the opposite.

"And we'll do the same should anyone inquire after Miss Ives," Putt spoke up. "It would only take one careless word to send Rose back to Chicago. And ruffians looking to cash in on a bounty are always on the lookout."

"Lookout for what?"

Emily turned, saw Caleb and Jake atop their horses and felt her knees weaken.

Caleb swung his leg over, slid down from his saddle and she saw an antelope, gutted and hanging across the rump.

She stood still, her relief palpable as Clem raced past her, throwing her arms around a startled Jake, who took his hat off and hugged her.

"What's all the fuss?" Caleb smiled, his eyes seeking Emily as she stood, unsure if she should greet him in the same way.

Then he was beside her, pulling her into an embrace, and she knew he was relieved to see them safe as well.

"I told 'em not to worry," Ruthie said, still bouncing James, who had turned in her arms at the sound of Caleb's voice. "Told 'em you left me alone for that three-day spell when you took off after-"

"You were right," Caleb said quickly, his gaze on

Rose, who stood beside her daughter, the resemblance plain for all to see.

"Ma'am," he touched his hat, and Jake came forward, did the same. "Pleased to finally make your acquaintance."

Rose nodded, her eyes darting to Putt, who stepped forward.

"Rose has always been good to me," he said. "Which is why I'm taking her and her daughter to Oregon."

"Ma'am?" Caleb asked. "I hate to ask—"

"There was some trouble in Chicago that the men at Laramie may know about," Rose answered. "We aim to keep them wondering."

"I don't blame you," Jake nodded. "As long as you ride with us, you're one of us."

Rose went still, then gave a brief nod.

"Much obliged."

It seemed at that moment that all the tension, all the talk of ghosts and Sioux and Skinwalkers, of derringers and fancy schools and soldiers coming from the fort drifted away and Emily took a deep breath, grateful now that the men were back and they would have fresh meat for their picnic at Chimney Rock.

She felt her body loosen in relief and Caleb noticed, pulled her aside from the others to the edge of the firelight.

"Em," he said, his voice low. "I didn't mean to worry you."

She shook her head. "There's no help for that now."

He smiled, pulled her to his chest, his lips grazing hers for an instant and she imagined lying with him beneath the wagon that night, his steady breath making sleep easy.

"Beatrice said there were Sioux on the high rocks," she said, not breaking from his hold, the feel of his heartbeat against her cheek as comforting as anything she had ever known.

"We saw two of them," he said, and she pulled back to look at him.

"What?"

"We'd just killed the antelope when they rode up on their horses. Said something about Waken Tanka and how it would paint the sky."

"What does that mean?"

He shrugged, pulled her back into his arms and rested his chin on top of her head.

"Damned if I know. But things are pretty close to perfect right now so I'm not gonna worry about it."

She smiled, leaned her head back as his mouth closed over hers.

"Eh- hem."

They opened their eyes, saw Ruthie holding a wiggling Jimmy.

"If you can kiss, you can feed this rascal."

She laughed, took her son as Caleb moved away to salt the meat.

She sank down in the shadow of the wagon, loosened her blouse and led Jimmy to her breast.

He was a healthy eater now, had no trouble taking his fill of her milk and the diapers she washed daily were a testament to how strong he was growing.

She sat, listening to the others, Putt and Rose lingering in the firelight as Clem talked about what they could eat with the meat tomorrow.

She looked down at her son, his little hands kneading her breast and remembered when Caleb put his mouth there.

She felt her cheeks burn, surprised by the feelings the memory stirred within her and wondered when they would be together in that way again.

She gazed at him as he worked beside Jake, the two of them cutting up the antelope and knew he would provide for her and Jimmy and whatever children they might have together.

"Miss Emily."

She started, unaware that Rose had come to stand beside her.

"I'm sorry," she said quickly, trying to draw her blouse closed.

"I've seen my fair share of bosoms, so don't bother covering them up."

Emily tried to hide her smile, her fondness for Rose growing.

"Working in a brothel, you learn to trust your instincts. And my instincts tell me I need to keep on with the story I began with the others."

Emily nodded, wondering what she could possibly add to what she'd already revealed.

"When I said I ran into some ornery fellas at the Golden Goose, I didn't just mean the man who cut me up."

"Oh," Emily said, unable to say more.

"You called your husband Marvin. And your son has red hair."

She looked down at him now, softly sleeping against her chest.

"Someone with that name came into the Golden Goose back about the time I had my trouble. Was asking about a wife who'd run out on him. Why he thought a bunch of whores would know anything was beyond my reasoning but that's not what struck me as strange."

She took a quick breath, Rose's words seeming to come from another world.

"He had a lady with him. She seemed real skittish."

Emily's skin went cold, her eyes seeking Caleb and at that moment he turned, looked at her.

"What was her name?"

Rose leaned back, her eyes on point.

"Maddie."

Chapter Twenty-Six

Rand Albright stood looking down the side of the mountain, his fringed coat and large hat blowing in a mid-summer breeze and thought of his wife.

He had left Ehawee two days before, and even though it was something that happened often, it never sat well with him.

He'd left her in their garden, tending to the berries she made into the preserves they ate through the winter months, her long hair plaited, her eyes watching his movements.

He'd left his speculating party safely on the border, had returned to his homestead and was now moving towards Laramie to collect his niece.

Ehawee wept when she read Emily's letter and had gone into the hills to burn sage and cedar. She loved Rand's family as if they were her own, if for no other reason than they had given her a loving husband.

And now they had been killed in a fire, and the niece was pregnant, and Rand knew everything would change when he returned home with Emily and the baby.

But Ehawee was kind, and her people visited often, and Rand knew Emily would come to love their way of life in the mountains.

He thought back to the letters he'd sent to the family back in Michigan, the care with which his nieces had responded, even from a young age.

And so, it came as no surprise when Emily asked for his help.

Rand shouldered his pack, used to carrying it for long distances, and swung his rifle against it.

At dusk he would make a camp and hunt the edge of the forest for mule deer.

If he was lucky, he would shoot one big enough to feed him for days, but he had enough hardtack and jerky strapped to his belt to get him through to Laramie.

He knew he could get a horse at the fort; knew he could ride safely with Emily to his cabin if she'd already delivered her child.

And he prayed she had.

He thought back to the early days of his marriage to Ehawee, remembered her family looking at them with suspicion. He worked hard to become a son to them over their twenty years of marriage, mourned with them when it was clear Ehawee could not bear a child, respected them by remaining close to her people, and wept when her father was buried in the sacred land the dark mountains sheltered.

He took a breath, preparing his mind and heart for the journey ahead, thinking back to the first moment he had seen his wife while checking his traps on the banks of French Creek.

She'd been washing clothes with the women of her tribe, and the man he was with, a trader by the name of Ezra Kind, was well known to the people and respected for his honesty.

Ehawee had smiled behind her hands, her dark eyes endless and Rand made up his mind then and there to let his heart decide his future.

And now he was doing the same, following a path that others might turn from, the sun beginning its slow descent over the mountains as he made his way towards the low country.

He stood for a moment, listening to the sounds of the forest and watching for game when he spotted movement to his left.

He knelt down, removed his rifle from his back in a synchronized motion he'd perfected over time. Bringing it to his shoulder, he watched the tree line.

Silence...

He knelt for some time, waiting for the animal to show itself and was surprised to hear a disturbance behind him.

Wolves... he thought- irritated for letting them get the better of him and spared a quick glance over his shoulder, expecting their eyeshine in the dimming light.

Nothing...

He readjusted his stance, ready and able to wait out whatever was hunting him and heard a voice rising from a dark glen of pine trees.

"Randall Albright," it said and for one absurd moment he thought it might be a member of the speculating party he'd left on the border, or one of Ehawee's people. Or Gerald Ives, returned from the grave.

A man appeared in front of him, wearing the rough gear of a bandit, two revolvers stuck in his belt, the handles reversed.

A gunslinger...Rand thought, his finger tightening on the trigger.

He did not recognize this man and had no idea why he was so deep in Sioux Territory. But he'd been shot at before, had killed his fair share of men who sought to cause trouble and had no doubt he could dispatch this one as well.

"State your business," he shouted. "You're trespassing here."

The man laughed, took a step closer when another person, large as a bear and dressed in a coat to match, stepped from the darkness.

A noise to the left caught his eye and he turned, saw a third man emerge and knew he'd walked into an ambush.

He stood, slung his rifle over his shoulder and held up his hands. Experience had taught him not to fight in situations like this. Only the element of surprise would work to his advantage now.

"Randall Albright," the gunslinger repeated, and his companions came closer.

Rand saw that they were just as dirty as he was, that they also carried revolvers on their hips.

"State your business," Rand repeated. "I'm on my way to Laramie and can't be delayed."

"To collect Emily?"

He froze, unsure how these men knew his niece's name, his thoughts wandering to Jack Hawkins.

"I'm taking a wagon train west," he said. "They need a guide through the Salt Desert."

The second man came forward, his hair dirty and greasy and tied back with a piece of rawhide.

"We know what you're about, old man. No hiding your business from us."

Rand adjusted his stance, ready to fight or run, whichever came first.

He thought of Ehawee in their garden, thought of Emily waiting in Kearny and prayed these men hadn't gotten to her first.

"Did you hurt my niece?" he asked. "Because I won't mind taking a scalp or two as payment if you have."

The gunslinger laughed again.

"You'll see her soon enough. And everyone else you've ever swindled."

"Swindled?" Rand repeated. "I live peacefully in the mountains with my wife, trading furs to the Sioux and Pawnee."

The second man shook his head, spit tobacco juice on the ground at his feet.

"Bet that's not all you've done."

Rand felt anger rise within him.

"You do not want trouble with my wife's people."

"Shut your mouth," the leader said. "My boss has business with you and your niece, and he intends to see it through to the end."

Rand swallowed, afraid for the first time in his memory.

"Where is she?"

The man with the dirty hair looked at his companions.

"Move," he ordered. "They're waiting in the meadow below."

Rand took a step forward. He knew the meadow they spoke of well, had intended to cook his breakfast there in the morning and began to walk, all the while looking for a chance to escape.

But did he want to escape if these bandits had Emily?

He thought these things as they led him down the mountain, his feet finding cracks and crevasses they'd known for years, coming upon the meadow in complete darkness.

A small campfire was burning, three people seated around it and he saw that one of them was a woman.

Cautiously he moved forward, and the woman turned.

Sister Patty had sent him a picture only a year ago of her family at Emily's wedding and he had looked at it several times, imagining what he might say to them if they ever met.

"Maddie-" he whispered, and she drew back, fear written plainly on her face.

The man beside her stood up, and Rand saw that he was tall, with auburn hair, his shoulders broad and well-muscled and recognized him as Emily's husband.

"What have you done with Emily?" Rand demanded.

Maddie looked down, and for the first time Rand saw that she was with him willingly- a sickness growing inside his stomach when he thought of the fire that killed her mother.

"Pleasure to meet you," the man said, stepping forward and extending his hand. "I'm Marvin Jones."

Rand looked at him, "Why have you brought me here?"

Marvin smiled, and Rand saw why his nieces had been taken with him.

"I have come to collect my property," he answered.

"Property?" Rand echoed. "You certainly have no right to Emily after what you did to her. And no right to her sister after the lies you've told her."

Marvin laughed.

"Maddie made her own choice. Although I do be-

lieve a man has a right to his son, and the gold his father died for."

"Gold?" Rand asked. "What-"

"My wife ran away with my child; your friend stole
my father's share."

"My friend—"

"Ezra Kind," Marvin said, his face still as he
watched Rand's. "I know you traveled these mountains together, know you aimed to find your fortune
here."

Rand swallowed, the name shaking him to the
core.

"What does that have to do with my niece? Or this
gold you speak of? Or *me*, for that matter?"

Marvin smiled, took a step towards Rand and the
man backed up.

"You, my good man, are going to help me get them
back."

Chapter Twenty-Seven

Emily laid with her head in Caleb's lap, the tall grass of the prairie shielding them from view, Chimney Rock in the distance, and tried not to think about her sister.

Rose had given her a name and described a man who could have been Marvin but there was no way of knowing if Maddie was really alive.

"Do you think Marvin took her?" she asked Caleb as they lay beneath the wagon the night before. "Why would he do such a thing?"

Caleb tried to comfort her, had touched the side of her face, his gray eyes thoughtful.

"There are a lot of people in Chicago. It might have been another couple altogether."

She knew he was right, and still the thought that her sister might be alive made her uneasy when it should have filled her with hope.

Her disquiet carried over from the night before to the meal they'd shared at Chimney Rock to now, as she laid her head in his lap.

She closed her eyes, the breeze blowing bits of her hair around her face, and felt herself falling, the fire that had taken her parents' lives reflected in Maddie's eyes.

She jerked awake, angry that this moment could be taken from her.

"Em."

She took a slow breath. "Did I fall asleep?"

Caleb smiled, his voice gentle.

"You're plum wore out."

She yawned, put her hands above her head and stretched, the strange vision forgotten as Caleb leaned forward, his eyes dancing with mischief.

"Anything I can do to help?"

She looked at him, a lazy smile on his face that made her forget about everything but the moment they were living in.

"You've already given me everything."

His smile went still, his eyes lingering on her.

"Not everything."

"Caleb—"

"I aim to show you why ladies up and down the Ohio fought like cats over me."

She smiled, rolled over onto her side, a wildflower tickling her ear and he broke it off, tucked it in her hair.

"How many times did the cat catch you?"

He touched the flower, his fingers brushing her temple.

"I only slowed down for Celia, but now it seems some girl who was *supposed* to stay in Fort Kearny has tripped me up."

She yawned again, put the back of her hand to her forehead.

"I could have hitched a ride north with one of the other soldiers, found Uncle Rand and left you to your everlasting sadness."

He leaned closer, his lips inches from hers. "Not a chance."

She took a slow breath, the buttons of her blouse digging into her skin. Unconsciously her fingers went to them, wanting to undo them, wanting *Caleb* to undo them.

"Where's Jimmy?" she asked, remembering that Ruthie had asked to walk with him when they finished eating.

"Over by the little valley we saw. Probably showing him spiders and grasshoppers and such."

She sat up again, straining for a glimpse and saw her auburn hair bobbing just above the grass.

"Lay down," he said, and she looked at him, beautiful against the burning sky, and obeyed.

Minutes passed in silence, Caleb's fingers resting against her face before tracing the side of her neck. She bit her lip, the feel of hot bath water rising between her legs- a sensation she had come to associate with Caleb's touch.

"What are you thinking?" he asked, his lips brushing her earlobe and she turned his face to hers, her mouth seeking his.

He leaned into her, his hands in her hair, the taste of the good food they had eaten on his tongue.

She imagined they were in California, his baby growing in her belly as they worked the earth God had given them and sighed against his mouth.

His hands were on her breasts now, kneading the fabric of her dress as he would her skin and she closed her eyes, hopeful the tall grass and prairie wind would disguise what they were doing.

But she didn't care if the others knew, didn't care if they were also enjoying the moments of privacy this place allowed.

"Em," he whispered, his fingers on the buttons of her blouse and she pressed into him, anxious to feel his mouth on the place where James nursed.

She looked down, pulled the fabric from her shoulders until it was bunched around her waist.

He bent his head, kissed the soft swell of her breasts, his fingers on the buttons of his shirt and Emily realized she longed to feel the press of his skin with no barrier between them.

She curled her fingers over his shoulders, pulled his suspenders down before yanking the bottom of his shirt free from his pants.

He drew back, looked behind them again and shrugged out of his shirt.

Emily drew in her breath, entranced by the smooth

stretch of skin over muscle, the dusting of hair on his chest and the width of his shoulders- freckled from the sun.

She heard him sigh as he lowered himself against her and for the first time there was no rush to consummate what burned between them. Instead, there was only a stillness as they lay against each other, the realization that their bodies were made to be touched by the other awakening a joy that seemed sacred.

She sighed; all thoughts of Maddie forgotten.

There was only this man, and the afternoon heat, and the large stone spire that guarded them like a sentinel.

"Em," he nuzzled her neck, his face buried in her hair. "I can't move. I don't want to."

She smiled, his breath mirroring her own.

Then she drew the skin of his neck into her mouth, biting on it playfully and he moved against her, his hands on her waist as he gathered her dress.

She felt his hand slip under her bloomers, his fingers wandering to the place he'd pleasured her before.

"No," she whispered, her hand wandering to the place between his legs. "I want you."

He paused, his hand stilling against her.

"Caleb," she managed. "Please."

"It's still too soon," he whispered.

"I'm fine," she said, desperate now. "You touched me before."

"This is different—"

"No, it's not," she said. "You've already begun it."

This seemed to disturb him even as she felt his arousal grow against her thigh.

"Don't worry," she reached up, touched his cheek. "I know what I want."

"No," he put his hand over hers. "You don't."

"I had a husband!" she said, her voice rising. "Don't treat me like a child."

Caleb pulled back, his eyes dark and Emily knew he was angry.

"You *have* a husband."

She turned her head, half naked beneath him and wished she could hide.

"I know I began this," he said. "Believe me when I say I want to finish it."

She felt her argument die in her throat, a part of herself warming with his words.

"But I won't until you're mine before God."

"Caleb—"

"It doesn't matter if it's a piece of paper or a bullet that sets us free," he smiled, touching the flower in her hair again. "I'll take it either way."

She smiled, wishing she'd let him continue in the way he'd wanted.

"I can only imagine what you must think of me."

He laughed, touched the tip of her nose with his.

"Don't ever apologize for wanting me."

She leaned in, kissed him softly and they stayed that way for a moment, the top three buttons of her dress still undone, the wind bringing the sweet smell of flowers that bloomed in the hot sun.

Emily knew she would have to pull away, knew they would have to gather Ruthie and James and move towards the waiting mountains with unanswered questions.

But Caleb loved her, and they were moving towards a place that would allow them to be together and she only needed to pray that Marvin had never gone to the Golden Goose brothel with a woman named Maddie.

A voice carried over the breeze and she pulled back, strained to see Ruthie and glimpsed Clementine instead.

She was moving towards them, Jake at her heels as something inside of her froze up.

"Caleb," Jake called, giving them warning and he stood, turned to face them.

"What?" he asked, irritation tinting his voice and at once his shoulders straightened as if he sensed the same thing she did.

"Where's Ruthie?" he asked, his voice rising above the wind and Emily stood, turned in a circle, searching for the girl.

"Where are they?"

Clem touched her shoulder, tried to calm her.

"I was tending to the oxen and Jake went looking for her. They could have wandered to the other side of the hill."

Emily felt numb, saw Caleb's lips form his sister's

name and didn't hear any sound. She stood, watching as the others began to search while Rose, Putt and Beatrice approached from their wagon.

She said her son's name, watched the wind steal her words and turned in a circle.

Caleb was moving away from her and towards the valley he'd spoken of, the prairie grass bending in the breeze when he cupped his mouth. Then he ran towards the hill, and she found the strength in her legs to follow him.

"Ruthie!" she cried, stumbling, and Caleb turned, took her hand.

Then he stopped, his eyes wild and she knew he needed her strength as much as she needed his.

"We'll find them," she said.

"Ruthie likes to wander."

Emily nodded, thinking of them lying together in the grass.

You have a husband...

Had he been watching them?

She ran, praying to see the two of them kneeling together, Ruthie pointing to some flower or bumblebee or bird, James's head cradled in her arms as she held him close to her heart.

He would be waving his fists like he always did, his head turning when he heard her voice, the eyes she hoped would remain blue straining to see her.

She thought again about Caleb, remembered his hands wandering over her body as Marvin stole the son he desired.

Guilt bathed her in heat, and she became breathless, slowed her run and Caleb turned, his eyes questioning.

"Em—"

"We shouldn't have been doing what we were doing."

"Don't think that."

"I should have been with Jimmy!"

"Then we'd be looking for you."

"You think he's taken them?"

"I don't know what to think."

She put her hand over her mouth, remembering everything she'd lost and could not go on. Instead, she sank to her knees.

Caleb stood for an instant, then bolted away and Emily waited for a cry or a whistle or anything that would tell her they'd been found.

All was silent aside from the distant cries of the others.

She put her head back, let the sun wash her face and wished she could die.

She sat that way for a long time, the wind blowing her hair and the fabric of her unbuttoned dress, her hands clasped in her lap.

She closed her eyes, praying to the God she felt sure had abandoned her and felt Caleb beside her.

She saw his pained face, knowing they'd done this to themselves.

"They're not here."

"You said she likes to wander."

"Ruthie's a lot of things, but stupid isn't one of them."

Emily felt dizzy and knew she was swaying on her knees, knew this because Caleb steadied her.

"It's gonna be okay, Em," he said. "We'll find them."

Out of the corner of her eye she saw Jake running, Rose at his heels.

"We found tracks."

She looked at him, one hand rising to Caleb's shoulder as he helped her to her feet.

"Two riders," Rose said, "Moving north."

"North?" she asked, her life in their hands.

Caleb pressed his lips together, glanced at Jake.

"They're heading for the Black Hills."

Jake looked at Caleb, tipped his hat.

"How do you wanna paint that sky?"

Caleb made a sound low in his throat, and Emily wondered why they were talking about things like this when everything was wrong.

"Guess we take our chances."

Emily came closer, gripped his arm. "What do we do?"

He looked down on her, his jaw set.

"Go after them."

Chapter Twenty-Eight

R uthie Merritt felt a hand shake her shoulder.

"Get up," a voice said close to her ear, and she swiped at it like a mosquito.

"Your baby's hungry," another voice, followed by laughter.

"Take your tit out and feed it, why don't you?"

More laughter, and a snort.

"Why don't *you*?"

Another shake to the shoulder and she opened her eyes, saw a low campfire surrounded by pines and had no memory of how she'd gotten there.

Two dirty men with trail dust and sweat stains on their shirts were sitting across from her. One had long hair tied back with rawhide, the other a pair of re-volvers turned backwards, and she tried to sit up, heard Jimmy crying and saw him lying in his blanket beside her.

"Better feed him," the man with the backwards revolvers said while standing up. "Before Slant tries his hand at it."

She felt a dull pain in the back of her head, saw blood on the sleeve of her dress and remembered the man with the long hair striking her with the butt of his gun as she walked with James.

She'd been close to the valley at the base of Chimney Rock when she saw them rise from the prairie like ghosts. She'd turned quickly, looking for the wagons only to realize she'd wandered from view.

They came at her quickly, Jimmy's cries the last thing she heard before darkness swallowed her.

And now she was their prisoner, and Caleb was probably mad as hell, and she knew Emily's husband was the reason behind it all.

"Get to it," Slant ordered while getting to his feet. "Casper ain't gonna peek if that's what you're worried about."

Ruthie hadn't thought about that, but now her cheeks burned when she imagined unbuttoning her dress in front of these men. Grabbing Jimmy, she adjusted him in her arms, crossed her legs and glanced up at the bandits.

"Turn your back," she said, and Casper chuckled, spit his tobacco juice into the fire and did as he was told.

"You, too."

Slant paused, his eyes on the swell of her breasts.

"Boss'll have your hide if he finds out," Casper called over his shoulder.

"Nothin' wrong with takin' a peek."

Casper turned; his eyes narrowed.

"Give the lady some privacy or I'll shoot you where you sit, you sick son of a bitch."

Slant laughed, wiped a streak of tobacco juice across his dirty face.

"I'd like to see you try."

Casper pivoted on his heel, stuck a finger in his face.

"Boss put me in charge, and he'll be pissed you knocked her out. Instructions were to make sure she could feed the baby."

"Looks like she can."

Casper cursed under his breath, then drew back and punched Slant square in the face.

The bandit fell onto his back and did not move.

"Stay the fuck down, you ignorant bastard," Casper grunted, his eyes rising to Ruth as she pulled James against her. "You nurse that baby, Ma'am. And don't mind Slant, he's spent most o' his life puffing on the end of a Chinaman's pipe."

Ruthie stared at him, the back of her head pounding again, and she touched it, surprised to feel dried blood on her scalp.

"He hit ya hard," Casper said, his eyes a cloudy color she couldn't decipher. "I'm sure Boss'll have somethin' to say about laying hands on his wife."

Ruthie bit her lip, trying to hide her surprise and

Casper bent down, his strange, milky eyes catching hers.

"Word is he used to rough you up."

She looked away.

"That's a bitch."

Ruthie sat staring at him until he turned his back again.

Unbuttoning her dress, she guided Jimmy to her breast.

At first, he wouldn't suckle, but rubbed his nose against her skin and she realized he'd become used to the scent of his mother. Momentary panic seized her until she remembered what had calmed him in the past.

She placed her lips where his soft hair was just beginning to grow, and whispered to him, her words spilling into a song her own mother used to sing.

She felt a longing then, the voice she remembered soft and clear as she sang of the wide Missouri, the words stirring a sadness in her heart.

"You've got a way with him," Casper said, and Ruthie tightened her shoulders, wondering what he would do if he found out she wasn't Emily. "Most mother's do. Except my own, of course. She wasn't much better than Slant."

Ruthie looked over her shoulder, hoping he would stop talking so she could think.

"I was sure the Boss told me you had yellow hair, and meat on your bones... No offense, but you're a scrawny runt."

Ruthie scowled.

"You ain't much bigger."

Casper laughed. "I got it where it counts, Ma'am."

Ruthie scrunched up her face, feeling the strange need to defend herself.

"I lost some weight on the trail," she said. "And changed my hair when I ran away."

Casper let out a slow whistle, his back still to her as he shifted from foot to foot.

"I've heard of ladies doing that, but they were whores."

Ruthie frowned, looked down at Jimmy, who had gone still against her.

"Boss said you might try to sweet talk your way out of here. Said you got a man on the wagon train to feel sorry for you."

"That's not true."

"Said you spread your legs for him behind some rocks."

Ruthie cleared her throat, remembering when her brother and Emily had gone for their sunset walk and prayed they hadn't done that.

"He's a good man," she said quickly. "And doesn't want trouble."

Casper chuckled. "Trouble's all he's got. Boss wants to cut his heart out and feed it to the wolves and I have no doubt he'll do it."

Ruthie drew a shallow breath and Casper took a

peek at her, saw that Jimmy was done feeding and turned around.

"You shouldn't be layin' with another man when you're married. Plain and simple."

She glared at him.

"And you shouldn't be hitting ladies on the head and dragging them off into the hills. Plain and simple."

Casper shook his finger at her and then tapped his head with it.

"At least I'm getting paid."

Ruthie laughed. "And you're calling *me* a whore?"

Casper's face hardened, his milky eyes moving quickly between hers.

"Boss said you had a mouth on you. You'd better mind it."

"Or what?"

Casper licked his lips.

"I'll leave that to him. Most likely more of what you're used to."

Ruthie laughed, propped a gurgling Jimmy over her shoulder and began to pat him on the back.

"He'll kill me before the week is up. I'll bet my soul on it."

The outlaw shook his head.

"Don't tempt the Lord."

She laughed again. "Ain't you a saint?"

Casper nodded, spit his tobacco juice in the fire.

"I do a lot o' things, but never that."

Jimmy burped, and it seemed to break the strange

dance they'd been doing. Ruthie laid him on the ground, saw that his diaper needed to be changed.

"Don't happen to have more of these, do you?" she asked, and Casper shook his head.

"Got some bandanas in my saddlebags."

Ruthie wrinkled her nose.

"Are they any cleaner than the one you're wearing?"

He smiled.

"A sight. You'd best clean that baby up and then yourself. There's a creek about two miles back the way we came."

"I'm not going to bathe in front of you."

"Boss's orders. He's only a day's ride away and will be right happy to see you again."

Ruthie's mouth went dry as she laid Jimmy down on his blanket.

"That makes one of us."

Chapter Twenty-Nine

Caleb felt the hot sun burn the back of his neck and reached back to rub it. Turning in his saddle, he saw Emily, trotting behind on Clem's palomino mare.

She'd stayed close the whole time, calling for Ruthie and James until her voice grew hoarse, but the last hour she'd gone quiet- and so he turned to check on her more frequently.

"Em?" he asked, and she looked up, her blue eyes seeming to look through him.

He'd suggested bringing Jake instead but knew that would leave the wagon party vulnerable. Marvin desired Emily as much as his son, and Caleb suspected he had either taken Ruthie by mistake or wanted to split the party in two on purpose.

Either way, the thought of leaving Emily alone

with only Putt for protection bothered him more than letting her come.

And Jimmy was her son.

"We'll find him," he said, and she looked up into the hills.

"How long will Jake wait?" she asked.

They'd left the others by Chimney Rock, with Rose agreeing to take over their wagon and drive on to Laramie.

But they couldn't wait long.

Caleb pulled his horse to a stop, remembering Emily's face as she waited to see if he wanted her to go and could think of nothing worse than leaving her behind.

So, Clem gave up her horse, a look in her eye that said she loved the animal and Emily kissed her cheek, saying they would see each other in Laramie.

"A week at the most," she promised, and her friend nodded, her eyes watery.

Caleb took off his hat, ran a hand over his head.

His hair was growing again, and he wondered if Emily would mind cutting it while they sat around the fire in the high country.

The picture brought a smile to his face, and she looked at him, her expression puzzled as he leaned towards her, touched her face.

"I might take you up on another haircut when this is over."

She smiled, her pulse beating in her throat and for

a moment wanted to place his lips on the side of her neck.

He thought of what that simple act would lead to, knowing desire would offer an easy escape from what they feared most.

He pushed the image aside, looked to the mountains and dismounted his horse.

He had experience with tracking and understood how to follow animals through the hills of the Ohio River Valley. But this land was hard and unforgiving, making it difficult to find the marks left by the bandits and their horses.

He walked a few feet, saw a disturbance in the earth at the base of a pine tree and moved towards it.

"What do you see?" Emily called from behind, her voice hoarse and he knew she'd been crying in the privacy of their wagon, and again while she followed silently behind.

"It's a campsite," he answered, his eyes finding the spot where a fire had burned, the logs charred and scattered within a circle of bare earth.

Caleb walked around it slowly, bending down on his haunches to examine the dirt.

"Ruthie sat here," he said, touching a spot where the grass was flat and rounded.

"How can you tell?" Emily asked, and he knew his knowledge was strange to her.

"It's small," he turned to her. "The other two are bigger."

She looked at him, her blue eyes glassy and he pointed to the places where the horses had stood.

"Two of the marks are deeper, the third one is faint. That means someone lighter is riding."

"Ruthie?" she asked, her face untwisting as she slid from her horse. "And Jimmy?"

Caleb nodded.

"How did you learn to do that?"

He stood straight, her admiration making him feel lighter.

"Most of my childhood was spent tracking critters that didn't want to be found. I taught Ruthie everything I know, so you can bet she's going to leave a trail those sonsabitches won't know about."

Emily nodded, as if thinking hard on something, and Caleb saw her touch the revolver she'd strapped to her waist with one of Jake's old belts.

They'd ridden through the night, only sleeping a couple of hours at daybreak to avoid lighting a fire, and Caleb knew she was hungry.

He went to his saddle, pulled out some hardtack and jerky and a couple of apples Clem had packed away. It wasn't a meal, but he could hunt when they got to the mountains.

"Sit down," he said, motioning to the spot where Ruthie had been. "You need to eat."

She shook her head, pushed her hair behind her ear.

"We need to keep moving."

He touched her shoulder. "We'll be no use if we're half dead when we find them."

She seemed to stiffen at his touch, and he handed her some hard tack, waiting a moment before speaking.

"Are you mad at me, Em?"

She looked down.

"Caleb—"

"I don't regret anything we did. I can't or it'll spoil something for us."

She shook her head, bit into the hardtack, her shoulders rounded against the wind and Caleb thought she looked like a child, so small and vulnerable and so he knelt beside her, put his arm around her.

She turned to him; her face pinched with worry.

"I'm so sorry, Caleb."

He shook his head.

"Don't say that to me."

She went on as if he'd never spoken.

"If you'd never met me Ruthie would be safe and you'd be on your way to California, not jumping at every shadow, praying it isn't my lunatic husband."

"Stop—"

"You could get married and have babies without worrying about a judge in some frontier town who doesn't know anything about us."

"I'm not worried about that."

"Yes, you are," she said. "You're just pretending you're not."

Caleb looked at her, wanting this part of them to be settled before he went any further.

"Emily Ives," he said, turning her so she could look into his eyes. "I've been managing my own affairs for a long spell, and I know my mind. If I say something, I mean it. You need to take me at my word, or this is going to be a hard road between us."

He waited, watching the wind blow her hair over her shoulder, the braid that had once been in place now a disheveled mess that made her more real to him.

She took the apple from her skirt pocket, looked at it for a long moment before answering.

"How do I do that?"

He touched her cheek.

"You just make up your mind and stick to it."

She laughed softly.

"You make it sound so easy."

He knelt down beside her, one arm resting on his bent knee.

"It's like the drawings in your journal. Or the stories you used to write. You decide what the picture is going to look like."

She worked the apple, passing it between her hands.

"Even if it's not true?"

He swallowed; memories of the brown bottles Celia had hidden in their pantry floating through his mind.

"Especially then."

She drew a shaky breath, seeming to understand.

"I won't lie to you, Em. Even if the truth hurts, I'm gonna tell it."

She looked down, swallowed hard.

"That's the nicest thing anyone's ever said to me."

Caleb put his hands in his pockets, drew out his own apple and took a bite.

"Glad to hear it."

Emily looked at him over the top of hers, smiled in a way that said she was his again and Caleb wanted nothing more than to place her baby safely in her arms.

Their baby...

James would be his son when they were married. And still his heart felt numb when he thought of the child, as though he'd been holding back for fear something like this might happen.

Once again, he was grateful Emily couldn't read his thoughts. But she was distracted now, her gaze skipping over him and when she fed her apple core to her horse, she seemed to have no awareness of what she was doing.

He knew they needed to keep moving, knew no amount of rest would quiet the storm inside of her.

And he needed to find Ruthie.

Jimmy was safe because his father wanted him, but there was only one thing Marvin would use his sister for aside from nursing his son.

"Let's get moving," he said quickly, and Emily

nodded, swung into the saddle in a seamless motion that spoke to how quickly she learned.

Then they were galloping towards the dark mountains, following a trail that seemed as mysterious as the Wakan Tanka the Sioux warriors had spoken of.

Crossing a stream, they stopped to water the horses, then picked their way across. Turning to look behind, Caleb saw her touch her gun and knew what she was thinking.

But he wouldn't let her.

Jimmy could blame him for his father's murder.

These thoughts haunted him as they rode north, the sky blackening as the rocks reached like crumbled fingers for the moon.

At dusk they scared up two mule deer and Caleb drew his rifle quickly, only to lose them in the darkened landscape.

He knew Emily was hungry, knew they needed to make camp, but a fire would attract attention, might call down bandits even though the night was cold, and they needed to stay warm.

He imagined holding her close beneath a blanket, wondering if he could keep his vow to not make love and wished he'd brought Jake.

He looked at Emily, a blur in the darkness and slowed his horse. She followed suit, reining the animal around as they looked for a suitable place to make camp when a rider raced between them.

His horse reared up and Caleb clamped his legs

around the flank, straightened his spine and the animal found footing again.

He looked to Emily, his fear rising when he saw the palomino do the same.

She fought to stay in the saddle, but her inexperience caused her to slide sideways. Then she was tumbling towards the earth and he watched her, his cry echoing against the rocks as she hit the ground.

"Emily!"

Suddenly she was rolling in a mass of skirts and braids as the rider bore down, intent on crushing her beneath the horse's hooves.

Caleb pulled his gelding to a stop and the animal went down on its haunches. He was out of the saddle and racing towards her when he saw the rider do the same, an agility to his body that said he would get to her first.

In an instant Emily was on her feet and yanking at her gun, unable to free it before the man grabbed her by the shoulders and spun her against his chest.

Caleb stopped dead in his tracks, the moonlight washing over them as Emily stiffened, the end of a knife pressed to the pulse point in her throat.

Caleb saw at once that the rider was Sioux- a man who may have been one of the pair he'd seen on the prairie with Jake.

He stood still, his eyes hard and unmoving.

Caleb watched Emily's chest rise and fall, her hands hooked over his forearm in an attempt to break his hold.

"Don't hurt her."

The rider grunted something and Emily's hands tightened, the fear in her eyes speaking to the pain the knife was causing her.

Caleb unholstered his gun, threw it aside and held up his hands.

"Let her go and we'll be on our way."

The rider grunted again.

"I saw you in the bad lands two days ago. I told you we would paint the sky for war if you came into these mountains."

Caleb shook his head, watched Emily's breathing become shallow, a hot terror making him dizzy.

"Bandits took her child," he said, his eyes drawn to the knife as he thought of how easy it would be for this man to end her life. "And my sister."

The rider was silent.

"They're hiding in the high country."

The man laughed.

"You and this woman are going to ride into the hills, kill the bandits and take back your people?"

Caleb didn't move.

"I see why you were foolish enough to come here."

Emily stiffened, tried to pull away but he tightened his grip.

"Your man should be horsewhipped for bringing you to this place. What happened to the other hunter?"

Caleb swallowed, guilt making him nauseous.

"He has a wife of his own," he nodded to Emily. "And this one's good with a gun."

The rider laughed again.

"Not as good as I am with my knife."

Emily shifted, dropped one hand and Caleb could see that she was getting faint. He felt his pulse beat in his temples, knowing no movement on his part would outwit the edge of that blade.

Then Emily was moving, and he felt his body jerk forward as though he had no control over it. He imagined the rider cutting her throat, imagined scrambling for his gun and killing him where he stood, only to have her bleed out in his arms.

His mouth went dry, his lips forming her name when he saw the man cry out, his arm loosening around her throat.

"Emily!" he cried, and she slipped under the man's arm, spun quickly, something silver in her hand.

The Sioux stumbled backwards, surprised to see blood on the front of his shirt.

Emily darted to the side, unholstered her gun and pointed it at the man.

"I have every right to be here!" she screamed. "Every right to find my child!"

Caleb moved towards his gun, picked it up.

"You are a trickster," the rider said. "Iktomi."

"I don't know what that means," she said, her eyes wild and Caleb feared she would shoot him. "I just want my son."

"We'll find him," Caleb said, trying to calm her

and when he looked at her other hand, he saw one of Clem's hat pins in it.

Had she hidden it in her skirt pocket? If so, he'd never been so grateful in his life.

She turned to him, none of the softness he loved displayed on her face. There was only terror and anger and a primal fear that would lead to death if he didn't seize control of the situation.

"You're safe," he whispered, moving closer.

"She is crazy," the Sioux said, his knife extended towards her. "Witko."

"Shut up," he grunted, watching Emily for any sign that she would pull the trigger.

"I'm tired of people telling me what to do," she said, and Caleb wondered if it was the rider she saw, or her husband standing in the Platte River. "Tired of burying the things I love."

The man stood with no fear in his eyes and Caleb touched her elbow, afraid for a moment she might turn her gun on him.

"Did you know I was coming to live in these mountains? That my Uncle Rand has called this place home for longer than you've been alive?"

The Sioux turned as if he could not hear, tilted his head.

"Rand Albright?"

Emily didn't move.

"You know him?"

The rider nodded.

"Tell me the name of his wife."

Emily shifted, her eyes moving to Caleb.

"Ehawee."

The man had no visible reaction, just straightened his shoulders, the tip of his knife lowering in the slightest.

"She is my sister."

Emily stood in place, the strands of hair blowing in the wind the only evidence that she had not been carved from stone.

"I have known Rand since I was a boy. He taught me to fish."

Emily took a breath, lowered her gun.

Caleb went to her, touched her elbow lightly and she turned, allowing him to pull her into his arms.

Her breathing was fast and short, and he tightened his grip, the nausea he'd felt while the knife was pressed to her throat rising again.

"I'm here," he whispered into her ear. "I love you."

It seemed that everything she'd been holding inside broke free and she began to shake.

The rider came closer, waiting until they turned to him.

"You are brave," he said. "But still *witko.*"

Caleb looked at him over the top of her head.

"My name is Caleb," he said. "This is Emily."

His mouth turned up at the corner.

"They call me Mahkah," he touched the blood on his shirt. "Your little knife did not do the thing you asked."

She pulled away, straightened her shoulders.

"Do you know who took my son?"

Mahkah nodded.

"My brother and I listened to the words they spoke around their fire. Tonight, they camp beside the Six Grandfathers. Tomorrow they will meet the man with fire for hair."

Emily glanced at Caleb.

"They have taken Rand," Mahkah said.

Emily looked at Caleb.

"Where's Ehawee?" she whispered.

The man turned back to his horse.

"I will take you to her."

Chapter Thirty

Marvin stood looking over the mountains, a cup of strong coffee in his hand, and thought about his dream. It was a rare thing for him to rest, but here, in the place that held the memory of his father, his sleep was sound.

Emily would be coming with their son, and if Slant and Casper had any sense, they would have taken the man she loved as well.

He imagined tying a rope around his neck and hanging him from the strong bough of a ponderosa pine. He would make Emily watch, make her think he was dead before cutting him down and doing it again.

And if she was found to be pregnant with another man's child...

Marvin wiped at his mouth, watched the people in camp ready themselves for the day.

Rand was amongst them, sitting on a stump, ever watchful for his chance to escape.

Marvin took another sip of coffee, remembering the dream and how it began in the place he called home, a little town nestled on the shores of Lake Huron.

He'd stood, looking for his father and found him standing in a graveyard.

He was leaning down to look at a stone and when Marvin approached from behind, he looked up at him.

"See that name, Red?" he asked, and Marvin squinted.

"Yes, sir."

"He needs to pay."

"He will."

There was no doubt of that now.

A shadow fell across the gravestone, and Marvin turned, saw Emily standing in the shade of a maple tree.

She approached, her face as lovely as he remembered from their evening walks.

Smiling, she touched the side of his face.

"I'm coming back to you."

He nodded, wanting the life he'd planned for them before she became a liar.

"I love you," he said, and she smiled, pulled him closer.

He was kissing her, his hands under her skirt, exploring as he had when they lived as man and wife, and she didn't pull away or make excuses as he'd come to expect.

Instead, she responded eagerly, pushing him back onto the ground, climbing on top of him as she had the night he'd found her in the rocking chair.

He sighed, unable to believe what was happening and let the pleasure her body offered erase all hatred for her.

"Someone's here," she whispered, and he turned his head, saw the man she'd been fucking in front of the rocks- a baby in his arms.

"He's mine."

He pushed at Emily, trying to get out from beneath her but she shoved his shoulders into the ground, her eyes boring into his as if the devil himself lived inside of her.

"You stupid bitch!" he screamed, clawing at her. "Give me my boy!"

"He was never your boy, Marvin," she hissed. "Your name dies with you."

Marvin screamed, felt hands shaking him.

He jerked awake, found himself rolled up in the blanket he shared with Maddie.

"Shit," he said, his body weak as he pushed her hands off of him.

"You were having a nightmare," she said, her voice small as he rolled away, got to his feet.

She stared at him, her face pale, and he wanted to slap her, to take her head and bang it against a rock so she wouldn't look at him that way.

"You said her name," she whispered, and he tried to suppress the rage he felt towards her, smiling as he always did when he lied to a woman.

"Whose name?"

She bit her lip. "My sister."

Marvin nodded, "We're going to see her today and my mind is in a twist."

Maddie sat up, pulled the open buttons of her dress together as if she were naked. "You promised I wouldn't have to see her."

"Did I?"

She nodded, her hair a mess and he knew she'd been restless in the night. "I can't face her after what I've done. And besides... she thinks I'm-"

"Dead?"

She looked down, tried to button her dress again.

"I hate to remind you, my love, but you are very much alive, and about to be reunited with her."

"I don't want to see her!"

"That can't be helped," he said, unmoved as Maddie covered her face.

"You said you would take care of her and the man she was with. You said she would never know the truth and that we could raise the boy as our own."

"And we will," he said. "But you must do what I say in this matter."

"Marvin-"

"Shut the fuck up, Madeline."

She shrank back, a look of fear on her face and he bit his lip, bent to touch her hair.

"I need you to do as I say, or we could both be killed. Rand Albright knows this land better than anyone else, and his wife's tribe will fight to free him. We walk a dangerous line, and I cannot abide your foolishness."

She did not answer, just sat staring at him as if she might cry again.

"Do you want to leave me, Maddie?" he asked. "Because if you do, feel free to walk towards Laramie. Although I believe the Sioux might sell you to the highest bidder before you get there."

She sank back down, her shoulders shaking, and turned away from him.

"I will take care of you. But you must never question me again."

She didn't answer, and after a moment Marvin moved away to the place he stood now, drinking the coffee Hawkins brought him.

The Sergeant seemed well-rested, if a bit irritated by the company he was being forced to keep, and Marvin was reminded of his sister and the way she would puff her cheeks out when the boys teased her.

"Why are you smiling?" Hawkins asked, his long, curly hair a jumbled mess and Marvin knew it bothered him.

"You remind me of someone."

Hawkins pursed his lips, used one finger to smooth his mustache into place.

"And who is that?"

"Doesn't matter," Marvin said. "Just be sure to be

on your toes when my wife shows up. She's a wildcat when cornered, and she'll be fussed up."

Hawkins snickered. "I have seen her wicked ways. And I need to remind you that my post will not wait at Kearny. The men will come looking if I have not sent word regarding the stolen mules."

"They will get word regarding the mules. Until then, your knowledge of the area is an invaluable asset to us. As are your friendships."

Hawkins puffed out his chest.

"Rand Albright was a comrade once, and now that is solidly in the pot. I'd hardly call a Pawnee I kept from the guardhouse a 'friend.' More of an acquaintance. And I barely had time to secure our next meeting before you pulled me from my post. It will be two days before any news can be brought to us here."

"Two days will be enough, my friend."

Hawkins dusted off his hat, placed it on his head and then turned it at an angle.

"If you had not shown Sophie kindness in her last hours, I would have told you to shove off long ago."

Marvin smiled, memories of the nights he'd spent in her company above the Lamplight Saloon tickling his fancy.

She'd spoken once of her brother and his post out west, remarking that he knew nothing of her new profession or the consumption she'd recently developed.

Marvin had taken a particular interest in her after that, had increased his efforts to the point that she had given him a ring as a gift- a certain family heirloom he had presented to Hawkins upon his arrival at Kearny.

The sergeant had been quite distraught to hear of his sister's passing, but Marvin had assured him she'd died in the company of the sisters of the Holy Cross and would be assured a place in Heaven.

"I'm glad Sophie's memory continues to keep me in your good graces," Marvin said. "And you will be well-compensated."

"You keep talking about money, but when the devil will I see any of it?"

Marvin gestured with his cup of coffee.

"Soon enough."

Hawkins muttered something as Marvin took another sip, remembering the day his sister died and how it had driven his father to leave them for good.

He'd been tasked with watching her for the afternoon and so he took her to the creek, where she liked to wade and look for stones.

Before long Betsy had wandered out to balance on an old log and when Marvin looked at her, she drew a penny out of her dress pocket.

"Pa gave this to me yesterday, Red. Said he'd give me another today if I was a good girl."

She'd held it up in the sunlight and it hurt Marvin's eyes. He remembered her laughing, then jumping up and down until her little feet slid on the slippery log, the cold water cupping her as she struggled to stay above water, her wet skirts pulling her under.

She'd cried out for her brother and at first, he considered going in after her.

But then he thought better of it, watching her head go up and down, her hands flailing for purchase until she went under for good, the stream carrying her away while a cold feeling that felt better than sadness spread to his chest.

He'd walked home then, his mother's face blanching when he told her Betsy was gone.

"Where is she, Red?"

He'd reached deep inside, the cold spot in his chest whispering words he needed to say.

They found her downstream on the opposite bank, her face blue and bloated, her eyes open as if searching for the brother who'd let her drown.

No one said anything at first, but as time passed his brothers would whisper under their breath.

What'd you do to her, Red?

And his father... a man already prone to drunken rages...

He beat Marvin with a belt one night after coming home from the tavern, then disappeared for the western frontier the next morning.

Marvin took another sip of coffee, his memory sharper than it had been before, and pictured the barn behind their house. He'd gone to use the outhouse, still sore from his father's beating, and heard a noise.

Sneaking to the barn, he saw his father and another man speaking in the low light of the lantern.

"I'll go with you, Ezra," his father said. "But this better not be a pipe dream."

"It's real, Jeremiah," the man replied, his face cast in shadow. "We leave at daybreak."

They shook hands after that, and Marvin saw that the mysterious stranger had something on his arm, a strange marking that seemed to take the shape of a bird in flight.

"I've already sent word to Rand Albright," the stranger continued. "He has knowledge of the Black Hills and will meet us at the outpost I told you about."

His father nodded before turning suddenly in Marvin's direction and he'd shrunk back, fearful of another beating.

He never told anyone what he'd heard, never tried to stop his father from going and after enough time had passed it seemed as if everyone in the family had forgotten him.

Until a letter came two months later describing his journey west.

Marvin remembered every word, had hidden it in a box with his treasured things after his ma tried to throw it away.

Tess and Boys...

Sorry to run off like I did, but I can't take the empty house and no Betsy to fill it. You will all manage. Boys, be sure to help your ma.

I've met a man who has dealings in the west as a

trader and knows of a Sioux guide in the Black Hills who talks sometimes of gold.

We are off to seek our fortunes. If you need word of me, inquire at the Fairview mercantile on the southern border. My companion has a sister and two nieces he writes to quite regularly.

I'd say I'm sorry, but you know that ain't true.

Jeremiah...

P.S. I'll send money if anything comes of it.

Marvin knew his father said the last part to ease his conscience, and still they waited for another letter.

But none came, and when Marvin suggested they find the sister in Fairview his mother just scowled, whispered "Good riddance to bad rubbish," and went about her business.

Time went on, and Marvin assumed his father had died when their brother returned from the flatlands of southern Michigan with a strange tale.

He'd been looking for work close to the southern border and was inside a saloon when he struck up a conversation with a man drinking whiskey.

His father had also gone west never to be heard from again. But his mother had received a strange letter from a remote outpost almost two years after he left, giving the family a glimpse of his fate.

They'd found gold in the rivers and were taking it out. But the Sioux were watching, and the guide they'd hired was turning his back on them. He feared they would be trapped, and if so, he wanted them to know he loved them.

Marvin's brother asked more questions, but the man just shrugged, drank another shot of whiskey.

"He said his companions went by the names of Ezra Kind and Randall Albright. We'd never heard of them, but word is Albright's sister runs a mercantile somewhere close to the border."

Marvin remembered his excitement when he heard they'd found gold, the name of his father's secret companion known only to him and he'd struck out then, determined to discover what had happened to the lost treasure and stake a claim to it, either through force or a familiarity with one of Rand Albright's nieces.

He remembered the moment he saw Emily in the store arguing with the woman with peacock feathers on her hat. The cold spot he'd carried in his chest since Betsy died had warmed when her eyes settled on him, something he'd never felt with another woman.

And when she grew to hate him, he knew his father's curse had followed him.

But that could be remedied.

Marvin stared at Hawkins, who adjusted his hat on his head.

"And what the devil does 'soon enough' mean?" he said.

Marvin knew he was getting impatient, knew the others were too, but he'd given them as much money as he could spare, all that came from his share of the farm after his brothers told him to go.

We know what you did, Red... Take your part and don't come back.

Marvin looked down the hillside and knew Rand Albright would die before he revealed what had happened to the gold.

But that could be remedied, too.

"You will be paid before the week is up."

"In a week I will need to be moving towards Laramie. There is a man who travels between and who I'm told lives in the low hills, and he will most certainly escort me in the way I must go. My Pawnee acquaintance will guide me—"

"Hawkins—"

"I've a mind to scout him out, see what the news is from the fort and if they intend to send some fellows up this way."

"Hawkins—"

The man began counting on his fingers, his voice laced with contempt.

"I measure four in our party along with the two who have gone to fetch your wife. That is a share split six ways and I do believe I have taken on more risk, with my post being abandoned and my reputation at stake."

"You will get your share and then some. For your risk."

"Sir—"

"The others can't count, anyway."

Hawkins made a little coughing sound, as if he hadn't expected the favor to be granted and then straightened his shoulders. "Well, I am... quite appreciative. I'd like to start a little nest egg for a special lady should she happen to come along."

Marvin chuckled, clapped him on the back.

"My advice is to stay far away from the weaker sex. Unless you can find one that is useful."

Hawkins laughed, pointed down the hillside.

"And here comes the woman you can't seem to set aside. I cannot wait to see the happy reunion."

Marvin felt his heart catch, hating the power Emily held over him. But Hawkins was right. Down the hill, just past Rand he saw Slant and Casper leading their horses while a woman walked behind, a bundle in her arms.

He threw his coffee cup aside, took off at a run and found that his injured leg could not keep up with him. Down he went on his bottom, but he didn't care how he looked as he slid down the hillside.

His wife was here… and his son.

He regained his footing, stood up only to run again as he came to a halt beside them.

He looked at Emily, but she had her sunbonnet up, her face turned to the side as the baby in her arms gurgled.

"Emily," Marvin said, and the child turned, his eyes and hair a reminder of the legacy he'd created. "Give him to me."

She would not look at him, but handed over the child and he felt the weight of him in his arms, the beauty and pain and love mixed up in one person.

The baby began to squirm, then pulled away. He

was looking for his mother, and when he saw Marvin, he scrunched up his face, started to cry.

"Shhhh," he said, unable to believe he was more concerned with comforting his son than what Slant or Casper might think.

The baby screamed, began squirming against Marvin and Emily stirred, holding out her arms.

"Give him back," she said, her voice a whisper and Marvin laughed.

"You steal him from me and then ask for his return? You have some nerve, you rotten *bitch.*"

Emily froze, every muscle in her body tense as she pulled her sunbonnet down.

Her hair was the color of a new penny, her eyes gray and her nose sprinkled with freckles.

He would have thought her pretty had the wind not been knocked from him, his gaze shifting to Slant and Casper.

"Who the fuck is this?" he demanded, and the bandits began to yell at each other, their words a jumbled mess and the woman used their confusion to grab the baby back.

"Kill me if you want but the child dies with me," she said. "I'm the only one who can feed him. The only one who can comfort him."

"What is your name?" Marvin demanded and Casper moved forward, his milky eyes darting between the two of them.

"My name's Ruthie," she spat. "I love this baby

and he loves me back, so if you wanna keep him, you better think twice about what you do to me."

Marvin watched her, saw how his son calmed immediately when she pulled him to her chest and understood that Emily had been unable to feed him, as she'd been unable to do so many things that came naturally to other women.

"Are you his wet nurse?"

She raised her chin, nodded quickly.

"My wife couldn't do it?"

Ruthie didn't answer and Marvin laughed, shook his head.

"What does she call him?"

Ruthie paused, shifting from foot to foot while she stroked the back of his son's head.

"Jimmy."

Marvin went still.

"You don't say."

Ruthie shifted him to her other hip.

"Is that short for James?"

She said nothing.

He thought of Emily, thought of putting his hands around her neck and squeezing until her tongue fell out of her mouth, until her eyes rolled back, and she stopped moving.

What'd you do to her, Red?

"Where's my wife?" he asked. "And the man she was fucking?"

Ruthie lifted her chin.

"You don't need your eyes or ears to feed my child," he said, and Ruthie swallowed, the small action telling him she was smarter than the two men who'd brought her here.

"Last I saw they were camped at Chimney Rock. But my brother won't take this lying down—"

Marvin smiled, and her eyes widened, realizing her mistake.

"Seems you might be worth more than I thought."

She struggled forward and Casper grabbed her, held her in place.

"He'll kill you where you stand, you sick sonofabitch!"

Marvin grabbed her chin, ran his thumb along her bottom lip.

"You should have your mouth washed out with soap. Or something else."

She raised herself on her toes, spit in his face.

He stood looking at her, then wiped his cheek.

"Take her to the low camp with Maddie and Gris."

One nod and Casper grabbed her arm, dragged her down the hill while Slant came closer, his hands out in front of him.

"We didn't know, Boss. She was holdin' the baby and was far from the others and I never got a good look at her in that wagon."

"Shut up."

"We'll make it right, Boss. We'll go back and get her."

Marvin smiled, the cold feeling settling back where it had always been.

"No need," he said. "She'll come to us."

Chapter Thirty-One

Clementine May pushed her food around her plate, her eyes blurred with unshed tears that seemed to sting in the sunlight.

They came easily now that Ruthie and Emily were gone, and Rose was in charge of the Merritt wagon. Jake led the way, and Putt helped when he could to make sure she was handling the oxen, but she missed her friends, worried that she would never see them again and was having a hard time tolerating Beatrice now that she had taken it upon herself to keep her company.

"Do you think Caleb and Emily have found them yet?" she asked, the bustle of Fort Laramie distracting her, and Clem shrugged, took a bite of the beans she'd boiled over their campfire.

They'd waited as long as they could at Chimney

Rock before heading west, watching all the way for any sign of their friends.

But none came, and this day marked the third since she had last seen them.

"We can't stay long," Beatrice continued, pushing her hair over her shoulder, her dark eyes scanning the grounds. "Two days and Putt will be anxious to leave. Mother should not be here at all-."

"Go, then," Clem snapped. "No one is making you stay."

Beatrice pursed her lips, took a bite and looked over her shoulder at the fort.

Soldiers were standing amongst the scattering of buildings, talking to travelers while their horses stood in place and Clem wished she could join them but knew she needed to watch their wagons.

"I'd hate to go on and have no word of their whereabouts," Beatrice said. "I wouldn't sleep for worry-"

Clem took a deep breath, trying to control her anger.

"Didn't that fancy school teach you anything?"

Her eyes widened, a look of bewilderment on her face.

"If you're waiting to see if Caleb returns alone that is the sorriest excuse I've ever heard," she said. "He doesn't love you. He'll *never* love you and you had best get that into your head before you embarrass yourself."

Beatrice coughed into her hand.

"Emily is my friend—"

"You'd sell her to the Sioux if you thought it would get you one step closer to Caleb."

Beatrice stood, turned in a circle, her fists clenched at her sides.

"I'll have you know it's Sergeant *Hawkins*, not Caleb Merritt, who was ever so gracious to me at Kearny. And if he shows himself, I'm likely to jump on his horse and ride away from this terrible place!"

"If that's the case, I'll help you look."

Beatrice sniffled; her lovely face mottled with hurt.

"I help you every day, and this is how you speak to me?"

Clementine paused, knew she'd better bite her tongue or risk upsetting the strange balance they'd created.

"I need to see to my laundry," she said, standing up.

Their clothes were drying on a rock, and she had no reason to check on them other than the hope she could get away and find her husband, who had gone to the Sutler's Store to replenish their groceries and get supplies to fix a cracked wheel.

They'd arrived at Laramie the night before, surprised to see no palisades and only a scattering of buildings that made the fort look like a small village.

Rose and Putt had stopped short of the other campsites, afraid to get closer and Jake had agreed that it was a good place to camp, telling them he would purchase whatever they needed the next day.

Beatrice seemed excited at first, but as she lingered

near their fire, talking of Caleb and Emily, Clem began to understand how unhinged her mind had truly become since running from the Golden Goose Saloon.

Jake noticed his wife's restlessness and pulled her aside, an urgency in his touch.

"Don't think it," he said, fear haunting the corners of his eyes.

"Think what?"

"You wanna hop on that horse and go find them," Jake said, angry and amused by turns.

"So do you," she said. "I see it in your eyes. And I can't help thinking about Jimmy."

"That baby is safer than the rest of them."

She stood, frightened by his words and he'd wrapped his arms around her, kissed her softly like he did in the darkness beneath their wagon, and she relaxed, the tension that seemed to live inside of her vanishing with his touch.

And now she stood by a rock outside of Fort Laramie, watching his underthings dry in the sun, wishing she could scream to the sky and have it answer.

She looked over her shoulder, saw Beatrice walking towards her wagon, a lone soldier patrolling the perimeter and knew she would not be returning anytime soon.

She looked back at the rock, racking her brain for some way she could help and could think of nothing short of what her husband feared most. The sun heated her neck, causing a trickle of sweat to run down her back and gather at her waistband.

She felt dirty, and wished for a moment she was back at her home- the claw foot tub waiting to be filled with warm water- instead of staring at the Laramie River.

She began walking towards the fort, unsure why she suddenly needed to stretch her legs so badly.

She passed the block buildings and a group of Sioux trading buffalo robes, heard the jumble of voices that reminded her of Kearny and scanned the area for Jake.

She didn't see him at first, but knew he was probably still at the store buying goods and so continued towards the center of the parade grounds, smiling at people who either ignored her or returned the gesture.

The store sat at the end of a row of buildings, long and squat and plain. People were milling around, holding sacks of flour and talking with their feet resting on barrels.

Two women stood looking in the windows, trying to catch a glimpse of their reflection while tying on new sunbonnets and Clem brushed past them, blinded by the dim interior.

She stood for a moment and saw her husband counting out coins at the counter. The journey had left little time for them to play husband and wife, and so she took a moment to admire him now for the handsome man he was.

Her mother recognized his physical appeal even as

she complained about his lack of breeding, and Clem believed it was one of the reasons her parents had finally allowed them to wed.

Jake could be charming when he chose to be, and when Clem found him seated with her mother on the front porch one evening, laughing so hard the dimples in his cheeks were showing, she knew the battle was won.

And here he was, leaning on the counter, the same easygoing manner guaranteeing them the things they needed.

He turned, saw her standing in the doorway, his eyebrows rising as if to ask what she needed.

She pressed her lips together, moved to the side and he excused himself, came to stand beside her.

"Who's watching the wagon?"

She sighed, annoyed that he would be thinking only of that.

"Most likely Putt, but I can't abide Beatrice another second."

"You're letting her get under your skin," he said. "There's nothing to be done but wait until we can't wait any more."

She hugged herself, looked down.

"We have to get over those mountains, Clem."

She met his gaze.

"I know."

Jake touched her arm. "I'm going to look for someone who can help us... just in case."

She pulled back, disturbed by his meaning and

looked out the window. A small grouping of gravestones stood in the center of a fenced enclosure, and she felt the need to be amongst their stillness and away from Jake's words.

"I'm going to step outside."

"Clem—"

"I just need some fresh air."

He raised his eyebrow, shrugged his shoulders and went back to the counter where the man was waiting.

Once outside, she circled to the back, the bustle of the fort behind her and entered the enclosure.

Headstones that had been worn smooth by time spoke of the sadness this place had seen. Most of the names were of soldiers, but a few women and children were amongst them, the cause of death being cholera or dysentery or some other sickness that made Clem fear for her own life.

She bowed her head, said a small prayer for those who hadn't made it any farther than this rise on the prairie and moved towards a grave that seemed to stand apart from the others.

Standing in front of it, she bent down to look at the name, wondering when Jake would be done and what Beatrice was doing at the moment and how long she could pass time until she went crazy.

The writing was faint, the date of death over twenty years past.

P.R. Albright... aged thirty-seven... died of scurvy.

She stood straight, a picture of Emily in her mind,

the letter from Rand in her hand and the signature at the bottom.

She'd asked about it, and Emily had assured her it was the way he signed his letters, the way he'd *always* signed his letters...

A scream jolted her, followed by a gunshot that sent her spinning in a circle and at once people began to pour out the door of the Sutler's Store, which suddenly seemed to be underwater.

She heard Jake call her name, saw him burst from the building and ran towards him.

He pulled her to the side of the store, forced her to her knees while he drew his gun, intent on shielding her as another shot sounded from the direction of their wagon.

All went quiet at once until a long, animal-like wail rose from what seemed like the prairie itself.

Beatrice.

"Jake," she gasped, and he looked at her, terror in his eyes as he pulled her to her feet, his long strides taking them towards their wagon.

She could barely keep up, her feet tangling with each other and skidding against her husband's. But he would not let go of her arm, would rather drag her along than leave her behind.

Which was why she loved him.

The wail rose again, and this time she saw soldiers and horses moving towards their campsite, words forming around her like a wall, and in the murmur, she was reminded of what had happened the summer before.

Jake had mentioned it the day they left Chimney Rock, had said something about a stolen cow and thirty soldiers being killed, and Clem had sensed a restlessness she hadn't felt in Kearny, a feeling that something was going to happen and now Beatrice was wailing, and gunshots had been fired.

They passed the rock and Jake's laundry, still drying in the sun, and saw people gathered around Putt's wagon.

Jake broke into a run, and she lifted her skirt, sprinted the remaining distance.

Her husband was pushing people aside, calling for Putt when he saw the man being held between two soldiers, Rose and another man lying bloodied and still at their feet.

Clem covered her mouth, looked to Beatrice who had gone to her knees beside her mother, blood on her hands and face as if she had been standing nearby when the shots were fired.

"Putt," Jake cried, and the man looked up, his face white, his eyes glassy.

A soldier stepped between them.

"We're taking him with us."

Beatrice wailed again; her long hair matted with the same blood that was smeared on her cheeks.

"Mother!" she screamed, and the people seemed to part around her as if they did not want to touch her.

"This man's with us," Jake said. "That woman as well."

The soldier shook his head.

"Seems she killed a man in Chicago. She was recognized and an argument broke out."

Clem went to her knees beside Beatrice, who looked at her as if she didn't see anything in front of her.

"Private Jenkins was called to sort the matter out when this man took matters into his own hands."

Putt shook his head, his face slack. "He killed her."

Jake looked at the soldier.

"Seems the man was only wounded and turned to draw on your friend. This woman jumped between them."

Clem heard the words and reached out to Beatrice, pulled her to her chest, blood soaking the front of her dress.

"Putt," Jake said again, and the man looked down at Rose as if his life had ended with her.

"I only wanted to protect her, to give Beatrice a better life."

The soldiers tightened their hold, shifted their stance.

"This man will stand trial for murder. I suggest you collect the daughter and take her to the post surgeon. We'll bury the mother and then find out what all this Chicago business is about."

Jake stood still, unable to say a word and it shook Clem to the core.

"I can spare a man to help you," the soldier said. "The store will buy what they can, and some might be willing to trade. And, if I may speak freely, this man will likely hang."

Jake put a hand to his head, looked helplessly at his wife as the soldiers moved away, dragging Putt between them.

The older man struggled to get back to Beatrice, his voice rising, and the soldiers took their gun, hit him on the back of the head and he collapsed between them.

Beatrice looked up, a fresh sob bursting from her throat as the soldiers carried him back towards the fort.

Minutes seemed like hours as Clementine sat holding Beatrice. She saw people talking to Jake, saw more soldiers come with wheelbarrows and take the bodies of Rose and the other man away.

"Jake," she said, her breath heavy and her husband kneeled beside her, his eyes on Beatrice.

"We have to go," she said. "We have to find Emily and Caleb—"

Jake shook his head, turned to look over his shoulder.

"We can't leave Putt."

"You don't understand," she said, still rocking Beatrice. "I found Rand Albright."

Jake stood quickly, turned in a circle as if the man would appear before him.

"Where?"

Clem touched the top of Beatrice's head, gently pulled her arms away and stood, one finger pointing to the graveyard.

"There."

Chapter Thirty-Two

Emily looked at the mountain known as the Six Grandfathers and knew her child was near.

Mahkah had said as much, but something deep inside of her lifted when she saw the peak, as though the forest itself wanted her to be at peace.

And still the thought of seeing Marvin made gooseflesh rise on her skin, her only consolation was the hope that Caleb would kill him.

At times her mind would wander to a dark place where Caleb lay buried, her heart torn and bleeding because aside from Jimmy, there was nothing in the world she wanted more.

They had ridden for three days, sharing campfires and rabbits Mahkah had killed, his knowledge of the forest a thing that seemed magical to her. And in the darkness, they would talk of Rand and Ehawee, of the men who had come into the mountains and the legend of the gold they'd left behind.

Mahkah spoke of his father, a guide called Indian Crow by the white men because he always knew the straightest path.

He spoke also of the shame his father carried, the way he had gone into the mountains for a time, unable to face his wife or children, known always as the man who had betrayed his people by leading the white men to gold.

"Afterwards, my father and Rand returned the treasure to the mountain," Mahkah said. "The other men were killed by my people on the high peak we call Owl Maker, to avenge what was taken."

Caleb sat looking at him, the firelight glinting off his hair, reminding Emily of how real he had become to her.

"What do you think happened?"

Mahkah shook his head, took a bite of meat from the end of the knife he'd held against her throat.

"My father was a mystery to me," he said. "At times a warrior, at others - a follower of shadows."

Emily looked at Caleb, a chill spreading over her skin.

"I do not believe he meant to betray us," he said. "But if the white men threatened his family, he would have sacrificed his pride to save them."

"Why would my uncle do any of this?" Emily asked, unable to reconcile the gold- hungry bandit described by Mahkah with the man from her mother's letters.

The answer came after considerable silence.

"Rand was just one man."

Emily thought about his words that night as she laid in Caleb's arms, his steady breath fanning her ear. She looked down at his calloused fingers, linked them with her own before sliding into a restless sleep.

She awoke hours later to find him watching her, his soft smile speaking to the love she prayed would remain between them.

Mahkah had risen early, telling them he would bring his sister down from the high camp where she kept watch for her husband and Emily's pulse quickened when she thought of their first meeting.

And now she was waiting in the shadow of the mountain known as the Six Grandfathers, wondering what Ehawee could do to help when she felt Caleb's hand on her shoulder.

She turned to him, saw him watching the horizon and knew he was thinking of Ruthie.

"We'll find her," she said, reaching up to cover his fingers with hers and he nodded briefly, his jaw set.

"I'm betting on it."

She raised herself on her toes, suddenly desperate to touch his skin with her lips, and placed them on his cheek, lingering until he turned to her, his mouth seeking hers.

They stayed that way until he pulled away, facing the mountains again.

"You're more than I deserve, Emily Ives."

She laughed lightly, ready to scold him when he shook his head.

"I've done a piss poor job of taking care of the things I love," he said. "Consider that your warning."

"Caleb—"

"God'll surely wash his hands of me if I don't bring Ruthie home."

"Don't say that."

"*I'll* wash my hands of me—"

She moved in front of him, struck by the brightness of his eyes, wondering if it was the clear sky or unshed tears that made them change color.

"No, you won't."

"She got pregnant when I was supposed to be watching her."

Emily drew a breath, wanting to comfort him but knowing he had to forgive himself first.

"I was so damn selfish," he said. "I couldn't see past my own face."

"You're anything but selfish."

He laughed. "Ask my mother if that's true. Or Ruthie or Celia."

She swallowed, her name a sore reminder of a past they didn't share.

"God," he put a hand to his face. "Sometimes I forget she's really gone."

Emily felt her hand drop on its own and Caleb took a quick breath, his face pained.

"Em," he said quickly. "I didn't mean—"

She smiled, straightened her shoulders.

"Of course, you did," she said. "She was your wife."

He cleared his throat. "I know, but-"

"And I'm just some woman you met on the trail."

"No," he said, running a hand over his head. "You're more than that."

She touched his arm, her heart galloping in her chest.

"Am I, Caleb? Because every thought you have seems to go back to her."

He seemed confused, wondering where the question would lead and Emily waited, her words hanging heavy between them.

"Not that I blame you," she said. "I *can't* blame you."

"Emily—"

"I don't want to compete with a ghost."

He opened his mouth to protest.

"And you shouldn't, either."

He paused, uncertainty in his eyes.

"Are you talking about the man you named Jimmy after?"

She looked away, wanting to hurt him like he'd hurt her.

"Did you love him?"

She dropped her eyes, not wanting to see the pain her pride was causing.

"Is that why your husband killed him?"

"He thought so."

"You're right, Em," Caleb said, his voice rough. "I won't compete with a ghost."

She felt shame stain her cheeks and tightened her hold on his arm.

"Marvin did what he did out of anger," she said, stumbling on her words. "But I never loved him."

He took a step to the side, putting distance between them.

"But you wanted me to *think* you did."

She looked down. "You said—"

"I wasn't using my head," he cut her off, his voice cold. "But you were."

She felt the sharpness of his words pierce her heart, unsure why they would argue when everything depended on standing together.

"I'm sorry," she said, feeling as miserable as she had on the shanty with Marvin. "I didn't want to hear Celia's name. Not here. Not now."

"Not ever," he finished. "Tell the truth, Em."

"You feel the same way about Marvin," she said, the color rising in her cheeks. "But I don't love him. I *never* loved him."

"Em—"

"I've never loved anyone but *you*."

He put his hands on her shoulders, bent to look into her eyes.

"But I have."

She felt tears building behind her eyes, unsure why she would cry now.

"Can you live with that?"

She swallowed, her words stuck in her throat.

"*Can you?*"

She opened her mouth, shut it again.

"That's what I was afraid of."

She shook her head. "No—"

"I'm going to fill our canteens."

Her heartbeat quickened, realizing for the first time the breadth of his anger.

"You're leaving me?"

"There's a creek at the bottom of the hill," he said. "It won't take long."

"Caleb, please—"

"I'm *mad*, Em," he said, looking at her for the first time with the passion she knew so well. "And I need to take a walk."

"But—"

"You need to let me."

She stood watching him, unsure what to say when he turned his back, yanked his suspenders up over his shoulders and for a moment she remembered them bare in the sun as he kissed her in the shadow of Chimney Rock.

"Stay put," he said, more an order than a show of concern. "And shoot anything that moves."

She swallowed, her own fear bubbling over as she watched him walk away.

"You were right when you said you take piss poor care of the things you love."

He stopped, his back to her, then continued down the hill.

Emily stood, regretting her words, the morning sun washing over their campsite and couldn't believe how quickly things had changed.

But she didn't know Caleb, despite all they had done with their mouths and tongues and hands- didn't understand his mind any more than her own and now she stood, watching a sunrise she feared could be her last.

She walked back to where they had tied their horses, touched the palomino mare and put her face against its neck. Breathing the scent of cold fur and sweet grass, she began to cry, knowing Caleb would see her swollen eyes when he returned.

If he returned...

She bit down on her lip, pushing the thought from her mind.

He was angry, but he wasn't cruel, and abandoning her now would make him nothing less than a monster.

She stood with her face in the mare's neck for several minutes, listening for the sound of his footsteps and heard nothing. Pulling away, she went back to the place he had left her and looked down the hill, squinting for a glimpse of the creek he'd talked about and realized there wasn't one.

Glancing behind, she saw their canteens hanging from the pommel of his gelding's saddle.

She pressed her lips together, her eyes smarting in the sun, watching for any sign of movement and touched the revolver on her hip.

When he came back, she could tell him she was

sorry, and that she would accept that he'd loved another woman.

But when she thought of the things they had done
to make their baby, when she imagined the hands that
had pleasured her offering the same to Celia, jealousy
wrung her stomach like a dishrag of water.

She thought of her son, wondering if Caleb pictured the same things and understood for the first time
why he hadn't held him.

But this was her road, begun on the dusty trail outside of Independence and it was up to her to decide the
best way to walk it.

Something shifted behind her, so subtle she might
not have noticed had the sun been higher in the sky
and she spun quickly, her hand on her gun.

Shoot anything that moves...

Mahkah stood watching her as if had been there a
long time, a woman beside him and her breath caught
when she realized who it was.

"Ehawee," she whispered, her feet numb when she
tried to move them.

The woman was more beautiful than she had
imagined, and she understood why her uncle had married her and made a home away from his own people.

She was dressed in the blouse and skirt of a home-
steader, a beaded buckskin vest overlaying it. Dark hair
streaked with gray fell over shoulders, her black eyes
kind but watchful.

"Child," she said, extending her arms and Emily
ran to them, letting the woman enfold her in an em-

brace that seemed as real as anything she'd ever experienced.

"Have you seen my son?" she asked, and Ehawee said nothing at first, just held her tightly.

"Where is Caleb?" Mahkah asked, and Emily pulled away.

"He went to get water."

Mahkah made a sound in his throat.

"There is no water down there."

Emily looked at Ehawee.

"He was angry with me," Emily said, not wanting to tell him more. "And he needed to clear his head."

Mahkah laughed.

"I do not think there is enough walking that can do that for him."

Emily raised her chin.

"He'll be back."

Mahkah crossed his arms against his chest.

"If he does, we will not be here."

"Did you see my son," she ignored him. "And Ruthie? She wears her hair in two braids."

Ehawee nodded.

"I have seen their campfires. Rand is with them."

Emily touched her shoulder. "We need to hurry. My husband-"

"The bands of the north are gathering."

"Gathering?" Emily asked.

"To make war."

"War," Emily echoed, and Ehawee put a finger to her lips as if she was listening.

Mahkah grabbed her by the shoulders, pushed her out of the way, an arrow in his chest.

"Koda!" Ehawee cried, and the man went to his knees, another arrow piercing his throat.

It seemed then that the sounds went dead in Emily's ears as she watched blood spurt from his mouth. Around her the horses reared up, neighed into the wind and ran away as she yanked her gun free.

Running now, she crouched behind a tree as Ehawee took her brother's quiver from his back. A moment later she'd slid behind a rock and Emily watched in horror as several figures began to climb the hillside Caleb had descended only a short time before.

"Who are they?" she hissed.

"Blackfoot," Ehawee answered, taking an arrow from her brother's quiver and placing it in the string of his bow. "They think we are a friend to the white man."

"Tell them we're not!" she cried.

Ehawee shook her head. "It does not matter what I say. They will not stop until they have you. Then you will wish you were dead."

Emily swallowed, watching as Ehawee pulled the bow.

One shot and a man fell to the ground.

A great cry followed, and they began to run.

She peered over a branch, ducking as an arrow sailed just above her head.

Ehawee made a noise and Emily glanced at her, saw

her looking over her shoulder as Mahkah writhed on the ground.

"Finish him," she whispered between gritted teeth.

Emily crouched, unable to move.

"I ask you as his sister," Ehawee said, her voice firm and Emily realized she had seen horror like this before. "To show mercy."

Emily thought of her son, thought of her parents-and Caleb, wandering somewhere in the valley and could not believe what she'd been asked to do.

"Please," Ehawee cried, putting another arrow in her bow. "You must not let them take him alive."

Emily looked at Mahkah, watched the blood pooling around his neck and chest, his legs slapping against the earth and aimed her gun.

One shot and he went still.

Bending over, she threw up her breakfast.

"Hurry!" Ehawee cried. "They are coming."

Emily wiped her mouth with the back of her hand, then turned to face the others.

She'd loaded her gun that very morning, which meant she had five shots left.

Crouching, she stuck the barrel of the gun in the crook of a tree and fired at the nearest figure.

He fell to the ground, only to have another take his place, a war club raised high, and she could only imagine what would happen if they broke over the hill.

Another shot and another man fell, followed by a third when Ehawee's arrow found its mark.

Emily readjusted her hold, wiped at her face and the sweat that had dripped into her eyes as a sharp pain ripped her breath away.

Looking down, she saw an arrow sticking out of her shoulder.

She screamed, rage fueling her lungs, and aimed again.

Her bullet hit the dirt, the man who had injured her drawing his arrow back for a second shot when she fired again.

His head exploded and she scanned the hillside, saw two Blackfoot remaining.

Ehawee was pulling back again, her dark eyes narrowed as she released her arrow.

The man stumbled, hit in the knee before Ehawee finished him with a second shot as Emily aimed at the remaining warrior, her left arm useless.

One shot would decide if she lived or died.

She thought back to the week spent in the woods with Quinn.

"Take your time," he'd said. "Pretend there's nothing to lose."

She looked at Ehawee, drawing another arrow from her quiver, her dead brother bleeding into the ground behind her, and aimed.

She pulled the trigger.

His club was raised high when her bullet hit him in the arm, spinning him sideways. He fell to the dirt, crawling forward when Ehawee stood and ran the short distance between them.

Suddenly she was on top of the Blackfoot, wrestling his war club from his hand.

Emily turned, unable to watch, and sank to the ground.

A minute passed, then two, and when Ehawee returned, her face was marked with blood even as her eyes went to Emily's shoulder.

"You are hurt."

Emily felt like laughing but took a staggered breath instead.

"But not dead."

"Lie down and I will tend to you."

She looked across a hillside littered with bodies, expecting to see Caleb emerge from the forest and knew something had happened to him.

If he'd heard the screams and the gunshots, he would have come... knowing she was in danger.

She shut the thought out of her mind, laid down on the ground and allowed Ehawee to place her hand around the arrow shaft.

"Here," she said, giving her a piece of rawhide to bite on.

Then she broke the arrow close to where it entered her shoulder, pulling it out, and Emily felt the deepest, darkest parts of herself spilling into her screams.

After a moment she felt Ehawee unbuttoning her blouse and knew she was cleaning the wound with cold water from a pouch.

Then she opened a haversack slung over her shoulder, drew out cloth and herbs made from the petals of yellow flowers.

"You will carry a scar to mark this day," she said.

Emily looked at her, tears forming in her eyes. "Your brother saved me."

Ehawee nodded, her face still.

"You gave him a good death."

Emily gritted her teeth, thinking of her parents, of James and Celia.

"There's no such thing."

Ehawee touched her forehead. "If they had taken us, you would know the difference."

Emily stirred, her head light.

"I need to find my son. And Caleb-"

"You will rest."

Emily tried to sit up, tried to look at the cloth wrapped around her shoulder even as Ehawee buttoned her bloodstained blouse over the top of it.

"I must move my brother's body until we can bury him. Then we will find the others."

Emily knew this was right, knew she needed to sleep to survive the journey, but her fear would not allow it.

"Caleb was down in that valley. He may be hurt or..." she felt panic tighten inside of her chest. "They may have taken him."

Ehawee's forehead creased. "The Blackfoot do not take men."

Emily's face collapsed, a sob retching free from her

throat when she thought about the last words she'd spoken to him.

"Let the medicine do its work."

Emily took a breath, tried to lay still and found the woman bending over her, whispering words she did understand, and they seemed to calm her.

She closed her eyes, pictures of Jimmy and Ruthie and Rand swirling in her mind. She saw Caleb yanking his suspenders up, saw the Blackfoot rushing towards her with an upraised war club.

She imagined Caleb seeing the same thing, imagined the club smashing down on the blond hair she'd cut only days before and felt like throwing up again.

I won't compete with a ghost...

But that wasn't true.

If she had to crawl on her hands and knees over the bodies of the men she had killed, she would find him.

And then they would paint the sky any damn color they wanted.

Chapter Thirty-Three

"Son," the voice was deep, reminding Caleb of the father who had died years ago. "Wake up."

Pain shot down the back of his neck, his last memory one of walking down the hillside, mad as hornet because of something Emily said.

It was foolish, he knew, but he'd never been good at recognizing his mistakes until it was too late.

"Pa?" he said, his mind a twisted heap of fear and confusion.

"My name's Rand Albright," the voice came again. "Can you open your eyes?"

He did as he was told, saw pine trees framing the blue sky, the face of an older man with a gray beard and mustache staring back at him.

He started, tried to scoot away but the pain in his head stopped him cold.

"Em?" he asked, remembering the moment he'd left her, a knot of worry pinching his stomach. "Where is she?"

"You were alone when they brought you here."

"Brought me here?" he asked, squinting at the sun, his hand going to his forehead. "Who?"

"Marvin's men."

His words startled Caleb and he rolled to his side, pushed himself off the ground.

"There, now," the man said. "Let me help you. We're in this together or we're sunk."

Caleb felt the back of his head and discovered a large lump, tender and throbbing, dried blood sticking to it.

Sitting up now, he scooted over to a tree, sat with his back against it and for the first time realized he and the old man's feet were tied together by a rope that had been secured to a root sticking up from the earth.

Looking around, he saw the smoking remains of a fire just down the hillside, two men standing in front of it with their backs to him.

"Where's my sister?" he asked, careful to keep his voice down. "And the baby?"

The old man nodded down the hill.

"She's at the other camp. They keep us apart, so we don't talk, but the boss went off to see about something, so they stuck you with me."

"Boss?" Caleb asked, and the two men turned, started walking towards him.

"Morning, Beautiful," the skinnier one said,

"Thought that whack on the head might keep you out a bit longer."

Caleb looked at him, rage making his temples throb.

"Where's Emily?"

The man smiled, something in his milky eyes making Caleb uneasy.

"Last I saw she was firing on a passel 'o Blackfoot that was rushing the ridge," he asked. "She was holdin' 'em off with that squaw, but we didn't wait around to see how things turned out."

The knot of worry tightened until he couldn't breathe, and he remembered the gunshots, remembered turning quickly and running towards the camp when everything went black.

"You left her?" Caleb asked, and the skinny man looked into his face, squinted for a moment before bending on his haunches to stare at him.

"I ain't about to stick my neck out for some whore what's screwed around on her husband," he smirked. "We'll tell the Boss they scalped her. Although they might keep the best parts just the same-"

Caleb lurched forward, catching him in the jaw with his fist before the rope sent him sprawling on his stomach.

The man fell back on his bottom, took a moment to rub at his face, then stood slowly and kicked Caleb in the side.

The old man began to yell as the bandit drew back and kicked him again. And then again.

"Boss wants this one for himself," the other bandit spoke up. "He'll be pissed if you take all the fight out of him."

The skinny one took a step back.

"Stay down, you sonofabitch," he spat. Then, pointing to the old man, "And you can quit hollerin."

The bandit with the cloudy eyes spit in the grass, waved at the other one to join him back at the fire.

Rand moved closer to Caleb, who lay on his side, his hands over his stomach, a rivulet of blood running from the corner of his mouth.

"The one that kicked you is Casper," he whispered. "And the one who called him off is Slant. Dumb as radishes but they seem to follow orders."

Caleb didn't answer, his mind spiraling on what that meant even as he pictured Emily fighting off a band of Blackfoot while he sulked in the valley like a spoiled toddler.

"Don't worry about my niece."

Caleb looked at him, then turned his face to the side, spit blood into the dirt.

"How are you here?" he asked, rolling over onto his back. "You're supposed to be on your way to Laramie-"

"Took me like they took you," he said. "Marvin has half the outlaws in Nebraska Territory working for him. And, apparently Sergeant Hawkins."

Caleb swallowed, the taste of blood still in his mouth.

"Why did you tell me not to worry about Em?"

Rand smiled again, his wrinkled face giving Caleb comfort.

"My wife was with her."

Caleb laughed.

"That makes me feel a whole lot better."

Rand chuckled; his eyes bright. "It should."

Caleb wanted to believe him, wanted to think that Emily and Ehawee had defeated an entire band of Blackfoot without getting killed or captured, but the very real possibility that they were now prisoners of a hostile tribe made his blood run cold.

"You love her, don't you?" Rand asked.

Caleb grunted.

"Drives you crazy, doesn't she?"

Caleb grunted again.

"I learned long ago the sweetest smelling flowers have the most bees buzzing around them."

"I'm starting to understand that," Caleb closed his eyes, swallowed. "Is my sister all right?"

"Seems to be. She feeds the baby. They keep her at the low meadow camp. Those two radishes seem to think she's funny."

"They're not wrong," Caleb managed a laugh.

Rand was quiet, watching the woods and the men at the fire, who were sitting now, talking in low tones, their shoulders touching each other.

"If I tell you something, you must use it to help my niece. And my wife, if need be."

Caleb nodded, his head throbbing again, the taste of blood in his mouth stronger since he'd sat up.

"My friend Indian Crow and I took gold from these mountains long ago. There was no excuse for it aside from flat-out greed."

Caleb held his tongue, curious how his tale would compare to Mahkah's.

"We were attacked on the Owl Maker, a high peak sacred to my wife's people. Marvin's father was one of the six men with us. We were the only two to survive. I know they spared my life because Indian Crow spoke for me, because he knew my heart was not like the others."

Caleb took a breath, his eyes on the men by the fire.

"I was left alone for a time, and while I sat there, I carved our story on a stone, hoping someone would tell our families if I was killed. I thought I could make up for what I'd done if I made these hills my home. I never wanted this to follow me, but it seems Marvin found out somehow, and if my instincts are right, married Emily to strengthen his claim."

"Claim?" Caleb asked, his head throbbing again.

"He thinks I owe him his father's share, and more than that, if the truth be told."

Caleb listened, the pain in his head no match for the fear that seemed to grow with every word.

He'd always thought Marvin was obsessed with Emily, but knowing now that she had been used as a pawn in a larger plan made her situation more dangerous.

"Where's the gold?" he asked, Slant and Casper standing suddenly as if someone was approaching. "Tell me and maybe it'll save our lives."

Rand looked over his shoulder.

"By the tall spires that stand next to the Owl Maker," he said. "I set traps around it so no one would be able to take it again-"

Then Slant was beside them, untying Rand's feet and dragging him to the edge of the fire where a man with hair the color of russet gold stood.

Caleb's stomach churned at the sight of him, rage propelling him to his knees.

Marvin saw him, a strange look passing over his face. Then he was walking towards Caleb, his limp pronounced, standing in front of him for a moment before kneeling to look into his eyes.

"You're Caleb Merritt," he asked, his tone cordial. "I've been wanting to introduce myself for some time."

"You put your hands on her, you sick bastard?" Caleb spat, but Marvin only tilted his head to the side and smiled.

"Is that what she said?"

Casper came closer, another man he recognized as Sergeant Hawkins behind him.

"She told me everything."

Marvin nodded, his face as calm as if they'd been discussing the price of corn at a feed mill.

"I'm sorry to break the news to you, but my wife is a known liar and whore. Poor James was foolish enough to believe her, and he paid with his life."

"No," Caleb said, the blood in his mouth again. "You're the liar, filling these men's heads with stories about gold you're never going to find."

Hawkins stirred, adjusted his hat while Slant and Casper glanced at each other.

"Oh, I'll find it," he said, his eyes shifting to Rand. "Won't I, old man?"

Rand looked at Caleb, then down to his feet. "Did you sell my niece out for money, Jack? I thought better of you."

"I say," Hawkins said quickly, one hand up.

"I wouldn't be counting on any big pay day if I were you, boys!" Caleb laughed. "Half that gold is probably washed down the mountain by now."

Marvin smiled again; his tone strangely soothing. "You'd best attend to your own affairs, Mr. Merritt."

Caleb gave a half smile.

"The only affair I need to attend to is how to tell Jimmy I killed the man who raped his mother."

Marvin went still, his eyes hardening. The next second he drew back, struck Caleb in the jaw and the blow took him to the ground, where he lay in the dirt, his breath coming in little pants.

"You won't get anywhere with me by beating the hell out of him," he heard Rand say and somewhere in the background Slant and Casper laughed.

Some time passed before the others drifted away and Marvin sat down cross-legged beside him, his voice soothing again, and Caleb understood for the first time why Emily had been fooled by him.

"How are you feeling, Caleb?" he asked.

Caleb coughed, spit more blood into the dirt.

"That's what I thought," he continued. "I figured you could use some company. I certainly could, after days in the company of these idiots. You seem like an intelligent fellow, and we have similar tastes, so to speak."

Caleb turned.

"How does she taste, Caleb?" he asked. "I'm sure you sampled her in front of those rocks."

"You sonofabitch-"

"I do envy you at times. My wife spent most of our married life trying to fight me off. I only experienced her true passion once, when she was drunk on whiskey and had pleasured herself. You, my good man, have undoubtedly known her in the way she was meant to be."

Caleb closed his eyes, imagining the things Marvin had said and prayed he would get a chance to put a bullet in his head.

"I had a sister once. She looked like yours, so pretty and spoiled. Pa loved her the most, and it got under my skin. The way she would brag. He even gave her a penny once, all because she'd behaved in church."

Caleb lay in the dirt, his chest hurting from the

kicks, his nose and mouth bleeding and wondered why Marvin was telling him this.

"One day my ma was busy and so I had to watch her. We went down to the river and ..." he smiled again, leaning closer. "She climbed out onto a log, held that new penny up for me to see and then she slipped, fell right in up to her fool head."

"She went down once, then again, and for a second, I thought about fetching her. But then I remembered that penny. And I let her go down again."

Caleb scooted away but Marvin reached down, pushed his shoulder into the ground to hold him in place.

"No one knew what happened," he whispered. "But I'm sure of one thing... our lives would've been worse with her in it. Just like Jimmy will be better off when I put his mother in the ground."

Caleb reached up suddenly, grabbed Marvin around the throat and squeezed.

"If you can find her," he spat. "Those assholes you hired left her alone to fight off the Blackfoot and took me instead."

Marvin's eyes went wide, his hands closing around Caleb's until he was able to pry them loose.

Once standing, he shook his head, then ran his hands through his hair, clearly disturbed.

"Casper! Slant!" he called, and the two men left Rand and came quickly from the fire. "Did you leave Emily in the company of hostiles?"

The two men looked at each other, and Slant slid his hat from his head.

"She was up by the Grandfather Rock, Boss," he said. "There was too many of 'em. An' we needed to get this one back to you."

Marvin moved closer.

"You left my wife and instead brought me a pile of shit?"

Casper shifted from one foot to another.

"We was just scouting out the edges like you said when we saw your lady up on top of that ridge. Then them hostiles came creepin' along real quiet like. Then we saw this fella off by himself and thought we better try an' snatch him an' there was no way we coulda climbed up that hill and gotten her-"

Marvin closed his eyes.

"Sorry, Boss," Slant said. "We can go back and look for her. She was holdin' her own right and good with that squaw."

"Hawkins has news from Laramie," he barked, and the sergeant came forward, hesitantly at first, bringing Rand with him.

"Do you know of a skirmish involving a known whore who was wanted for murder in Chicago?"

Caleb felt his heart jump in his chest.

Rand shook his head. "Why would I?"

Hawkins smoothed his mustache.

"My acquaintance says there was quite a ruckus, and that one young lady who was involved in the matter inquired about a particular headstone in the cemetery. It seemed a strange request, but it seems she was quite convinced the grave contained *you,* Mr. Albright-"

"Sir?" Rand asked, and Caleb watched, his heart in his throat.

"How can someone with your name be here, in the Black Hills, but also in the graveyard at Laramie?"

"Obviously there has been some mistake-"

"My acquaintance reports the man in the grave was found to be one Phineas Randall Albright, born in Michigan, who died of scurvy 20 years before."

"Sergeant—"

"Seems the man was a trader who had knowledge of the Black Hills. All the things you are known for."

Caleb looked at Rand, who had lowered his head.

"Who is the proper man, Mr. Albright? You, or the one moldering at Laramie?"

Marvin came forward then, a strange look in his eye, and took hold of Rand's arm.

"I think I can set this matter at rest."

Rand tried to pull away, but Marvin would not let go. Slant and Casper came to the other side, holding him still, anxious to see what their boss would do.

"I remember a man visiting my father when I was young," he said. "They hid out in our barn and talked by the light of a lantern. No one knew I was there. I was very quiet, you see. Very still, and even though I couldn't see the man's face, I did see something else."

Caleb felt his breath stop in his throat, watching as Marvin shoved Rand's sleeve up to his elbow. The man began to struggle, but not before Caleb saw what Marvin was looking for- a tattoo of what looked to be a bird in flight.

Marvin chuckled, shaking his head, then stepped back as Rand continued to fight the two bandits.

Hawkins came forward, bending to look at the mark.

"What is this, sir? And why all the fuss? Is this the man we have been hearing about or some ghost risen from the grave? I believe I have a right—"

"Hawkins," Marvin interrupted, bowing low before Rand, who had gone suddenly still. "I'd like to introduce you to Mr. Ezra Kind."

"Ezra Kind?" Hawkins bellowed, removing his hat and slapping it on his elbow. "I'm quite sure I've never heard of him. Who the devil is that?"

Marvin smiled, reached out to clap the old man on the shoulder.

"The son of a bitch who stole my gold."

Chapter Thirty-Four

Ehawee looked back over the hill where she had buried Mahkah beneath a scattering of pine boughs. She would return with her brother and make his scaffold, but now she needed to move, needed to find the war-makers before they killed Rand.

She turned, saw Emily on the palomino mare and knew she was in no condition to ride.

And yet, she seemed intent on finding Caleb. So intent, in fact, that she slid from the horse when they reached the bottom of the hill, searching the ground for anything that would explain what had happened to him.

Ehawee dismounted as well, her eyes focusing on a spot where the earth had been disturbed.

"He was taken by surprise here," Ehawee said, glancing at Emily, whose face had drained of color.

"Bandits, maybe. They took him and returned the way they came."

Emily put a hand to her shoulder, her fingers touching the bloody bandage as if it could help in some way. Then she looked down at the spot where the pine needles were scattered, leaving only bare earth, and went to her knees.

Ehawee came to stand beside her, looked closely and found a small splatter of blood.

"He was hit with something," she said. "And bled here."

Emily touched the spot with her fingers, then rubbed them together.

"There is not much," Ehawee said. "These men wanted him alive."

Emily looked up, her eyes worn and Ehawee regretted not letting her rest longer. But then she thought of Rand, thought of what he might be suffering and knew there would be no waiting on her part, either.

"We need to go," Emily said, standing now, moving towards her horse with slow, measured steps that spoke of her pain.

"I will change your bandage, first," she said, and the girl paused, nodding as Ehawee unbuttoned her dress, unwrapped the bloody bandage.

Ehawee looked at the wound, red and angry, and knew she should be resting, knew they should be at their cabin where she kept her medicines.

The shaft had not gone through, but the Blackfoot

were known to poison their arrows, causing infections even the yarrow could not soothe.

She opened her pouch, took out more herbs and used water from her canteen to clean the wound again.

Emily gritted her teeth.

"I am sorry," she said. "If we were at my cabin, or the tipi of my mother, there would be more help for you."

She shook her head. "I just need to find my son. And Caleb."

Ehawee tucked the cloth, buttoned her blouse over the top of it.

"Then we must go. The way is not good for horses past this valley. Then you must climb."

She nodded, and Ehawee looked at her, saw that her breathing was fast and knew she could not argue any more. If the arrow was poisoned there was nothing she could do for her.

She touched her own cheek, cut in the same way and wondered if they would die together somewhere in a forgotten glen, Rand and Caleb never knowing their fate.

They rode into the afternoon, watching as the sun sank against the mountains, the horses growing tired and Ehawee knew a time would come when they would have to leave them. She knew her people would take them if they found them wandering, hopeful the beautiful mare Emily rode would be cared for.

They did not speak, but instead stayed silent and

watchful, stopping every now and again to rest. Ehawee took to foraging at one spot and was able to find some juneberries and they sat down cross-legged in the meadow and ate them.

Emily laid down afterwards, slept for a short time and Ehawee wandered down the hill, the snowy blooms of the windflower giving her hope.

She had walked these hills with her mother, a woman of great wisdom when it came to healing plants, and she thanked her now, lifted her eyes to the darkening sky and spoke her name.

Moments later she dug the plants up, took the roots and smashed them between two rocks, making a poultice that would fight the infection that was making Emily sick.

"I will return you to your son," she said while making it, lifting her words to the Great Spirit who protected these hills. "I will return you to the one you love."

She touched Emily's head, feeling affection for this young girl, and she started awake, her blue eyes fearful until they focused on Ehawee.

"I have something for you," she said. "But you must sit up."

She took a breath, pulled herself from the ground and allowed Ehawee to remove the bandage she'd changed that afternoon. The poultice was cool to the touch, and Emily's face relaxed when it touched her skin.

"Thank you," she said. "I can never repay you for what you've done."

Ehawee smiled. "You can repay me by being a good mother to your son. And a good wife to Caleb."

Emily smiled, nodded in a way that said she would do as she asked.

Then they were climbing back on the horses, riding down to the bottom of the valley as the moon began peeking over the edge of the hills. Soon it was dusk, shadows playing tricks on their eyes when Ehawee decided it was time to let the horses go.

"This is not my mare," Emily protested. "She belongs to my friend, Clementine."

"My people will care for them when they are found," she said. "The creek runs through this valley, and my mother's people live at the end of it. The horses will follow the grass and the water."

Emily looked at her, then climbed down from her horse, stood in the moonlight while Ehawee dismounted, taking the things they would need from their saddlebags.

Then they were walking towards the place where Ehawee had seen the campfires, and Emily followed behind, her steps slowing the higher they climbed, the mountain called Owl Maker stabbing the sky like a spear.

Ehawee listened as they walked, stopping now and again and the silence seemed to breathe with them, the wind carrying to them the sounds of voices in the distance.

"Did you hear that?"

Ehawee did not answer.

"Do you think-"

"Yes," she said, unnerved, a noise to their left drawing her attention.

She dropped to the ground, unsheathed her knife and Emily pulled her gun, aimed at the darkness.

A man emerged from the shadows and Ehawee stood for a moment before taking a step forward.

"Kohana," she said, speaking slowly, not wanting to tell him what had happened to their brother. "We were to meet in the long meadow."

"I came from our mother," he said, his eyes moving to Emily. "She asks about you. And our brother."

Ehawee took a deep breath, told the tale of the Blackfoot coming from the valley, and her brother's face went still.

"Why is she here?" he asked, looking at Emily and Ehawee raised her shoulders, ready to speak in the girl's defense.

"He was not taken because of her," she said. "She gave him a good death."

Kohana's eyes narrowed, his hair blowing in the breeze.

Then he unsheathed his knife, took a handful of hair and cut it.

Emily stood, her gun never wavering even as her left arm hung useless at her side.

"My brother does not mean to harm you," Ehawee whispered. "He will help us."

Emily nodded, lowered her gun, all the while watching Kohana.

He stood in the moonlight, his head back, the wind blowing his black hair over his shoulders before moving towards a clearing. Once there, he stood for several minutes, saying words that were meant only for the darkness.

Then he was in front of them again, his eyes on Emily.

"We must walk slowly," Ehawee told him, "She is hurt."

Kohana made a noise low in his throat.

"An arrow pierced her shoulder," she said, and he looked at her, the same fear in his eyes she felt in her heart.

"Our way is through the high country."

Ehawee nodded, telling him without words that Emily would not be left behind.

The moon climbed higher, and as time passed, they heard voices more plainly, and began to see the glow of the campfires. Ehawee listened for the sound of Rand's voice and heard the soft cry of a baby instead.

Emily began to move faster, gathering her skirt with her good hand and Ehawee touched her arm.

"Slowly," she said. "We must watch and wait."

"My son—"

"Is with his father," she said.

"If Caleb knew I was coming... or Rand," she began, "We could overtake them. I'm a good shot and so is Ruthie-"

"We must be careful," she paused. "Or all is lost."

Emily's mouth tightened, and Ehawee understood her impatience, made worse when they found a rocky ledge above the campsite where the captives could be seen plainly.

Her husband lay next to the fire, bound by his feet to a younger man with fair hair. Emily gave a soft cry and Ehawee looked over, surprised to see her leaning forward.

"Emily."

"It's Caleb," she whispered, and Ehawee bent down, climbed as close as she could to the edge and noticed movement between the two.

"They are alive," she whispered. "But they are hurt."

Emily's mouth tightened.

"It's my fault," she said, and Kohana glanced at his sister, a quick jerk of his head telling her he was going to scout from another location.

He moved off and Ehawee drew close to Emily, touched her arm.

"He went down the hillside because of me," she mumbled. "Because of my pride. And the awful thing I said to him."

Ehawee did not move. "You must know when to keep quiet."

She shook her head.

"I'm no good at that."

"Then learn."

Emily swallowed, bent down to watch and after some time had passed, a figure appeared in the firelight that made her stiffen. He stood beside two of the bandits, his hair the color of fire.

It seemed as if he turned suddenly, looking up at the rocky ledge.

Emily backed away, her breathing shallow.

"He knows you are here," Ehawee whispered.

Emily nodded, slinking down behind the rocks but the man did not move, did not take his eyes from the rocks and Ehawee knew a spirit lived inside of him that allowed him to see what others could not.

Another voice rose to their hiding spot, and Emily seemed to recognize it because she stood on tiptoe, the top of her head just visible above the rocks.

Ehawee glanced down, saw a young woman with long, brown hair speaking to Emily's husband.

"Maddie..." Emily whispered, leaning forward again, her hands gripping the rocks.

"Above!" Marvin shouted, pointing to the ridge and the bandits pivoted on their feet, began to fire.

Stone shards exploded around them, showering on Emily and she ducked down, crawled back to her hiding place while Ehawee peered between a crack.

She saw Caleb kick out with his bound feet, saw him knock one of the gunmen over while Marvin drew his own revolver against the other, ordering him to stop.

"We must go," Ehawee hissed, knowing her brother would be waiting.

Emily shook her head. "My sister..."

"Come," Ehawee ordered, pulling on her arm. "Get up!"

The girl stumbled to her feet as shouts came from below.

"Emily!" Marvin shouted. "I know you're up there."

She paused, his voice seeming to rise like the embers from the fire.

"We have Caleb and Rand with us. And Jimmy is safe with Ruthie."

"Jimmy?" she said, moving forward and Ehawee touched her arm, willing her to run but wanting to hear what the man had to say.

"Show yourself to me," Marvin said, and at once there was a shout from Caleb, followed by Rand and Ehawee knew the bandits were dragging them away. Peering over the rock, she saw the two men shoving bandanas in their mouths to keep them from speaking.

"Show yourself to me, and I'll let them go."

Emily looked at Ehawee, then moved forward and stepped into the open, her hand on her gun.

It was a long moment before Marvin spoke again, and Ehawee saw the look on his face that said he desired his wife, saw the sickness that had taken hold of his heart and whispered lies into it.

"What do you want?" she asked, and Ehawee took an arrow from her quiver, placed it in the bow.

"You," he said. "All I have ever wanted is you."

"If you're thinking of shooting me, there's an arrow pointed at your heart right now."

Marvin held his hands up, laughed lightly.

"I don't want to kill you, Emily."

"Like hell you don't!" she cried, her hand tightening on her revolver and Marvin took a step back, motioned for the others to lower their guns.

"Meet me at dawn at French Creek," he said. "Beneath the Ponderosa Pine that is shaped like a pitchfork. Ehawee will know-"

"And then what?" she broke in, her eyes on Caleb as he lay struggling at the bandit's feet.

"I'll let this man and his sister go."

Emily waited, her voice rising with the wind.

"What about Rand?"

Marvin paused, his voice seeming to drift to the mountaintop as the woman stood silently beside him.

"The old man can return to his cabin after the gold is in my hands."

Ehawee's jaw tightened, knowing the treasure would not be found on French Creek.

She looked at Emily, shook her head.

"It is by the Owl Maker," she whispered. "Rand must be trying to trick him-"

Emily spoke, her eyes on her sister.

"And what will you do with Maddie?"

Marvin's laughter rose like a ghost, echoing against the moonlit rocks.

"Nothing she hasn't already allowed me to."

Emily pressed her lips together and watched her sister step away.

"What about my son?"

Marvin paused.

"We'll raise him together."

Emily closed her eyes, her hand dropping to her side and Ehawee thought she saw her lips moving, wondering if she might be praying.

After a moment she raised her head, nodded at the man before turning her back on him.

"I'll be there."

Chapter Thirty-Five

C aleb laid on the ground beside the man who'd pretended to be Rand Albright, the dirty bandana Slant had shoved in his mouth tasting of spit and whiskey and fought the urge to throw up.

He'd tried to sleep, images of Emily on the ridge above giving him hope.

He couldn't believe it when she first appeared, had thought she was a vision brought on by delirium but when she spoke, he knew she was real.

He'd seen blood on her blouse, and knew she'd been injured in the Blackfoot attack. And still, her determination to find them made him that much more willing to fight.

He'd kicked out with his foot, hit Rand in the side and the old man started, looked to where Slant, Casper and Hawkins had gathered around the fire, some sleeping, some drinking whiskey, but all in no state to bother with them.

Caleb scooted over towards him, motioned for him to bend down so he could take the bandana out of his mouth.

Once done, Rand returned the favor.

"Where's Marvin?" Caleb hissed.

"I saw him go off with Maddie."

Caleb rolled over onto his back, hoping it would look like he was sleeping.

"Ready to tell me what the hell is going on around here?"

"Caleb—"

"Should I call you Rand? Or Ezra? Or Santa Claus?"

The old man chuckled.

"I don't think this is funny."

"I have to laugh, or I'll go crazy. My wife was up there. And my niece."

"*Rand's* niece."

The old man signed, waited a moment before speaking.

"He was a good man. And I took advantage of that. We traded together when he first came to the mountains, along with a fellow named Marquardt who was friendly with the Sioux."

"Seems Indian Crow found gold in French Creek and told Rand about it. At first, he wanted to take it out and make our fortunes, gave me the name of a man back in Michigan who would help, and I traveled east, rounded him up and a few others that happened to come along at the right time."

"When we returned to the Black Hills, he'd changed his mind. Indian Crow had gone back to his family and Rand was sick, didn't want to waste what time he had left and so he abandoned the mountains, never to be seen again."

"And he died at Laramie," Caleb said, thinking of Clem and Jake. And Beatrice. "That was my friend who was killed."

"I'm sorry for that," Rand said. "Just like I'm sorry for everything else. After Albright left, we decided to do the job without him, and got as far as the Owl Maker before the Sioux came for us. Indian Crow found us there and became my blood brother when he spoke for me."

"Spoke for you?"

"I'd written my name on that rock, left it on the Owl Maker thinking we would die but when I went back to destroy it and the record of what I'd done, it was gone. Indian Crow said the mountain took it back and that's when I knew I had to become a new person. I'd known Rand for so long, it seemed like I just stepped into his skin."

Caleb looked at the sky, saw embers floating towards the treetops and wondered what would become of them when dawn broke over French Creek.

"Does Ehawee know?"

Rand laughed again. "She is my wife."

Caleb stiffened, his thoughts on Emily.

"And she let you write your letters, let that family think you were one of them-"

"It saved my soul, I think. And when Emily told me about the fire, there was no question about helping her."

Caleb swallowed, grateful for this man despite the trouble he'd caused.

"When I became Rand Albright, I left the name of Ezra Kind behind me. In all ways. I'd be obliged if you remember that."

Caleb nodded; his throat full.

"And what exactly am I supposed to do when we get to French Creek tomorrow? Did you tell Marvin that's where the gold was?"

Rand looked over his shoulder, sat up as if he saw something and Caleb turned quickly, surprised to see Ruthie running towards him, Jimmy in her arms, the large man who wore the bearskin coat lumbering after her.

"Caleb!" she cried, rushing past Slant, Casper and Hawkins, who turned to stare at her.

She skidded to a halt beside him, went to her knees and touched his face.

"Did they hurt you?"

He chuckled.

"Does it look like it?"

She smiled.

"Still a smart aleck, I see."

Settling Jimmy on the ground beside her, she faced her brother.

"You look beastly, if I'm being truthful. Gris must have been worried because he told me I could leave the low camp and come up here."

"Gris?"

She motioned to the large man, who stood a few feet away, his shotgun pointed at the ground, watching them.

"Was Emily here?" she asked.

Rand nodded. "She was on the ridge with my wife."

"Your wife?"

"Ruthie," Caleb began. "This is Rand Albright. Or at least the man we thought was him."

Ruthie raised an eyebrow.

"I'll tell you later."

She turned back to her brother, her eyes narrowed.

"How did you and Em get split up?"

His face fell, a darkness gathering in his eyes.

"What muttonhead thing did you say to her?"

He shrugged his shoulders, and she could tell he'd been gnawing on the words since the moment he'd said them.

"Just that it was hard to believe Celia was gone."

Ruthie reached out, smacked him in the shoulder.

"How could you be so stupid?"

"I wasn't thinking... but the truth is the truth. I miss her, Ruthie."

He watched his sister's eyes soften, watched her gaze down at Jimmy, who was wiggling on the blanket, excited by the fire.

"I miss her, too. But it's best if you don't mention the woman you used to love to the woman you love right now."

"I know I'm an ass, okay," he snapped. "And believe me when I say I'll never forgive myself if something happens to her."

"You'd best worry about yourself," she said. "Because I do believe Emily is the brains of your little outfit."

"And you'd best worry about keeping your hands on Jimmy," he added.

"I *am*."

"I warned you not to get attached to that baby-"

"You should talk," she spat. "Just admit you love him, and you're fit to be tied right now."

"I'm fit to be tied all right-"

"You two put on quite a show," Rand said, a strange smile on his face and Caleb broke down laughing, a thing that felt as good as anything he'd ever done before.

"You're impossible," she spat, her face blazing red. "Did you ever think Em was trying to get your dang *attention*!"

"I give her plenty of attention."

"Sure, you do," Ruthie laughed. "When you want something."

A movement caught their eye and Gris raised his shotgun, motioned for Ruthie to grab the baby and come with him.

"They're taking us to French Creek in the morning," Caleb said quickly. "Emily will be there, trading herself for our freedom."

"No—"

Gris lumbered forward and she bent down, kissed her brother on the cheek as Marvin came into view, Maddie trailing behind him.

"Don't run off on my account, Miss Ruth," he said, in good spirits. "I was sure Gris would bring you up here sooner or later."

Stopping at the fire, he said something to the men sitting around it, then came over to Caleb and Rand. Standing above them, he stretched his arms above his head, smiled at the moon.

"I have to say, Madeline Ives never fails to lift my mood. You might want to give it a go, Caleb, see how she compares to her sister—"

He stopped mid-sentence, his attention drawn to a movement in the trees.

"Caleb," Ruthie whispered, falling to her knees beside him.

A woman, her dark hair spilling over her shoulders, had stepped from the darkness of the forest.

Caleb sat upright, unable to speak until Marvin did so for him.

"Stop, there!" he cried, unholstering his gun and the woman came forward, stumbling now, until she collapsed beside Hawkins.

"Miss," he said quickly, kneeling beside her, lifting her chin so he could see her face. "Are you hurt?"

She didn't answer, and Marvin moved forward, bent down to look at her as well.

"I know this woman," Hawkins exclaimed.

"Like hell you do!" Casper whooped. "She's mine!"

"No, she ain't!" Slant cried, edging forward until Marvin pointed his gun in the air and fired a shot.

The noise didn't seem to startle her, and Hawkins looked into her eyes, swept his hat from his head.

"Miss," he whispered, his tone soothing. "Tell me who you are."

"Beatrice," Caleb spoke up, his mind in a freefall. "Her name is Beatrice."

Chapter Thirty-Six

E mily laid on the hard ground beside Ehawee and Kohana and could not sleep. She thought about her mother and father, and Maddie, wondering when she had begun to love Marvin.

She remembered the dinners at their house, remembered Marvin glancing between the two of them as he sat across the table, spinning his stories about the north country.

Had her betrayal found footing in a lingering glance, the soothing tone he used while speaking of the large house he hoped to build.

Had he made love to her, sweetly the first time, only to remind her of her failings later?

But maybe she hadn't failed. Or if she had, just pretended otherwise.

She'd always followed the rules more closely, always wanted to please their parents so desperately.

Would Marvin be any different?

She thought back to all the times she'd told Maddie secrets about Marvin, the times she'd glanced away in discomfort.

Emily had always thought she pitied her, when in reality she hated her.

She turned to her side, pulled the robe Ehawee had given her over her throbbing shoulder.

She touched her bandage, wishing for Caleb and Jimmy and Ruthie, for Clem and Jake and the wide, blue ocean that called from California, the scent of oranges on the wind.

She looked into the darkness, saw Kohana sitting on a stump and knew he was sleeping. It was strange how he could do it with his back straight, his bow and arrow across his lap, a revolver in his belt.

But even a man like him could become careless without meaning to.

A single gunshot, muted by wind and distance made her spine stiffen and she saw Kohana stir, his eyes opening before slowly falling shut again.

For one wild moment she imagined Caleb killing her husband.

Then she pictured the opposite, a tightness spreading to her chest as she pulled herself from the ground.

It would not work to spend the night here, listening for ghosts in the woods.

She stood slowly, watching Kohana and Ehawee but they did not stir.

French Creek lay in a valley below Marvin's camp, and she knew it would take time to get there.

She thought of going to the Owl Maker instead, thought of bringing the gold to Marvin and ending everything once and for all and knew he would kill Caleb and Ruthie and maybe even her uncle if she did not do as he said.

But if she could get to French Creek first, maybe she could turn things to her advantage.

Before she knew it, she'd walked down the hill, the moonlight covering her like a bridal veil, her thoughts wandering to the names she'd been called by.

Daughter, Sister, Wife, Mother, Friend, Lover, Orphan...

The last one cut to her core, causing other memories to tumble free as she crept silently through the darkness...

Murderer, Adulteress, Liar, Whore...

And she couldn't argue that she wasn't.

The moon sailed higher, cresting above the pines before moving downwards, the shadows long and lean, an army of ghosts standing sentinel in a haunted wood.

She touched her bandage again, pain jumping through her skin and stopped to catch her breath. The world seemed to whirl around her, causing her to brace herself against a tree. Reaching into her pocket, she pulled out some juneberries Ehawee had given her and ate them.

For a moment she felt better, then sick to her

stomach as she emptied the last of her stomach's contents into the grass.

Disgusted, she wiped the back of her mouth, bent to pick some grass and chewed on it for a moment before spitting it out.

The wound was making her weaker, and she found herself weaving on her feet, surprised that she could move at all.

Instead, she straightened her spine, walked on until she came to a sloping valley. Gathering the last of her strength, she stumbled to the bottom of it, losing her footing one moment, tumbling the next until she landed beside what she believed to be French Creek.

She crawled to the riverbank, unwound her bandage and soaked it in the cold water.

Pressing it to her shoulder, she felt instant relief and took a breath. She stayed that way for several minutes, washing out the bandage several times while trying to preserve the poultice Ehawee had placed there.

She felt the throbbing subside and wished for a drink of the whiskey she'd enjoyed while sitting alone in the rocking chair.

She sat for several minutes, trying to decipher the landscape when she heard a twig snap across the creek.

She drew her gun, ready to fire, and saw a figure moving against the trees.

A figure she knew all too well.

"Clementine!" she shouted, unsure if she was

dreaming and the woman stopped, called her name in return.

Then Clem was waving her arms, rushing across the creek, and Emily stumbled forward, intent to meet her halfway.

Her feet slid on the wet stones, and she fell, the current pulling at her skirt and it made it hard to stand, hard to get anywhere when a hand hoisted her to her feet, helped her cross the water to the opposite bank.

"Em," Jake's voice sounded like heaven and Christmas and clean bedsheets and a million other wonderful things. "We found you-"

"Found me?" she asked, the next words gone as Clem threw her arms around her.

She sucked her breath in, pulling away and they stood, the blood on her bodice suddenly visible.

"I was hit by an arrow," Emily said, and the others were silent, unable to speak. "Ehawee tended to me."

"Emily," Clementine said again, pulling her friend into a more careful embrace and she folded against her, tears she'd held back running down her cheeks.

"How are you here?" she asked. "We left you at Chimney Rock."

Jake looked at her, and she could tell he was weighing his words.

"There was a shooting at Laramie and Rose is dead. We had to take Beatrice and run but before we did... we found something out, Em. Something that might be hard for you to take in."

Her heart sped up, the pulse beating in her shoulder, and she reached behind her, sat down on the grassy bank.

"We found your uncle's grave," Clementine said softly, and Emily listened to her words, not understanding what they meant.

"We knew we had to come and find you, and so we rode north until we came to the hills and then followed your tracks to the campfires," Jake continued. "Beatrice offered to distract them, and I was able to sneak to the edge of the camp and talk to Caleb and Ezra Kind. That's how we knew you'd be here."

"Ezra Kind?" Emily echoed, unable to understand how this one last thing could be taken from her.

"Your uncle Rand was a good man, too good to take part in what the others wanted to do, and so Ezra Kind took his name, used it after he died in Laramie."

"But he wrote to us," she said, her words hollow and senseless. "He said he loved us."

"He does," Jake said. "They both do."

Emily sat up straighter, remembering the care Ehawee had given her.

"She knew?"

Clementine put a hand on her arm and nodded.

"Ezra Kind became Rand Albright, Em. He's sorry for what he did back then, and he wants to make it up to you."

Emily said nothing, just sat on the grass and put her head in her hands, memories of the long-ago days in the front room coming clear, her journals in front of her, a packet of paints Gerald had purchased on the table.

She'd chosen yellow for the flowers she had drawn, and then green for the stems, and then purple... one by one... she'd decided how her picture was going to be.

She could do the same thing now.

Lifting her head, she looked at her friends.

"Uncle Rand hid the gold at the high peak called Owl Maker. You're going to go there and find it. I'll wait here for Marvin."

"No," Clementine protested.

"After he lets Caleb and Ruthie go, I'll take him there."

"Rand set traps," Jake said. "He told us about one of them. Right next to the rock they call the Needle."

"Use it," she said. "I'll make sure that sonofabitch finds it."

"Em—"

"French Creek was a diversion. But Uncle Rand's cabin is here."

"Where?" Clem asked.

Emily looked over her shoulder, saw the moonlight spilling over the creek and the Ponderosa Pine Marvin had spoken of.

"Past the next bend," she said, her heart lifting. "Hidden behind a copse of trees."

They helped her to her feet, walked with her to the place where the cabin had been in her dreams and when they rounded the corner, it stood dark against the forest, a blanket of moonlight making it seem as bright as midday.

"It's here," Emily breathed, the picture she'd painted coming to life and she moved faster then, the door opening before her and at once they were looking through cupboards, taking out food and medicine that would help with the journey to come.

It wasn't long before the sky began to lighten and Emily looked to her friends, knowing what she had to do.

"Emily," Clementine said, her eyes watery as Jake stood at the door.

"Stop crying," Emily said, the picture in front of her as clear as if she'd painted it herself. "And go find that gold."

Chapter Thirty-Seven

Ruthie laid beside her brother, James cradled against her chest, and listened to the men snoring in various volumes around the fire. The flames had died to embers, the night almost spent, and she knew they would have to get up soon and make their way towards French Creek and the gold Marvin was counting on to get out of these mountains alive.

She reached out, touched Caleb's hair and wondered if he would live to see the end of this day.

After Beatrice had stumbled from the woods, there had been quite a ruckus, so much so that Jake was able to crawl to the edge of the firelight and speak to Caleb.

He'd explained what happened in Laramie and Ruthie did her best to give them time by rushing up to Beatrice, asking all sorts of questions that seemed to rile up everyone and before Marvin was any wiser, Jake had vanished again.

"Miss Beatrice was left with vagabonds and will stay under my protection," Hawkins announced, his arrogance roused, and Ruthie went back to sit beside Caleb, her heart lifting because her friends were alive and trying to help them.

She sat there for some time, Jimmy asleep in his blanket beside her and was grateful Marvin hadn't come over and asked to hold him.

She'd been using the blanket as a sling, just like Emily, and he fit comfortably inside of it. So comfortably, she hoped everyone would see how wrong it was to separate them.

Straining further, she saw Jack Hawkins propped up against an old stump, half awake, Beatrice sleeping with her head against his knee.

The young woman had braided and unbraided her hair several times while Ruthie sat watching, her words strange and slurred and the girl knew the death of her mother and Putt's arrest had damaged her mind.

"I'm not waiting around until morning," Caleb's voice startled her. "Try loosening this rope."

"Try again, you mean," she said, the chafing on her fingers testament to her earlier efforts. She'd tried hard not to arouse suspicion, and labored quietly under the rheumy eye of Slant, who seemed angry now that his whiskey was gone.

Everyone seemed angry, come to think of it, and Ruthie hoped it was because the gang was wising up, realizing no amount of gold would make up for what they'd already sacrificed.

Birdsong jarred her thoughts, and she realized she'd been asleep as Hawkins sat straight, gently waking Beatrice before rising to his feet to rouse the others.

One by one the party rose and stretched. The fire was built up again and coffee warmed over the top of it.

Slant came over to where Rand lay and kicked him in the shoulder. The old man sputtered and spit, then rolled over onto his back and heaved himself into a sitting position as Marvin and Maddie stood on the other side of the fire.

Gris lumbered to her side, bringing a plate of biscuits and beans.

"Coffee?" he asked, and she shook her head, nodded to Caleb.

"He'd like some."

Gris looked at him for a beat, then handed him the cup he'd brought for Ruthie.

"Maybe if we get out of this you can keep him as a pet," Caleb joked once he was out of earshot.

Ruthie frowned, then placed Jimmy over her shoulder and burped him as if it were any other day.

And it could have been, had Marvin not come to stand before them, cutting Caleb's bonds himself with his pocketknife before ordering him to his feet.

"Run and I'll cut your sister from neck to navel."

Caleb shook his head. "You might have to go through that grizzly bear first."

Marvin smiled, but something in his eyes told Ruthie he knew his hold was slipping.

"Get moving," Marvin ordered, and Ruthie rose beside her brother, tucked Jimmy into his sling and began following the others as they walked slowly downhill.

All the while, she scanned the forest for signs of her friends, half expecting to see Jake ride up on his brown gelding. She saw Rand watching the woods as well, no doubt looking for his wife and her people, but all remained silent, the only sounds the talk of those in their company and the rushing of the wind through the tall pines.

It seemed an hour had passed before they heard the song of French Creek. The land was rugged, the trees towering above their heads as Marvin left his place beside Maddie and moved to the front of the group.

Ruth watched as he ran to the riverbank, standing on the edge, gazing into the rushing water for what seemed like forever.

"No cabin in sight," he mocked. "Just that Ponderosa Pine you keep talking about, old man."

Then he jumped on a rock, seeming to leapfrog across the water, looking for a calm spot where the current was settled.

The men seemed restless, shifting from foot to foot, turning in place, watching for any sign that would tell them what they were supposed to do.

"They won't find anything here," Rand chuckled under his breath.

Ruthie turned on him, wondering what sort of trick he had up his sleeve when Marvin leapt back across the rocks, his boots sliding at the last, so he had to jump for shore. Once there, he came towards Rand and struck him in the gut before anyone could move.

"Where's the gold?" he asked as the man doubled over. "You said it would be here."

A silence descended on the company as they waited for him to answer.

"Where is it, old man?" Slant cried, and Casper nodded, touching his backwards revolvers.

"Maybe my niece knows," he answered at last. "Or my wife."

"Is this a joke?" Marvin asked, his voice rising, and the others began to whisper until Casper spoke up, his voice close to a whine.

"Where's the gold, Boss?"

Marvin strode up to him, stuck a finger in his face.

"You shut your fucking mouth; you hear me? The gold was swept downstream and we're going to get it."

Slant slid his hat from his head, scratched at his dirty hair.

"That sounds like a lotta work."

"I don't pay you to sit on your ass—" Marvin began.

"You don't pay us at all," Casper spoke up and Marvin drew his gun, placed it beneath Casper's chin.

"Another word, and I'll blow your brains into that tree."

Casper stood still, as did the others, watching what

Marvin would do, fear and frustration and just the smallest spark of anger in their eyes.

"There's a spot where the water's shallow," Rand spoke up. "The gold likely washed out there."

Marvin turned his head slowly.

"Would Emily think the same? Or your wife?"

Rand chuckled. "Emily would tell you there's all sorts of hiding spots out here. And not to count your chickens before they're hatched."

"Would she, now?"

Jimmy, as if in response to his father's voice, began to fuss, and Ruthie took him from his sling, bounced him on her hip and it caught Marvin's attention.

"Take that baby," he said, jerking his head in Maddie's direction.

She stiffened, shook her head.

"Take him," he ordered, and Maddie's face turned white as she took a faltering step forward.

"Let Ruth keep him," Slant said. "Maddie ain't got no business with that kid."

"I agree," Hawkins said, his tone dry. "I believe the young lady has done an excellent job nursing and burping and changing those awful diapers."

"Shut up," Marvin growled. "I run this outfit."

"Do ya?" Gris grumbled from behind and Marvin opened his mouth, took one look at the man in the bearskin coat and shut it again.

"Get the baby," he said to Maddie and Ruthie tightened her grip.

"Stay where you are, Miss Maddie," Gris said. "We don't want no one gettin' hurt."

Marvin stood, his control toppling around him and turned suddenly. Looking downstream, he pointed to a thick copse of trees.

"I think I see the place," he said, his tone softer. "Let's scout it out."

Hawkins looked at Beatrice before putting his arm around her.

"This lady needs to rest-"

"She can rest later."

"I will not allow it, sir," Hawkins said. "I have been pushed too far and wish to assert my authority as a member of the U.S. Army-"

Marvin took his gun out, marched up to Beatrice and put the barrel against her temple.

"You wish to assert your *what*?" Marvin asked and Hawkins held his hands up, looking in horror at Beatrice, who began to laugh.

A shot rang out and Ruthie jumped, her terror complete as Beatrice fell like a ragdoll into the grass, the side of her head gone.

Jimmy began to cry as Hawkins went to his knees, a wail rising from his chest that made Ruthie cover her face.

"*Shit,*" Caleb cursed, turning her into his shoulder and she bit down on her lip to keep from screaming.

"Do you believe I can lead this outfit now?" Marvin screamed. "Or have you still been *pushed too far*?"

Ruthie heard Hawkins mutter something, heard Maddie softly crying as Jimmy's cries turned into muted sobs, then hiccups.

"Do you doubt I will end each and every one of you, if you do not do exactly as I say?"

More silence, and Ruthie prayed they were pulling their guns, ready to overtake him.

"We're moments away from becoming rich men," he said, turning suddenly to Hawkins and clapping him on the back. "Then you can buy any woman you want."

"You killed her," he whispered.

"He's gone loco," Slant echoed. "I ain't ever seen no one blast at a lady that a way-"

Marvin walked away as if he didn't hear, waved at them to follow.

"Come this way if you want the gold, otherwise I will keep it all for myself and blow the rest of you to bits."

They stood looking at each other, their eyes on anything but Beatrice.

"Okay, Boss," Casper nodded after some time had passed. Then he moved to join him, motioning to Slant who in turn motioned to Gris, who stood looking at Hawkins, still kneeling beside Beatrice.

"Let's go," he said, his tone gruff. "Get up."

Hawkins sat, and Ruth went to him, put a hand on his shoulder, her eyes skipping over what lay in the grass.

"She didn't deserve that," she whispered. "I'm so sorry."

Hawkins nodded, then got slowly to his feet.

They moved downstream, past the tree that looked like a pitchfork and at one point Marvin jumped into the water, waded to the center where he stood, howling in laughter.

"You see something, Boss?" Slant asked and Marvin laughed again, his head back.

"You fucking bitch!" he cried to the mountains. "Where's my gold?"

The others stood, unsure what to do and Gris looked at Ruthie, nodded in the slightest and she knew this was her chance to run.

But she couldn't.

On the other side of the river a woman emerged from the forest, as wild and brave as Ruthie remembered and she felt Caleb tense beside her, his voice an agonized whisper.

"Emily..."

Chapter Thirty-Eight

Emily knew everything in her life had led to this stepping forth from the wilderness, this change from darkness to light.

And so, she did.

Scanning the faces of the people on the other side of the creek, she prayed everyone she loved was there and saw Caleb and Ruthie- a small bundle she assumed was Jimmy nestled at her chest.

A joy so pure it was painful washed over her, and she bit down hard on her back teeth to keep from weeping.

Waiting in the darkness, she thought of her parents, of James and Carrie and the man she had come to call Uncle Rand, of Ehawee and Kohana and Mahkah, praying she would have the strength to finish what had begun the day Marvin walked into the store.

She stood now, her eyes on Caleb and knew he

wanted to run to her as Ruthie grabbed his arm, holding him in place.

"Where's my gold?" Marvin asked, Maddie standing silently beside him, her eyes down. "Ezra Kind said you might know where it is."

"I do," she answered, her gaze returning to her sister before she realized someone was missing.

"Where's Beatrice?" she asked.

No one spoke at first, but then Hawkins approached the riverbank, pulled himself to his full height and straightened his shoulders.

"Your husband killed her," he said, his arrogance reminding her of their time in Kearny. "In cold blood, as she stood by my side. I intend to bring the matter to the attention of the authorities once I have returned to my post."

"She was the daughter of a whore," Marvin cried, jumping onto a nearby rock, his bad leg causing him to totter at first. "And as crazy as the day is long."

Hawkins cleared his throat, then turned back to Emily as though he were addressing the Queen of England.

"Nevertheless, a crime has been committed and I will not stand by and allow such a travesty-"

A shot rang out and Hawkins clutched his chest, pitched forward into the creek as blood pooled around him.

Maddie screamed while the others jumped in different directions, unsure if Marvin or some unseen enemy had shot the soldier.

Her husband holstered his gun, ending speculation as Slant and Casper ran to the edge of the creek, looking down on the fallen man while the others stood in silence.

"He talked too much."

"Dammit, Boss!" Slant cried. "You gotta stop killin' people."

"More gold for you," he paused. "Which brings me to my original question."

"I'll take you to it," Emily said. "On one condition-"

Marvin smirked, "You want me to let your friends go? What assurance do I have that you will keep your word?"

"The same assurance I had when you married me."

At that moment Hawkins' body hit the rock Marvin was perched on. He looked down, pushed him off with his boot as though he were nothing more than a weed caught in the current.

The soldier turned belly up, his eyes open and staring, then continued downstream before disappearing around the sharp bend.

Marvin looked at her, a smile yanking at his mouth.

"I'll take you up on your offer," he said. "But we must go alone."

She saw Caleb move again, the large man in the bearskin coat reaching over to help Ruthie hold him in place.

"Let them go, first."

Marvin touched his chin. "What of our son, my sweet?"

Emily looked at the woman holding him.

"He stays with Ruthie."

Marvin did not speak at first, but stared at her, his eyes slowly filling with hatred.

"You would keep him from me?"

A snicker from one of the men and her husband turned quickly on his rock in the middle of French Creek, surrounded by those who either feared or hated him.

A deadly silence descended on the group until all that could be heard was the rushing water.

"Make a choice. Your son or the gold."

He stood still for seemed like forever before pointing his finger at her.

"Fuck it, then," he shouted. "And fuck *you!*"

"Is that a yes?"

He paused, considering. "What happens after we find it?"

She paused, her eyes on Caleb.

"I'll go with you."

Caleb moved again, his voice piercing her heart.

"Don't do it!"

Marvin turned then, leapt from his perch and strode to where Caleb stood. Pulling his gun, he held it against the side of his head.

Emily pulled her revolver and placed it against her temple.

"Kill him and I'll do the same to myself," she shouted, her eyes on Marvin.

No one spoke or dared to move.

"You would leave our son motherless?"

She looked at Ruthie.

"He has one. And she's a damn sight better than me."

She saw Ruthie's shoulders shake, saw her cover her mouth with her hand.

Marvin paused, readjusted his hold on the gun.

"Step away," she said. "Or you'll never find your gold."

Marvin paused, seeming to consider her words.

"And what if I don't care, Em? What if I only want to see the look on your face when I blow his brains all over Gris, here?"

She stood straighter; her face impassive.

"Do it, then."

Something shifted in Marvin- she could see it as plainly as she saw the sun, or the wind blowing the hair on Gris' bearskin coat. It was a feeling as well, a change in the way he'd always seen her, and in the way he would think of her from this moment on.

He lowered his gun.

She waited a moment before doing the same.

"I'm going to enjoy this time with my wife," he said while turning to look Caleb in the eye. "It's been a long while since we were alone."

Caleb struggled forward, caught again by Gris as Marvin turned to his men.

"Meet me at the Owl Maker," he instructed his men. "You'll get your share then."

They grumbled, unhappy with his decision.

"Set them loose."

"Boss-" Casper began.

"*Do it!*"

"Marvin," Maddie spoke, and Emily turned to see her standing alone beside the bandits.

She began to move towards him, but he raised a hand.

"Stay with the boys," he said gruffly. "And meet me at the peak."

"But-" she began.

"On second thought," he said, and Emily knew it was anything but. "You'd best take that baby. Just in case my wife gets any funny ideas."

"No," Emily whispered, watching as Slant and Casper began to walk towards Ruthie.

Gris reached for her just as Slant and Casper drew their guns.

Maddie paused before reaching into the sling. Jimmy began to cry, his tiny head turning towards Ruthie and Emily felt the world begin to go black.

"Give him back," she begged. "Please."

"When things are settled up," Marvin said. "Can't expect me to take all the risk, can you?"

"Listen here," Gris said, and Marvin shook his head.

"You're going soft on me. Keep it up and your share becomes mine."

The large man stepped back, and Emily listened to her son's wails, feeling like her skin was on fire.

Not wanting to see the faces of the people she loved, she turned quickly, plunged blindly into the forest and up the opposite bank.

One step at a time, she climbed the sloping bluff, her shoulder burning, and Marvin came to stand beside her once they'd reached the top.

"I had to do it, Em," he said, as if reading her thoughts. "You understand."

She stood, her breath labored, the wound pounding with her heart.

"Maddie can't feed him."

A pause.

"Can you?"

She nodded quickly.

"Then we'd better keep moving."

She took a step, pain radiating down her arm and stopped short.

"Did you take an arrow?" he asked, and she did not know what to say, so she kept quiet.

"Damn," he whistled. "You've come a long way from that prissy thing I saw standing in the store that morning."

She didn't answer.

"Let me look at it—" he reached for her shoulder.

She pulled away.

"You're no use to Jimmy like this."

The name jarred her, made her think of all the things he would grow up to be.

"All right," she said, standing still and he came closer, touched the buttons at the collar of her dress, undoing them as he had so many times before.

"That's a bad shot and those hostiles like to smear their spearheads in shit. Might not make it through the night if that thing festers much longer."

"That should suit you just fine."

He bowed, motioned for her to lead the way.

An hour passed.

And then another.

She thought of Ehawee and Kohana, wondering if they had awakened to discover her gone and made their way to the creek, watching from the forest while she bargained with her husband.

Another hour passed before she saw the spires Jake had told her about.

They were close now. Emily glanced at her husband, surprised he had climbed so far with a bad leg.

Moving forward, she picked her way towards the tallest one, the Owl Maker rising to the east.

They would be hiding behind it, guns drawn, ready to spring the trap once he stood in the place they had marked.

But things had changed now that Maddie had Jimmy.

"Are we close?" he asked, "Our son's getting hungry, I'm sure."

Far up on the rocks, she saw a glimmer catch the sun and knew what it was.

Marvin saw it too and began to run.

"Stop!" she called, unwilling to see what the bandits would do to her son if she returned to the high peak without their leader.

What *Maddie* would do...

He didn't listen, just plunged headfirst towards the gold watch Jake had placed there.

"I'll be damned," he whooped. "I thought you were pulling my leg!"

"Marvin," she raced to him, hopeful Clem and Jake would do something when they saw her.

"I'll be damned," he said again, as if to himself. "It isn't possible."

Grabbing his arm, she yanked him back and he spun on her, his hand raised to strike her when the earth caved in, and they tumbled into darkness.

Chapter Thirty-Nine

Caleb stood holding his sister, watching the bandits as they walked towards the north country.

Slant glanced over his shoulder.

"Follow us an' you're dead."

Maddie stood, unsure what to do with a squirming, crying baby and began to walk.

"No..." Ruthie cried again, and Casper turned this time, pointed his gun at her.

"You shut your mouth. I stood up for you once but that baby there's gonna make me rich and I don't care how good a wet nurse you are. You can't keep him!"

She looked at Gris and the man shook his head.

"You stay away, now," he said, his tone wavering. "I mean it."

And so, Caleb had no choice but to let them go, his heart beating hot in his chest.

It had taken everything inside of him to let Emily leave with Marvin, and still he couldn't believe he was standing free beside his sister, able to walk back to Laramie and continue west as though nothing had happened.

A dusty feeling came into his mouth, and he knew there was no way in hell he would leave the mountains without the woman he loved.

Rand waited until the others were out of sight, then came to Caleb.

"She's some lady," he said. "Saved our skin more times than I can count and got what she wanted to boot- aside from losing Jimmy."

Caleb looked at him, disturbed by the way he was acting.

"Maybe we should climb up after them," Ruthie offered, looking to the spot in the forest where they had vanished. "Stay behind so they don't notice."

Caleb rubbed at the back of his neck, thinking of the blood on Emily's blouse.

"Do you think it's possible?" he asked. "Marvin's armed."

"So is Em," Ruthie said. "And she's a better shot."

"We could," Rand said, stroking his beard. "But I'll do you one better."

Caleb looked at him sharply.

"What do you mean?"

The old man smiled, the first real one Caleb had seen in days.

"We could go to my cabin and get my guns."

Ruthie looked up, her nose red from crying. "Your *cabin?*"

Caleb looked at his sister, afraid of the hope that had risen within him.

"There's nothing here."

Ezra Kind laughed. "If Marvin had gone past that copse of aspen trees he would have seen it. I'm sure Em raided my cabinets and found herself some medicine. Might have eaten breakfast, too."

"Your *cabin*?" Caleb repeated. "Is right here. And Marvin missed it?"

Ruthie jumped up and down, clapping her hands. "And you're saying it has food and water and—"

"Guns," Rand finished. "All the makings of a daring rescue."

Caleb felt a power surge into his lungs and heart and mind, alive for the first time since he'd walked down the hillside and away from Emily.

Then he was running, everything else forgotten in his rush to see if Rand was telling the truth.

The cabin was where he'd said it would be, and he couldn't believe the stroke of luck they'd had in Marvin missing it.

But maybe it was more than that, like the coming together of all the things he and Emily were- the starting over, and *loving* over, and taking the past and making it into something better because they'd decided to.

He'd learned about things like that in Sunday school, had felt the stirrings inside himself when Mahkah and Kohana spoke of the spirit that lived in these hills.

You will paint the sky for war or peace...

He'd tried to make things right.

And now he was going to finish the job.

He didn't dare think about it for long, couldn't imagine what it would be like to live with Emily on their farm by the ocean. He could see her face in the morning light, her eyes soft and sleepy as she kissed him. He would reach for her, finally able to touch her in the way he wanted.

He thought of their baby growing inside of her and yanked the door of the cabin open, his eyes scanning the room for anything he could use.

A trunk lay at the end of the bed, and he ran to it, opened it.

A rifle and two revolvers lay on the bottom, a packet of cartridges beside it.

"Throw me the Dragoon," Rand spoke from behind and Caleb grabbed it, tossed it to him.

"Ruthie's good with a rifle," he said. "I'll take the Navy."

A clamoring in the cupboards told him she was gathering food for their journey, and he turned, strode outside with the gun in hand.

He stood, feeling the power restored to him after

so long without a sidearm, and aimed at the rock Marvin had been standing on.

Leveling his arm, he shot at it, saw splinters of rock shoot into the sky.

The next moment Rand and Ruthie were beside him, anxious to get moving.

"How do we get there?" Ruthie asked, and Rand pointed to the hillside, started walking towards it.

"I know another way. With any luck my wife will be waiting for us."

Caleb looked at him, amazed at the confidence he held and understood it had grown over their many years living together in this place. Then he thought of Emily, remembering the moment she'd held the gun to her temple, betting on Marvin's pride to be his undoing.

Rand seemed to sense what he was thinking.

"That was a helluva thing she did up there."

He nodded, holstered the gun.

"And you would do the same for her. As you are right now, heading into these hills instead of walking back to Laramie like a sensible fellow."

Caleb smiled. "Ruthie'd never let me leave that baby."

Rand laughed. "*You'd* never leave that baby. And you shouldn't. He'll be yours soon and you'll have to raise him to rise above all of this."

Caleb felt the heaviness of his words settle on his shoulders.

Jimmy would be his. And it would be his job to

show him how to become a man when he'd barely learned the trick of it himself.

His mind began to take him down darkened paths and Rand was quiet for some time, picking his way over rocks that would have made a younger man stumble.

"You will be his father," Rand said. "Remember that. And don't doubt it."

He stopped, taking a moment to catch his breath when a strange sound rose like the call of a great bird above them.

Rand seemed to snap to attention, moving faster than Caleb thought possible.

"Ehawee," he called, jumping from rock to rock and Caleb fell behind, a large boulder blocking his view until he reached the top.

Rand was running now, into the arms of a woman who stood in the meadow as if she had always been there.

They embraced, and he saw him kiss her forehead, pull away and look at her to make sure she was sound from head to foot.

It was then Caleb saw the man standing beside her, his face hardening and he recognized him as the second warrior he'd seen while hunting on the prairie.

"Kohana," Ehawee began, and the man stepped forward, his finger in Caleb's face.

"I warned you," he said. "And now you have brought war."

Rand put his hand on the man's chest, spoke to

him in his own language as Ehawee came to stand beside Ruthie, her face telling the girl she had nothing to fear.

"This man is not the reason we are here," she said. "It is my husband's shame, and now we must bury it once and for all."

Kohana's eyes did not move from Caleb's face, but his jaw tightened.

"We're going to find Emily," Ruthie spoke up, her lower lip trembling and Caleb realized she had never seen people like this before. "And we're going to get Jimmy."

"The bandits are headed to the Owl Maker," Rand said. "Are you able to gather your people and bring back the child?"

Kohana looked at the old man, his face like stone.

"Our brother is dead," he said. "He was protecting the woman—"

Caleb's spine stiffened.

"She was hit with an arrow," Ehawee said. "I have tended it the best I can, but the wound will fester without medicine."

"We need to move," he said, his eyes seeking Rand. *"Now."*

"My mother can tend to her," Ehawee said. "She makes her home on the eastern meadow."

"Ina is not well." Kohana spoke, his voice like ice.

"Emily gave our brother a good death. You must not forget that."

Caleb stood dumbly, struck by her words and

wondered what had happened while Slant and Casper were carrying him back to the campsite.

Kohana turned to Rand, his shoulders straight.

"We will go to the high peak and bring back her child."

Ruthie shook her head, looking to Ehawee.

"There's a man. He was good to me—"

"The others will be killed," Kohana cut her off. "For Mahkah."

Ruthie stood, looking miserable and Caleb touched her arm.

"Go with them," he said. "Jimmy needs you."

She stared at him, fear in her eyes until Ehawee came closer.

"Can you use the rifle?"

Ruthie straightened her shoulders, nodded quickly.

Kohana waved his arm, made a sound in his throat. Then he was moving ahead, his feet silent against the earth and Ruthie looked at her brother.

"Go," he said quickly, afraid he would change his mind. "Find Jimmy."

She nodded, hugging him quickly. "Bring her back."

Then Rand was embracing his wife, and she nodded at him, telling him all would be well as he turned, leading Caleb towards the east and a valley of pines that reached towards the noon day sun.

They did not speak for some time, not until the

land began to change, the rocks taking on strange, sharp forms.

"Are we close?" he asked, lowering his voice and Rand nodded, putting his hand back as if telling him to slow down.

They picked their way over the boulders, climbing at times and Caleb did not dare look down, did not stop moving for fear he would fail Emily again.

Soon they came to a rock-strewn plain, and at the far end of it sat a cluster of spires, cutting the sky like a row of fangs.

In the distance two figures moved, picking their way down the side.

Rand crouched down; his Dragoon drawn.

"Can you see them?" Caleb asked, and the old man nodded, leveling his gun.

Caleb looked closer, his eyes narrowed against the sun and saw a flash of dark hair.

"Wait!" he shouted, standing up.

"Get down!" Rand cried, grabbing Caleb's arm but he shrugged him off.

"It's not Emily," he said, watching as they drew closer.

"Who the hell is it, then?"

"Clem!" Caleb cried. "Jake!"

They looked up, began waving their arms and he took off running, jumping from rock to rock, unaware of the danger until he stood beside them in the middle of the jagged plain.

Clem threw her arms around him, her breathing ragged.

"Emily," she gasped.

"What?" Caleb asked. "Where is she?"

Rand was behind him, rushing to the edge of a pit that seemed to have opened in the earth before them.

"Dammit," he cursed, going to his knees and Caleb looked at Jake.

"Where is she?"

He swallowed, nodded towards the hole.

Caleb ran to the edge and looked down into the blackness.

"Emily!" he cried, praying for a reply. Dropping to his knees, he called out again. Silence echoed against the landscape, and he looked to Rand, who stared down into the pit as though hell itself had opened up.

"This was one of my sinkholes..." he muttered, more to himself than the others. "Looks like it worked..."

"We found it," Jake said. "And set the trap like Emily wanted. I don't know why she tried to pull him off it— "

"They took Jimmy," Caleb said, and Clem covered her face, shook her head.

"No—"

Caleb gripped the edge and swung his legs over, ready to climb down or jump, whichever came first.

"Wait!" Clem cried, grabbing his arm. "You can't."

Caleb looked up, not really seeing her, a single thought stopping him cold.

"*Where's Marvin?*"

Jake bent down beside him, his jaw set.

"Down there with her."

Chapter Forty

Maddie felt sweat pool under her arms. Shifting her nephew to her other hip, she thanked God for his silence.

He'd cried much of the first hour they'd been walking, so much, in fact, that Gris offered to carry him.

His bearskin coat seemed to muffle the infant's sobs, but not before he grew weary and gave him back.

Now he lay like a rag doll in the sling she'd taken from Ruthie, his small fist up against his mouth as he suckled in his sleep.

Maddie looked at him and couldn't help but see Marvin in the red hair that lay plastered to his sweat-soaked head.

She wondered what part of him looked like her sister, seeing it in the blue eyes that had opened wide when she first held him.

For a long time, she prayed he was James's son, fantasizing about the moment Emily's deception would be revealed, but his resemblance to Marvin proved otherwise.

She'd been angry with the way he treated her, and he'd come to her before Beatrice appeared, speaking sweet words around the fire and she'd gone with him into the shadows, allowing him to lie with her on the dry earth, praying a child would fill her womb.

She touched her stomach, wondering if she was pregnant.

Slant stopped, turned back with the strange, confused look he always wore.

"What're you planning to do when you get to the high peak?" he asked, and she shrugged, not wanting to talk to him.

"She'll be second fiddle to that yellow- haired she-devil," Casper laughed, spinning on his heel to look at her.

"You can be my girl, Maddie," Slant said. "I'll be a rich man. Take you straight to Oregon and build you a fine, fancy house."

"She don't want any house you would build her," Gris said. "Might come up short in the wrong places."

Slant and Casper looked at each other, then began to walk again.

Gris stood beside her, one hand on her arm.

"You should take that trip, Miss Maddie."

She looked up at him.

He'd never spoken more than three words to her, had always spent his time with Ruthie and because of that, she felt he hated her.

"Why do you say that?" she asked, her chin high.

Gris lowered his voice, letting the others gain ground.

"The Boss acts different when you're not around."

She laughed, ducked beneath a low-hanging pine branch as a mule deer darted from the brush.

"I imagine he does."

"You need to get away."

She stopped, spun to face him.

"My family is dead. My sister hates me. I have no friends who will help me make my way to California or Oregon or whatever *trip* you think I should take."

"Your sister doesn't hate you. I saw it in her eyes-"

Maddie laughed. "Oh, yes... she does."

"When she meets up with you, try to have a word. You can take that baby and go away from here. Leave the Boss behind."

She laughed again. "And how could I possibly leave a man like that behind?"

Gris stared at her, his face still.

"You know."

She paused, her heart in her throat, and touched the baby that lay curled in the sling.

"He's Jimmy's father."

"No denying that."

"Gris—"

"Give him a better one."

She drew a breath, then moved ahead so she wouldn't have to talk anymore and soon found herself on high ground, struggling to climb the rocks that seemed to grow from the earth.

After some time had passed, Slant and Casper circled back to her, their faces drawn with worry.

"No way to make the meeting spot," Slant said. "Not with that baby."

"I'll wait here," she said, taking a seat on a flat rock. "Marvin will see me."

"You wouldn't run off, would ya?" Casper elbowed Slant in the side, laughed again.

"Boss fucked her good last night, so she'll likely stay put."

Maddie looked down at her lap.

"Heard you plain as day," Slant smirked. "Saw you, too, stuffing your hand against your mouth like that would keep you quiet."

"Shut your dirty traps," Gris growled. "And remember this is a lady."

"Lady?" Casper chuckled. "W*hore* is more like."

Gris swung at the man, his enormous fist making contact with Casper's jaw and the bandit went flying.

"Shit..." Slant cursed, scrambling away as Gris pulled his shotgun.

"Stop where you are."

Slant turned, his eyes large.

"Miss Maddie is gonna stay here and keep Jimmy and one of my Colts company. You two, on the other hand, are dragging your sorry asses up those rocks and never looking back. Understand me?"

"Boss won't like it!" Slant cried. "He said to stay with that kid."

"I'll answer for it," he said. "And take his thanks when he sees a living son is better than one with a cracked head."

Slant nodded, his hands out in front of him, and stumbled forward.

Gris moved to Casper, kicked him in the ribs.

"Git up," he growled.

Casper moaned, rolled over onto his side and dragged himself to his feet.

"We'll be back to fetch you, Miss Maddie," Gris said, laying his revolver on the rock beside her. "If you've a mind to wait."

She felt her breath hitch, unable to answer and the next moment he was turning, poking the other two in the back as they stumbled up the hill.

She sat, listening to the birds that made their home in these hills, imagining the life she would've had if she'd never met Marvin in the storeroom.

Would her mother be sewing her a new dress, or letting her take afternoon walks with a beau? Would her father allow her to take the teacher's exam she'd asked about, or would she be standing at the upstairs window, watching life pass by.

She thought of her time with Emily, the evenings of gossip and laughter, summer afternoons spent in the hot, Michigan sun. She'd loved her, never questioning her intentions until Marvin did.

She remembered their time in the darkness the night before, his hands on her shoulders, and then her throat. It seemed he was thinking of someone else, his movements reminding her of their time at Fort Kearny when he'd used her like an animal.

But she'd pushed it aside, grateful he wanted her.

She gritted her teeth, thinking of the show he put on in the middle of French Creek- treating her as an afterthought when he'd buried himself inside of her the night before.

She looked down at James, still sleeping, and understood for the first time what Emily had suffered in the making of this child.

She looked into the branches of the pine trees, sunlight spilling over her and picked up Gris' revolver. She'd found her father's Colt in a drawer not long after Emily's wedding, and taken it out, wondering at the power one person could hold over another.

She remembered her father coming in, his eyes wide with horror when he saw what was in her hand.

He'd taken her outside, shown her how to use it.

"I never did this with your sister," he'd said, his voice low. "And now I must live with the consequences."

A snapping branch caught her attention, and she slid off the rock, her hand instinctively covering her nephew. Peeking over the top, she saw two Sioux- a man and a woman- approach the high peak.

Trailing behind, her rifle drawn, was Ruthie.

She clutched the side of the rock; fearful she would see and did not know if she would help her or kill her.

Ruthie paused, her eyes seeming to sense the presence of the child.

If you've a mind to wait...

She remained still, watching the young woman and then stood slowly.

Ruthie swung her rifle around as gunshots exploded on the high peak.

The Sioux took off running and still Maddie didn't move, just waited while Ruthie came closer, her eyes seeking the sling.

"Give me Jimmy," she said, the tree above them shedding its skin as birds flocked to escape.

Maddie pulled the hammer on the revolver, aimed it.

"I go with him."

"Like hell you do," Ruthie spat. "I'll drop you where you stand."

Maddie looked at her, remembering her father's face.

"Same here."

Ruthie narrowed her eyes, looking over the rifle sights.

"Sounds like quite a tussle up there," Maddie said. "We might want to head in another direction."

"I ain't taking you anywhere," she said. "And Gris' up there."

"He told me to go," she said, and the girl's face

softened, her hold on the rifle slackening. "He wants better for Jimmy."

She watched the girl swallow, the muscles in her throat working.

"He said that?"

Maddie nodded, her aim never wavering.

"Why do you think he left me sitting on this rock?"

Ruthie tightened her hold.

"You wanna run?"

Maddie took a deep breath, nodded.

Ruthie watched her, the sound of battle bursting above them, and lowered her rifle.

"Let's get going, then."

Chapter Forty-One

Emily felt pressure on her chest, keeping her breath at bay as something hit her face. It was gritty, and smelled like the prairie after a hard rain, or the earth after it had been scorched by the Nebraska sun.

She swiped at it with her hand, heard someone call her name.

Caleb... But she didn't understand why he would be on the outside of the darkness that seemed to be holding her gently.

She tried to answer, to make her lips form his name but the heavy thing on top of her would not allow it.

It seemed as though she had felt it before, the sharpness and softness, as if it had always been there.

She thought back to her nights in the shanty, picturing Marvin's sweaty face, his lips pulled back in a way that made her think he was in pain.

And maybe he was.

She heard her name again, this time in a different, higher tone.

"Clem," she whispered, pushing at the thing on top of her and it moved, then rolled back to where it had been before.

Pain pierced her shoulder like a hot poker and she cried out.

The voices stopped, followed by-

"Emily!"

She gathered her breath, pushed it forth in a way she hoped he could hear.

"Caleb!"

The same grit fell into her mouth, and she coughed, spit it out and opened her eyes.

A small circle of sunlight fell from a piece of sky far above her head and she remembered grabbing Marvin's arm before the earth fell out from beneath them.

She looked at the thing that was lying on top of her and stifled a scream.

Her husband's face was buried at her breast, his arms askew and dangling on either side of her hips, making movement impossible without pushing him.

She gasped for breath, this dark place a grave they inhabited together.

"Emily!" Caleb cried again and she knew he was part of that small circle of sky. "I'm coming to get you!"

Marvin stirred, turned his head to the side.

She gasped, taking as much breath into her lungs as his weight would allow. "He's waking up!"

Darkness fell across her and for an instant she thought she saw Caleb crawling down the side.

A rock fell beside her head, making her jump. And then another.

"Stop!" she cried. "It's caving in on me."

Silence, followed by Clem's voice.

"Are you hurt?"

She wiggled her toes and fingers, moved her arms and legs as much as she could and felt the familiar pounding in her shoulder.

"No more than before."

Marvin moaned, raised his head to look at her and she reached for her revolver. Felt nothing.

"I lost my gun!"

"Get away from him, Em!" Jake cried. "We'll find a rope."

She almost laughed, wondering where they would get such a thing and if she could pull her own weight up it and groped on either side for something she could use against her husband.

"Look for a tunnel," Rand called. "There are old caves all over the place. I know where this one come out-"

Marvin groaned again, pushed off her and rolled to the side. She took the opportunity and flipped onto her stomach, then rose to her knees.

"Emily!" Caleb cried again and his voice awakened the monster inside of Marvin, because he sat up, pulled his gun and fired at the dot of sunlight above their heads.

"Stop!" Emily screamed, throwing herself on top of him.

His elbow found her cheek and the gun went off again, hitting the dirt wall and she saw a glimmer in the dim light.

Then she was scrambling away, grabbing her revolver with both hands but not before Marvin got to his feet, yanked her back by her hair.

She cried out, the revolver flying from her hands. Pulling free, she ran away, pressed her body against the wall while trying to cover herself in darkness.

There are old caves all over the place...

She moved away from Marvin, ran her hand along the soft dirt wall until it began to harden under her fingertips.

She quickened her step, followed the passage by touch alone.

"I'm coming for you, Emilou," Marvin called. "No hiding down here."

Turning back, she saw Marvin standing in the spill of sunlight, squinting in her direction, his gun drawn. For a moment she considered going back, taking her chances if it meant she could die in a place where Caleb could find her.

"Leave her alone," he cried, and Marvin looked up, fired another shot at the circle of sky.

She covered her mouth to keep from crying out,

horrified by the thought of Caleb's body tumbling to the bottom of the shaft.

Silence, and she stood, wondering why they didn't fire back, realizing it was because they didn't know where she was.

"I'm in a tunnel!" she screamed, praying they would hear her. "Shoot him."

Marvin spun in the direction of her voice as a bullet hit his left arm.

He grunted, his teeth drawn back in the way she remembered, then plunged headlong into the darkness.

She turned back, dove into the black passage.

"I see you, Em," his voice, laced with pain, echoed behind her and she knew he was lying, knew he was just as blind as she was. "I can feel you. *Smell* you."

She took another step, then another, her hand on the wall, praying it didn't end in nothing.

And it didn't, but seemed to go on forever, her arm numb and throbbing when his voice shocked her, making her spin to the left.

"I have your gun, my sweet. All you have to do is come and get it."

Emily put her head down, tried to swallow her terror.

"We can take the gold and start over with Jimmy."

She slid her foot again, drug herself forward.

"Those were the best times of my life."

She didn't doubt he meant it.

"I won't even ask you about him."

She stopped, the mention of Caleb making her chest hurt.

"Did you feel it when he touched you, Em?" he asked, "Because I forgive you if you did. I could have been a better husband. But you wouldn't let me. You need to *let me,* Emily."

She took another step, her hand sliding on the wall as a rock came loose in her hand.

"Stop running and *talk to* me!"

She paused, threw the stone and it hit the opposite wall.

Marvin's gun went off, the flash illuminating the tunnel.

He spun, saw her before they were plunged into darkness again.

She dropped to her knees, began to crawl as another blast rang above her head.

If he was lying about having her gun, he had two shots left.

If not... eight.

"You'd rather bleed out like a rat in this hole than be with me?"

She crawled forward, every reach of her arm an agony that reminded her of the moment the arrow hit her.

"Maddie didn't feel that way. She wanted me so bad we made love in your parents' store."

She stopped, closed her eyes, the image of what they'd done making her sick.

"It was her who set the fire, you know," he said. "I had nothing to do with it."

She covered her mouth, a sob bursting behind her hand.

"She was tired of you being such a bitch. And I can't blame her. You just told your lover to shoot me, after all."

She reached in front of her, the pain in her shoulder making her head fuzzy. Ehawee had told her she needed proper medicine and now, in this place with the bandage loose and the healing herbs gone, she understood how dangerous her situation truly was.

"Your ma and pa were killed with the club he kept under the counter. Maddie was there and so was Slant. I had *nothing* to do with it."

She pressed her lips together, drew her breath through her nose and felt the earth shift beneath her.

"Your pa went down right away, but Patricia... she fought a bit. Slant said it took four blows to finish her off."

"Stop it!" she screamed. *"Stop!"*

He laughed then, the sound thickened with pain, and she heard him pull the hammer back. Then she was on her feet, dragging herself to the opposite side of the passage as the flash of his shot blinded her.

Emily saw a second tunnel, waited for the darkness to descend before stumbling down it.

She wasted no time, but ran as fast as she could, well aware she could hit a wall head-on when a pin-point of light made her heart skid to a stop.

A scuffling sound behind, followed by the heavy breath of her husband made her pitch forward. Her shoulder exploded, her heart beating against her temples as she began to run, the pinpoint of light widening even as the edges seemed to narrow.

She had no knowledge of Marvin behind her, no sense of anything other than getting to the light.

I know where they come out...

"Caleb," she whispered, praying he would be there.

Words behind her, lost in the pounding of her pulse, her arms and legs and chest and throat numb.

She was so close now, and the breathing was there, at her neck, his ragged steps telling her he was in as much pain as she was when she tumbled outside, suddenly blinded by the sun.

She went to her knees, covered her eyes with the back of one hand.

"Got you!" Marvin growled, and she crawled forward, felt his hand on her arm as he flipped her onto her back.

She kicked out with her foot, but he stepped away, a single revolver in his hand.

One shot left...

"Leave me alone," she gasped. "Take the gold and go."

He staggered forward, his left forearm glistening with blood, his hair dusty, his face covered in grime.

"I can't, Emily," he said. "I've got to end this."

"No," she gasped. "Think of Jimmy-"

Marvin laughed.

"He has a mother."

"Please," she begged, scooting backwards, her hands out in front of her. "Please..."

Marvin stepped closer, raised the revolver.

"You're only thinking of Caleb now. Just wanting to live so you can run away with him. But everything has been leading to this moment. James, Lester... that crazy old bastard who helped you in the woods."

She pulled in her breath.

"Quinn?"

"I killed him after he dropped you in that wagon yard," another step forward, and she tried to move but the pain in her shoulder would not allow it. "And that lovely dunce... what was her name?"

"Beatrice," she whispered.

"And Hawkins. Although I'm surprised I didn't shoot him sooner."

She watched him, her eyes on the barrel of the revolver.

"Betsy..." he said, his eyes going soft for an instant. "It all started with her."

"Betsy," she whispered, sensing an advantage. "Who-"

He smiled.

"Caleb knows. But you'll never get the chance to ask him, will you?"

"Please," she begged. "Don't-"

He stared at her, not really seeing her, and pulled the hammer back. Emily shut her eyes, ready for the blackness that would end everything and heard a shot ring out.

She winced, her breath suspended, and waited.

Opening her eyes, she saw Marvin swaying on his feet, a hole in his stomach. He stumbled forward, the gun still loaded with his final shot, and collapsed onto his side, his breath labored.

A shadow fell over her from behind and she turned, her senses beginning to fade as Maddie stepped from the forest.

"Finish him," she said, holding the revolver and Emily took it with a shaking hand, staggered slowly to her feet.

"Madeline," Marvin rasped, his eyes wide as he focused on the two women in front of him. "Emily."

"It's over," she said, raising her arm. "Your name dies with you."

His face went still, then contorted in fury, his screams piercing the air as he swung his revolver around for the final shot.

Emily fired.

The bullet hit him between the eyes, and he went still in an instant, a small rivulet of blood pouring over his nose and into the dirt.

She stood with her arm raised, looking into her husband's unseeing eyes, her breath coming in short pants and felt Maddie touch her arm.

Turning, she lowered the gun slowly, her ears ringing, her head numb.

"Maddie-"

"I'm sorry, Em," she said, reaching for her as she went to her knees, darkness closing in around her. "Please-"

Emily felt her body begin to sway, her sister's face the color of sunlight.

"I am, too."

Chapter Forty-Two

Caleb sat beside Emily, his hand in hers, and put a cold cloth against her forehead.

She'd been resting in the tipi of Ehawee's mother for two days.

When Ina, as she was called by her children, heard of Mahkah's fate, she'd wandered to the edge of the meadow, asking about his death and Ehawee lowered her head, told her about Emily.

Soon she was bustling quickly between this place and the hillside, gathering herbs and tonics, soaking bandages and burning cedar and sage while her daughter and son helped as they could.

There were a handful of other tipis, some occupied by the family of Ehawee and Kohana, some by others who wandered between this place and another camp closer to the Mountain of the Six Grandfathers.

There was a time when Ina did not know if Emily

would wake up. The wound had festered too long, and there was an infection running through her body. How she had survived was a wonder, and Caleb looked away, unwilling to think of what might happen.

Ruthie, with Jimmy in his sling, hovered nearby with Clem and Jake, not knowing what to do until Ehawee gave them chores meant to keep them out of the way.

Caleb remembered the moment he'd heard the gunshot in the forest, his heart jumping to his throat. He'd left the others behind, skidding to a stop when he found the mouth of the cave.

Ruthie was standing over Marvin's body, while Emily lay with her head in her sister's lap as if she'd simply fallen asleep in the forest.

He felt unable to move, unable to take a step towards the woman he loved. Maddie's eyes met his, and in them he saw everything she'd lost while Marvin lived.

"I told her I was sorry," she said, her voice low. "She said she was, too."

"Maddie," he said, wanting to move quickly. "We need to get her to the tipis-"

"Yes," she'd said, as if in a daze. "Take her."

She'd moved then, allowed him to take her in his arms and Ruthie motioned for them to go. He'd looked over his shoulder, wondering if she would follow but she just stood, her revolver in her hand.

The others were shouting now, and Rand was calling to them, telling them how to get to the tipis and

Caleb turned, began walking down the mountain when a single gunshot echoed against the rocks.

Jimmy wailed again, and Caleb stood, his gaze cutting to his sister.

"Don't look," she whispered, rocking Jimmy. "Please."

It was almost sunset when they reached the tipis, and at once Ehawee emerged from one.

Rand ran to her, kissing her soundly on the mouth this time, embracing for what seemed forever before leading them to a woman whose face bore the heavy creases of wisdom, her brown eyes milky.

It was during that first long night that Ehawee pulled him to the tipi door, telling him what happened on the Owl Maker.

Others from their band had climbed the peak and fired upon the bandits. Kohana killed the man named Slant and she had done the same to Casper.

They had taken gunfire but had not been hit, a sign of protection from Waken Tanka.

The large man who wore the skin of a bear was at the peak as well but had stepped aside as if he wanted no part in the battle, and when it was over, he'd come to stand beside them, asking in their own language about Ruthie and Jimmy and Maddie.

Caleb remembered the moment his sister caught sight of Gris, the shout of delight as she ran into his arms and knew she had found a lifelong friend.

But even these memories seemed bitter in light of what lay before him.

He looked down on Emily, pulling the cold cloth away and she turned her head, mumbling something under her breath.

"Em?" he whispered.

She moaned again, moved her hand and he caught it in his.

"Emily."

"Caleb?" she whispered and the darkness that had been living inside of him lifted.

"Where am I?" she asked, blinking as though the light hurt her eyes.

"Ina's tipi," he paused. "Ehawee is here."

She took this in, as if struggling to understand, and then looked him in the eye.

"Jimmy?"

"He's with Ruthie."

"Clem, Jake—"

"They're fine."

A pause.

"Maddie?"

He swallowed, not wanting to burden her.

"She's gone."

Her brows came together, as if she did not understand what he meant and he touched her cheek, his thumb lingering.

"She saved me."

He paused, remembering the sound of the gunshot as it echoed off the rocks.

"There was nothing we could do."

No words, and for a time he watched her, holding

her hand while she mourned her sister for a second time.

Ina went into the tipi, saw Emily and left quickly. Soon others were peeking through the elk skin door and Ruthie pushed past them, tears in her eyes as she placed Jimmy in her arms.

The baby turned at the smell of his mother, began to gurgle in his throat and Emily laughed, her tears for Maddie mixing with those for her child.

Caleb stood then, walked out of the tipi and to the meadow where Ina had stood mourning her son two days before, the whole of the Black Hills spread out before him.

He waited while voices gathered, while a fire was made, and meat was cooked over the top of it. The sky began to blacken, and still, he did not return to Emily.

It was nightfall when Kohana came to stand beside him.

"She wants to see you."

He nodded, knowing he'd stayed too long.

"She should not have to ask."

"I know."

Kohana did not speak, just looked at him.

"I left her-" Caleb said. "Out there on that ridge."

"And you are leaving her again."

He shook his head, hardly believing he was speaking the words.

"My wife," he muttered. "I did the same thing to her. Even when I knew it was wrong. I needed the work, yes, but the truth was I couldn't look at her anymore. Couldn't stand to see the sickness in her eyes."

Kohana gazed out at the hills, his face still.

"It was the same with Emily. I saw something I didn't like and ran away. And she almost died because of it."

Kohana nodded, the wind ruffling the feathers in his hair.

"When a hunter finds the place where the game rests, he uses a different trail each time he takes a kill. Otherwise, they will smell him and run away."

Caleb put his hands in his pockets, rocked back on his heels.

"And if they run away, no one eats."

"What does that have to do with me?"

Kohana smiled, reached over and laid his hand on his shoulder.

"It is time to take a different trail."

He stood, silent, thinking on the way he had loved his wife and sister. The way he had loved Emily.

"What if I can't?"

Kohana looked up at the stars.

"What does the sky tell you?"

He looked at the man, unsure, then drew himself up, thinking of all that had happened since the day he'd brought Jimmy into the world.

"When I found you on the prairie, I said you could paint the sky for war or peace."

Caleb stood, his throat thick. "What does it tell you?"

Kohana stood still for a moment.

"It tells me that you should stop wasting your time with me and take your new family west."

Caleb chuckled. "Sad to see me go?"

Kohana laughed, and the sound echoed down the hillside, scaring mule deer from the darkened glens.

"Not as sad as you are to see me stay."

Caleb shook his head, a smile dusting his lips and after some time had passed, Kohana spoke again.

"Did you know I was the one who took the stone Rand wrote on? I would not have my family shamed and was going to break it into a million pieces. Then Mahkah came to me, said the stone belonged to the mountain, said it should remain so we would never forget."

Caleb looked at him. "He never knew—"

Kohana shook his head. "I buried it on the hillside. And he became a new man because of it."

Caleb stood, listening to the sounds of laughter, the smell of cooking meat reminding him of their nights on the high prairie, his fiddle dancing on air.

"Come and eat."

Caleb smiled.

"I have to tend to something first."

Kohana nodded, moved away while chuckling to himself and Caleb turned, walked towards Emily's tipi.

He pushed back the elk skin flap, took a step and saw her sitting up in bed, the color high in her cheeks, her hair spilling over her shoulders.

"Em—"

She lifted her chin.

"Where have you been?"

He paused. "Out in the meadow."

She looked down at her hands, picked at something in her lap.

"What were you doing?"

He paused, wishing this moment could be different.

"Thinking."

Her hands stilled, as if she were afraid to move, afraid of what his next words might be and he went to her, sat down beside her.

"I need to tell you something."

She shook her head.

"You don't need to say anything."

"Yes, I do."

"We'll stay here with Rand and Ehawee."

"Em—"

"We'll make a new life—"

"Like *hell* you will."

She looked at him, her blue eyes widening, and he smiled, touched the side of her face.

"I'm sorry I left you on that hillside. Sorry I walked away when I didn't like what I saw and sorry I couldn't see what was inside your heart. I was no better with Celia or Ruthie, but I promise I'll keep trying. And if you'll have me, I'll take you to California and build us a house by the sea."

She put a hand over her face, held it there for a moment and when she lowered it again, she had tears in her eyes.

"With orange trees?"

He smiled.

"A million of 'em."

"And Jimmy?"

"I'll be a father to him. He won't ever know any different."

She dropped her eyes again, fiddled with the blanket that covered her.

"I'm sorry, too," she said, her voice so low he could hardly hear it. "I should have told you the truth about Marvin, should have trusted that you loved me in the same way as Celia."

"No," he shook his head. "It will never be the same. And that's what's beautiful about it."

She smiled, the tension lifting from her body.

"Ruthie can get a house beside us... and Gris, if he has a mind to. Hell, Clem and Jake can join the party."

She stopped him with a kiss, and he deepened it, his mouth opening before pulling away, whispering in her ear.

"And we'll need to get started on Jimmy's brothers and sisters."

Emily pulled back to look at him, her jaw set.

"Aren't you forgetting something, Mr. Merritt?"

He tilted his head, his gray eyes questioning.

"You never asked me to marry you."

He looked at her sheepishly, scratched the back of his head and Emily touched his cheek, her blue eyes promising the one thing he'd spent his whole life looking for.

"The answer is *yes,* if you need to know."

Caleb smiled, touched his forehead to hers.

"I suppose I do."

Chapter Forty-Three

Emily stood between Ruthie and Clem, turning from left to right while they tucked wildflowers into the braids Ehawee had woven into her hair.

It was her wedding day- two weeks since Ina's medicine had saved her life and she'd opened her eyes to find Caleb beside her.

She'd filled the days between with good food, long naps and walks in the mountain air with people who wanted her strong again. And on those walks she thought about all that had happened since leaving Independence, and before, even- a warmth taking root where fear had pressed for so long.

The horses had even returned, as Ehawee said they would, and Clementine had spent many moments with her face pressed to the palomino mare's neck, whispering words meant only for her.

"You look pretty, Em," Ruthie beamed, stepping back to smooth the skirt of the blue gingham dress she was wearing- a gift Ehawee had retrieved from the trunk in her cabin.

"Rand said I needed a white woman's dress in case we ever traveled to a town," she said while handing it to Emily. "But I do not see that day coming anytime soon."

Emily remembered the moment she tried it on, remembered Clem and Ruthie's faces and almost forgot the sadness she felt for the people who could not be there.

She thought back to her wedding to Marvin, remembered the nervous flutter in her stomach, the strange glances passed between her parents and knew the feelings stirring inside of her today were made from entirely different things.

She thought of Caleb, waiting for her at the edge of the meadow where Ina would say the words meant to bind them until they could stand before a judge in California.

"You look like a wood nymph I saw in a picture book," Clem said, reaching out to tuck another flower in her hair. "Caleb will be beside himself."

Emily caught her hand, squeezed.

"I owe all of this to you," she said. "If you hadn't let me ride in your wagon—"

"Hush," Clem said, her eyes glistening. "I only did what any decent person would."

"No," Emily said, extending her hand to Ruthie as well. "Both of you are anything but ordinary."

Ruthie cleared her throat.

"Much as I hate to admit it, Caleb deserves some credit, too."

Emily nodded.

"I intend to show him how grateful I am," she paused, a sly smile dusting her lips. "Starting tonight."

Clem gave a little gasp, and then covered her mouth. Ruthie just stood with her hands on her hips, shaking her head.

"Jimmy's shaping up to be a handful and a half. I wouldn't add more to the mix anytime soon."

Clementine smiled, shrugged her shoulders. "You won't need a midwife, at least. Caleb could hang a shingle and hire himself out."

Emily laughed, and then Clem, and finally Ruthie until they were all doubled over, exhausted and hopeful and grateful for this moment- which was better than any other.

"Are you ready?" Ehawee's voice startled them, and Emily turned to the woman, her face awash with the happiness the day had already given her.

Then she was moving through the door, the sky a dusky mix of purple and red and pink painted just for her.

She strained for a glimpse of Caleb but did not see him at first- the tilt of the land and the people who had gathered seemed to be in her way.

She passed them one by one, smiling in turn, laughing at Jimmy who wiggled in Gris' arms, the man's long beard the only distraction her son seemed to need.

Ina stood on the edge of the meadow, Kohana and Rand on either side of her and Ehawee paused, linking her arm through Emily's.

"Is this what a father would do?" she asked. "To give you away?"

Emily stopped, her heart in her throat as she thought of Gerald Ives.

"Yes," she managed. "Just like this."

Ehawee leaned closer, touched her head to hers.

"They are with you."

Emily pressed her lips together, her mind traveling to the flatlands of Michigan, where the creek she used to wade in gathered afternoon sun. Then she was standing in the store, measuring out beans and flour and putting them in a sack for Lester while her mother looked on, her golden hair caught in a pair of combs.

Maddie was there, smiling behind her hand when a handsome farmer came in, rushing to help him, stealing a piece of candy from the penny jar when Patricia wasn't looking.

Her father would check on them before closing, talking of how he had the best workers in town, and the prettiest, and was it any wonder they never ran out of customers.

At night there would be the smell of pipe smoke,

and Uncle Rand's letters to go over, and stories to write in the warmth of a glowing fire.

Then she was watching Clementine talk to Jake in the wagon yard, her heart in her throat, the memory of the first time she'd seen Caleb smile at Alcove Springs making her feel like she'd swallowed a bumblebee.

She remembered Ruthie teaching her to shoot as they aimed at the cottonwood tree and the miracle that had become her son- his face pressed against her as they knelt in the middle of the Platte River.

She leaned her head back, the breeze sliding over her cheek as a million memories lingered in a place she would treasure, their legacy marked by the way she would live from this moment on.

She stood at the edge of the meadow, her eyes settling, at long last, on Caleb.

She stopped, unable to breathe for his beauty.

He wore a linen shirt rolled at the sleeves, his thick hair streaked with gold, a belt made of beads that was a gift from Kohana tied at his waist.

It seemed he lost his breath as well, his body going still as his gaze traveled the length of her.

He reached out, took her hands, the warmth of his flesh speaking to what would happen between them tonight.

Ehawee took a bundle of sage and handed it to Ina, a gift symbolizing the customs of their people and the old woman began to speak in her language.

It only took a moment to become husband and

wife here, in the shadow of the Owl Maker, but to Emily it meant more than what would take place anywhere else.

Caleb touched her face, kissed her gently and she wanted to take his hand, lead him to the tipi that had been set aside for them, but the time had not come.

Then there was feasting, and dancing around the fire Kohana had built as Rand brought out a fiddle he used to play in his youth.

Caleb looked at it, his eyes shining as he took it in his hands, tuning the strings.

She stood, looking at the person she'd thought was her uncle and knew he was still the man she'd believed him to be.

Caleb began playing a song, and she lifted her skirts, twirled in the firelight with Clem and Ruthie until she was breathless, her braids coming undone, the flowers falling from her hair.

More music followed, carried on the wind by spirits until Emily moved to the edge of the firelight, waiting for her husband.

Caleb's eyes caught hers and he handed the fiddle to Rand. Then he was before her and she stood on tiptoe, wrapped her arms around his neck.

"I think I've waited long enough," she said, and he smiled, kissed the tip of her nose.

"Me, too."

The others cast glances their way, continuing to eat and dance and Caleb took her hand, leading her down the hill and away from the others to the tipi Ehawee had prepared for them, a deerskin laid in the center.

He stood for a moment, and Emily touched his shoulder, marveling that this man was hers.

"What?" she asked, a strange fluttering inside of her.

He just smiled, reaching down to grab the deerskin.

Gathering it in his arms, he began to walk away from the tipi, and she had no choice but to follow.

Soon they came to a glen of pine trees set in the path of the rising moon.

A creek skirted the bottom of the hill, its song one of water and stone and Caleb stopped, his face full of the things she had dreamed about as a girl.

He laid the deerskin down, put his hands on either side of her face.

"This place is for us."

She nodded, placing her hands on his chest, the need to have her skin pressed to his consuming all other thoughts.

He leaned forward, kissed her softly while unbuttoning her dress, sliding it from her shoulders. She felt the fabric skirt past her shoulder and drew her breath between her teeth.

Caleb stopped, ran his finger over the newly healed skin and bent to place his mouth there, his lips as soft as moonlight.

"I love you," he whispered, moving to her throat,

his hands sliding the dress over her hips until it puddled at her feet.

She stepped out of it, kicked it aside while he unbuttoned his shirt, then his pants.

Soon they were standing naked before each other, looking, touching, his fingers in her hair as he kissed his way to her breasts.

She felt her knees weaken and he lowered her to the deerskin, the ghosts that wandered these hills binding them to this place.

Emily closed her eyes, wound her fingers in his hair.

She'd imagined this from the moment Caleb had kissed her under the cottonwood tree, had prayed for it even as turned his back on her at Kearny.

And now, in the glen of moonlit pines, the reality was almost too much.

She turned her head to the side, saw the rush of moonlit water sliding by and felt it running inside of her.

His hand cupped her knee, parting her legs and she let them fall wide of each other, wishing she could erase every touch before this.

"I don't want to hurt you," he whispered, his voice wavering and she smiled against his neck.

"You won't—"

"It," he paused. "It hasn't been long."

She knew his fears, knew he carried the weight of another child on his shoulders, and she touched his face with her fingertips, looked into his eyes.

"I've painted a picture in my mind," she whispered. "And it's with you."

Her words seemed to relieve him, the muscles in his back relaxing. She slid her hands to his waist, lifting her hips, and at long last, he was inside of her.

She tensed against him, the feeling so different from Marvin, and went still.

"Em," he whispered, his voice pained. "Are you—"

"It's good," she said, her lips on his neck. "Please—"

He paused, his eyes on her as he began to move, the ebb and flow natural- sacred, bringing with it the small flame she knew would grow into what had overcome her in front of the rocks.

She said his name, her nails digging into his shoulders as he whispered words in her ear, telling her what he felt, what he wanted her to feel and she closed her eyes, undone by what Marvin had denied her.

She opened her eyes, saw her husband silhouetted against the stars and felt as if she had become one of them, the very core of her being a thing of mystery she had yet to understand.

"Emily," he whispered, feeling her release, her cry of pleasure an offering she laid before him.

She felt him tense, his body returning what she had given, his breath rough on her neck as he buried his head there.

They laid that way for a long time, the evening air cooling their skin, hands stroking, lips seeking, words whispered and hidden away in secret places.

"You've given me so much," she said at last, and he raised himself on his arms.

"No more than you've given me."

"We're even, then," she whispered, knowing whatever path they chose would lead them home.

He smiled, touched his lips to hers.

"I'd say."

Epilogue

E mily sat in the grass, the scent of salt in the air, and stretched her legs in front of her.

They'd been in California for eight months now, arriving in late September after leaving Laramie to continue their journey over the western mountains.

Clem and Jake had come as far as Sacramento, saying they would visit after establishing their claim, but the lure of the sea had kept her and Caleb moving until they found the land they'd dreamed of.

Nestled on a hill crowned with two orange trees, Caleb built them a cabin, talking all the while about the crops they would raise and the fish they could catch.

He'd paid a pretty penny for it, but Rand Albright's gold had helped with the sting.

They hadn't wanted to take anything, but Ina had insisted.

You have driven the war children away, she said. *That is worth more than any gold we could give you.*

And so, they'd gone to the place where the Needles brushed the sky, taking a small portion of what the mountain had to offer.

Emily let the wind whip through her hair, looked over at Jimmy as he toddled in the grass, falling squarely on his behind the next.

He'd learned to walk the week before - a small event that had upended everything in their life.

She said his name and he turned on the grass, smiled in a way that said the past would never touch him.

She heard a door slam, saw Ruthie standing on the threshold of the neighboring cabin. Raising her hand, she waved, and the girl returned the gesture before moving off to tend the garden that would see them through the winter months.

It seemed the lure of a place to call his own appealed to Gris, as well as Ruthie, who'd discovered a handsome man beneath the beard and bearskin coat.

Emily felt a hand on her shoulder, looked up into the face of her husband.

"It's a fine day," he said, his hair blowing in the breeze, and she made a note to cut it later that night as they sat in front of the fire.

"It is," she nodded, wondering if they would take a walk by the sea, or if he would hunt despite the shed full of meat Gris had provided before leaving to set his traps.

Caleb dropped down beside her, the affection that came so naturally displayed plainly as he kissed her softly, his hand wandering to the swell of her stomach.

The baby would be coming soon, of that she was certain - just as she remembered the night she'd conceived as they camped beneath the Sierra's starry eastern skies.

"I have something for you," he said, handing her a package.

"What's this?"

"They just got some at the store in San Jose and-"

She laughed, hushed him while opening the brown paper she'd used to wrap parcels in her own store.

Her fingers closed around something square, and she drew out a journal, touched the cloth cover with reverent fingers.

"The paints will come next week. And some pencils-"

"Caleb," she said again, undone by what this meant, and he leaned forward, his hand running from her stomach to her knee.

"It was a long time coming and I'm sorry for that."

She smiled, sat the journal off the side as Jimmy tried to stand back up, his smiles turning to laughter now that Caleb had returned.

"Think we can handle two of those?" he asked, and Emily shook her head.

"Better pray it's a girl."

He put his hand to his chin, stared up at the sky.

"A girl," he mused, his eyes widening, and she laughed, knowing their daughter would have him all sewn up.

"What should we name her?"

Caleb shrugged. "Heck if I know. I'm terrible at this kind of thing."

Emily watched as Jimmy stood slowly, his faltering steps bringing him close to his father and felt her heart open in a way it never had before.

"What do you think of Alice?"

Caleb smiled, his eyes on the sea.

"That'll do just fine."

The End

Acknowledgments

I want to take this moment to express my thanks to all the people who have helped make this project a reality.

To my parents, Charley and Peggy, my husband, Scott, and children, Stone, Meg, Ana and Aubrey- thanks for your understanding when I spend long hours in front of the computer, or stare blankly into space, trying to fill in a plot hole.

To my readers, thanks for encouraging me to keep writing the stories of my heart. I'm so blessed they found a place in yours.

To those in the arena who have helped me along the way, I appreciate your faith and dedication. Special thanks to Rob Samborn, Nola Nash, Denise Birt, Terry Shepherd, Shanessa Gluhm, Wade Rouse, Gary Edwards, Elisha Morales, and Sharon Bippus.

I first imagined writing a western when I was young, and the earliest whisper of this novel appeared in my early writings- a 'Goonies' like adventure that was set in Arizona near the Lost Dutchman Mine.

As books of our youth often do, the manuscript

vanished- most likely to the dark confines of a moldy box in my parents' basement.

Still, the allure of the American West, and the brave people who traveled the Overland Trail always seemed to be in the back of my mind, and so I returned to the idea, setting my new novel in the Black Hills of South Dakota.

I hope I've done service to those who have called this sacred land home for thousands of years, and to those who remain faithful stewards of their legacy.

About the Author

Laura is a teacher who loves to write about her home state of Michigan. She has a B.A. in Creative Writing from Western Michigan University where she studied under Stuart Dybek, and has had her short fiction and poetry published in Chicken Soup for the Soul, Word Riot, Tonopalah Review, SaLit and SLAB: Sound and Literary Art Book. "The Pursuit of Happiness," – a short story she wrote while at WMU, was chosen as a finalist in the Trial Balloon Fiction Contest. She is the award-winning author of the Lantern Creek Series, and the historical romance 'I Paint the Sky.' When not writing, she enjoys singing and participating in community theater as well as spending time with her husband, four children, two dogs, two cats, and seven chickens.

Made in the USA
Columbia, SC
29 April 2025

57322362R00286